A CYPRESS HOLLOW YARN

# How to Knit a Heart Back Home

## Rachael Herron

**KENNEBEC LARGE PRINT**
*A part of Gale, Cengage Learning*

GALE
CENGAGE Learning™

Detroit • New York • San Francisco • New Haven, Conn • Waterville, Maine • London

This book is a work of fiction. The characters, incidents, and dialogue are drawn from the author's imagination and are not to be construed as real. Any resemblance to actual events, or persons, living or dead, is entirely coincidental.

Kennebec Large Print® Superior Collection.
The text of this Large Print edition is unabridged.
Other aspects of the book may vary from the original edition.
Set in 16 pt. Plantin.

**LIBRARY OF CONGRESS CATALOGING-IN-PUBLICATION DATA**

Herron, Rachael.
How to knit a heart back home : a Cypress Hollow yarn / by Rachael Herron.
p. cm. — (Kennebec Large Print superior collection)
ISBN-13: 978-1-4104-3920-8 (softcover)
ISBN-10: 1-4104-3920-8 (softcover)
1. Knitters (Persons)—Fiction. 2. Knitting—Fiction. 3. Large type books.
I. Title.
PS3608.E7765H66 2011b
813'.6—dc22 2011028263

Published in 2011 by arrangement with William Morrow, an imprint of HarperCollins Publishers.

Printed in the United States of America
2 3 4 5 6 15 14 13 12 11

FD326

For Lala Hulse,
for putting on her thinking cap at all
the right times.

# ACKNOWLEDGMENTS

My deepest thanks go to Susanna Einstein for reading and rereading my many rewrites, for brainstorming with me, for believing in me, and best of all, for being my friend. I am so lucky. Deepest thanks also to my editor, May Chen, who is a genius, pure and simple. Thanks to the wonderful people at Harper-Collins who have made working on this book such a joy: Amanda Bergeron for knowing how much overnight delivery means to an author, Catherine Serpico for being excited with me, and Kendra Newton for bringing the noise. Thanks to Ann Mickow and her mother, Josephine A. Mickow, who was nothing like Irene except for inspiring a moment of hand-washing grace. Thanks to Susan Wiggs for her unparalleled generosity, Stephanie Pearl-McPhee for the laughs, and Barbara Bretton for everything. Thanks to Cari Luna, for making me believe I could pull it off. Thanks also to Stephanie Klose of *Romantic Times,* for bringing the knitters with her, and to A. J. Larrieu for her keen eye. I couldn't have written this (or any other) book without MacFreedom (which kept me off Twitter long enough to write it) or Zocalo Coffeehouse (where I write all my first drafts). Thanks to the Pigeon Point Lighthouse for being a refuge, and to Pescadero's Duarte's, for allowing me to eavesdrop on the ranchers. Thanks to our Night of Writing Dangerously NaNoWriMo fairy godmother. To my PensFatales, I don't know where I'd be without you: Martha Flynn for pushing us to make things *happen,* Gigi Pandian for your gracefulness, Adrienne Miller for knowing everyone needs a hero, L.G.C. Smith for knowing just about everything else, Lisa Hughey for caring so hard, Juliet Blackwell for hotel sauna pillow fights, and for Sophie Littlefield who makes everything happen exactly as it should. Thanks also go to Elizabeth Sullivan, for making my pattern-math work — any mistakes are mine, not hers. Thanks to my dispatchers: you really do save lives, and I'm so proud of you. To the readers of Yarnagogo, I adore you and thank you. And to my family, Dan, Christy, and Bethany Herron; Lala, Tony, Jeannie, Richard, Won-Ju and Isaac Hulse:

you are my everything. I'm sorry I get so busy writing that sometimes I forget to tell you.

# One

> If you cast on with joy, your stitches will dance. If you cast on with your eyes to the floor, your stitches will likely run that direction the first chance they get.
>
> — Eliza Carpenter

In the dim light of the bar, Lucy could barely see the sock she was knitting, but it didn't matter. These were bar socks, meant to be knitted in the dark.

"This is the best kind of night," said Lucy.

"It's dead," said Molly, seated at the next bar stool.

Lucy sighed in happiness and took a sip of what she always ordered, a Manhattan with two cherries, no ice. "I know. Just a regular night. It's perfect."

The crash that followed was deafening, the sound ripping through the bar, tearing metal, shattering glass. A hubcap flew in through the open door. It fell to the floor and then rolled and wobbled across the bar, toppling over with a clang at Lucy's feet.

Lucy opened her mouth but nothing came out, and Molly's wide eyes met hers. Lucy's brother Jonas threw his cloth onto the bar and reached for the phone.

With the other bar patrons, Lucy ran outside. A small blue compact car was crumpled like aluminum foil against a pole. A white car was nose to nose with a fire hydrant and a potbellied older man tried to emerge from the driver's side, saying out his broken window, "I didn't see her. I swear I didn't see her." Blood ran down his forehead.

The blue car hissed and spat as the engine protested its demise and a flame growled underneath the chassis of the engine.

A man in a black leather jacket pulled on the handle of the door of the vehicle, trying to wrest it open while the woman inside struggled with the seat belt. She screamed and looked out at them, her eyes wide, her mouth twisted in pain.

Lucy's stomach lurched as if she were seasick as she recognized first the car, and then the hair through the broken driver's-side window. "It's Abigail. Oh, God, it's Abigail MacArthur. We have to get her out of there." Lucy peered through the back window to look for a child's car seat. "Do you have Lizzie in there?"

Abigail shook her head and said, "She's home. With Cade." She gasped as something under the car made a horrible noise. "Please. Get me out."

Lucy looked at the man in the leather jacket fighting with the door handle. "She's pregnant." She glanced over her shoulder at the potbellied man. "Were you with that driver? Why are you . . ."

"I was going past and saw him T-bone her." The man put his entire body into trying to get the car door open, but the metal was too bent. A crackling sound came from the pole's wires, which dangled just above his head.

Lucy's brother Jonas, now outside, said, "Back, all of you get back." He used his arms and body to push the crowd onto the sidewalk. "Lucy! Get away from that car!"

The potbellied man who had caused the accident yelled something from behind them about his insurance company.

"Fire department's on the way," Lucy's mother yelled.

"There won't be time," the man in the leather jacket said to Lucy. "In a second I'm going to need your help. Don't move."

Lucy had no more breath to hold. Under

the warped metal at the front of the car, the orange glow of the fire grew brighter.

He jerked his elbow through the rear driver's side window, somehow still intact. Then he reached through and fought with the lock on the door and pulled until the back door popped open.

"Don't move her!" someone in the crowd yelled. "She's injured!"

Leaning into the car, he reached forward and then retreated. "I can't," he gasped, putting a hand to his hip as if he'd wrenched it. He looked pale and off balance. His eyes met Lucy's and her heart skittered into overdrive. "Push in," he said. "See if you can drop her seat backward. I can't fit in there."

Lucy took a deep breath, like she'd done in training exercises. She'd worked car fires before, but never with a person inside, never from this close. "It won't explode, right?" Her voice shook. They had to hurry.

"It won't. Not just like that. I've seen lots of car fires. You can do it."

Lucy moved forward.

It was hot and loud inside. Lucy leaned in to the backseat area and drove her hand up the side along the front door. She could feel the heat growing beneath the car. What if she got stuck and burned to death along with Abigail? Would it be fast? Would it hurt?

"The latch is on the side of the seat," said the man behind her. "Feel for it and pull up."

"I can't find it!" Lucy yelled.

"Please, please, please," said Abigail, in a strange, singsong voice.

"Hang on, Abigail, we've almost got you," Lucy said.

"You can do it." His voice came from behind her shoulder.

There. Lucy could feel the hot plastic under her hand. She pulled and the driver's seat dropped back. Lucy pushed herself out, away from the heat, away from Abigail's awful bloodied mouth and panicked eyes.

He said, "Okay, now we pull."

"Her neck could be broken, you fucking morons!" someone yelled.

His voice was low in Lucy's ear. "I know what I'm doing."

Lucy only hesitated for a split second as a tendril of fear bloomed in her heart. Moving Abigail was against all her training. They had no backboard. No C-spine.

But then something gave a loud *boom* underneath the car, and it got suddenly hotter. Lucy helped him, dragging Abigail over the top of her seat, being as careful of her stomach as they could be. They wrestled her out of the car and moved her toward the sidewalk. Lucy's younger brother Silas was now next to them, holding Abigail by the legs.

As they set Abigail safely on the ground in front of the bar, the car went from glowing underneath, a flicker or two licking the front end, to completely engulfed in flames, erupting into a fireball. The heat drove the crowd back even farther, some people retreating back inside the bar to peek out the windows.

Lucy heard the sirens coming. She saw the flashing lights reflecting against windows even before her fellow volunteers made the turn onto Main.

The same drunk guy who'd called them morons for moving the woman was babbling, "They saved her. She woulda gone up in flames . . ."

Abigail was crying now, weeping.

Lucy felt a sob rising in her own chest that she wouldn't give in to. Molly stopped digging her fingers into Lucy's arm and moved to clutching her hand. "You saved her. *You* saved her."

Lucy could only stare.

She watched them move Abigail into a stable position. Her brother Silas used his arms to steady her head, one hand over her forehead to keep her from lifting it to look around. The man in the leather jacket moved his hands over her body as if looking for the source of the bleeding.

God. It couldn't be him, could it?

And just like that, it came back to her. Owen Bancroft. The man she thought she'd never see again. Holy hell.

Where had he *come* from? Lucy looked down the street, and her eyes closed in on it as if drawn by magnets: that damn blue Mustang was parked over by the art-supply shop. So he still had that car. She wasn't even really surprised.

Paramedics moved in and loaded Abigail into the ambulance.

Captain Jake Keller and some of the local volunteer fire brigade extinguished the blazing car. The street went dark as they shut down electricity to the pole. The only light now was from the moon and the lights on the firefighters' helmets. The salty smell of the Pacific mixed with the metallic smell of the charred car.

Lucy couldn't take her eyes off Owen. He stood with Silas, shoulder to shoulder, their backs to the crowd. They watched the ambulance tearing up Oak Street toward the hospital, siren whooping.

The men turned. Silas said something and

Owen jerked his chin, as if in agreement. Owen's jacket was ripped and his cheek was smudged. He was limping.

Lucy tried to breathe around a sudden judder in her chest and examined Owen more closely. She tried to focus on stilling her breath and not on the black spots dancing in front of her eyes.

If it was possible, Owen looked even better than he had in high school, seventeen years ago. She willed his dark blue eyes to meet hers, and then didn't know if she'd be able to meet them if he looked at her.

Owen stood on the street, alone, as Silas walked away from him. He'd just saved a woman's life. He still looked perfect, dammit to hell.

Then Molly pulled Lucy into the bar, and she lost sight of the man she'd never forgotten.

Jonas lit the bar with candles. Lucy peered through the dim light at her knitting. Her hands were shaking too violently to even make one stitch, but it didn't stop her from trying. Always, after working an incident, she got this — the shakes, the queasiness, the sense her body had suffered an interior earthquake. It was the worst part of working with the volunteer fire brigade — the aftershocks.

"Yeehaw!" said Jonas, slamming down the bar phone. "Captain Keller says Abigail's fine, and so's the baby. Drinks on the house!"

Molly said, "Are you sure that's your cheap-ass brother?"

"I feel like I'm going to throw up." Lucy fought another wave of nausea. Thank God Abigail was going to be okay. *Owen Bancroft was back.*

"Did you have too much to drink?"

"Didn't you *see* what just happened?" Lucy looked around the bar. People were already telling one another the story. The legend was already being crafted.

Lucy's mother held court in a booth, waving her knitting needles around.

Her father pumped his fist in the air, letting out a yell that was drowned by her younger brother Silas's whoop as he smacked the eight ball into the side pocket.

Jonas was behind the bar, moving as if he were in fast-forward.

Molly said, "I saw. You okay?"

"She would have died. Ten seconds later, if we hadn't gotten her out of there, she would have been on fire. Her whole body, burning. While she was alive. The baby . . . And Cade, with little Lizzie at home wouldn't have . . ."

Molly shook her head. "You were awesome. I've never seen you work; you just usually answer your pager and run out when you're on call. But I even saw Abigail's legs move when the ambulance guy told her to wiggle her toes. She's gonna be fine. You get to do that all the time? And that tall firefighter was *hot.*" Molly reapplied her lipstick, using a metal candleholder as a mirror.

Lucy clapped her hand over her mouth. She would *not* be sick here, not in her brother's bar. She slid off her bar stool and dashed past the pool table into the women's room, where she knelt in front of the toilet. She just made it.

A few minutes later, she splashed cold water on her face. In the mirror, she barely recognized herself. She was pale — white, really — with high pink spots on her cheeks. Her eyes looked too big for her face. Dammit.

No. She didn't do that all the time. Most car fires didn't have someone trapped inside. When she took the pager four days a month, the medicals she ran were usually older people with difficulty breathing, or fall victims. She'd had a couple of CPR calls, but they'd been elderly, expected deaths.

Lucy didn't wrestle her pregnant friends out of the jaws of imminent death regularly.

And he hadn't recognized her. Of course he hadn't. She looked like hell. And why would Owen Bancroft remember who she was? He'd left town right after his high-school graduation. Sure, he'd kissed her. It was a kiss she'd never forgotten, even though she wished she could, but there was no way he remembered it, not after all these years. Most people had interesting lives, after all.

Lucy grimaced at her reflection and made her way back out into the main room. As she passed the table where her mother was knitting with her friends, her mother stopped her.

"Honey, do you know anyone that wears a size-eleven shoe?"

Lucy's mouth dropped open. "Really, Mom?"

Toots Harrison nodded, her knitting needles flashing. "I got some cowboy boots at the thrift store that are divine, purple and red and green, but I can't find anyone that they really belong to. They're so big."

"Did you see what just happened out there? To Abigail?"

Toots closed her eyes and nodded happily. "It was so good she got out in time. I wonder if *she* has big feet. Do you think she does?"

Lucy sighed. "I don't know, Mom. I'll ask her when I see her, okay?"

"Okay, darling."

Lucy made her way back to Molly and crawled up on her bar stool.

Jonas handed out the last shot from his free tray and leaned across the bar. "You gonna live, kiddo?"

She nodded. "Don't call me that." Her voice only wobbled a little bit, but Jonas wasn't paying attention to her anyway.

The lights blazed as power was restored. The jukebox kicked back on, blaring "I Will Survive," mid song. Lucy squeaked, startled.

Silas swaggered past Lucy's bar stool. He held up his shot glass and raised his eyebrows.

"You had your round," said Jonas. "Pay up for the next one."

Silas flipped Jonas off with his free hand. But they grinned at each other, and Lucy watched something pass between them. There had always been a bond between the brothers, something that Lucy was used to being left out of. She looked down into her empty glass and decided against a refill.

Jonas turned to Lucy and said, "That guy that helped out, that was Owen Bancroft, wasn't it? He was in my class, so he was a year older than you, right? Do you remember him?"

"Maybe." Lucy shrugged.

"He was a bad seed, that one."

"Oh, my God," said Lucy. "You sound about a hundred years old. And weren't you the one who got busted with weed in Mr. Dwight's shop class, speaking of bad seeds?"

"Yeah, but Owen barely graduated. And then there was his dad, with the drugs and arrests, and dying in prison and all."

Lucy dropped her gaze to the top of the bar again. "Just because his dad screwed up didn't mean no one could trust him." She could feel Jonas staring at her but she didn't look up.

"You seem to remember him pretty well, huh?"

"Are you serious? That's the one you told me about, right? The one? From high school? Your bad boy?" said Molly, nudging Lucy in the side.

"Hey, I gotta go." Lucy stood, grabbing her knitting bag. She shoved the sock into it unceremoniously, knowing she was losing stitches that she'd regret later.

Molly raised her eyebrows but stood also.

"I'll go with you. I'm on call in the morning, and I hate being woken by the phone."

Silas was looking deeply into the jukebox. Lucy kissed him on the cheek. He looked surprised, but as usual, he didn't say anything. Then she went around to the back of the bar and kissed Jonas's cheek, too. His face relaxed and he laughed and flicked her with the cloth he was holding. "God, Luce."

Lucy waved at her father, but he was already back to watching the game.

Her mother was with the knitters, their needles flashing as their heads bobbed, rehashing what had happened. Lucy blew her a kiss. Her mother reached up, grabbed it and mimed putting it in her pocket, and then blew one back.

At the crash, police officers were filling out forms, and a tow truck beeped as it backed up toward Abigail's car.

"How are they possibly going to move that?" Lucy pointed.

"That's what they do."

"What if Abigail was still in there? What if she was . . ."

"Then they probably wouldn't be towing it yet," Molly said. "Geez. It's all fine, okay? It was exciting! Different! Weren't you just complaining it was too quiet? And then you had to work on a day you weren't even scheduled to volunteer. But you loved it, didn't you?"

Lucy didn't say anything. The damp ocean air was cool. In the distance, the surf crashed in rhythm that Lucy knew like her own heartbeat. She wrapped her scarf more firmly around her neck, bringing it up over her nose.

"So Owen *is* the guy you told me about from high school," said Molly. "Didn't you say he was in San Francisco?"

Lucy shook her head. She didn't want to talk about it.

But Molly wasn't going to be put off, just like that. "He was your bad-boy crush. The only onc you cvcr had."

It hadn't felt like a crush at the time. It had felt bigger than that. Oh, kids were dumb. "Yep, not like you. You chew up bad boys and spit them out for breakfast."

Molly laughed. "I like a challenge. Or three."

"He never knew I was alive."

"Not true," said Molly. "You said he kissed you. And that you saw stars."

It hadn't been that simple. "Why do you like jerks, again?"

Molly shrugged. "They're just more interesting sometimes. They need more. And they give a lot, too. But I do end up going through them quickly, that's for sure."

They walked in silence for a few minutes. Then Molly veered sideways and nudged Lucy's shoulder with her own.

"Some calls are harder than others, and when a friend is involved, it's always worse."

"You've had to handle calls with people you know?" Lucy was surprised. She'd never heard this. "Were you scared?"

Molly's face was soft as she turned to look at Lucy. "Hell, yeah." Molly worked for a language-translation line, translating Cantonese into English for 911 centers around the country. "I recognized my aunt's voice even before I heard the client ID. My uncle wasn't breathing, and I couldn't even tell my auntie who I was, who was helping her, I just had to translate the other dispatcher's words and translate my aunt's words back."

Lucy stared. "Did he make it?"

Molly shook her head, her eyes searching the dunes.

"I'm so sorry."

Molly seemed to shake herself like a dog after the rain. "Oh, hell, girl, now I don't even have to stop stirring the chili while I'm translating, you know that."

Molly's old Victorian loomed in front of them.

"Any home sales recently?" asked Lucy.

Anything to change the topic. She should never have brought it up. She felt raw.

Molly grimaced. "Someday I won't have to have two jobs, right? Nothing in a month. But Cypress Hollow is a beach town. That's why I moved here. It'll get better."

"Yeah, so you say. And anyway, you moved here so you could live in Eliza Carpenter's hometown. I know the truth."

"It's the knitting vortex. It sucked me in. Now go home. You're in a mood, and I'm tired of you. Love you, though." Molly wrapped Lucy in a bear hug. "You're fine, honey. You did good tonight. Okay?"

Lucy nodded and hugged back. She stood at the gate and watched Molly run up the porch stairs and heave open the massive front door.

Then she kept walking.

She turned her head to look back down the hill at the moonlight reflected off the ocean, and smelled smoke in her hair. The fear rose again, threatening to bring with it the nausea.

Home. She wanted to be home, on the couch, her fingers wrapped around her bamboo needles, the merino flying through her hands, a book balanced on her knees, safe, with Grandma Ruby's sweater around her. That was the only good place for her.

# Two

> Sometimes a knitter needs the familiar feel of her favorite wooden needles in her hands — the ones worn and bent. Like favorite shoes, they fit no one else but her.
>
> — E. C.

The next morning, Lucy walked past the bar on her way to open the bookstore. The power pole was still leaning. Most of the glass from the crash had already been cleaned up by the streets department, but shards still glittered by the storm drain.

Abigail almost lost her life at this spot. Lucy almost saw her die.

For one second, right where Abigail had been lying last night on the pavement, Lucy's knees refused to lock the correct way. Her gait felt wrong, as if she were drunk. She looked down to steady herself, and there, next to a dropped matchbook, was a stain. Abigail's blood.

Everything went dark. She sucked extra air in through her mouth and touched the outside wall of Jonas's bar. It was fine. Everything was fine. It was a great morning to be alive, wasn't it? If she could keep the fluttering in her stomach to a minimum, and if she didn't pass out right here and now, it would be an even better morning.

Come on, now. A member of the prestigious Cypress Hollow Volunteer Fire Brigade didn't act this way. Lucy knew that. She could handle blood. She could dress a wound and apply pressure to a hemorrhage and hold people down in the back of the ambulance, even when they were begging and screaming bloody murder. For someone who normally flew under the radar — quiet old bookstore Lucy — Captain Keller always said he was impressed with how she came through under pressure.

So what the hell was this about?

Her brother's bar was shut up tight. Jonas would be in soon, though — even in Cypress Hollow, some people drank in the morning. When he'd bought it, he'd changed it from a seedy rundown bar filled with old men and a perpetual cigarette-smoke haze to a clean, friendly gathering place. Drinkers and teetotalers alike met at the Rite Spot to have Trivia Night, to play board games, to toast weddings and mourn deaths. On Friday nights, Jonas hired live bands to play, and on Sunday mornings, he opened early so the book club could meet over donuts and coffee. Lucy's mother's knitting group met there on Thursday mornings, and if some of them added a little Baileys to their coffee, no one ever complained.

But for now, it was still closed, and no one would mind if Lucy leaned against the post next to the front door and pretended to read the list of bands lined up for the next month. The words swam in front of her eyes, though, as the images from the night before played against her eyelids: Abigail's open, bloody mouth; Owen's hands, working against the metal frame of the car door; the flames underneath the engine.

It was okay. Gooseflesh rose along her arms and legs, and her heart raced again as she looked at the stain on the sidewalk, but she told herself it was all right. She pulled the yellow sweater her grandmother had knitted for her so many years ago tighter around her and resumed walking to work.

Lucy walked past Tillie's Diner, the perennial town favorite. The main room, mostly booths, was already full of patrons, and she peeked in the plate-glass window to see all the ranchers in the side room. They gathered after their chores in the morning, as if they'd been there forever in their cowboy hats and lived-in jeans, gossiping about girls walking past the windows and the price of hay, and she tried not to think about the fact that every year, there were one or two less of them in the room.

She avoided looking at the old art deco movie theater, its red-and-yellow sign curving out over the street and back in again. The windows were boarded up and it broke her heart to look at it. And she hated how it matched the other closed-up, battened-down businesses that hadn't weathered the recent financial storms.

The Book Spire was across the street. After she unlocked the huge front door with the biggest key on her key ring, she flipped on the overhead lights. The building, constructed at the turn of the twentieth century, was originally a small Gothic Revival church. Its central stained-glass window used to showcase a dour Jesus, but when Lucy's grandmother Ruby bought the desanctified church, she'd had the Lord removed and replaced him with the stained-glass image of a pen breaking a sword over a tower of brilliantly colored books. Ruby had kept some pews as seating, lined with cushions. The nave and narthex held dark wooden bookshelves now instead of hymnals, but the air was still scented with the ghost of incense and lilies.

Lucy moved into the coolness of the store, flipping on the standing lamps and three space heaters, trying to shake the images of the downed power pole and broken glass out of her mind.

*Owen Bancroft was back.*

Starting the coffee was the most important thing now. Besides the books, she was known for it: strong and dark, but never bitter. She ordered a special blend of beans from a roaster up the road. It was pricey, but worth it.

She counted out fifty dollars' worth of change left over from the woefully slim deposit yesterday, enjoying the everyday sound of paper money whispering, the coins clinking. She placed the till in its drawer and then swept. Blessed normalcy. It soothed her.

Until a rap at the front glass made her jump.

Already? It wasn't even nine yet. But Elbert Romo looked like he couldn't wait. He jiggled the handle of the door and tapped again.

"I'm coming!" Lucy unlocked the door

from the inside and swung it open. “Jeesh, Elbert. You’re early today.”

“I couldn’t sleep. I’ve been at Tillie’s since six this morning. And you know that I . . .”

“You hate their bathroom.”

“They don’t clean it. Not so it smells clean. Not like yours . . .”

Elbert had already pushed past her, and his voice trailed off as he bolted into the bathroom. Lucy didn’t hear him lock it. Why would he? Elbert was one of a group of customers who treated her store as if it were their home. Elbert wouldn’t lock his bathroom door at home — why should he do it here?

Lucy turned on the stereo. It was a Chopin kind of day. Most Saturdays were.

Elbert came out a few moments later, smiling beatifically, still tucking in his shirt. “That’s better. Man, that was a lot of coffee today.”

He went and poured himself yet another cup from her first pot, which had just finished brewing. At eighty-four, Elbert was no spring chicken, but he still had some of his hearing and all his own teeth. He reminded Lucy of a seed catalog, colorful, cheerful, simple. His eyesight, he was happy to tell anyone who would listen, was just fine, and he trained that vision on any lady pretty enough to grab it.

But he was sweet. He hummed sometimes, without knowing it, and he brought her little presents for the store: a bouquet of local flowers that he'd pilfered out of gardens along the way, or a box of crumbled cookies for her to put out with the coffee.

Lucy flipped the sign to Open, and rolled the postcard rack out. She'd keep an eye on the skies and rush it back inside if it started to rain, but she wouldn't roll the clearance cart out at all. She didn't want to risk ruining a whole cart full of books, even on sale, in a spring shower if she could help it.

As she put out the postcards, she saw Greta Doss and Mildred Elkins turn the corner and head in her direction. They smiled. Mildred shook a white bag in the air.

Lucy sighed in happiness. She never let herself buy donuts, but if someone else wanted to get her one, well, who was she to stand in the way of their joy? Mildred knew her special weakness was the thick, gooey bear claw. Happy Donuts stuffed theirs with almond paste and raisins, just the way Lucy liked them.

As much as an octogenarian could, Mildred scampered up to Lucy, thrusting the bag at her.

"See? No calories if someone else buys it for you!" Mildred was always pleased when she made this joke, like she'd never made it before. Lucy laughed as hard as always. Small price to pay for a bear claw.

"Come on in, ladies. Elbert's already here."

Both Greta and Mildred groaned. They made fun of Elbert Romo behind his back, calling him Elbert Oh-No, and to his face they mocked that he ate every meal at Tillie's. But Elbert was the oldest surviving single man in town, and the three of them spent enough time together at the Book Spire to qualify them as actual friends, even if none of them ever admitted it out loud.

Elbert stood as Lucy ushered Mildred and Greta inside. He always stood when a lady entered or exited, or when they sat down or stood up at the reading table. His knees creaked and popped ominously when he did, and Lucy told him not to do it, but he said, "That would be like not breathing air, my dear."

Mildred took a serving plate out from the cabinet below the coffeepots. She ripped open her other white bag and placed four donuts on it, a glazed, two chocolate crullers, and an old-fashioned. Greta took the mugs they always used off their hooks and filled them with coffee, adding cream to Mildred's and nothing to her own.

Both women moved then to the table and sat with contented sighs.

Greta, the younger of the two women, had been a schoolteacher for many years, and had never married. She'd taken care of her mother until she died, thirty years ago. Right around the same time, Mildred's husband had dropped dead of a stroke, and after finding out about some bad investments he'd made, she'd had to sell the house to pay things off. She'd moved in with Greta then, and the pair had been inseparable ever since.

Greta was the quiet one. In Lucy's mind, she was like an Edwardian novel: leather bound, tiny print. It might be difficult to turn the fragile pages, but the color plates made it worth it.

Mildred, on the other hand, was a child's picture book: colorful, and loud. She never wore anything that wasn't bright, and she said that if she wore a pink blouse, she didn't want to hurt red's feelings. So she wore red pants with a purple sweater, an orange scarf at her neck, topped with a green jacket and blue hat.

"Lucy!" Mildred called imperiously.

Darn. Lucy had thought she might get the

new magazines out. Oh, well, it would have to wait. She'd never hurt their feelings by ignoring them.

"What's on your mind, Mildred?" Lucy asked.

"Were you there last night?" Her fingers flashed as she held her knitting in her lap. She was doing something with two strands, knitting with both hands.

Would it help to play dumb? Lucy wasn't sure. "Is that Noro? What are you making?"

"Does this look like Noro? You're not stupid, child. Jamieson's. Sleeve. And don't give me that. At the bar. Did you see the crash? Did you really get stuck inside? And did Abigail really lose three fingers and a toe?"

"God!" Lucy lost her breath. "No! Where did you hear that?"

"On the news."

"You *didn't.*"

Mildred shrugged. "Okay. No, we heard it from Phyllis Gill, who was there."

"She's legally blind," said Lucy. "And she must have had a few too many. Because in no way, shape, or form did that happen. There was a crash. Abigail was trapped. But she got out, and then the car burst into flames."

Mildred and Greta both looked disappointed.

Lucy shook her head. "Don't you think that's exciting enough? Just the way it is?"

"Well, at least you were there," Mildred said. The most tech savvy of the eighty-plus set, she pulled out an iPhone and started tapping notes out on it. "What were her injuries? I may talk about it in my podcast later, and I want the details. And was Irene Bancroft's son there, too? Back from the City?"

Elbert said, "Never liked Irene's husband, that Hugh Bancroft."

"Well, no one minded when he died," said Mildred.

Greta gasped. "You can't *say* that."

Mildred keyed something into her cell phone with extra force and looked up. "I can. Good riddance to bad rubbish, I say."

Elbert nodded. "And if the son is back in town . . . You know what they say about apples and trees, after all."

Greta said, "But he became a police officer, didn't he? In San Francisco. And I think Phyllis said he helped get Abigail out of the car, too."

Mildred raised her eyebrows and kept staring into her phone. "You really think that being a cop makes him trustworthy? In a big, corrupt city like that?" Then she hit a button on the phone twice and looked up at Lucy. "So. What was Owen really doing there last night?"

Lucy reached for a pen but it slipped from her fingers, falling to the slate floor with a small clatter. "Mildred, I have *so* many things I need to do. I'm going to let you three catch up this morning, and we'll call the hospital later, how about that?"

She rolled the dolly stacked with magazine bundles to the periodicals area. Now was not the time to think about Owen. Lucy knelt on the floor and reached down to grab some extra Interweave Knits that had slipped to the very back of the rack. As she hauled them out, she took a moment to survey her store. The lower-than-usual viewpoint made everything look different. It pleased her, but it took her a minute to realize why.

When she'd first started coming here regularly to help her grandmother, she'd probably been as tall as she was now, seated on the floor. The two huge front doors seemed even bigger than usual and the stacks of books looked so much taller and more impressive and exciting. This was what she'd fallen in love with.

She'd spent so much time as a child at the bookstore with her grandmother, curled up in various corners reading or scribbling story ideas on scraps of spare paper, that it had been a natural transition into working here through high school. She'd been the one to talk her grandmother Ruby into carrying new books, as well as the used books she specialized in. Lucy had ordered the microfiche from Ingram, and opened an account with Baker and Taylor. Ruby let Lucy make the decisions, and Lucy would carefully order one bestseller and watch, thrilled, as it was paid for and carried out of the store. So she'd order a few more authors, until she had a good sense of what her customers wanted.

The Book Spire might be mostly used books, but Lucy took pride in being able to order almost anything for anyone. When internet selling had hit the book trade, she'd seen the magic in it from the start. Now, even out-of-print books were available, at a price, leaving little she couldn't track down for her customers.

There. That was the last of the magazines. She looked over at the table. The three of them were still fine. Elbert was trying to talk to Greta about fly-fishing, and Greta was staring at a spot on the ceiling just over his right shoulder.

Lucy stayed sitting on the floor.

A spot of sun had broken through the overcast sky, and she was sitting directly in its beam, like a cat warming itself. Her grandmother, had she been here, would have come over and stood in the sunlight with her. Her feet had always been cold, and Lucy had loved watching her follow the stained-glass-colored sun puddles all over the store.

The left door creaked, letting someone in. Lucy didn't move from her spot. She was half hidden by the second magazine shelf, and she'd be able to spy on whoever it was. For a moment, she felt six years old.

Then Owen Bancroft entered the store carrying a box, and she felt sixteen.

Damn. That thick brown hair that stuck out as if he'd rumpled it when he arose and hadn't touched it since — men in magazines paid a lot of money to have their hair look like that. She hadn't noticed last night how broad his shoulders were. Could they have been that wide in high school?

And he was still limping, like he had been last night. As he moved forward, his motions were smooth, but there was a distinct hitch to his gait. So she hadn't imagined it, then.

And his eyes . . .

When they landed on her in the corner, his dark blue gaze burned into her.

# Three

When you start a project, have respect for the fact that it may turn out to be something completely different than the item you originally intended it to be. It may be prettier, longer, shorter, or stranger altogether. It will certainly be better.

— E. C.

The Book Spire smelled like books and paper and something sweeter. Owen's eyes scanned the room as he struggled to hold the heavy box while still retaining his balance. It didn't help that the three people sitting at the central table turned and stared as he opened the door. But the staring had been happening all over town, and he supposed it would get worse before it got better. He hadn't been a local in a long time, and even when he had been, this town hadn't trusted him.

Owen knew the moment he stepped inside

the store that there was a person hiding in the corner, felt it with a vestige of his old profession, but he reminded himself that he wasn't a cop anymore. A female, from the size of the person. Crouched low. Armed? His hand moved to his side, where he still carried his gun.

Shit. He was off duty. For good. Goddamn, that still hurt like a punch to the gut.

He had to remember that a girl staring at him from behind those magazines wasn't the enemy. Owen didn't need to worry. Except possibly about her well-being.

Maybe she was a special-needs resident of town; maybe the people at the table took care of her.

On second glance, he revised his opinion. He recognized her with a jolt — she was the woman from last night, the one who had helped him pop the seat back just before the car was engulfed.

Holy hell, she was a looker, with long dark hair that fell forward over her shoulder, and dark brown startled-looking eyes. All he'd really noticed about her last night was that she was small, just the right size for forcing her way into the car where he couldn't.

Crazy that he hadn't noticed how pretty she was. Even in that weird outfit — ratty yellow sweater over overalls, with purple and blue sneakers — she was a knockout. He should ask her about last night, see how the woman was . . .

But the old man who sat at the big wooden table in the middle of the room pushed back his chair and teetered to the front of the store to stand in front of him.

"Elbert Romo. You're Irene's boy, ain't you?"

"Owen Bancroft. Yes." He had to put this box down, soon. His hip was killing him and his knee kept locking.

"You played football for two years."

Owen winced. Just because he'd had wide shoulders, even back in high school, didn't mean that he was a great athlete.

Elbert said, "I do seem to remember hearing you spent more time under the bleachers smoking than on the field."

"Hey, I gotta put this box down. The counter?"

"Come over here and meet the ladies. Mildred, Greta, this is Owen Bancroft, Irene's boy."

The woman named Greta gave him a half smile and looked into her coffee cup as if she were reading tea leaves.

But the one Elbert had called Mildred also stood. She met him, lifted the box out of his hands like it was full of tissue paper and set it on the table. Then she pumped his hand so firmly that he reached out to balance himself against the table.

"I'm sorry about your mother. How is she doing?"

*Whoomp.* The suddenness of the question rocked him. He knew his mom was bad, but to hear this, to see the concern written all over this perfect stranger's face . . .

"She's okay."

"At Willow Rock now, isn't she?" She was the type of woman who knew everything in town. He'd never liked this particular type, and he was remembering why.

Owen nodded. "Yep."

"It's a good care facility. Sometimes we carol there at the holidays, some women from the church and I."

He smiled thinly. "Very kind."

She fluttered her hands, "Oh, we just do what we can. Your mother and Eliza Carpenter and I used to knit together. That is, when your mother wasn't in a mood. But that was a long time ago now. Don't worry, they take good care there. So what brings you here? Something we can do for you?"

Good, she must be the owner. Owen pointed to the box. "Books. I think. You buy them?"

More fluttering. "Oh, you need Lucy."

Mildred pointed to the woman in the yellow sweater who had come up out of her crouch and was now skittering out of sight, crab-like, through a back doorway, dragging a dolly full of magazines. “Lucy! Over here! Come meet Owen Bancroft!”

At that moment, there was a loud crash from the back room. Owen looked at the three people at the table. None of them were young enough to move as quickly as he’d be able to, even if he was a gimp.

In the back room, he found the woman on the floor. It looked like she’d slipped and had taken down a tall stack of magazines with her when she fell. She looked up at him with wide eyes.

“Are you okay?”

Mildred came up behind him. “What happened?”

Owen said, “She slipped.” Then he turned back to the woman and said, “Don’t move.”

From the floor, the woman winced. “I’m fine. Just had the wind knocked out of me.” She stood, brushing off her overalls, looking at him expectantly.

“Are you sure you’re okay?”

“Positive,” Lucy said. “Is there something I can help you with?”

He cleared his throat. “Oh, yeah. Books? I have some.”

Lucy nodded but didn't say anything. He followed her back out into the main room of the store and pointed to the box he'd brought in. "Probably just junk."

"I'll be the judge of that. What's on top of it? It's covered with . . ."

"Cat hair. I'm sorry," said Owen. "I tried to clean off most of it, but a lot of it seems to have embedded itself into the cardboard. Cats have been sleeping in my mother's storage unit."

Lucy raised her eyebrows. "It looks like a felted rug."

"But as far as I can tell, no cats have peed on the boxes."

"Small mercies."

"Two more of them in the car. Just as fuzzy."

She barely glanced at him, just pulled her sweater tighter. There were holes at the hem of the sleeves, Owen noticed. "Go get them, then," she said.

When Owen finished carrying in the third box, she was leaning against the counter, laughing at what sounded like a stupid joke about two peanuts and a bar, told by the old man, Elbert.

She had a great laugh. But when Owen leaned against the counter and smiled, Lucy's laugh trailed off, and she moved the last box to the left.

"I'm sorry, I don't think that —"

Owen interrupted her. "How is the woman from last night?"

"Abigail?"

"Yes."

Lucy's face softened. "I called when I woke up this morning. She's got a few bruised ribs and a couple of lacerations, but she's fine and the baby's fine."

"You did a great job."

She looked down at the box and then back up at him. "Yeah."

"You're just a natural, I guess. You were the perfect person to have right there. You couldn't have come out of the bar at a better time. You helped save her life." Owen smiled, and hoped for a similar response. Her brown eyes were more familiar than they should be from just seeing them last night. Owen knew her, and he could almost place her. God, had he dated her? He couldn't remember having a girlfriend named Lucy, but the name rang a bell in his head. If he could just remember . . .

Lucy was still looking at him, her head tilted to the side, a surprised look on her face.

"What?" he asked.

She jumped. "I'm sorry. Nothing. Okay,

your boxes. I've only poked through them a little bit, but they look like they're just full of old romances. Let me look at this one." She leaned forward, her hair falling in front of her face. She smelled sweet, the hint of incense that remained in the old converted church mingling with whatever she was wearing.

Lucy looked up at him. Those lips . . . Damn. Had it been that long that he was this easily distracted? Owen forced himself to listen to what she was saying.

"I'm sorry." She held up a ripped Barbara Cartland. "I don't buy old romances. I have too many already."

"Hell. Don't you buy books? Isn't this a used bookstore? Those are used books."

"Too old. And too used. Look, these are losing their pages. Even I have my book principles."

"What do you suggest I do with them, then? A library?"

She snorted. "I'm sorry, but no library wants these."

"A Dumpster, then? You got one out back? If you have a Dumpster I could borrow, I'll bring the rest of my mother's junk and chuck it all in, once and for all. I just don't know —" Owen cut himself off. She didn't need to know what he was going through, dealing with the stuff Irene had just crammed in that storage unit with no regard to what he was going to have to deal with to get through it. He picked up the first box he'd brought in. "Thanks anyway."

"Wait," she said, and her voice was softer now.

"What?"

"Fine, I'll take them. But I can only give you . . . five bucks a box."

Owen turned, slamming the box back on the counter with more force than he'd intended. "Deal."

Lucy turned to open the register and Owen took a deep breath. They were only books. Goddammit.

"How long are you staying, Owen?" Mildred called out from the table. Nosy broad.

But he turned and gave what he hoped passed for a smile, and then deliberately didn't answer the question. "Over at the Starlite Motel, on South Street."

Mildred gasped and pressed a beringed hand to her ample bosom. "I knew a man who caught something at that fleabag place that we don't like to talk about in polite company. Why don't you rent a place? A nice place?"

"I'm not staying long."

The register slammed shut with a loud jangle.

Mildred smiled, showing all her teeth. "Still, you should at least rent something better while you're here. Good thing the parsonage is rented, Lucy, or you'd have to show it to him, wouldn't you?"

From behind him, Lucy said in too loud a voice, "Fifteen dollars! Here you go! Thanks for stopping by, please come see us again."

She slid the cash across the counter instead of placing it in his hand.

"What's the parsonage?"

Mildred was up and moving over toward him. She was a force of nature, he could tell.

"It's in the back, here, past the little cemetery. Lucy rents it out, fully furnished, but she has a tenant now, don't you, Lucy?"

Mildred's voice set Owen's teeth on edge. It was as if she were rubbing it in — that Owen didn't deserve to stay in a nice place in town. Yeah, he understood that. He always did.

Lucy looked up at the high beamed rafters as if the answer were hanging there. "Well, she moved out last week," she said, finally.

Mildred's look turned to one of concern. "Well, now, that wouldn't mean that . . ."

"So it's available?" Owen asked.

Lucy said, "I just usually don't rent it to grown-ups."

This conversation was difficult for him to follow. "Excuse me? I'm thirty-five, but . . ."

"I rent it to girls who are at the local junior college, usually. There's a high turnover, but they're nice. I've never . . ." She cocked her head to the side for a moment and surveyed him. "You're a cop, right?"

How did she know that? "Retired."

"You're not old enough to be retired."

"Medically retired." The next question would be whether he'd ever shot anyone. He fucking hated that question.

"Huh." She studied him some more. She didn't ask the question. And then, just like that, he remembered.

"You were Lucy Harrison."

"It's the darndest thing." A smile broke like sunrise across her face. "I still am."

"Well, women's last names change all the time."

"Mine tends to remain stubbornly the same."

"Mine, too," said Owen. "You were my tutor."

"You were really terrible in math."

"I was."

And then a blush slid across her cheeks, staining them a dusty pink. Owen had to curl his fingers around the lip of the wooden counter — the urge to reach out to touch the soft skin of her face was astounding. And it would have scared the crap out of her, rightly so, had he done it.

Owen wondered if she even remembered that one kiss.

Probably not. What teenage girl remembers some stupid guy who bails and never comes back? She probably didn't remember that night at all. He did, though. *Now* he remembered Lucy Harrison.

Elbert Romo cleared his throat from behind them. "It's more of a cottage, really. Way more house than someone like you needs."

Owen nodded, using an amazing feat of will to look away from Lucy's mouth. "It sounds perfect, actually."

Greta, who had been very quiet until now, said, "I know a very nice bed-and-breakfast run by a friend of mine who's always looking for a man around the house to help her with things. I bet she'd even give you a discount. Lucy's right, her little place is better suited to younger people."

Mildred's voice cut Greta off. "Lucy won't rent to Owen. That's enough of that."

Owen raised his shoulders. "Well, considering I haven't even seen it yet, maybe I could just do that."

"Out of the question," said Mildred, pushing her chair in to the table with a thud. "You're just not what she's looking for."

Mildred's voice buzzed like an insect, but Owen kept his eyes on Lucy. God, she was pretty. Had Lucy been this hot in high school? Maybe he'd missed her because she was short — still was — but damn, those perfect curves made up for whatever she lacked in height. How had he only kissed her that one time?

Owen backed up and stuck his hands in his pockets. Mildred was right. He didn't need pretty right now. He didn't need a complication. He just needed a place to figure out what the hell his next move was going to be. The Starlite Motel was as good a place as any, close enough to his mother, and quiet enough when the desk clerk wasn't singing lousy opera at the top of her extremely loud lungs.

Without meeting his eyes, Lucy said, "You can come look at it. Can you come back at five, when I close?"

# Four

> We can't help but feel sorry, can we, for those who don't knit? What do they do when they're nervous? When they don't know where to look? What is knitting if not directed fidgeting?
>
> — E. C.

Lucy flipped the Open sign to Closed. Although he was still a block away, she could see Owen approaching on foot. Punctual.

What was she doing, anyway? Thinking about renting to him? After he'd graduated a year before her, she'd spent her senior year of high school — not to mention the first couple of years of college — trying to recover from him. Trying not to remember the kiss he'd given her, the one that had changed her completely. He'd disappeared without even saying good-bye.

And he was even better looking now. How

was *that* fair?

Lucy held the door open for him.

His eyes were much bluer today. She'd remembered that they were dark blue, but not how very deep, very dark they were — practically the color of the deep water out over the breakers. She'd never seen that particular shade on anyone else. And those lashes! She had to wear mascara every day to have any lashes at all.

His mouth twitched.

"What?" she asked.

"You're staring."

"Oh, sorry." God, how embarrassing. She had to pull it together. "I'm just tired. I was just . . . um . . ." Lucy would be professional. This was business.

Why had she decided to show him the parsonage?

He nodded and stepped into the store, the slight limp marking his gait. Lucy turned her back to lead him and was conscious of what a rat's nest her hair always looked like by the end of the workday.

"Just through here." She led him out through the middle of the store and turned left at the side door leading out of the transept.

Owen paused behind her and looked up at the high ceiling vaults. "It doesn't look like a bookstore. More like a . . . I don't know." He put a hand on the lintel. "I think I remember coming in here as a kid sometimes. It hasn't changed much, huh?"

Lucy smiled. "This is just the way my Grandma Ruby had it." She loved her store at this time of day, when the sun was setting, the red-and-orange light streaming into the nave through the clerestory windows. It felt sanctified, like her own cathedral to books. But that was a bit much. She wouldn't tell him that.

"The old bones of the church make it feel like a temple."

Lucy's eyes widened. She cleared her throat and led him out. "Here, through the garden." The heavy door slammed behind them.

"Would I always have to walk through the bookstore?"

She should have led him through the outside gate. She wasn't thinking clearly.

"Of course not. Sorry. There's a walkway there, see?"

"Nice roses," he said, and he actually sounded like he meant it.

"I pay a kid a few bucks to prune and water and weed. I don't have a green thumb."

"My mom loves roses."

Lucy didn't know how to answer that, so she hurried up the path to the front door of the tiny house.

"This is it." She unlocked the door and pushed it open. Damn, she should have aired it out this afternoon. It still smelled of the last girl's penchant for patchouli.

"Kitchen," she pointed. "Gas appliances. Washer and dryer are just off there."

"Fine."

"It's tiny," she said. Why did she feel like she should apologize? "It was built to be the parsonage, but I think that was a fancy name for what's more like a one-bedroom house. No study, no library, no servants' quarters. Just the threadbare carpet and lots of candle sconces to earn its name."

She flipped on the lights in the hallway and led him to the far door. "Also, there's a parlor, with the original furniture. I don't recommend the blue chair. There's an unruly spring I haven't been able to fix. But that settee is actually comfortable."

He nodded. She couldn't tell what he was thinking, and it made her nervous. And nerves made her chatty. "It was originally an Episcopalian church, and the parsonage was built at the turn of the last century. But the church went rogue in the twenties, with a pastor who bought the buildings and took the church in more of a fundamentalist direction. By the sixties, that same old pastor was caught hoarding guns for the Apocalypse and had lost all but three of his church members. When he died, his widow sold everything to my grandmother and moved to Florida to be with her grandchildren. My grandmother Ruby lived happily back here for the rest of her life."

"How did you end up with this? And with the bookstore?"

Lucy turned her back to him, and then she pulled open a small door. "Extra storage here, next to the hot water heater. When she died, she left it all to me. I'm the book girl. My brothers are big readers, but they didn't want the store."

"It's what you always wanted? To follow in her footsteps?" Owen sounded interested, and Lucy couldn't remember the last time someone sounded that way.

She nodded. "I was always the reader in the family. And when I was little I wanted to be a writer, but then when I realized writers didn't make any money, I wanted to sell books instead. And I've always been a knitter. It's what I do. I know it must sound pretty boring to someone like you . . ." Lucy felt a small flame of embarrassment.

But he smiled at her instead. Laugh lines

she didn't remember folded at the corners of his eyes. "You never lived back here, though?"

"No, too small. So many memories, and I can't get rid of one thing that's in here. I don't like to change it around from the way she had it. You know? The income from the store and the rental allowed me to buy a little house in town a few years ago. Better that way. God, these shelves are dusty. And oh, there's a cemetery out there. Guess I should mention that. No one's been buried in it for ages, though." Lucy brushed off her hands and shut the small closet door.

Owen nodded. He touched the base of a silver candelabra still propped on a low table. "The ceilings are nice." He looked up at the exposed wooden beams.

Lucy felt her stomach flip. "Yeah," she said. "They're my favorite part."

Lucy's cell phone rang, blaring "I Shot the Sheriff" from the pocket of her overalls. She hit the Ignore button on the side of it as fast as she could but the damage was done.

"Nice," said Owen.

"My brother Jonas. He programmed it." She was going to kill him.

"Not a fan of the boys in blue?"

"Just likes Marley, I guess. The bedroom

is back here."

It was the largest room of the small house. All open space, a queen-sized bed in one corner, a large desk in another. A green couch faced a bookcase, and one of her grandmother's comfy old recliners sat next to the window. "See? Big closet. And lots of shelves, for your stuff. The girls ran in cable and internet — if you have a TV I'm sure it would hook right up."

Her cell phone rang again.

Owen winced. "Do you need to get that?"

Lucy looked at it. "Jonas doesn't usually call me, and he never calls twice in a row. It might be important. I'm sorry." Owen nodded as she flipped open the phone. "Hello?"

Owen looked out the window that overlooked the old cemetery.

"I just heard some crap that you're going to rent to Owen Bancroft." Jonas didn't bother saying hello.

Lucy took a deep breath. "I can look into ordering that for you, but it might take a while."

"Dammit, Lucy, you know you can't trust anyone in that family. I'm just looking out for you. Old Bill told me his father was in prison three times for assault with a deadly weapon."

Lucy frowned. "That doesn't sound like

any of your business." Then, glancing at Owen who was trying to open the window, she hastened to add, "To order a book like that, I mean."

"We're just looking out for you. There are a million people better than him. Why can't you just . . ."

*"Goddamn!"* Owen jumped away from the window, cradling his hand.

Lucy jumped. "Jonas, I have to go."

"What's going on? What's he doing? Are you safe there? Do I need to come over?"

"Don't you dare! He cut his hand on that window latch I keep asking you or Silas to fix." Lucy hung up without saying goodbye. "Owen, I'm so sorry. Let me see your hand."

"You should get that fixed. It's booby-trapped." Owen came toward her, examining the blood dripping from his arm.

Lucy felt terrible, but at the same time, as she reached for his arm, she was conscious of the fact that she'd forgotten that a man could smell this good. It wasn't cologne — he didn't strike Lucy as a cologne kind of guy. It was a clean soap smell, not flowery, just brisk. Efficient. And something else, something richer. Nicer.

Lucy realized she was inhaling deeply. Too deeply. He was going to notice.

And then Owen looked at her.

She forgot to breathe. He really did have the most amazing eyes: deep blue shot with streaks of gold. She willed herself not to look at his lips but failed. She licked her own out of nervousness, and his eyes followed.

Then she remembered the important part — Owen was bleeding. Just what she needed. Would he sue? *Could* he sue? Did insurance cover that kind of thing?

Damn. The wound. She focused. It wasn't deep, wouldn't need stitches, but it did need to be covered.

"Stay right here," Lucy said. "I'll fix you up. Stay. I'm sorry." She raced out of the room, leaving Owen staring at his hand.

She ran out of the parsonage and into the bookstore. In the bathroom, she grabbed a tube of Neosporin and a box of Band-Aids. She found a clean washcloth and ran back through the garden.

A nice quiet girl, a student, would be better anyway. School would be starting back up for the spring quarter. It was just easier that way. Not that she even wanted him to rent it. She didn't know why she'd volunteered to let him see it in the first place — it just hadn't seemed fair, the way they'd been going on about how he *shouldn't* be allowed to.

Lucy prayed Owen wasn't the lawsuit type.

When she entered the bedroom, Owen was using Kleenex from the box next to the bed to wipe away the blood.

"No, let me. It's the least I can do. It's my stupid broken window." She sat next to him on the edge of the bed.

Lucy used the washcloth to clean up the blood that had trickled down his hand.

"I'm happy to bandage you up. I know how. Or I can take you to the hospital. I'll pay, of course, for any treatment." She tried not to think about what that would do to her slim bank account.

Still Owen said nothing. He was too quiet. Was he furious with her? Wouldn't she feel scared if that was so? And Lucy wasn't scared. She felt nervous, yes, but none of her regular fears plagued her, sitting next to Owen.

She put the antibiotic ointment on her finger. "I washed my hands. So they're clean. Um. You should know that . . ." This wasn't the way they would ever do it on the ambulance. God, Captain Keller would be laughing at her right now. Why was she so flustered?

"I'm just going to put this on your hand. I mean, on the wound. Damn. But I don't think it will hurt."

She took a chance and stole a glance at him, looking up for a split second at his face. She needed to know whether she was going to need to run or not.

Was that a smile? Were the corners of his mouth really twitching?

Lucy dropped her head again to his hand. "Here I go. There. That wasn't bad, was it?" She made sure the wound on the side of his hand was carefully covered with antibiotic ointment, and then turned his hand over to see if there were any other wounds that needed care. She ran her fingers over his skin.

His hand was huge. Strong. Warm. Completely, jarringly masculine.

And still bleeding.

"Okay. Good." Lucy cleared her throat. She flipped open the top of the box. "Oh, crap."

She looked up at him and then back into the box. Surely she had a normal Band-Aid. She flipped through the bandages, then she looked again. Oh, how embarrassing. She was an emergency medical technician, for the love of God.

"Um," she said. "You have your choice between rainbows, dinosaurs, or cowboys. It looks like I only have novelty Band-Aids. There are some sushi ones, too, but . . . I'm kind of saving those ones."

Owen started laughing. It was a deep, rolling laugh, sounding like it came from the middle of his chest. "Cowboys. Of course I want cowboys."

It was the last reaction she would have expected from him. He went on laughing as she continued to bandage his hand. At least it was better than him yelling at her, or suing her. Which he could still do later.

"I'm sorry, it's going to take more of these than I thought," Lucy said as she struggled to open yet another bandage. These really were crappy, she thought. They didn't seem to have any stick at all, and they were brittle. Good for nothing but putting on imaginary boo-boos, which Owen's boo-boo, sadly, wasn't.

"There. I think that'll do it." Lucy stood and looked at her handiwork.

The back and side of Owen's hand was covered in little cowboys riding horses and wearing chaps. He held it out and nodded in what looked like satisfaction.

Lucy couldn't help it. "Why aren't you mad at me?" she asked.

"I just cut my hand on the window latch. It's not like you bit me."

"I wouldn't bite you!" And she blushed.

She busied herself picking up the bits and

pieces of the wrappers that seemed to be everywhere. He stood up but she didn't look at him. "So, I can suggest a few more places, if you'd like. A friend has a cottage that I think is vacant, and another friend owns that little motel down on Pine Street. Then there's that bed-and-breakfast that Greta mentioned."

"Why?" Owen asked. The smile slipped from his face as if it had never been there. "Because I hurt myself? I'm too much of a liability?"

The way he said the last word turned something inside Lucy, made her ache for him. There was more to this than a cut on a window.

"No. I just assumed . . ."

"I've gone through worse." Owen frowned.

Lucy tried to steer the conversation. "How long do you really think you'll be here, anyway?"

"I have no idea. I know I'm not staying."

Lucy twisted the cap of the antibiotic cream tighter and then loosened it.

Owen went on, "I'm trying to figure out what I'm doing when it comes to my mother. She's just down the road, at Willow Rock."

"Why is she there?"

"Alzheimer's. Couldn't live alone anymore." Still seated on the bed, he ran his fingers along the Band-Aids. "I haven't decided how I'm doing all this yet. I sold most of my stuff before I left and what little I kept is in storage in San Francisco. But I'd like to take this place while I work it all out. It's perfect. Great location, just around the corner from my mom, and it's furnished. I won't ask you to make a decision right now. Will you just let me know after you think about it? You need my cell number, and here." He pulled a piece of folded paper out of his pocket and handed it to her, the paper warm from being so close to his skin. "A few references. They're officers, sergeants, and lieutenants I used to work with. They all think I'm great. If you want the full story, I listed dispatch's phone number. They may not all like me that much, but you'll get honesty from them. My credit score is on there, and it's okay if you confirm it."

"Do you smoke?"

"Depends on what you mean. Smoke what?"

Was he serious? "Cigarettes?"

He half smiled, and she saw him, suddenly, in the hallway of the high school, his arm slung around yet another blond, that same teasing look in his eye. "I don't smoke anything."

Whew. "Do you, well . . . I'm not sure how to ask this."

"Just ask." His voice was gravelly. She liked it too much.

"Do you carry a gun?"

"Do you really want to know?"

"Heck, yeah!"

"Then, yes, I do carry a gun. Is that a problem?"

Lucy thought for a moment. He studied her while she did. She made a conscious effort to still her hands. She wished for her knitting, wished she could feel the wool slipping through her fingers, but her bag was still inside the store.

"It makes me nervous. Didn't you say you were retired? Ex-cops still carry guns?"

"It's like carrying your driver's license. Even if I'm not a cop anymore . . ." Owen's voice trailed off. Then he went on. "After that many years, it gets to be a habit. I don't feel clothed if I'm not wearing it."

And just like that, Lucy pictured him with no clothes on. The image flashed in front of her eyes, superimposed against his actual clothing. Instead of the blue button-down shirt, she could see his bare, muscled chest. No clothes, no pants, no gun.

How long had it been for her? she wondered. Obviously, too damn long.

God. Maybe he hadn't noticed her fade-out. "Guns scare me," Lucy said. "But I think that's probably a good thing."

"You should go to the range sometime."

"No way. Not me."

"I'll take you."

"Not my thing. I'm the biggest chicken you'll ever meet. Ask anyone." Man, did she sound lame.

"You don't seem like a chicken to me."

Lucy nodded vehemently. "Scared of rats. And heights. Really scared of heights. Can't even go up a ladder. Lightning. Don't like that much either." Why was she *saying* this?

"Chickens don't drag pregnant women out of exploding cars."

Lucy sucked in her breath. "That's different."

He stood, grimacing the slightest bit as he did. His hand moved to his hip in a seemingly unconscious gesture.

"Does your hip hurt a lot?" Lucy asked.

Owen frowned. "Not always."

"Can I ask how you injured it?"

"You can ask." But the tone of his voice told her that he wasn't going to answer.

"Never mind," she stammered. "I should probably get on my way . . ." She glanced at her watch. It was even later than she'd thought.

"Hot date?"

"Oh! No. I mean . . ."

Owen said, "It's okay. You let me know what you decide. My cell's at the bottom of the reference paper."

She led him down the dim hallway and out the front door. Owen thanked her and then headed down the walkway toward where his Mustang was parked on the street.

Standing on the steps of the parsonage, Lucy paused and listened. She looked over the small white headstones flanked by overgrown roses, almost lost in the deepened dusk.

She couldn't hear anything but the wild beating of her heart, and there was no stopping the grin that spread across her face.

Owen Bancroft was back. Hot *damn.*

# FIVE

When your knitting makes you cry, at least you have something with which to mop up your tears.

— E. C.

Owen hated the sign in front of his mother's residence: WILLOW ROCK, A HOME FOR ALL.

It wasn't a home, it was a fucking capital-H Home, that's what it was. It was what his mother had always lamented about. *When I'm old, you'll just put me in a home. No one will care about me. I'll die alone if you put me in one of those.*

Then he had done exactly that. His mother's nightmare had come true, but it was the only thing he could do, the only avenue left open to him.

It still broke his heart, every time he thought about it. She hadn't been here long before the shooting, and while he was recovering, he'd stared up at the ceiling from his hospital bed in San Francisco, two hundred miles away. The first thing he'd done as soon as the doctor cleared him to drive was to head straight for Cypress Hollow, the three-hour trip making his hip and knee burn like acid was being poured into the bones.

His mother hadn't registered who he was that day, nor had she the next day, or the next. He'd had to go back north and leave her behind, but at least he finally knew she was in good hands.

This time he would stay a little longer. Not that she'd know it.

He should get out of the car. Drumming his fingers against the steering wheel, he tuned the radio dial, searching for a song on the radio, any song that he could cling to for another minute. He'd take just about anything. An eighties pop song, nineties grunge. Just one song. Couldn't he find one on this wasteland of a radio dial in among all the commercials?

With a curse, he flipped the radio off and jerked the keys out of the ignition.

He supposed he could use those Windex wipes to work on the windows. . . . No. It was time. Every day he did this. Dammit.

He could be a grown-up. For the love of God.

His fingers itched to restart the car and drive back to the Book Spire, to talk to Lucy Harrison some more. He never would have guessed that seeing her would have made him feel like a dumb eighteen-year-old again, but that's how he'd felt. Like that kid he'd been that awful night, running away from home, getting the hell out of town, hitting the highway in his Mustang with no intention of ever coming back to Cypress Hollow, regretting that he'd never see Lucy Harrison again. That same blank ache that he'd almost forgotten about.

Dammit.

Owen got out of his car and locked the door even though people here left their keys in the ignition in case a neighbor needed to borrow the car. But old habits ingrained by years of city living died hard.

Miss Verna was on duty tonight. Good. At least there would be Oreos.

"Owen! I haven't seen you for months!" She bustled out from behind the desk to hug him. She smelled of chocolate and plastic utensils.

"I've been by, but I keep missing you."

"Janie told me you were in town. I'm so glad. How long are you here this time?"

"I just rented a place. I'm staying for a little while, until I figure where I'm going next."

Miss Verna clapped her hands to her prodigious bosom. "Oh! That *is* good news. We deserve to celebrate! Go see your mama, and then I'll bring you both some cookies and milk."

"Greatest place in the world," Owen said, and kissed her cheek. He didn't mean it though; he never did.

Willow Rock was a small facility, only eight residents. Right now, most of them were in the TV room. He wondered what people did with their elders before television existed to keep them quiet. He sure as hell didn't want to spend his dotage staring at *Judge Judy,* but he supposed it made things easier for everyone.

His mother didn't like TV either. But that's not what made her the most difficult patient the nurses had. She would have been anyway.

Irene Bancroft had always been a pain in the ass. Even when she was younger, when Owen was still in school, she was famous for shooing kids away from her prized rosebushes. She spent most of her time out in the garden, but it didn't make her sweet, like it did the other gardening ladies in town. It seemed to make her cranky. The only thing that made her crankier was the winter cold and rain. She became an indoor cleaning machine during those cold months, and it had been hard for the teenaged Owen, struggling to keep his muddy shoes off the carpet and his dirty clothes off the floor.

The only time he'd ever seen her crankier than that was when he'd moved her here, but after the two small fires she'd accidentally set, he'd had no choice. To pay for moving her into Willow Rock, he'd had to get power of attorney and sell her house, breaking her heart.

But now he was here. He could start trying to make it up to her.

His mother was standing at the window staring at the curtain when he entered her room, her back to him. She looked fragile, but her back was still straight.

More than he could say for her mind.

"Mom, it's me." She jumped as he switched on the overhead light but she didn't turn around.

"How are you doing, Mom?"

She flapped a hand at him as if he were interrupting something, as if he were bothering her when she was in the garden. He'd seen that particular flapping too many times in his life to count.

"Hey, Mom, if you want to look out the window, you should pull back the curtain, huh? It's dark out there, but I bet the outside is more interesting than looking at that brown fabric." Owen reached for the curtain cord and pulled.

The floodlights in the backyard lit her face. His mother, for one second, looked like she did back then, back when she could still tell time and remember his name on a regular basis.

Then she pulled back into herself. She moved to the left, out of the light. "I had a good view of my garden. Now I can't see it. Ruined."

She stalked to her bed, head held high, and sat. "Home."

"Did you already eat?" he asked. Dinner was served so early in this joint, sometimes at four-thirty or five. But he supposed it made sense; it probably helped the staff get them to bed at a reasonable hour.

"Waiting for the bus. *Home.*"

The statement never failed to hurt, but he couldn't do anything about it. Normally, he chose to ignore it completely. Every once in a while he could get her turned around and on to something else.

Her hands jumped in her lap. They had

never been still. A single tear rolled down her cheek, and her lips moved, as if she were trying to say something.

This was what he hated most.

Owen tried the stop-gap method — the small TV that neither of them would have normally chosen to watch. He flipped through the channels until he found something that caught her eye, a show on home renovations.

"You like that, Mom? You want to watch with me?"

But within two or three minutes she was slumped again, her shoulders rounded, looking toward the windows.

"Anything good happen today, Mom? That you can remember?"

Silence.

"I met a girl named Lucy and she knows knitting people who know you. I bet she knits, too. This whole town is crazy for it still, aren't they? I guess it wasn't just some fad here, huh?"

Irene didn't even so much as blink.

"You used to knit, remember? Remember that lady who used to come over? What was her name? You used to sit outside in the garden and knit for hours. She brought me a book once, when I was a kid, about a magical knitting needle that made . . . God, sweaters into gold and then back or something. . . . Mom, do you remember her? Eliza somebody?"

No dice.

Sitting on the bed, she cleared her throat.

"Mom, you okay?"

"Not here most of the time now, am I?"

"What?"

She turned to face him. Her eyes, a rheumy blue, met his, clear for the first time.

"How did you get hurt?"

She was here. His mother was with him, right now. Miss Verna had told him this happened sometimes: times when she knew exactly who she was and that she was sick.

"I was shot, Mom. In the hip. And leg." Just saying it made the joint burn below him where he sat.

"Shoulda been an accountant."

Owen laughed, feeling an almost painful stab of joy. This was his mother, not some old woman concerned about a garden she didn't have anymore, a home that was lost, but here, now, criticizing him. It felt like coming home.

"Who shot?" Irene's voice was sounding confused, and Owen wasn't sure she was tracking the conversation anymore, but he desperately wanted her to be able to.

So he took a moment to frame the answer.

"An ex-cop gone bad shot me."

Irene didn't say anything.

"He'd been a friend of mine. A really good friend. I'd just found out about him when it happened."

Irene's eyes stayed on his. Was she still listening to him? If so, she was probably judging him, sure, but there wouldn't be anything new or strange about that.

Keep talking, keep her present.

"He was high, and when he found out we were at his house to take him in, he went crazy."

Owen broke off. No matter how present his mother was, he couldn't tell her this story. He couldn't even think about the story, not about how it had really gone down.

"He died," said Owen. "And I got shot."

"You killed him?" Irene's voice wavered. She really *had* been tracking the whole conversation. God, if it wasn't so macabre, he'd feel like breaking out the champagne.

"I don't know, Ma. There were a lot of people shooting."

"Maybe you did."

Owen felt like he'd been shot, all over again. Only higher this time. In the chest.

"Maybe." He paused. "Mom. I'm okay. Let's not talk about this. Tell me something else. Tell me about how your nights are."

She looked blankly at him and pulled at the sleeve of the pink robe she insisted on wearing most days. It was wearing thin at the elbows and had strings hanging from the hem.

"Why don't you wear that other pink robe I bought you? The new one? It's warmer."

"Gave it away."

Owen felt anger rise inside him. No. He took a deep breath.

"Who did you give it to?"

"Don't know."

"Great, Mom. *That* makes sense."

"Am I going to stay here until I die?"

Shit. Owen looked at his tennis shoes. Her feet were bare on the tile floor. "Will you put your slippers on, at least?"

"Is my house still there, Owen? How are my roses?"

His mother's voice was, for this moment, like it used to be. Sharp, steady. Her eyes were piercing again, and looked straight into him.

"The house is still there, Ma." It wasn't a lie. The house itself was still standing. He hadn't looked at the roses.

She went limp with relief. Her hands stopped twisting and dropped, still, into her lap. She almost smiled.

Then she looked up at him, sharply. He didn't have time to mask the guilt he felt.

"Whatever." She looked back out the window. Her eyes went unfocused again. "Cops. And aphids."

Time for the big guns.

"I'm thinking about planting a Moondance tree rose. I'm going to do it in very dry soil. I don't plan on giving it much water, and I don't like to prune. Do you think it will do well?"

She frowned and looked right at him and then she said, "Ridiculous. It will die. You can't."

His mother sat up straight, perched on the side of the bed, her bare feet together, her hands moving in her lap. She told him about roses with halting, jumbled words that didn't always match, but their meaning was clear enough to her son. Owen sat in the chair next to the bed and let her talk for as long as she could.

# Six

Every once in a while, knit in the dark. Or even better, by candlelight. It makes picking your work back up again the next day that much more interesting.

— E. C.

"For the second time this week, we're at the bar," said Lucy. "Does that mean we have a problem?"

Molly shook her head. "It just means we need a coffee shop in this town that stays open later than six o'clock. Thank God your brother put in the espresso machine."

Jonas was behind the bar, doing something with the register, and Silas was in the side booth near them, reading a book that had a dragon on the cover, his signature red earflap cap pulled low over his forehead. Otherwise, with the exception of two drunk college-aged guys playing pool and a canoodling couple that Lucy was trying desperately not to look at, the bar was almost empty. The cool spring night had turned drizzly, and most people in town appeared to have stayed home for the evening. And the two who had their hands all over each other probably should have done them all a favor and stayed in, too, Lucy thought.

She took a sip of her latte. "I wish this was a decaf, though. I'm going to be up all night." She shook her bar sock in the air. "Although insomnia would help me finally finish this, I suppose. And I'm carrying the fire-department pager tonight, since Nadine has the flu, even though it's a work night, so I could be called in at any time. Suppose it's all right it's caffeinated."

"Is that really what's going to keep you awake?"

Molly knew her too well. She ignored the question. "He has a limp. Did you notice that the other night?"

"In the glow of the car fire? No. But how romantic!" said Molly.

Jonas propped his arms on the bar and leaned forward. "How the hell is a limp romantic?"

Molly sighed. "Isn't it obvious? It's a weakness, and any weakness in a strong man is an attractive quality."

"You mean you want to emasculate the

man and make him into a child by taking care of him?"

Molly said, "You've been watching Oprah again, huh?"

Jonas said, "No, that's what Aggie said once. Right before she returned my Wii."

Aggie left Jonas in the middle of the night two years before, running off with a beer delivery guy. Lucy thought Jonas still looked broken sometimes.

"You weren't good together. Everyone knows that. You're better off apart," said Lucy, taking another sip of her latte.

Molly slid off the bar stool. "I'm going to play some music."

As Molly moved toward the jukebox, Jonas said, "So. About Owen Bancroft moving in."

"I'm in love. It's serious, and it's moving fast," said Lucy. Then she shook her head. "He wouldn't be moving into my house, you dumbass, just into the parsonage. And I haven't decided yet, anyway. It's been two days, and I haven't called him. He hasn't called me, either. He's probably found somewhere else by now."

"You can't just let him move in. How do you know he hasn't turned into a serial killer since high school?"

"You're the one who was in his class in

high school. Was he a killer then?"

"I'm serious, Luce. It honestly worries me." Jonas leaned back, folding his arms across his chest, giving her that look that said he meant business. He'd been giving her that look their whole lives.

"He used to be a cop. He gave me references."

"Did you call them?"

"Well, no. Not yet. But Mildred Elkins said that he's home to be closer to his mother, who's in some care facility, and he confirmed that. It sounded pretty sad, actually."

Jonas raised his eyebrows in obvious disbelief. "He was one of the bad kids, Lucy. Not little punk stuff, cutting class, not weed. His friends carried guns, stole cars. You're the one who tutored him, you should remember this even better than I do."

Lucy tried to look confused. "Did I? Now that you mention it . . ."

A look crossed Jonas's face, and Lucy watched him remember. Her heart fell.

Jonas said, "You had that *crush* on him."

"I did not."

"Did *too*. Something about a party, right?" He snapped her arm with his rag. "Dude, it's all coming back to me."

"That thing is dirty! Don't do that!"

"The first time you got drunk? I remember Dad being mad at you for like the first time ever. Owen had dropped you off that night. That was the night the puke picture got taken, the one in the yearbook."

Lucy clucked her tongue and shook her head. She would *not* discuss it with her brother. "Nope. Not ringing a bell."

Jonas laughed. "You're full of shit."

"Okay, okay. God, that picture is from *hell*. Yeah, he's that one. But don't remind Owen of it if you see him, okay? I'm hoping he has a bad memory for that part of it."

"Hey, Silas!"

Silas looked at them from his booth, his eyes unfocused, clearly still deep in his book.

Jonas said, "You remember Owen? Lucy's big crush in high school? That's why she's thinking about letting him move in."

Silas frowned.

Lucy laughed. "He has no idea what you're talking about."

"God. Silas. Pay attention once in a while."

Silas nodded and went back to reading.

Molly settled back onto her bar stool, back from the jukebox. "I'm flashing back, kids. Dire Straits, straight ahead."

Shaking his head, Jonas said, "No taste in music."

"It's your jukebox."

One of the college guys at the pool table said something about the other's mother and a ball hit the floor with a clatter.

"Hey!" yelled Jonas. "Keep 'em on the table!"

Lucy stirred another packet of sweetener into her latte even though it didn't need it. Desperate to change the subject before Jonas led it back to Owen, she asked Molly, "How's Booty-Call Barry?"

Jonas snorted and leaned backward, watching them.

Molly grabbed Lucy's stir stick and broke it, then set the pieces neatly next to her coffee. "I told you, quit calling him that. Besides, booty calls don't stay over, and sometimes he did."

"And?"

"I haven't called him back. He said I needed to watch my calorie intake, so I said he needed to watch his back."

Jonas rolled his eyes and walked away toward the dartboard. "You're not fat."

Molly was a little on the padded side, it was true, but she was the kind of woman who wore it beautifully. Every part of her body was proportioned, and she had a waist, and hips, and breasts. She had a figure to die for, Lucy'd always thought, but she never listened when Lucy told her so. She reminded Lucy of a chick-lit book, pink and fun, with hidden depths not appreciated or noticed by everyone. Masses of straight black hair fell around Molly's shoulders as if she'd just had it professionally done. She had a perfect ivory complexion, with a bloom of rose at her cheeks. She had the longest lashes Lucy had ever seen. She had Lucy Liu freckles and a perfect small gap between her two front teeth.

Lucy patted Molly's hand. "You know you're not, right? And has your body shape ever slowed a man down?"

Molly gave her a smile. "Believe me, I know I'm not. And no, my body shape just speeds 'em up, usually."

"It's true. You were telling me about Larry."

"Barry. Prize jerk. But never mind about him, because now I've got a new thing going on with Theo down at the TV repair shop."

"Since when? A thing?"

Molly shrugged and grinned. "A naked thing. Which is awesome when we're not arguing. He's spicy. Not like Barry, who was just an asshole."

Lucy said, "What if you like the fighting with the bad boys more than you like the relationship itself?"

Molly didn't deny it. "What's better than make-up sex? It's like a mental challenge. Better for your brain than crosswords."

"I'm glad about Theo, if it's what you want, and I'm sorry about Barry," said Lucy. "You want me to put flaming dog poop on his porch?"

Molly brightened. "Would you?"

That was the thing about Molly. She might be serious. Lucy shook her head and said, "No, not really. I don't want to touch dog shit, let alone light it on fire, which I'm sure is some kind of arson. I'll snub him if I see him in the grocery store, though."

"Damn." Molly looked disappointed. "I've done it. I don't think it's a crime. But okay. Snubbing is good. But while Jonas is gone, let's go back to you. Owen Bancroft? Would you really rent to him? Is he as cute as he looked the other night while he was dragging that woman out of the car?"

"Yeah, if you like that rugged McDreamy look, sure." Lucy shrugged.

"Who doesn't? Three words: Hit that shit."

"Ew! No." Lucy's answer was too quick and she tried to cover it up. "You know. Not really my type."

"What kind of book is he?" Molly knew how Lucy categorized people.

Lucy thought before carefully choosing her words. "I think he's a thriller. Like a paperback espionage novel. Suspenseful. Guns and forged passports and spies."

"Hot," said Molly. "But you're a really bad liar. That's not what book you think he is."

"I hate you sometimes."

Molly held up a finger. "One quick sec." She looked to see that Jonas was busy clearing a booth before scuttling around the back of the bar. She shot a finger of Baileys into her coffee and raised the bottle toward Lucy's cup.

"No, thanks. I'm on call, remember?" Lucy pulled the pager out of her pocket and waggled it at Molly.

"Oh, yeah." Seated next to her again, Molly said with a satisfied air, "Now. Really. What book?"

Lucy sighed and said in a whisper, *"Wuthering Heights."*

Molly laughed so hard she almost came off her bar stool.

"It's not that funny."

"Oh, God!" Molly tried to gasp for air. "Yes, it is. Heathcliff. To your — your Cathy . . ."

Lucy sat. She waited.

"You done yet?"

Molly giggled. "I think so. I'm sorry. It's

just funny. Thinking of you on the moors . . ." She wiped her eyes with a cocktail napkin.

"Stop! Seriously."

"That's why you wouldn't read it with me last year for book club? Too" — Molly choked — "difficult?"

Lucy spun on the barstool to face her, trailing the yarn behind her. "Shhh! Look, it's not funny, and I'm well aware that it's moronic, but that was a hard time for me."

"It was high school. I was in New York, not out here on the Wild West Coast, but it was hard for all of us."

Molly had no idea. Looking at the stitches on her needles as if they held the answer, Lucy said, "I was his math tutor. I was the bookish one. The smart one. And then one night . . . I thought he really saw me, that someone finally had seen me. And the best part was that the someone who had seen me was *him.*" With each word, she jerked a stitch. They'd be tighter than the rest on her next row.

Molly leaned over and put her head briefly on Lucy's shoulder. "I'm sorry. You don't talk about him, and I'm just trying to figure out what happened in high school to my best friend. Will you forgive my teasing and tell me?"

Lucy groaned and gave up. “Long story made blessedly short. It was the grad night party of his senior year. I was a junior. I had a nice boyfriend, Tim Snopes, who was on the football team: running back. We held hands and necked on Friday nights, but he had strep throat and couldn’t take me to the party. Owen had twenty-two girlfriends and he did more than neck.”

Molly snorted. “Yeah, right.”

“I could list the girls for you. In either alphabetical or chronological order.”

With a whirling hand motion, Molly indicated for Lucy to go on.

Lucy made sure Jonas was still over by the dartboard. She sure as heck didn’t need her older brother hearing about her sad love life. Behind her, Silas’s nose was still buried in his book. He’d never hear them talking, even if he were sitting closer.

“I’d been his tutor for six months. I was crazy, horrible, sick-to-my-stomach in love with him. He never even really knew my name. We’d meet in the public library on Thursday nights and I’d take bets with myself whether or not he’d get my name right or not. Laura or Lisa or Luann — every once in a while he got it right and called me Lucy. I told myself he was teasing me, but I wasn’t sure if he was or not. He wasn't good at math, but it wasn't because he wasn't smart. There was stuff going on at home — he'd come in with dark circles under his eyes, and kids told stories about the screaming coming from his house, his father beating his mother, and he came in with black eyes sometimes. He blamed it on his motorcycle."

"Swoon," said Molly.

"I know, right? Remember Matt Dillon in *The Outsiders*? Dallas Winston? He was that tough and dark and scary and sad. And *hot.* I sat next to him and we talked numbers. He never met my eyes."

"And you went to a party . . ." Molly prompted her.

"I'm getting there. I tried the punch. My first alcohol. I was practically begging to be a John Hughes movie, I know. I was a moron. I wore this fuchsia dress with big puffed sleeves and a net bodice — it was horrible. I had dyed fuchsia shoes to match that made my toes pink for weeks. My mom still has the outfit in a closet somewhere, I have no idea why. I drank too much, of course. I saw him standing in a corner when I was waiting for the bathroom and when I came out, I saw him go into a side bedroom. I followed him on a drunken whim, and as soon as I entered . . ."

Molly said triumphantly, "A la John Hughes, he stole your panties and put them on the bulletin board at school!"

Lucy groaned. "I wish. He'd been waiting in the dark for a girl. I'm not even sure which one, but he thought I was her, so when I wandered in, not knowing what I wanted, and suddenly he had his . . . hands all over me, I was surprised. But I went along with it." She stared across the bar into rows of colorful bottles.

She had shut the bedroom door behind her, and the noise of the party that had been roaring like an unfamiliar train behind her was suddenly silenced, and all she could hear was his breathing, close, right in front of her.

"You came," Owen had said to her.

And even though the small part of her brain that was still processing normally knew he hadn't meant her, knew that he'd been waiting for someone else, she irrationally hoped he'd seen her backlit by the open door and that she was, in fact, exactly who he'd been waiting for. She'd nodded, even though in the dim light he would barely have seen it.

Both of his hands slid around her waist, and he pulled her tight against him. Her breath left her body as if she'd fallen from a great height, as if it had been knocked out of her. Her head felt light. He didn't take his time. His lips moved to just below her jawline at the same time that his hand crept up to cup her breast. Then his mouth claimed hers.

And time stopped.

She swore it did. For Owen, too.

The kiss deepened. Their breath became ragged as their lips touched, danced against each other's, parted and returned. She couldn't bear her mouth to be far from his and she noticed that his hand at her breast became less insistent as all their focus spun around this one kiss, this perfect, perfect, kiss. Everything depended on this moment. Just to breathe against his mouth, to feel him gasping against her, was enough. Their hands touched each other's faces, they drew back and gazed in the dimness at each other in wonder, and then returned to what was the ultimate kiss, the kiss Lucy knew she'd been waiting for her entire life.

"Lucy," he'd whispered raggedly. "I never . . ."

He'd known her name. He *knew* her.

"What?" she said, breathless.

Then the overhead light snapped on.

Whitney Court, dressed in a pale pink strapless dress with lots of tulle, danced into the room, camera flashing. "Smile, kids, this is history in the making!"

Lucy watched Owen's face go from completely unguarded to totally closed and spitting furious in the space of half a second. It was frightening, like watching a lightning storm move in over the ocean.

Whitney was still snapping pictures, the flash bouncing around the room, making Lucy's head hurt. She couldn't smile. Probably shouldn't smile. More people had followed Whitney into the room, kids laughing, carrying red plastic cups full of the toxic punch.

"What the *fuck,* Whitney?" snapped Owen.

"We heard you were in here with an A student, just wanted to document it for posterity," she trilled. "Don't worry, darlin', it's all in fun."

Owen's eyes met Lucy's for one desperate instant, and for that one second Lucy was sure that he'd felt the same thing that she had, that his heart had been beating as hard as hers, with the same amount of passion that wasn't just lust stirred by youth and hormones, but by something more.

Lucy covered her mouth with her hand and ran out of the bedroom just as Owen said, "Whitney, you're a fucking bitch."

He followed her out of the room and into

the living room, Whitney on his heels.

And there, in the middle of the party, in the living room, where the only kids who hadn't witnessed her humiliation had been, if not dancing, then swaying to the music, Lucy threw up, splashing Randall Lawson with green punch and bile.

Giggles followed, laughter turning to full-blown drunken roars. It would be legend by Monday morning and carved in stone by her senior year. Lucy's head spun. Her eyes felt wobbly, and her legs followed suit as she stumbled outside into the front yard, desperate to go home.

"It was the lead photo in the *Moments We'd Like to Forget* section of the yearbook. Whitney submitted it. Me, in my fuchsia net dress, vomiting all over the outgoing seniors, the juniors watching. Me, with a whole year to go. I still can't believe they printed it."

Molly's cup was suspended halfway to her lips. "But what about Owen? He took you home? And?"

"Oh, yeah. He took me home, all right. He put me in the front seat of his blue Mustang. Held my hand all the way to my house. I sat there praying for the courage to tell him that I loved him, that he meant everything to me, but instead I worried too much that he'd try to kiss me when I'd just thrown up, so when he pulled up, I ran inside and slammed the door. He left the next day, left town completely and pretty much never came back. Never called, never left a note. . . ."

*"Vile."*

Lucy took a sip of her latte and shrugged. "I thought so at the time, but really, we were just kids. Right? But you can see why I was —"

"So madly in love with him? Oh, yeah. You're in trouble, for sure. And . . ." Molly leaned sideways so that she was looking just to the left of Lucy.

"What?" asked Lucy.

"You might want to . . ."

Lucy turned, but she already knew. The front door was still swinging, and Owen was three bar stools down from them. He leaned forward, one hand on the top of the bar, the other stuck in the pocket of his black leather jacket that looked as well-worn as his jeans.

Her heart rattled like the dice in the cups Jonas carried toward them.

Jonas thumped them down in front of Lucy and Molly. "Wanna play?"

Molly shook her head. "I always lose at Bullshit. Which is ironic, because I'm so good at it in real life."

"Nah," said Lucy. "Too rich for my blood." Then she waited for Jonas to go back and serve Owen.

Instead, Jonas started washing glasses.

Owen took his other hand out of his pocket and put it on top of the bar also. He cleared his throat.

"Jonas," started Lucy. This wasn't like her brother.

"What?" Jonas said.

"Can I get an Anchor Steam down here?" Owen's voice was polite, but firm.

Jonas folded his lips together and nodded, without looking at Owen. He drew a beer and slid it across the bar, accepting payment without ever appearing to make eye contact.

"Thanks," said Owen.

Jonas jerked his chin in response and returned to stand in front of Lucy and Molly.

"What's your problem?" hissed Lucy, hoping the sound of the jukebox covered her voice.

Jonas shrugged. "Nothing."

Lucy felt the pulse at the front of her throat beat wildly as she turned as casually as she could. "Hi," she called down the bar stools.

"Hey there." Owen half smiled, but there

was a reserve to him, a set to his mouth that Lucy didn't blame him for. Jonas had been deliberately rude, and Lucy was embarrassed.

Lucy wanted desperately to ask him to move down and join them, but she couldn't seem to make her vocal cords say the words. Her mouth opened and closed. She knitted faster.

"Come down here and sit with us," said Molly.

Lucy smiled.

Jonas harrumphed and went into the back room, where he started rearranging kegs with thumps and bangs.

"I'm Molly," Molly said, turning on her signature full-wattage smile, "and that's Silas over there."

Silas barely looked up from his book before dropping his eyes back to the page.

Lucy found that her voice worked again. "You'll have to forgive my brothers," said Lucy. "One has no social graces. And the other one, well, he has no social graces either."

Molly smiled. "Silas wouldn't notice if a bomb went off in here."

"If the bomb made him lose his place, he'd notice. But not until then," Lucy agreed. She turned the row on her sock, flipping the yarn, and noticed that Owen was watching her hands. She was conscious of the way her fingers were moving in a way she usually never was.

"So Owen, I hear you're the local black sheep, returned to pasture." Molly cocked an eyebrow.

Owen's eyes darted to Lucy's, but then he nodded. "Yep. The proverbial bad penny."

That wasn't right, thought Lucy, but correcting Molly would make it worse. Owen was neither of those, not a black sheep returning nor a bad penny turning up. He was just a man coming home.

But before she could say something, the door to the bar swung open with a bang. Whitney Court entered, holding a large plate covered with cookies.

"Hello, darlings!" Whitney's voice was a trill. "I went a little overboard in the butterscotch-pecan-cookie department tonight right before I closed, and I thought you all might like a little sample of my wares."

Silas's head rose from his book so fast Lucy thought he might get whiplash. Owen said, "Cookies?" Molly grinned. Jonas poked his head out from the back room. And the two drunk college guys who had been arm wrestling over who got to break the rack on the next game of pool unlocked hands and tripped over each other in their haste to get to Whitney.

The eponymous Whitney's Bakery sat next door to Lucy's bookstore. Lucy was used to people tromping through her store, a muffin in one hand, a fancy caramel latte in the other, browsing books with sticky fingers. And even though she kept trash cans at the front of the store just to catch their empty wrappers, she still found cookie crumbs behind the biography section and empty coffee cups perched on the romance shelves.

The college boys slapped each other's hands in their rush to grab a cookie, elbowing each other out of the way. They were obviously drunk and they were making Lucy uncomfortable, but Whitney seemed relaxed. She always seemed at home around men. It drove Lucy crazy.

"Oh, now, boys. There's plenty for everyone." Whitney's laugh was gorgeous, light and silky. She wore a sweet pink dress with a full skirt, cinched with a red belt. The wide red headband that held back her long chestnut brown hair matched her red belt, as did her red patent kitten heels. She looked perfectly sexy and wholesome at the same time, and as usual, Lucy felt a mixture of both admiration and jealousy, and didn't like either feeling.

Whitney held the plate in front of Silas, who was still seated at his booth. "Cookie, Silas?"

He nodded, the bobbles on the end of the earflaps on his cap bouncing up and down.

"My darling, you have to say the magic word."

Lucy felt heat rise to the top of her head, and she inhaled sharply. It wasn't that Silas had a speech impediment, or that he stuttered. He just didn't like to talk. And no one made him, no one *told* Silas he had to talk.

No one, that was, except for Whitney, who was drawing the plate back away from Silas's outstretched hand.

"What's that teensy little word, you handsome brute?"

Lucy looked at Jonas for help, but he only seemed amused, the traitor.

Silas frowned, a deep furrow across his forehead. Then he finally muttered, "Please."

"That's it! There, now was that so hard? You can have *two* cookies for that, you sexy thing, you." Whitney smiled in triumph and looked up at Lucy.

"Oooh! The gang's all here! Goodie! You have to have one of these." The skirt of her dress swayed, a full bell, showing off her shapely legs to full advantage as she brought the plate to Lucy.

Whitney's eyes never met Lucy's, though — she was too busy staring at Owen. Holding the cookies dangerously high under Lucy's nose, she said, "The rumors are true, then."

Owen leaned backward, his elbows resting against the bar, his head at an angle. Lucy couldn't read his face. "Depends on what they're saying."

"That Owen Bancroft is back in town to stay."

"Sounds like a rumor to me."

"So you're only passing through?"

"Not planning on sinking my roots in too deep."

Whitney said to Lucy, "Do you mind?" and gave her the plate to hold.

Lucy looked at Molly, who rolled her eyes. Twisting, Lucy placed the cookies on the bar behind her. Jonas snatched three of them, scarfing two before Lucy could even snarl at him.

Whitney stood directly in front of Owen, placed her hands on her hips, and struck a pose. "Do you remember me? I'm sure you do. I'm positive you couldn't forget."

Owen pressed his lips into a thin line and

crossed his arms. "Can't say that I do."

Lucy felt a wild surge of relief. He didn't remember that party, then, if he didn't remember Whitney. Maybe he didn't remember that night. Or that kiss at all.

"Oh, you! I know you do." Playfully smacking his knee, Whitney said, "Come on, remember the tree house?"

A grin broke across Owen's face. "I'm just teasing you. Of course I remember you, Whitney. You haven't changed a bit."

"Oh!" Whitney gave a small, well-pitched noise that sounded like something Cinderella might have intoned if the prince had slapped her bottom. "You're so bad. I believed you for a minute! That was just awful of you. I shouldn't let you have a cookie at all. But it is good to see you again. We have to catch up. Maybe all of us can go out sometime. Get some dinner?" She looked at Lucy and Molly. "Wouldn't that be fun?" Without waiting for an answer, she turned back to Owen and said, "Now, tell me everything you've done since I last saw you. I have all the time in the world."

Lucy spun around on her bar stool. It was enough that she was going to have to hear it, but to have to watch it was just too much. Sure, history repeated itself, but did high-school history have to? Because that wasn't fair for anyone.

"I'm going to the bathroom," she said to Molly, who was texting someone on her phone.

"What?" Molly glanced up, smiling. "Okay."

"Are you setting up a date for after I leave or something?"

Molly looked guilty.

"Oh, my God," said Lucy, "I was kidding."

"I'm sorry. Theo's into me right now. I mean, he will be," Molly looked at her watch. "In about . . ."

Lucy held up her hand. "Stop. I don't want to know. I'll be right back."

In the bathroom, Lucy took a minute to compose herself. It was fine that Owen was out there with Whitney. They were all adults now. Lucy was used to dealing with Whitney — they had to work on the Chamber of Commerce together, and they were co-chairs on the Christmas Lighting Committee every year. Whitney's saccharine smile was something Lucy had learned to suck up as a responsible member of society.

Just because Whitney had been instrumental in her humiliation on what had been the worst night of her high-school career didn't negate the fact that the same night had also been the night that Owen Bancroft had kissed her.

Lucy leaned in toward the mirror. Same brown eyes, flecked with hazel bits at the edges of the iris. Funny, she'd had these eyes then, when he'd kissed her, when he'd taken her hand and moved her firmly across the line from girl to woman, with just that kiss. It hadn't taken more than that. Maybe she was extra naïve, but when her other friends were busy giving their boyfriends hand jobs and having sex in the backs of their parents' cars, Lucy had been content in the knowledge that the one thing she had that they didn't have was the one perfect kiss.

And now, seventeen years later, looking into the same plain brown eyes that hadn't changed a bit, she wondered the same thing she'd been wondering at random moments over the years — how many other girls had felt the same way about a kiss from Owen Bancroft? Was the Central Coast of California littered with them? Girls who still, years later, pined for the perfect kiss?

Or on the other hand, maybe the coast was littered with girls who had figured out way back then what Lucy hadn't — that it had just been a plain old regular kiss, nothing to write home about, and Lucy had made too big a deal about it then, just like she was doing now, thinking about it at all.

God, she was pathetic.

Lucy pulled open the door of the bathroom.

In the small hallway, Owen leaned against the wall, as if he was waiting for her.

"What are you doing?" Lucy hated the thin sound of her voice.

"I was wondering if you'd decided whether or not to rent to me."

Even the very rumble of his voice did things to her insides. She remembered that from tutoring him. She hadn't grown up at all, had she?

"Why my parsonage? Have you looked at other places?" Lucy felt cornered, and gauged whether she'd be able to slip past him, whether she'd fit around him in the narrow hall. Or whether she'd touch him moving past, and what that would do to her . . . No, better to stay here.

"Nothing that I liked as much as yours. Did you call those references?"

She hadn't. Lucy had picked up the phone a few times at the store, but the idea of asking other people about Owen Bancroft, hearing them talk about him, made her nervous, and each time, she'd put the phone down and picked up the romance she was reading. Better to get lost in a book, always better to be lost in fiction.

Taking a deep breath, Lucy pushed past Owen. She'd just made it around him, just cleared him, when at the last moment, he reached out and touched her wrist. Static electricity jumped between them, a snap of blue that cracked and hurt. Lucy jumped. Owen jerked his hand back.

"I'm sorry," he said.

"No, I always pick up charges. I drag my feet," Lucy said.

"You should know that I'm still interested," said Owen.

And for one long second, the tone of his voice made Lucy think that he wasn't talking about the rental.

# Seven

Man learned long ago that two sticks, rubbed together, can create a spark. It took a little longer to realize that if you attach a string, you can create a whole lot more.

— E. C.

"Just let me know." Owen peered at her. "Okay? You have my cell number, right?"

Lucy shook her head and then nodded. "Yeah, I have it." Her cheeks flaming, she made her way back out to the main bar area, leaving him standing behind in the hallway.

Molly was laughing with Whitney. Some best friend she was. The frat boys had eaten all the treats and seemed even drunker now. Jonas looked like he was trying to serve them coffee, but they were more interested in lining coasters up along the edge of the pool table.

She sat down and picked up her knitting.

It was really too dim in the bar to try the short-row heel she usually worked on toe-up socks, but she'd reached the place for the turn, and there was no way in hell she was going to sit here and not knit. Maybe she'd just keep knitting straight, a long useless tube, and rip it back and fix it tomorrow.

Molly leaned sideways and nudged her shoulder. "Whitney was just telling me the funniest story about her employee Thomasina, the company SUV, and a Venetian gondolier. You have to hear it."

The two women dissolved into giggles, and Lucy tried to smile. "It sounds like a good one."

"Oh, it was! You should have seen Thomasina's face, when I caught her and Paolo in the back of the Phrosting-mobile. She's worked for me for ten years, and suddenly she pretended she didn't speak English."

Lucy gave what she hoped passed for a laugh. Then, when Molly and Whitney were talking again, she sighed.

It wasn't even that she hated Whitney Court anymore. Who could? They weren't in high school anymore. The throwing-up photography incident was behind them. Whitney had not only grown up to be incredibly beautiful but had also become a remarkably savvy businesswoman, respected by the community of Cypress Hollow. Her bakery supported a good number of small ventures in town. She was successful, a small dynamo. Cheerful. Positive. Influential. She had an employee, for Chrissake. Lucy had to do her own taxes.

And Lucy wanted to run whenever she saw her.

Owen made his way back out from the bathroom, limping slowly. He picked up his leather jacket from where he'd draped it over a chair and shrugged into it. "I'm going to get out of here. You all have a good night."

Whitney hopped lightly off her bar stool and said, "You know wasn't it you and Lucy who pulled Abigail MacArthur out of that wreck earlier this week? Or was that just a rumor I heard?"

Molly said, "That wasn't a rumor. They were heroes. I saw it all."

"Well, heckola," said Whitney. "I think that deserves a little fanfare or something." Her voice was sweet. Light.

*Too* sugary. "That's okay, Whitney," Lucy said.

"No, we should get some press for you. It would be good for the bookstore!"

"It's fine."

"I'll call the paper tomorrow. We can do it

up right. Get a big front-page spread on the small-town heroes, the local boy finally makes good, alongside the quiet bookstore girl who never has a moment's excitement, thrust into the heat of action. And I'll cater the desserts at the reception."

Aha. That was her angle.

Owen's face flushed, and he tugged the zipper up on his jacket. " 'Night," he said, nodding.

"Wait," Lucy said. *Local boy finally making good, my ass.* She took a deep breath. "You can have the parsonage."

Jonas stuck his head out from the back room and glared at her.

"Good," said Owen. He shoved his hands into his pockets and looked at her, his face impossible to read. His eyes, though, were the same as they'd been in high school, filled with the same intensity they'd had then.

"If you walk there with me now, I'll give you the key. You can have it tonight."

Jonas spoke from behind her. It was a warning. "Lucy . . ."

Owen said, "Deal."

Then he smiled at her. Lucy's heart flipped a somersault, and she dropped most of the stitches on her left needle.

■ ■ ■ ■

The walk to the parsonage was quiet and short, the waves crashing on the far side of Main Street louder than their footfalls.

At the front of garden walkway, next to the side wall of the Book Spire, Lucy flipped the gate open. "Look, if you jiggle the latch here, you'll keep it from sticking. I haven't been able to fix that."

"I can do it for you, if you want," Owen said. "I'm good at things like that."

Lucy nodded. "That would be nice. Thank you. We can take it off your rent."

She led him down the pathway, past the old cemetery, and up the steps. Unlocking the door, she led him into the parlor.

"I really appreciate this, you know," Owen said. "It's the perfect place for me right now. I wish I could tell you how long I was staying, but . . ."

Lucy shook her head. "It's really all right." She got the rental agreement from the kitchen, and he filled it out in silence. She gave him a key, showed him where the fuse box was, and how to relight the heater's pilot light.

Then she stood in the hall and held up her hands. "That should be it. I'll leave you here to get settled in. There are fresh sheets in the linen closet, just make the bed, and you're good to go."

"I'll walk out with you," said Owen. "I'll grab my stuff from the motel. Won't be sad to dump that joint." Moving forward, he stumbled on the old, worn runner.

"Careful!" Lucy put her hand out and caught his forearm. His arm was warm, the sinews of muscle below the skin taut, rope-like. She swore she felt another spark jump between their skin, a snap of electricity that jolted her through to the ground. As quickly as she touched him, she withdrew her hand. Had he felt it, too?

God, he looked sexy as hell. That black leather jacket over those jeans, looking enough like a bad boy to make her heart beat fast and enough like a hero to make her knees knock.

*No.* That line of thinking just led to trouble, and she had no need for that.

"Thanks," he said.

She jerked her chin in a nod of sorts and started toward the stairs. He followed, holding the handrail.

"Steps are the hardest for me. Any more than three and I'm doomed."

His voice didn't invite pity, so she didn't give any. "It's a good thing there are only three, then."

Lucy swung down a step, her hand on the porch rail, gazing out into the yard.

"So who's buried out here anyway?" In the cold air his voice floated over the headstones, which gleamed pale in the moonlight.

"There aren't too many, really. The Snodgrass family has a few members buried out here, and they put flowers out sometimes. The very first minister and his family. The drummed-out minister's first two children, who were stillborn. A couple of drifters, I think, that they took pity on, if I'm guessing right, since their full names aren't given, just their first names and the dates of death. No one's been buried here for sixty years, though." She glanced at him. "In case you were worried. They've been sleeping a long time."

Owen said, "Live people give me enough trouble. I don't worry about the dead ones. I think it's kind of . . ."

"Companionable?"

He nodded.

"This used to be one of my favorite places to read as a kid. There's a baby's tomb over there, almost invisible to us right now, under that huge oak." Lucy pointed into the dark. "In the summer, that marble was the coolest thing to curl up against. My parents could never find me when I hid on the far side of it, but my Grandmother Ruby, always knew where I was. She didn't ever tell my hiding spot — she'd just come out here and give a whistle if she really needed me."

Lucy stuck two fingers in her mouth and whistled, an ear-shattering blast that split the night.

"I never could do that," he said admiringly.

Lucy shrugged. "It's easy." She moved down another step. Only one more and she'd be on the ground, leaving.

"How old were you when you last hid out there?"

"Last summer. I closed the store early one afternoon when it got into the hundreds. There's no air-conditioning in the store — hell, nothing's changed since you left. There's still no air-conditioning in town, except at Williams Brothers Grocery — never need it here on the ocean. And I hate the heat. So I closed and came out here with a book and my knitting. I fell asleep on the baby's grave. I didn't wake up until after dark, and I had a crick in my neck, but it was cool and the air was so sweet. . . ." Her voice trailed off. "I must sound like some dumb hick to you."

"I'm from here, remember?"

"I remember," she said. She looked down at the ground and then back up at him. Then she felt it again. That frisson of energy that went from the soles of her feet, right through her blue-and-green Keds, all the way up to the crown of her head.

God, she wanted to kiss him. It wouldn't hurt to do it, right? Just a quick peck. It would be brave of her. And around Owen, Lucy felt different.

She skipped up the two steps until she was back up on the porch with him and pressed her lips lightly to Owen's. "Thank you." His lips parted in surprise.

It was meant to be light. Fun. Daring.

But he was quicker than she was, and instead of stepping away, as she'd meant to, he caught her in the circle of his strong arms — they came around her, catching her against his chest.

"Did you mean to do that?" Owen asked, his mouth an inch from hers.

Lucy had no breath left to speak but managed to say, "No."

He didn't let her go — he pulled her more firmly against him. "What did you think would happen next?"

"I didn't . . . have a real plan."

The corners of Owen's eyes crinkled and

as he lowered his mouth to hers, she felt his smile against her lips.

For one moment, Lucy was aware that she was kissing Owen Bancroft for the second time in her life. That first time hadn't gone so well, all things considered.

But then all conscious thought left her head as the kiss deepened. Her mouth opened under his, and he tasted of hops and something dark, somehow sweet. His tongue rasped against hers, and Lucy's hands reached to clutch the fabric of his shirt, under the leather jacket. She needed to hold herself up — her knees weren't capable of doing the job.

"Lucy," he whispered against her lips, and the sound of her name jolted her back.

What was she doing?

She'd started this. Lucy pulled back and stared into Owen's eyes. They were as turbulently clouded as she'd ever seen the ocean on a stormy day. She'd kissed him, right after giving him a *lease* to sign. How damn professional was that?

"I'm sorry," she gasped. Pushing against his chest, she broke out of his arms, and stumbled backward down the steps.

"Be careful!" Owen reached to keep her from falling, but Lucy caught herself on the railing.

"I'm fine. I'm sorry. I wasn't thinking. Forgive me. That was dumb." Oh, God, just *saying* that was stupid. She had to get out of here. Lucy felt like she was that high-school kid again, a clueless loser, her unrequited crush the size of the Pacific.

"Wait a minute, Lucy, just let me . . ."

Beeps broke though his sentence, blessed beeps, and she felt the vibration of the pager against her waist. The fire-department pager. Thank God.

Even before he'd finished his sentence, she was down the path and through the gate, not turning once to see if he was watching her run.

# Eight

I believe in the goodness of knitters everywhere. I've seen it evidenced over and over, in charitable works and kindness to strangers and community alike. But while knitters don't normally lie, don't trust them not to exaggerate yardage.

— E. C.

After lunch, before school let out, was Lucy's favorite time of day at the Book Spire. When no one was in the store, Lucy usually had her feet up on the shelving cart and a novel propped open on the counter. Ruby's yellow cardigan would be wrapped tightly around her, except in the warmest weather. Lucy would knit a while and take a bite of her apple and then knit some more, flipping pages as needed. Any book — it didn't really matter. She had six or seven of them behind the counter at all times, Post-its marking her spots. If a customer asked what she was reading and expressed interest in it, rather than ordering her a copy, she was happy to sell it to her on the spot. It would come back around soon enough, and she'd get to finish it then.

But Lucy was having trouble focusing on the historical romance she was reading today.

Owen was just a door away. He'd been in residence for two days, and she hadn't seen him once.

He hadn't called with any questions, or stopped by for a magazine, or even waved as he'd walked by the window.

It was probably because she'd attacked him.

She'd launched herself at Owen without provocation, then she'd run away without any explanation. She must have looked like a crazy person, running away like that.

Lord, that pager had been the best thing she'd ever heard in her life. Of course, he hadn't known what it was, so he still probably thought she belonged in a mental institution.

And the page hadn't even been for a medical or a fire, it had just been for backfill to the station — the ambulance had been sent out to difficulty breathing down in the valley, and whenever that happened, dispatch paged in two volunteers, in case another medical call came in while the primary paramedics were out. Lucy had raced to the station, wild-eyed, breathing heavily, still completely shocked by her behavior. She'd hidden it by hunkering down in one of the La-Z-Boy chairs, knitting on the sock until the truck captain, Milton James, asked if her needles were smoking.

Now, days later — still no sign of Owen — Lucy sighed and tucked the book under the counter. Maybe she'd write something down, jot ideas, like she used to in her old journal, the one she hadn't seen in so long. She missed the feeling of the pen on the page. She wondered when exactly she'd given up that old habit of writing everything down. It had fallen to the wayside at some point. . . . But then she might want to write about Owen, and that would *not* help.

Maybe she needed a mystery novel instead. Something more involved, something to keep her brain busier, keep her from thinking about him.

Yesterday she'd seen Owen walking by the store, going down the path to the parsonage, but he walked with purpose, limping just the slightest bit, staring at the ground.

He never looked up at her. Just as well, too.

Lucy shivered, remembered the feel of his lips against hers. That fine, slight evening stubble that she hadn't expected. . . . That taste of him that she'd desperately wanted more of, and *more.*

When she remembered that kiss, the way he'd held her, just for that moment, she wanted to run back out there and try it again. But just as soon as the thought passed through her mind, she knew it for what it was: Crazy. Dumb. Irrational.

He'd left once. He was going to leave again. Everyone did.

She pulled Grandma Ruby's sweater more tightly around herself and felt an ominous soft *pop* under her left thumb. Yet another strand had broken, another fiber worn through. No one would wear a sweater as ratty as this, Lucy knew, no one but her.

Lucy sighed and pulled the front left side out, holding it up to the light, examining the damage. It wasn't good. She'd darned everything she could already, but now in some places there were holes next to other holes.

Grandma Ruby had made this sweater shortly before Lucy had graduated from college, when she'd been home on spring break. The Book Spire had been closed on the soft, warm evening, and Ruby had woven in the last few ends of the sweater. "It's done." She put it on, the yellow color suiting her soft gray curls and pink cheeks. "Let's go for a stroll to celebrate Eliza's clever pattern and my nimble fingers, shall we?"

The two of them had walked down to the edge of the water, as they often did together at dusk. It had been the perfect walk, up till that last moment, when they'd been standing there, looking at the last of the fading light, and Lucy'd heard her grandmother make a funny noise.

Grandma Ruby's skin was ashen, her eyes closed. Her hand clutched at her left arm, and she swayed for a minute before she dropped to her knees in the wet sand.

"Grandma!"

"Help," Ruby whispered. "Help me."

They were the last words her grandmother ever spoke to her. Lucy raced up the beach to get help as fast as she could, her feet sinking into the sand which sucked at her heels as if she were in a nightmare. The volunteer fire brigade arrived and gave her grandmother CPR. Lucy watched helplessly, hot tears streaming down her cheeks.

Ruby died at the hospital, hours later. Lucy looked at the pile of clothing in the small emergency room, the yellow wool still bright and happy.

In the cold hospital, Lucy slipped the cardigan over her shoulders. Sand fell out of it to the tile floor.

It would be the sweater she wore in the bookstore. Always.

The bells on the front door jingled as it opened, jolting Lucy out of her memories. So much for a break. Lucy looked up and quietly groaned.

"Yoo-hoo!" Whitney Court gave a prom-queen wave as she entered. Her perfect brown hair fell in shining waves, her bright green eyes sparkled, and she was dressed in a sweet blue gingham dress that had to be vintage. Just looking at her caused an extra layer of bookstore dust to land on Lucy.

Whitney placed a plate of beautifully frosted cupcakes on the counter in front of Lucy. "I made too many, and they're not all going to sell today. I thought you or your customers might appreciate a sweet little pick-me-up!"

"Thanks, Whitney," said Lucy on a sigh. Sometimes she thought Whitney was one of those women put on the planet in order to make other women feel badly about not channeling their inner domestic goddess. If Lucy had spent two hours in front of a mirror, she still wouldn't be able to pull off that kind of perfect wave in her hair, those beautifully made-up eyes that looked sweet and sultry all at once. Lucy was just lucky if, on the rare occasions she applied eye-liner, she didn't stab herself in the eye.

And the problem, aside from Whitney's immaculate presence, was that Lucy would have to eat a cupcake. Or a couple. Or all of them. Whitney's creations were the best in town, hands down. She was a baking genius. Damn her.

"What's new in the land of books?" Whitney leaned against the counter, her perfect manicure resting on top of a pile of Cliff's Notes that needed shelving later. Weren't bakers' hands supposed to be burned and scarred from baking?

"Not much," said Lucy, looking around for something to work on. There: those boxes she'd bought from Owen. She hadn't gone through them yet and maybe she could convey just how very busy she was. Maybe Whitney would get the hint and leave. She put the top box on the counter.

"Pretty slow, huh? Oh, eww! That box looks like it has the skin of a . . . what is that on top?"

"Old cat fur, matted into the cardboard."

Whitney wrinkled her nose. "Well, that's disgusting. Whoever it belonged to should have cleaned that off for you. It looks like half the cat is still there."

Lucy looked up at perfect Whitney. "Don't watch, then. This is going to be boring. Is there something I can help you with in the meantime?" She opened the lid, parting the matted cat hair, and peered through.

Whitney wandered a little way, looking up to the stained glass overhead. "So, quiet day?"

Lucy ignored her and lifted out the top layer of old romances and studied them as if they were the most interesting books she'd ever seen. Everyone brought them to her, thinking she had a use for them. But her romance section was strained to the limit as it was. No one wanted to read bodice rippers from the seventies anymore, not when there were so many new love stories out there, with more than just bodices being ripped.

Whitney went on, "But you must be doing okay, though, right? My goodness, the bakery has been doing so well; I've almost doubled my receipts in the last two years. I heard something on the news that said in times like these people may be cutting back, but they still allow themselves the little treats, and that's where we come in, right? They may not take their big vacations, but they'll still buy lipstick from the drugstore, or éclairs from me, used books from you." Her laugh was a perfect harmonic lilt, hitting just the right note of friendly conspiracy. "We'll ride this recession all the way to the bank, right, Luce?"

Luce. No one but her family and Molly called her that, and while Whitney may be doing well, Lucy was just scraping by. She didn't feel like hearing about Whitney's fabulous life right now.

The second most difficult thing about her grandmother's death thirteen years ago, after the grief Lucy had felt, had been saving the bookstore. No one in her family knew how close Lucy had come to losing it entirely. She'd kept it from them, not wanting them to worry. When Lucy took it over, when she opened Ruby's bankbooks for the first time, she'd been horrified. The creditors had been breathing down Grandma Ruby's neck for years, and it was only by playing every single one of her cards perfectly that Lucy had managed to hold on to the store. Even now, Lucy never felt like she was making enough to feel truly comfortable, and she certainly couldn't say she'd doubled her receipts recently like the lucky Whitney had.

Gritting her teeth and wishing Whitney

would say whatever it was she needed to say, Lucy finished emptying the box. Harlequins galore, circa mid-seventies. Basically worth nothing. She'd wasted fifteen bucks on these three boxes, fifteen dollars she could ill afford.

Lucy forced herself to smile at Whitney as she lifted the second box up to the countertop. She would get through this.

On top were more yellowed romances, the covers curled and worn. Great. Straight to the recycle bin.

"Is there something I can help you with, Whitney?" She kept her voice light. Polite. Get to the point.

Whitney's smile lit up her whole face like a CoverGirl commercial. Were those false eyelashes? Who wore those anymore? She reminded Lucy of an exercise regimen book — equal parts chirpy encouragement and patronization, made of rules impossible to follow.

"Well, I was on the treadmill last night — you know I go an hour on it every evening, right?"

Lucy jerked her head in what she hoped looked like encouragement.

"I was thinking more about that party we should have."

Lucy sighed. She found a layer of old Life

magazines. Not worth anything more than a buck or two on eBay, but she'd enjoy looking at the pictures later.

"You and Owen are heroes," Whitney said. "You need to be feted. Like I said the other night, I want to be the one to do that. Whitney's Bakery will throw the celebration."

Frowning, Lucy continued pulling out books. A couple of hardcovers, but nothing special, nothing more recent than 1980 that she didn't already have three of on the shelf. "No way. That would be embarrassing. I don't want that. Throw a party for Abigail if you have to do something, but not for us. I called the hospital, and she's been released, but Cade said she doesn't want visitors until the bruising goes down."

Whitney clapped her hands lightly and said, "What if we did something together? A night to celebrate Abigail, where you have a sale on knitting books, and I bake cupcakes in the shape of knitting needles and sweaters and maybe we can hire a band! I've been meaning to approach you anyway. Our businesses are perfectly suited to work together, don't you think? It could be the start of something good, something ongoing. We could do a night together once a month, and celebrating Abigail, and your heroism, could be just the start. . . ."

Entrepreneurial Molly was always going on about things she could try to make a bigger splash in town — have reading nights, clever themes, book parties. Lucy assumed Molly would love the idea of her working with Whitney.

But those ideas took work, and required taking risk, whereas going along as she always had was safe. Simply selling books and providing coffee was working out fine so far.

Safety always won.

"Mmmm. I don't want to make money on Abigail's tragedy."

Whitney held a hand to her heart. "Of course not! I didn't mean that!"

But Lucy wondered if she hadn't. And a party wasn't a horrible idea. But Lucy didn't want to work with Whitney. Period.

She pulled out the next hardcover.

"Oh, holy crap." A grin spread across her face. The book was an old Barbara Walker, a book of stitch patterns that was still popular and still in print. But this was an early one, a really early one. She opened the book to the copyright page. "Oh, man."

Whitney looked on with interest. "Something good?"

"First edition." Lucy couldn't keep the

excitement out of her voice. Was Owen's mother a knitter? She had to be, this was just too good.

"Is it worth a lot?"

Of course, that would be the first thing Whitney would ask about. But Lucy nodded, a grin spreading across her face. "It's worth some. But mostly, it's just awesome."

"Really?" Whitney asked.

Lucy moved another layer of paperbacks, this time old mysteries and put them to the side. Come on, early Meg Swanson. Or Elizabeth Zimmerman? Maybe a first edition of *Knitting Without Tears*? It was too much to hope for, and she knew it, but she couldn't help feeling the same as when she rubbed off the coating on the lottery tickets she rarely bought.

Her fingers felt it first. Another hardcover, this one wide and heavy.

It couldn't be what she thought it was. . . . Closing her eyes, Lucy took a deep breath before opening them again.

It was. Lucy whooped.

*Silk Road.* In perfect condition, although for this particular Eliza Carpenter book, it didn't matter what condition it came in. It was the Holy Grail for knitters.

She looked at the copyright page.

It was another first edition.

And it was signed. Eliza Carpenter's clear hand, those loops that were so recognizable, trailed up the page in ink still dark.

Chills ran up and down her spine. This was the find of a bookstore-lifetime.

Lucy ran her fingers over the cover. The "Cypress Hollow Lighthouse" pattern was in this book. Generally agreed to be one of the most beautiful sweater patterns in the world, it was a fine-gauge, tightly cabled sweater that suggested the sweep and scope of the beam from the old lighthouse, the way it used to shine out to sea before the light became an auto-strobe and the lighthouse itself closed and became too dangerous to enter. In real life, she'd only ever seen one sweater made from the pattern, since the book hadn't had a large print run and had gone out of print so quickly. She couldn't even imagine how much it would go for on an auction site.

"You look stunned," said Whitney.

Lucy held up the book. "The best. Absolutely the best."

"Worth a lot?"

Lucy placed the book reverentially on the counter. "Oh, yeah. But I'd never sell it. No one lets this book go. Look at this." She opened to the Lighthouse pattern. "Who wouldn't be dying to make this?"

Whitney frowned, a slight crease forming between her nicely shaped eyebrows. "It's really pretty, I guess. If you like a sweater that looks like it needs shoulder pads."

"That was just the style then. It's amazing. I've never been able to even read the pattern before. I can't wait to read it, let alone cast on for it."

"Isn't there some kind of black market out there? Someone making photocopies?"

"No!" Lucy was horrified. Then she considered the question. "Well, yeah. Some people make photocopies of patterns, but it's under the table and it's not cool. But no one, no knitter worth her stitch markers would ever make a copy of a pattern from this book. The first knitter who saw the sweater would want to know the story of how the knitter found the book. Then they'd want to see it for themselves. . . . It would get ugly, fast."

"What else is in that box?"

She shrugged. "Who cares?"

"Come on, finish it. What if there's another copy?"

What if there was another copy? Lucy would keel over and die, that's what. Right after she called every knitter she knew to rush to the store for an insta-auction.

But the box didn't hold much more. Just

a large packet of papers, tied with a piece of nondescript gray yarn. Each page was covered in tiny, handwritten script.

Lucy squinted. She pulled the first page out of the bunch.

It was a pattern of some sort.

"Do you know what those markings mean?" Whitney leaned forward.

Lucy nodded. Of course she knew what they meant.

"You do? Is it some kind of code?"

Lucy laughed. "The code of my people."

"What?"

"It's a knitting pattern. It's really familiar. Hold on a second." Lucy kept reading. She read down to the bottom of the page, then turned it over. "This is so weird. I swear I've never seen this pattern before, but it reminds me of someone. And it's missing a part. There's nothing on the back. There must be another page — there aren't any sleeve directions on here."

She pulled out the next brittle page.

"Do they match?"

"No, this is only half a pattern."

"For what?"

She took a moment to glance over the papers again. The dry smell tickled her nose. "Looks like a cardigan. It's funny, though . . . the way it's written is familiar. I swear I know who wrote this."

"You can tell?"

"It's like a signature. Some people have stronger styles than others. I'd take a bet this was Eliza Carpenter."

"Who's Eliza?"

Lucy gaped at her. That's right, there were people in the world who hadn't been raised to revere Eliza as the modern-day patron saint of knitting, weren't there? She'd forgotten that. She tapped *Silk Road* and then turned it over to show Whitney the small picture of the older woman with the long silver braid on the back cover.

"Cade MacArthur's great-aunt. She revitalized knitting in this country, took it mainstream. How could you live here and not *know* her?"

"She looks vaguely familiar. Is she the one who started that whole knitting-is-the-new-yoga thing?"

"That's just a fad — there were knitters before, and there'll be knitters after. Eliza self-published her patterns in the fifties and taught her readers how to design patterns themselves, using unconventional design ideas. She moved knitting from fussy to easy, attainable, wearable. And she wrote with a voice that was entirely unique. And she was local. You know, Abigail's knitting shop? That was Eliza's cottage, so we take even more pride in her than most knitting areas do. We *claim* her."

Lucy heard the passion in her own voice and tried to tone it down for the non-knitter.

Whitney asked, "You knew her?"

It felt weird to Lucy that she and Whitney were talking. They rarely spoke alone like this. "A little, I guess. She and my grandmother were knitting friends. Eliza moved south about ten, fifteen years ago, to San Diego, and she died there not that long ago. But when she lived here, when I was in my teens, my grandmother would close the bookstore and would take us kids to spend long afternoons on Eliza's ranch. Mom and Grandma and Eliza would knit in the parlor while the boys tore around outside. I usually wanted to be alone, so I read books up in the hayloft more often than I knitted with them."

She turned the pages, looking at the smiling face of Joshua, Eliza's husband, leaning against the railing of the house Cade and Abigail now lived in, wearing a rugged Aran that looked so thick it seemed like it had been knitted right off the sheep, barely spun at all. Lucy touched the page. When she was a kid, Eliza had always taken the most interest in her knitting. Lucy's mother and grandmother taught her to knit, of course, but Eliza was the one who came to stand behind her, moved her arms so she held the yarn in her left hand, "Like me, so you don't flap like a chicken. There, isn't that nicer this way? Now you can read at the same time."

And once, Eliza had given Lucy a hand-tooled leather-bound journal from Italy. "To record your dreams. I noticed you write. Keep writing, and you'll remember your life. If you don't write things down, it's like they never happened."

A sudden film of hot tears sprang to Lucy eyes. Where was that old journal of hers? Up in the attic at home? She should find that. In honor of Eliza.

Words and knitting had always been her favorite things. They still were.

Whitney pointed at the stack of loose papers. "So that's good?"

Lucy snapped back into the present. "Oh, hell, yes." She looked again at the two pages. The reality of it began to sink in.

This was more than good. This was huge.

She sat on her high stool behind the counter.

If this was really Eliza's work . . .

She pulled out more of the sheets. More

patterns, all in the same delicate hand. She shuffled pages. There had to be at least twenty, maybe thirty patterns here, as well as pages that appeared to be journal entries or letters. None of them, at first glance, looked anything like Eliza's other published patterns, although they shared a similar voice. Lucy didn't recognize any, and she practically knew Eliza Carpenter's patterns by heart.

The bell on the door jingled. Mildred Elkins and Greta Doss entered.

"What did you forget this morning?" Lucy called.

Mildred waved both hands over her head. "My umbrella! My purple umbrella!"

"Is it raining?" Lucy hadn't even noticed that it was overcast.

"No! But it might someday! And I love that umbrella. Do you have it? Oh, hello, Whitney. How are you?"

Before Whitney could even open her mouth, Mildred said, "Greta, go look under the table, I'll check the bathroom."

Greta, quiet as usual, nodded and checked the table. Mildred came out of the bathroom, satisfied.

"Got it. Thank goodness. What are you two up to?"

Lucy had a flash of brilliance. "You'd

recognize Eliza Carpenter's handwriting, right?"

Greta smiled at Mildred, who shot a look back at her. "One of our favorite people," said Greta in a soft voice.

Mildred used her umbrella, striking it on the floor for emphasis. "She certainly was. What do you have there? Move, young lady." Mildred pushed a startled-looking Whitney out of the way.

Mildred took the loose pages out of Lucy's hands. She only glanced at the first page before laughing.

"Oh, Greta, look. This is Eliza." She held the page up, first to Whitney and then to Lucy. "This is Eliza."

"How certain are you?" Lucy tried not to get excited, but it was almost impossible.

"Two hundred percent. I have letters from her at home that we can compare, but I know with all my heart that these are Eliza's." Mildred riffled through them and then handed them to Greta. Shaking her head, she said, "I've never seen these."

Lucy clapped her hands and jumped off her stool. "I knew it! I knew it! This is the most exciting thing ever!"

Whitney laughed.

Lucy blushed. "Okay, it's not your kind of exciting, I'm sure." Coming around the counter, she stood next to Mildred, looking over her shoulder.

"Unbelievable," breathed Greta, as she examined several sheets.

"And look," said Lucy. *"Silk Road."*

Their jaws dropped.

"Where did you get all this?" Mildred demanded.

Hell.

In the space of a second, Lucy thought it through. She couldn't keep the boxes. It wasn't right to keep it, to profit on such a treasure, when she hadn't fully looked through them before buying them from him.

And everyone in the whole world would want these papers. There would be a run on them. Knitters from all over the globe would descend, wanting to study them, to examine them, to parse their contents and take them away from her. Lucy wouldn't be the right person to keep them.

No one would let Lucy keep these. Nor should they.

Lucy swallowed her disappointment. It had been lovely to own them for even a moment.

"I bought them from Owen Bancroft. Boxes from his mother's storage unit."

"Oh, the luck of you!" Mildred banged her umbrella against the tile floor. "This is unbelievable. Are there any more?"

Dumbly, Lucy shrugged. Oh, if Irene had more treasures from Eliza stashed away . . .

Mildred jabbed her forefinger into Lucy's arm. "You *ask* him," she hissed. "You ask him as soon as you can. And then you put them in a safe-deposit box until you decide what to do with them." Mildred pulled her iPhone out of her crocheted purse. "I have to Twitter this."

Whitney smoothed the skirt of her dress. "So those looseleaf papers? They're knitting patterns?"

Lucy nodded.

With a butter-couldn't-melt voice, Whitney said, "So if they're unpublished, wouldn't they revert back to her estate? You said she was local?"

Mildred gave Lucy a stricken glance. "Don't tell Cade," she hissed. "We can hide them."

Lucy sank into a chair at the table. She'd have to tell Cade and Abigail. Soon. Of course she would. But she wanted just a moment more with them — to hold them, to read them, to pretend they were hers.

But even though the words galled her, she said them anyway. "Whitney's right. And I'll talk to Owen. We'll tell them."

Waving her hands modestly, Whitney fluttered toward the front door. "I just do what I can to help. Now I have to get back to the shop. I'm sure Thomasina's overwhelmed, with a line a mile long. Please, ladies, have a cupcake, won't you? Lucy, we'll plan our little party soon. We'll combine our business savvy soon enough, won't we? We can take over Cypress Hollow together!"

Cold day in hell, thought Lucy, but she nodded.

Then she lowered her head to the papers, letting Eliza's quiet voice sing in her ear.

# NINE

> A mother's needles, in particular, are the strongest needles of all.
>
> — E. C.

At Willow Rock, Owen's mother was crying.

Miss Verna whispered, "She's been like this for about fourteen hours. Nothing is stopping it."

"What's she upset about?"

"No one knows. She doesn't seem to want anything, she's not even angry. She's just crying."

It was awful. Owen looked at his tiny mother, lying curled up on top of the narrow twin bed, weeping into her pillow. She didn't heave with sobs, she just cried quietly and shook.

He sat on the bed next to her. She didn't seem to notice.

"Mom. It's me."

Nothing but more tears.

Somehow, somewhere, this was probably his fault. He took a deep breath. He was here now. That was the point.

For one second Owen allowed himself a dangerous fantasy — that a woman was here next to him, and that she loved his mother, also. That she could lean over and say something, *do* something, and ease whatever pain his mother was in, just by saying the right womanly thing. And if, in that brief daydream, that woman happened to look a lot like Lucy, well, it was just a damn fantasy, right?

But dreams didn't come true, Owen knew that for sure. Especially his. And he needed to stay the hell away from Lucy Harrison — he could feel it. Bancrofts didn't deserve much in this town — he needed to remember it, and get out fast, as soon as he knew his mother would be all right.

He took a deep breath and shook off the thoughts that had gone in a direction he hadn't wanted. "Mama. What's wrong? Is there anything I can do?"

"Will you drink something, Mrs. Bancroft? You're gonna dehydrate yourself with that crying." Miss Verna held out something that looked like an adult version of a sippy cup.

Owen hated it, but he supposed it was necessary.

Irene just turned her head farther into the pillow and cried.

Owen looked up at Miss Verna. "Really? Hours?"

"Without even falling asleep once. Just crying. I didn't sleep much myself, too worried about her."

"Does the date mean anything today?"

"Honey, she don't know what the date is today. Or any other day."

That was true. It was a stupid question.

"Can I take her out?"

"You could . . . But . . ."

"What if I took her out for a ride? We could go get a *drink*." Owen put air quotes around the word for Miss Verna's benefit, but his mother, who couldn't see him, seemed to pay attention. Her crying grew quieter.

Miss Verna said, "Well, I don't think she seems in any mood to go. But you could ask her."

"Mama, do you want to go for a ride?"

Irene turned her head on the pillow and nodded.

Miss Verna helped him change Irene from her nightdress and robe into jeans and a sweatshirt. It was exactly the kind of sweatshirt she would have hated when she was younger, but his mother had changed drastically over the years. Instead of mocking clothing covered in animal appliqués, she was drawn to the puffed fabric, running her fingers constantly over the design, speaking to the animals as if they were real.

The sweatshirt today was one that he'd bought in Florida for her: it had dolphins leaping over a glittery moon. As she sat in the passenger seat, one finger stroked the top of a dolphin's head.

He'd transported lots of prisoners over the years. Some had been chatty, some sullen. But even the drunk ones hadn't been like this. Owen began to doubt the wisdom of what he was doing.

He hadn't taken his mother out of Willow Rock since the time he lost her in the mall last Christmas when he'd been visiting. It had been his own damn fault: he'd sent her into the women's room while he used the men's room as fast as he could. But when he'd sent another woman in to look for her, his mother had vanished. A half hour's worth of searching with every security guard on duty had turned her up, tucked into a display bed in Macy's, a box of half-eaten powdered doughnuts under the covers.

Now, even though small sobs wracked her

body every fifteen seconds or so, and the tears streamed down her cheeks, Irene's face was relaxed, and she watched out the car window as if pleased to be moving. Her fingers played over the door handle.

"Anytime you want to tell me what's wrong, you just let me know."

She looked at him blankly, wetly, and then turned back to the window.

So what if he was seen leading his crying mother into a bar at two o'clock on a Monday? Oh, God, what if the bar wasn't even open on a Monday afternoon? It was possible. Probable, even. What the hell would he do then?

It wasn't even like his mother had been a big drinker when she was younger. That had been his father.

But every night at Willow Rock they offered the residents a drink, fixing them a glass of bubbly water with a splash of grenadine. Owen supposed it calmed the ones who remembered the evening tradition. Sometimes Miss Verna added a little drink umbrella that she provided herself. This pleased Irene and made her tractable enough to tuck into bed for the night.

They were smart there.

Smarter than he was, bringing her out in public crying like this. People would think he was beating her.

Best to move quickly, then.

He parked. Of course there was a spot in front — normal people didn't go to the bar at two in the afternoon. Just lushes and sons with crazy mothers. Come to think of it, there was probably a good amount of overlap between the two groups. He was dying for a beer.

He unlocked the doors and got out. Opening her door, he said, "Here we are, Mom. Dry your face. You don't want people to see you crying, do you?" Owen said, and then felt immediately ashamed.

She had Alzheimer's. Who cared if she cried, if she wanted to? He straightened his shoulders as he helped her out of the car.

This was his mother. Who cared if anyone stared?

But he sure as hell wished she would stop crying. His mother looked up at him with a puzzled frown, tears still streaming.

"We're getting a drink. You want a drink, Mom?"

She nodded.

"Here, hold this handkerchief, all right?" Owen handed her a white one that Miss Verna had given him as they left. Maybe if she had it in her hand, she'd use it. "Can you dry your face a little before we go in?"

Irene patted her face with the handkerchief. The tears didn't stop rolling, but now at least her chin wasn't dripping like it had been. There were already big wet spots on her blue sweatshirt. It looked as though the dolphins really *were* leaping through the seas.

"Come on, Mama. In here."

Quickly, into the bar, before anyone suspected elder abuse.

The high windows let the afternoon light stream in over the polished bar down to the dark wood floor. The large room was empty. Not even Lucy's brother was visible, which was a relief.

Owen led his weeping mother across the room to a booth. Irene, still holding the handkerchief, dabbed it under her dripping chin. It was eerie, really, how placid she looked. No emotion crossed her face, which was unlike her. Usually her irritation showed. Sometimes, when listening to him talk about her house and her roses, she looked happy. But this calm face with tears still flowing as if she'd sprung a leak, this was something he'd never seen before.

Jonas came out from the back room, whistling. He stopped, pitching forward, his lips still pursed, when he spotted them in their booth.

"I didn't hear anyone come in," he said coldly.

Owen took a deep breath. Maybe he should have gone to Tillie's, or the ice-cream shop, but those places were so crowded, so loud and confusing for someone like his mother. If it had to be game on with Jonas, then so be it.

"Just here for a drink."

"Fine," Jonas said without meeting Owen's eyes. "Get something for you?"

"A beer for me. Whatever you have on tap. And for Mom, she'd like a virgin old-fashioned, I think."

Jonas looked surprised. Irene gazed past him into the room, tears rolling down her cheeks.

"Is that possible?" Owen tried to sound nonchalant, tried to keep the desperation out of his voice. He slung his arm up onto the back of the booth and hung his head to the side.

"Everything all right?"

"We're working on it."

Thank God for beer. In a couple of minutes, Jonas delivered their drinks. "The lady's old-fashioned." Under his breath and speaking rapidly, he muttered to Owen, "It's iced decaf coffee with a little sugar and a cherry."

Feeling a gratefulness he didn't want to betray, Owen said, "Good. Thank you."

Jonas jerked his chin. "We all have keys to the parsonage, you know. We drop by. To check on things. A lot. All the time. We don't call first."

He had to say it, Owen knew. He was the older brother. If he'd had a sister like Lucy, he'd damn-straight be protective, too.

"I'm not the same punk I was in high school."

Jonas looked at him like he was sizing him up, as if he was trying to see if there were a visible way to tell if this was true or not. "You can say that all you want, but you're still the guy living in my sister's rental, and I don't have to trust you farther than I can throw you."

Owen felt his gut clench, the same way it always did right before a foot pursuit, or before a perp tried to twist out of his grasp. It took everything he had to still his breath and remain seated, his hands quiet, open. "What's your problem with me? Are you like this with all the people she rents to?"

"Only the men."

But Jonas looked away when he said it, and Owen knew that it wasn't the men that Jonas felt this way about. It was him, in particular. He wondered if Jonas's father had known his dad. God help him if he had. Hugh Bancroft hadn't left Owen a legacy to be proud of, but if he had to make up for the sins of his father, there wasn't enough time in the world.

"Fine," said Owen. "I gave your sister a list of references. I can give the same list to you." The words burned like liquid nitrogen in his throat.

Slowly, Jonas shook his head. "I'm going to give you the benefit of the doubt. But you only get that once."

Irene finished her drink and burped. Her shoulders still shook with sobs.

"Seriously, guy," said Jonas. "Is she okay? Do you want me to call someone?"

"Could we have another one of those drinks for her? Maybe even more watered down? I'm worried she's crying out all her hydration."

"Yeah, sure. I'll be back in a minute."

"Thanks." Owen felt relief he wasn't going to have to fight Jonas. Not that he would have, not in front of his mother, of course. It wouldn't have come to that. But the relief he felt was palpable.

The front door opened. A middle-aged woman dressed in a purple sweater with snowflakes on it entered. She seemed to bring noise and light. Were those bells attached to her shoes?

Irene noticed her as well. Her face, so still and unmoving, lit up as she looked across the room.

The woman waved both arms at Jonas. "You have to help me! I think one of my tires is going to go flat! It looks funny. I touched it and it doesn't feel like the other ones — it feels like it's just not really confident about wanting to be a tire."

"Mom, now?"

"I'm just outside, it won't take a minute."

Grumbling, Jonas followed his mother outside. Irene's face went back to disinterested. And wet. Still very wet.

A few minutes later, Jonas reentered the bar and brought over the second drink to Irene. "Here you go. Sorry. You know mothers." Jonas gave Irene a half smile and for one moment, Owen saw Lucy's eyes in his face.

"Are her tires okay?"

"They're fine. She has strange ideas sometimes."

Jonas's mother, entering the bar again, heard this last. "Don't be silly. It's worth getting my son to check on these things for me. It's about my safety, isn't it?"

Jonas rolled his eyes, but turned to face his mother. "Yeah, Mom. I made sure that you're safe. You feel better?"

"So much! Thank you, my darling boy!" She went up on her toes and embraced her son's neck. She kissed him twice on the cheek.

"Look at him!" she said across the room to Irene. "Isn't he just the most handsome thing? Oh, Bart and I made some good babies. How nice to see you out, Irene. Is that your son? He's handsome, too."

"Mom," said Jonas.

Irene's eyes opened wide through their tears. The woman crossed the room, bells tinkling.

"Owen Bancroft."

"Toots Harrison, so nice to meet you." She shook Owen's hand and then held her hand to Irene.

"She probably won't . . ." started Owen. But then his mother folded the damp handkerchief, placed it carefully on the table, and shook Toots's hand.

"Wow," he said.

"Pleasure," said Toots. "Honey, what's wrong? I haven't seen you in a long time. You look so sad."

Toots didn't let go of Irene's hand, and Irene didn't pull hers back. There was a quiet moment as Owen and Jonas watched their mothers stare at each other. The tears didn't slow on Irene's face, but her eyes softened.

"We don't know what's wrong," said Owen. "The nurse said she's been doing this for hours now, without stopping."

"Well," said Toots. "We'll just have to deal with that, won't we, Irene? Crying is good for the soul, but then it has to stop, too." She gently pulled her hand away from Irene and gave her back the handkerchief.

"You just hold that tight for a minute, honey. I'll be right back. I can fix this."

Owen was too surprised to say anything.

"Mom?" said Jonas, looking startled. "Mom, you're not going to do anything like . . ."

"Just a little bit, Jonas. No one will mind." She was already darting out of the bar. "Be right back!"

Jonas groaned. "She's out of her mind."

"So's mine."

Owen took another gulp of his beer. Thank *God* his drink wasn't virgin.

Back through the door Toots jingled, carrying a red tote.

She said, "Scoot a little, honey," to Irene, who did indeed scoot, to Owen's surprise. Toots sat next to her and took things out of her bag: alcohol, cotton balls, long thin needles.

*Needles?*

"What the hell?" said Owen.

"Mom, you can't do this to just anyone."

"Do what?" Owen held up a hand.

Toots grinned and crossed her eyes at Owen. "Just a little acupuncture. It'll fix her right up."

"Acupuncture?" Owen almost yelled the word.

"Mom, that's not sanitary. Not in my bar. I'll lose my license!"

"Hush. No one's going to see me doing it. You boys pipe down."

Irene leaned forward to look, and tears dribbled off her chin and onto the tabletop.

"You see that?" said Toots. "She's interested. She knows this is good stuff. You want to try this, honey? Here, wipe some of those tears away again, I don't want you crying into my kit bag." Her touch looked light as she used the soggy handkerchief on Irene's chin and cheeks.

Owen blew a puff of air from his cheeks. How bad could this be? "You know what you're doing?"

Toots nodded. "Of course. It's one of the many things I was meant to do."

She stripped paper from the needles. At least they looked sterile. Small comfort.

"Mom, you're not even licensed yet.

You've only had like four classes."

"Licensed, schmicensed. I don't need the government to approve of what I do, and neither do you, my boy."

Owen said. "*Excuse* me?" That's what every gun-toting off-the-grid libertarian had ever said to him, right before he arrested them.

Toots held a finger in front of his nose. "Shhh. Don't disturb the process. Irene, take a deep breath in for me."

Irene drew a shuddering breath.

"Now, this won't hurt a bit, and it will make you feel better, all right?"

Owen knew he should jump in, but he felt frozen. He couldn't do anything, couldn't move, and he couldn't stop it, either.

Toots raised a needle high and then stuck it, quickly, with a small tap, into the very top of Irene's head.

"Are you *crazy?* Her head?"

"Quiet. Don't scare my patient." Toots's voice was stern, and Owen fell silent.

"Just two more. One here," a swab with a cotton ball and then a needle went into the flesh between Irene's right thumb and first finger. "And one here." Another needle, just the very tip, went into Irene's other hand.

"Put your hands on your thighs, love. Lean back into the booth. Close your eyes.

Rest in the breath."

"Mom? Does it hurt?" Owen didn't think Irene would answer him, but she rocked back and forth in a no gesture as she kept her eyes closed.

"Let me see one of those," he demanded of Toots. She nodded and handed him a needle. It didn't even look like a regular needle — it was so thin it was almost transparent at the end. Barely the width of a hair, the whole needle moved and bent with the lightest touch.

"Do one in me," Owen said.

Jonas raised his eyebrows. "You sure, man?"

"Yes. Put this one in me. I want to see if it hurts."

"Just one?" asked Toots, sounding disappointed.

"One."

"Just one place for it, then." She swabbed a place between his eyes, up about a centimeter. Then she held the needle to his forehead and gave a slight tap. She drew the outside casing back, leaving the tiny wire bouncing above his eyes.

It didn't hurt. It was more of an electrical feeling. Owen felt as if it was plugged into something, a tiny current. It didn't feel bad, just kind of twitchy.

Jonas laughed. “You look funny.”

Toots said, “Quiet, or you’re next.” She turned back to Owen. “Now, just sit here with your mother for ten minutes. I’ll come back then and take them all out. You just relax.”

“Can I still drink my beer?”

“Of course, if you think that helps.”

Toots and Jonas retreated to the bar. Owen could hear Jonas chastising his mother again in low tones, but from the sound of her giggles, she didn’t seem to be taking him very seriously.

Owen stared at his mother. Her cheeks were still wet, but her eyes were closed, and she looked content to rest the back of her head against the red leather seat.

He closed his own eyes. The beer was hitting him hard, and he hadn’t even had half his pint.

Beer never made him feel like this.

It couldn’t be the needle, could it?

Nah.

Owen rested, enjoying hearing his mother breathing in and out. Less sniffles, more oxygen.

It didn’t feel like it had been even ten minutes when Toots came back, but when he looked at his watch, he was shocked to find it had been more than twenty.

"Time! Here we are, honey," said Toots as she unceremoniously pulled the three needles out of Irene's head and hands. She plucked his out. Again, he felt that tiny jolt but no pain.

"That felt weird," said Owen.

"Looked weird, too," said Jonas.

"I'd like to see Mrs. Luby's roses," said Owen's mother.

All three of them went silent as they stared at Irene.

Irene wasn't crying anymore. The tears had dried. There were streaks down her cheeks that showed where she'd been crying and the bottom of her chin still looked damp, but she wasn't crying. Her eyes met and held Owen's eyes, and she looked like his mother.

Bullshit. He wasn't going to let *his* eyes fill up. One crier in the family was enough.

"Okay, Mama. We can go see the roses." Owen looked up at Toots. She appeared completely satisfied, standing there in her purple sweater, jingling every time she moved. He wondered if Lucy ever favored clothes that had bells attached. "How did you do that?"

"It's just a really good point." She put her head to the side as if evaluating him. "You're the one living in Lucy's parsonage."

"Yes, ma'am."

"Do you like it?"

"I do."

"Do you see her much?"

"No, ma'am. We both seem to be pretty busy."

"Jonas said you used to ride a motorcycle when you lived here."

"I did."

"And that you were a troublemaker and you were either a criminal or a cop. Or maybe both."

Owen didn't say anything.

"Do you still?" Toots asked.

Owen shook his head, confused. "Still what?"

"Ride a motorcycle."

"No, ma'am. Not for a long time."

"Too bad. I'd ask you to take me out on it sometime. Always wanted to feel one of those rumbling between my legs, and my kids are too conservative."

Owen laughed in surprise.

Owen's mother smiled and dropped her eyes to the table. "Slip the first stitch of every row."

"Mom. Come on."

But Toots looked pleased by Irene's random statement. "That's exactly right, my dear. Once a knitter, always a knitter, isn't that right?" She slid into the booth next to Irene and pulled out a different set of needles and started knitting something bright orange.

Owen said, "I guess we'll have another round."

# Ten

Wool is magic — even wet,
it retains heat.

— E. C.

Lucy gasped as she threw herself down the walkway between the store and the parsonage. Just that short distance had been enough to soak her to the bone and the sound of thunder reverberated inside her chest. The spring storm had come up fast, black clouds scudding up from the west, heading inland with furious haste. Thank God for Grandma Ruby's bookstore sweater — the rest of her was freezing, but at least her torso was warm.

Lucy huddled under the small eave and knocked.

No response.

Oh, God, she was nervous. Seeing him again was making her heart beat double time.

*Chicken.*

She knocked again.

Still nothing. The lights were on, and his car was on the street.

Lucy tried the door handle. It was unlocked.

She fought with her baser self as she jiggled up and down, rain water sluicing off her hair and down her back.

Her baser self won. He might be hurt inside, for all she knew. Shouldn't she check?

The door gave the telltale creak it always had, the sound that had always alerted her grandmother that Lucy was visiting after school, or coming over for the night. But Owen didn't call out.

"Owen? Hello?" She hoped she didn't startle him. Was he armed right now?

But Lord, it smelled good in here. Like garlic and steak. Like Owen was cooking. His back was to her as she entered the kitchen.

"Owen? There was no answer at the door."

He didn't turn around.

"Hey, Owen." Her heart now beating so fast she could hear the blood pumping in her ears, she tried to keep her voice even. "What are you cooking?"

He just began to shake his hips.

*That's* what he was cooking?

Then, while he continued to lean over the sink and peel potatoes, Lucy watched Owen proceed to get his groove on. White cords trailed out of his ears, and Owen danced to music she couldn't hear. She could see from the side that he was mouthing words to go along with his motion. His hip shaking got bigger, more exaggerated. He was better at moving one side than the other, but he was still working it.

Did he really just do a *Saturday Night Fever* move? He put the potato peeler down for a second and used his right hand to do a little pointing dance move. He shuffled his feet to the right. Then he scooted toward the left again.

He looked exactly like Lucy felt when she was having her own little dance parties. Only she'd always suspected she looked pretty dumb and wouldn't have ever wanted to be caught.

He just looked relaxed. Like he was having a ball.

Like he had *no* idea he was being watched.

On a twist move, bent knees with slight pelvic thrust, he burst out singing in a falsetto: "Oooh! Got to give it up!" As his twist turned toward her, Lucy tried to duck out of the way to remain unseen, but it was too late.

His eyes met hers as his voice sailed up to another "Oooh!"

He came to a complete stop and his voice cracked.

Holding up the potato peeler, he gave it a little wave. He tugged the iPod headphones out of his ears. He jerked his chin in a manly way and said in a deep voice, " 'S'up?"

Lucy grinned and raised her hand in greeting.

"How long you been standing there?" he asked.

"Long enough . . ." She giggled.

"Man . . ." Owen said in disgust. "It's Marvin Gaye. What are you doing in here?" He turned back to his potatoes.

"I'm sorry I startled you. It's pouring. You didn't hear the door."

He looked over his shoulder at her and raised an eyebrow. "You know you just broke the law, right? You have to give me twenty-four hours notice before you enter my rental."

Lucy took a step back, the smile falling from her face. She hunched her shoulders. "I'm — I'm sorry. I didn't think. I've never . . ." She turned to bolt. Dammit. He was right. She was such an *idiot.* She should have thought it through before barging in.

"It's fine."

She paused at the edge of the kitchen where the linoleum met the old rug. The rug was lifting, she noticed. She'd have to get that fixed. He could trip and hurt his other hip.

Owen spoke without turning away from his peeling. "What's up, anyway?"

In a halting voice, she said, "I had something to talk to you about. Those boxes you sold me."

"You hungry?"

Lucy wondered if she'd missed something. "Excuse me?"

"Steak in garlic and onions. And I'm making garlic mashed potatoes, too. Lots of garlic." He glanced at her from the sink. "Want some?"

Lucy held up her hand. "Oh, no. I'm fine."

"I didn't ask that, I asked if you were hungry."

She paused. "Really?"

"I've got plenty. I'd be glad if you stayed."

And just like that, Lucy heard it in his voice. He'd be glad, honestly pleased if she stayed.

And she would be, too.

"You want to chop some more garlic for me? I forgot I wanted to make garlic bread, too."

Lucy nodded and picked up a knife. This certainly wasn't the way she'd seen her evening going. But she'd give it a shot.

He sure was going all out for this meal. Did he do this often? Or was this just something he did once in a blue moon? And how often did he dance like that?

Lucy suddenly felt impetuous — a stirring that matched the feeling she'd had on the porch when she'd kissed him. She pointed to the speaker dock sitting on the kitchen table. "Does your iPod plug in to that?"

He glanced back at her, obviously surprised. "You want to hear?"

"Yeah. Looked like you were having fun."

Owen dried his hands on a paper towel and plugged in his iPod. The dance strains of "Give It Up" filled the room. Owen walked deliberately back to the sink to finish rinsing the last of his potatoes.

She mentally shook herself. He wasn't going to sit next to her at the table over his math textbook and ask her again to solve the equation for him while he watched so he could "get the gist" of it, and he wasn't going to ask to borrow her pencil and forget to give it back yet again. He wasn't going to pass her in the hallway the next day, a different girl on his arm, never noticing her once.

There might be no more dancing from him tonight, she thought. But that was okay. It was enough that the music filled the room. Enough that she could rest her eyes on his broad shoulders while he turned the faucet off.

When she was done with the garlic he asked her to mash the potatoes as he worked on doing something to the steak. He handed her a beer, and she drank it out of the bottle, like he did.

Owen put heavy plates on the table and turned on the light outside so they could see the rain sheeting down through the sliding glass doors.

But as Lucy reached to take her first bite, the rain slowed. It eased so quickly that the resultant silence from the roof was unnerving.

Lucy chewed, conscious of every move she made. Then she said, "So. Those boxes."

Owen took a bite and then leaned back in his chair, the front legs lifting off the floor a few inches. He looked comfortable, and a half smile played at the corner of his mouth. "Big boxes o'crap."

"Yeah. Not so much. They're full of treasure."

Owen raised an eyebrow.

"A knitter's treasure," said Lucy.

"There was yarn in there? I really thought there was only paper."

Lucy moved the mashed potato into a peak with her fork. "There were a couple of really valuable books. . . ."

"Lucky you. Looks like my loss, your gain."

She looked up at him quickly. "It's way more than that. There were papers in the box. Undiscovered patterns of a really famous knitter."

"Knitters are famous?"

"A few of them are legendary. Elizabeth Zimmerman. Barbara Walker. And Eliza Carpenter. And these are Eliza Carpenter's papers. The most important knitter of all."

Lucy scooted to the edge of her chair and tugged on the hem of her old bookstore sweater. She had to explain to him her favorite find of all in the boxes. "See this? This was my grandmother's sweater. She made it from Eliza's pattern. I found half the pattern for this, the body part. But not the sleeves. I have to know if the sleeves exist."

Owen looked bemused. "I can see that the sleeves *do* exist. Full of holes, but they're there."

"No, in her words. Her pattern." How to explain it for the non-knitter? Lucy didn't know how to make it clear how important it was.

"Can't you do something like un-knit it? Figure it out backward."

"Reverse engineering. You're good." Lucy was impressed. "But it wouldn't be half as exciting as finding her real, original pattern — what Eliza Carpenter really intended."

Owen shifted his weight on his chair, obviously redistributing his weight off his hip, and Lucy was aware of the smallness of her grandmother's old kitchen.

"Will you make money from me?"

"No! I can't keep them. I have to give them back to you."

"What if I don't want them?"

Lucy paused and then said, "Well, I think you might actually have to give them back to Cade and Abigail MacArthur anyway, since they're unpublished, and depending on laws that I probably don't understand fully, they'll revert to her heirs."

Without warning, Owen leaned forward, putting his mouth next to her ear. "What if we don't tell anyone?"

Lucy felt his warm breath against her cheek as he spoke. She focused on the corded muscles on the back of his hand resting on the tabletop.

She froze in place. If she turned her head

to the left, her mouth would brush his.

No way was she doing that again.

Leaning to the right, she reached for the salt her steak didn't need. "Cat's already out of the bag. Some of the knitters already know, and Mildred tweeted it, so now the whole blogosphere knows, I'm sure of it."

Owen leaned back, easily. Was he even dimly aware of what he did to her? "So what now?"

"Are there . . . more? Of the boxes?"

Owen shrugged. "The storage unit is packed like an insane person filled it."

"Who packed her stuff up?"

"I did. But I was in such a hurry back then, when we were moving her out of her house, that if things were already in boxes, I just shoved them in. I couldn't tell you if there were more of those or not." He gave Lucy a searching look. "Maybe you could help me."

Lucy's heart skipped. "Okay."

He grinned that devil's smile, and Lucy saw the teenaged boy she'd had such a crush on again.

"Come by anytime. We'll go over there. It's not pretty, I have to warn you. Hey, that gal . . . How is she, anyway?"

"Abigail? She's good." Lucy smiled, and she refolded her paper napkin. "She's really good. I'm glad we were there."

Owen nodded. "You did everything right. Not the normal kind of citizen assistance I'm used to."

Lucy didn't feel like telling him that she wasn't the normal citizen — trained in CPR, fighting fires, hose lays, search and rescue . . . She just wasn't used to dragging pregnant friends out of imminent fireballs. "Are you going to miss that? Being the hero?"

Owen shook his head and frowned.

"What?" asked Lucy.

"It's not like that. You never feel like a hero. It's not like you're looking for a parade or a medal or something. You're just the guy people call when they want someone to be in the right place at the right time."

"Still." Lucy leaned forward and put her chin in her hand. "What are you going to do instead for excitement?"

Owen's face clouded and Lucy regretted the question as soon as it left her lips.

"I mean," she said, "of course you're taking some time off, and figuring things out, you said that . . ."

"I might do some handyman work. You know, pick up some odd jobs. Fix-it stuff." He held up his arms and wiggled his fingers as if they didn't belong to him. "I'm good with my hands."

"Oh?" she said politely. But how could someone go from being a police officer to being a handyman? From wielding a gun to a hammer? His eyes looked deadened, and his voice was flat.

"My brother Silas does that," Lucy went on. "He does home remodeling. Painting and electrical work. Plumbing. He's slow to help his sister, though, and I have an ornery garbage disposal. It must be nice to have that talent."

"I can help you with that sometime, if you want," Owen said, but it sounded as if he were injecting enthusiasm into his words artificially. "Maybe doing that kind of thing will keep me busy. If I figure a way to get it off the ground. Get a business license or something . . ."

A flash lit the yard. The rumble followed shortly after.

"Feels like the eye of the storm," said Owen.

The hair on Lucy's arms stood up. "I hate lightning." It was right up there with rats and heights in her book of favorite things.

"You do? I love it."

Lucy looked at him.

That was the difference. After having such an exciting life and getting out of Cypress

Hollow, living in the big city, he probably just wasn't scared of anything at all.

"I'm going to go watch it," she said. Before she had time to change her mind, before he had time to say anything in return, she let herself out the door.

It was pitch dark. Terrifying. Lucy thought about turning around to let herself back in but the thought of him watching her from inside pushed her into the middle of the yard. She looked up.

The wind gusted and knocked against her, spitting in her face. It was still a little wet, even though it wasn't really raining. The air was cool and had a sharp, metallic smell.

A huge gust blew through the yard, pushing Lucy. She moved sideways but retained her ground. She was terrified, but she ignored the part that told her to cower, to cover her head with her arms. She wasn't going anywhere.

The wind lifted the porch swing behind her and sent it sailing, four feet, then seven, loudly scraping the paving stones. Lucy flinched but stayed put. Shutting her eyes, she moved with the wind. It felt almost like being in the water at the beach, rocked by waves: a push-pull motion that left her in the same place.

It was liberating. Exhilarating. Dangerously fun. She could see the appeal in this, standing in the middle of a good, scary storm.

Then her head exploded.

It was as if she had invented the loudest noise she'd ever heard. Nothing outside her could possibly be that loud. At the same time, the yard lit up. Everything — headstones, trees, the old sundial — went blindingly white and seemed to stay that way for a long time, even though it was probably only for a second. She could see every detail of the tree trunk across the yard, each knot and burl clearly delineated. Then blackness.

Everything in her body collapsed.

From a noise that refused to fit in her body, to nothing.

She was sinking, falling.

Strong arms from behind caught her. Lifted her. She closed her eyes.

She didn't understand anything.

When she opened her eyes again, she was inside, in the parlor. Her head was cushioned by a magenta afghan her grandmother Ruby had knitted the last winter before she died.

"Are you okay?" Owen knelt next to the couch. He was touching her, running his hands over her face, her shoulders, her legs.

He put his hands at her waist and left them there.

Her breathing, already rapid, quickened.

"What happened?"

"A bolt of lighting hit the tree right next to you. Not even twenty feet away."

"But I didn't see it."

"You're shaking. Are you sure you're all right?" His hands, large and warm, wrapped around her forearms. Lucy liked the way they felt.

In fact, she liked everything about him right now.

"Yep. I'm fine." She smiled.

"Are you burned somewhere and we just can't tell?"

She thought about it. She wiggled her fingers and toes. "Nope, not burned."

His face was so funny, this close to her. He looked so concerned and at the same time so restless, like he had to do something. It was probably what he'd been trained to always do: Do something. Cops ran to help.

But she didn't need help. She wasn't a damsel in distress who needed saving. Maybe she needed something else.

Even though he was more dangerous to her than lightning.

As he gave her another once-over, she slid her hand into his. He stilled.

"What? What is it?"

She reached her other hand up and put it behind his neck. He appeared so concerned about her that he didn't seem to understand what she was doing until she brought his head down and lifted her lips to his.

For the third time in her life, Lucy Harrison kissed Owen Bancroft.

Even then, he didn't seem to get it. Lucy felt wild elation in her chest. Almost struck by lightning. Kissing a man just for the hell of it.

His lips were soft. Warm.

His lips were gone.

Lucy opened her eyes. Owen had pulled back and was staring at her.

Oh, God. She hadn't planned further than the initial kiss. Now he was going to ask what the hell she'd been thinking, and she wasn't going to have an answer, that was for sure. She had no idea what she'd been thinking.

But he didn't look mad.

Then his head came down fast. His mouth was demanding, strong.

Her lips parted, and his tongue stroked the tip of hers. He bit her bottom lip and kissed her again.

Lucy couldn't breathe. She could only kiss him back.

As his mouth held her, kept her, his hands moved again. They'd just been all over her a moment ago, but this was different. His touch before had been exploratory, testing, worried. Now it was different. The pressure was firm. His hands more demanding.

Lucy moaned against his mouth and arched her back. Where had this come from? This hot need? This overwhelming desire for more?

Owen grazed the side of her face with the back of his knuckles, keeping his lips on hers, while his hand slid under her shirt. He cupped one breast without hesitation and instead of being shocked, Lucy pressed herself into his hand. She wanted more. She needed him to slip the fabric down, yes, like that, like he was doing. His thumb and finger found the sensitive nipple and played with it, twisting lightly, as his mouth stayed on hers, nibbling her bottom lip.

Brave. She was still brave, even though her blood raced through her veins in frenzied surges. Lucy pushed against his chest and sat halfway up. She stripped off her cardigan, then her tee shirt.

What the hell was she doing? She never took the lead like this.

But Owen was different.

She reached to unclasp her bra, slipping

the straps off her arms.

Owen's blue eyes darkened. He groaned, low, under his breath, a sound that quickened Lucy's pulse and made heat flare inside her, rapid flames that spread to her fingers, her toes.

He pushed her back against the couch cushions, claiming her mouth again, harder this time, greedier. Then he kissed his way down her neck, rasping his tongue along her clavicle, dipping it into the hollow at her throat, winding it between her breasts, and just when she thought she couldn't stand it one second longer, he took the peak of her breast into his mouth and sucked, using his finger to massage the other one. Lord have mercy, he *was* good with his hands.

Lucy writhed against him. She needed more. She wanted him, wanted him fast, and she needed to either cool off or figure out a plan, because in about three seconds, her brain wasn't going to work at all.

"Owen," she whispered into his hair.

He looked up at her and ran his tongue around her nipple again, and then bit it. She bucked, bringing her legs around him, pressing her hips against him as hard as she could. He groaned and sank against her, his face twisting in what looked like a combination of pleasure and pain.

"Oh, God, am I hurting you?" Lucy had completely forgotten about his hip.

"Do I look like I mind?" Owen ran his knuckles down her stomach, dipping his fingertips into the waistband of her jeans.

"We have to . . ."

Owen's hand stilled. "If you tell me to stop, tell me soon. Please. Because you're . . ."

She was what? Lucy ached for him to finish the sentence. But like the breast damp from his kisses and cold to the air, his sentence was left incomplete. She was something to him, and she had to know what it was.

"I'm what?"

"You're so . . . hot . . ." His voice trailed off.

It wasn't what he'd been going to say, Lucy knew it. She had no idea *what* he'd been going to say, but it wasn't "hot."

Lucy sat up, her spine straight. She pulled the cardigan over her breasts. "We don't want this. I should go."

This was where he would push her back into the couch and cover her with more of those intoxicating kisses and tell her what he really meant.

Instead, he sat up straight as well, adjusting the weight on his hip, and said, "If you think that's best. . . ."

Lucy looked at him.

No one ever stayed. He'd just been the first to go. Lucy scrunched her eyes shut and then opened them again.

He stood. "You sure you're all right?"

Lucy didn't know if he meant the lightning strike or the kiss, but she closed her eyes and nodded.

"Can I have a glass of water?" she asked in a low voice. She wished for the excuse of the pager's beeps, but she wasn't on call tonight.

While he was filling a glass in the kitchen, she put on her clothes and bolted out of the house and into the rain. Sitting dripping in her car, she saw him silhouetted in the light of the opened door. Then the door was shut. The porch light was turned off.

Lucy's hand shook as she reached for the ignition.

# Eleven

Knitting disasters are never exactly that — yarn, even tangled to the point which resembles something beyond hope, really isn't. Enough patience — and swearing — can resolve every snarl.

— E. C.

As Lucy shut her car door and started up the walk to her parents' house, she could see her breath. She thought briefly of the lightning storm a week before, and the kiss, and then, even though it was cold and she only wore a thin red turtleneck and a ratty red wool sweater she'd knitted years ago, she paused on the walkway to crane her neck, looking up at the home she'd lived in for the first eighteen years of her life.

This rambling old house, at least a hundred years old, three stories, many, many windows, all of them lit and shining out into the darkness, was where Lucy felt safest.

Lucy loved the way it looked at night. Her mother, while always going on about conserving one thing or recycling another, didn't feel badly about using electricity. She said she made a difference in the world in many ways, and she remained unrepentant about leaving lights glowing in every room. White twinkle lights left over from Christmas ran along the eaves in the twined wisteria vines that would bloom soon, and Lucy saw her father pass in front of the hallway window, his hand jammed absent-mindedly into his hair, holding a book in front of his face. Without even being inside, she knew that in five seconds, he'd stumble on the old rug in front of the stairs and curse, dropping the book, losing his place. It was home.

Owen's mother was in Willow Rock. His father, she'd heard, had died in prison. What would it have been like to not have parents creating a safe home? To not be able to peek in from outside, into a place where you were loved?

Lucy pushed open the door and tried to push Owen from her mind at the same time.

Inside the house, her mother caromed past, barely seeming to notice she had entered. Lucy moved into the dining room and poured herself half a glass of red wine from the carafe on the table. She looked up at the wall where Toots's self-portrait hung — a study in green and yellow, the mouth off-center and drooping, the eyes wilder than they ever really were.

Lucy's mother, Toots, reminded her of a self-help book with a bright blue cover that proclaimed freedom from all problems in thirty days with a money-back guarantee. She was a dynamo, a force to be reckoned with. Lucy knew enough of her friends' mothers to realize even at a young age that her mother wasn't like anyone else. Back when she was a kid, her mother was a little eccentric. She'd hung her laundry and didn't believe in dishwashers or microwaves. She was into everything, always. If there was a cause, she rallied behind it. She fought for animals, for plants, for peace, for all groups' sexual rights. She was pro-choice, anti-war, and sex-positive in a small town and had taken flak in the past for it. But everyone loved Toots.

Especially Lucy. She didn't even mind very much that Toots had usually been too preoccupied to ever pay much attention to her only daughter. That was just her mother, just her way. Toots was always busy, usually making a difference in someone's life in a meaningful way. Lucy wouldn't have changed a thing about her.

As Toots raced past again, going in the other direction, she said over her shoulder, "How are you, my little parsnip?" She wore a long gray cabled sweater with a belt and a red velvet floor-length skirt. A black snood-like hat perched on her gray curls.

"Hi, Mom. Where's the séance?"

"Have to get the lamb out of the oven, sweets. Will you go light the fire in the living room, please?"

Lucy wandered into the living room. Good, no one here. Lucy wasn't that great at building fires. While her brothers had been Boy Scouting, she'd been busy knitting. Fire scared her. She usually preferred to play it safe, make someone else do it.

But not tonight. She'd build a great fire. Two big sips of wine, and then she started.

Grabbing the newspapers from their pile, she balled up some pages, placing them under the grate. She piled kindling, the small twigs and branches that her mother gathered on her long, rambling walks. A few more pieces of driftwood on top of these — they'd flash blue and green flames later.

From behind her, Lucy heard Molly's voice say, "You have too much paper in there."

"Hey! I didn't know you were coming

tonight!"

Molly leaned down and gave Lucy's shoulder a brief squeeze, and then said, "Your mother hasn't fed me in a while. And if I didn't get a break, I was going to go stark raving crazy. Between the translation, with the phone ringing off the hook — you have no idea what it's like to translate for a teenager screaming that her brother just overdosed while you have the worst PMS of your life — and at the same time you're online, watching the comps for the house you're selling change before your very eyes. And meanwhile, Theo is in my bed, telling me he loves me."

Striking a match, Lucy held it to the newspaper. Her father said a fire was well laid if it caught at just one point. No moving the match around, no lighting more than one place. Just one match, one spot, and if the fire started, he'd been successful.

"That just sounds like a normal day for you."

"The love part? No love. I don't do love. You know that. I do need and I do now, but not love."

Nothing. Just a little flickering of the paper. It lit, briefly, and caught the edge of another sheet, and then died.

"Dammit," Lucy muttered. So much for

her dad's method. Lucy lit the paper in three places, then struck one more match, and lit two more areas.

With a surprisingly loud *whoomp* the fire caught. It blazed so fast and so hard that Lucy scuttled backward in fright.

"I told you there was too much paper!" said Molly.

"It looked right to me!"

The fire wasn't settling down. The small kindling and the larger pieces of driftwood were flaring into flame. Smoke poured out of the fire and started to fill the living room. Flames leaped higher in the grate.

Molly said, "You opened the flue, right?"

The flue?

*Shit.*

"I can't remember which side the handle's on." Lucy ran to the doorway and yelled up the stairs, "Dad? Dad! We need you! Now!"

The smoke thickened.

"Can't you put it out?" Molly said through coughs.

*"Dad!"*

Lucy's father raced into the room. "Is the house on fire? Call the fire department!"

"I *am* the fire department, Dad. It's just the wood in the fireplace. But I can't remember where the flue handle is. . . ."

"You forgot to open the flue?" He sounded

incredulous.

"I guess so."

"Good God."

Grabbing a plaid wool jacket from the coatrack, he zipped it up and pulled one sleeve down over his hand. Then he plunged through the white smoke, and sticking his arm into the fireplace, he leaned into and over the flames.

"Be careful!"

He yanked something hard, and then drew his arm back, leaping away from the fireplacc.

"Dad? Are you okay?" Lucy coughed.

Toots came in the room. "Bart! Are you *on fire?*"

Bart slapped at the jacket, which smoked in several areas, and he checked the arm that had opened the flue. He held up the blackened sleeve triumphantly.

"It's dirty in there, but I got the job done."

Toots patted his arms. "Thank God for wool."

"Naturally fire retardant," Bart said, smiling at her. "You always say that. So I grabbed it."

"You remembered!" said Toots, and kissed him. Then she turned to face Lucy. "What did you *do?*"

It was more like what she hadn't done. "I

forgot the flue."

"How many times have I told you to check it?"

"Really, Mom, too many times to count. That's why I normally don't light the fires around here. I'm sorry."

Lucy drank from her wineglass while Toots waved her hands around and pushed open two windows. "All's well that ends well. Bart, go get the fan from our bedroom. We'll blow this smoke out, and that nice smell will linger for days. We'll pretend we're at a beach bonfire."

Molly patted Lucy on the shoulder and said, "There. And you call yourself a firefighter."

"Stop it." But for one moment, Lucy imagined what it would have looked like had they not been so lucky, had Bart not been able to open the flue, had the fire escaped the safety of the fireplace. What if the house had gone up in flames? What if Lucy had lost the very meaning of home? And it would have been her fault. The thought made her stomach heave.

She *did* sometimes call herself a firefighter. Four times a month, when she carried the department pager, she did. And for the love of fiber, she must be the worst firefighter in the world. Lucy bit the inside of her cheek.

Toots yelled up the stairs for Jonas and Silas to come down for dinner and shooed the rest of them to the table.

Once they were gathered around the table, Toots looked at Lucy and said, "Thank you for not quite burning down the house, my firefighting daughter. Now pass me the pepper and tell me how your new tenant is doing."

Lucy sent the pepper to her mother via Molly. "Fine, I guess. I haven't seen him much, actually. He's pretty busy with his mother, I think. Out of the house a lot . . ."

Toots nodded. "Because I met him at the bar and I think we should set him up with Whitney."

Lucy felt the heat of the wine hit her veins. Whitney? *Whitney?* "Yeah, Mom, I *think* he's fine, if you don't mind that kind of mama's boy. He's back in town to be near her, you know? Cute enough, I guess, if you like that kind of thing. But remember when I tutored him in high school? Anyone who dated him would have to help him pay the check just to get the change right."

Molly gaped through the thin remaining haze.

Lucy went on, "And who knows where he got that limp? Maybe he tripped walking out of the doughnut shop when he was still on duty." The sharp words felt unfamiliar, acrid, in her mouth.

Lucy's father stopped serving the mashed potatoes. Silas stared at her. Even Jonas's eyebrows went up in surprise.

"I thought you were a fan of his, darling," said Toots lightly.

Jonas said, "I *told* you she shouldn't have let him move in."

Lucy said, "I just don't think he's right for Whitney." She curled her toes into balls at the ends of her canvas shoes.

"He was shot by his best friend," said Toots. "While on duty. It ended his career. Your tone is unkind and I don't like it at my table. Would anyone like some fried Indian okra to go with the lamb?"

Lucy stared at her mother. "How do you know that?"

"He told me." Toots smiled at her daughter.

"He *told* you?"

"I asked. I met him at the Rite Spot the other day. Jonas and I had a lovely time with him and his mother. Eliza and I used to knit with his mother, and Irene and I had a nice little catch up. She doesn't look well, poor old thing."

Lucy just shook her head.

"And I think it's just the saddest thing, a

man who loses his career like that, even a job that involves potential violence and the need to carry a deadly weapon, as his did. Must be like losing his whole identity. I think Whitney, such a bright, sweet thing, would be good for him. Or Molly!" Toots sat up straight, as if seeing Molly for the first time all night. "What about you, sweetheart? Are you seeing anyone right now?"

Molly gaped for a moment. "Well, no. Yes. Kind of?"

"Oh, that's fine. I'll set my sights on Whitney."

"What about Lucy?" asked Molly, with a giggle in her voice. "You won't set them up?"

Toots looked startled for a moment. "My Lucy?"

Lucy said, "Molly!"

"Why not?" asked Molly. "They already have the advantage of proximity, with the bookstore and the parsonage — you already like him, and Lucy's single. What's wrong with that?"

"Oh, but . . ."

Lucy's father frowned. "I don't think anyone should be setting anyone up with anyone. Let people make up their own minds."

Jonas said, "Dad's right."

Toots winked at Lucy. "Lucy's looking for a different kind of man, anyway."

"I am?" Lucy still felt awful about what she'd said about the doughnut shop. She'd been kidding. How could she have known he'd been shot on duty? Of course her mother *would* get the low-down before anyone else.

Toots nodded. "Lucy needs someone gentle. Someone sweet, like her. Someone who can understand her quiet moods, her peaceful nature. Someone . . ." Toots held up her hands and let them sway. "Someone who is like the ocean on a gentle summer's day."

"Someone like Gary," said Jonas around a mouthful of potato.

"Come on, I didn't *know* he was gay. And for the record, he says he didn't, either. He was finding himself," snapped Lucy. "And I loved him. He was sweet."

"As a lamb," agreed Molly, but her cheeks were pink, a dead giveaway she was about to burst into giggles.

It wasn't fair. Lucy used to date more often than she did now, and she even fell in love sometimes. She hadn't always been this scared. But every single time she'd fallen in love, she'd been left. There'd never been a time that she'd been the person causing the breakup. She'd never been the one doing the leaving. Tim had left her for a taller, thinner version of herself who owned a chain bookstore in the city. Gary had left her (lovingly) for a man. Randy had just left. One morning, he was gone, leaving only a note that said, "I'm sorry," and a dirty pair of jeans next to the washing machine.

After Lincoln broke up with her, saying he was moving to Alaska to work in the canneries, Lucy had adopted a cat. After six months, Mr. Pickles had moved next door, into Mrs. Zaimo's house. Lucy suspected a tuna lure, but couldn't ever prove it, and now just satisfied herself with rubbing Mr. Pickles's head whenever she saw him sunning himself outside.

It was just safer to be alone. It hurt so much less.

"I found a bunch of unpublished patterns." Her voice came out too loudly.

Lucy's father said, "Well, that's nice, honey. Hey, Jonas, did you ever . . ."

"They're Eliza Carpenter's."

Toots all but came out of her chair. "Eliza Carpenter? *Our* Eliza Carpenter?"

Lucy picked up her knitted bag that she'd set next to her chair. "Look, patterns that the world has never seen. And some journal entries, too."

Toots's voice was low. "Let me see those." As she reached out to take a page from Lucy, her hand was shaking.

Molly said, "Are you kidding?"

Toots, after a moment, said, "This is her work. This is her handwriting." She looked up at Lucy, her eyes shining. "How amazing, Lucy. Where did you find them?"

"Old boxes I bought from Owen, actually. They were his mother's. And look." She fished clumsily through the papers and gave one to her mother.

"Look at the title of it."

Toots peered at the page and her eyes filled with tears. "Ruby's Book Spire Sweater."

"It's a cardigan. It's *my* cardigan. The yellow one of hers I wear all the time, the one that's shredded into tatters. She wrote this one for Grandma, who was always chilly at the store. . . . Look at the scalloped edges. Now I can re-knit it, if I find the other page, the page with the sleeves." Lucy's voice was passionate.

Toots sighed and touched her lips with two fingers. "She wrote it for Mom." She turned the paper over. "But where's the rest of the pattern?"

"I haven't gone through everything yet. I hope I find it. But no matter what, there are enough patterns for a whole book. I'll take it to Abigail and she can edit a whole new Eliza Carpenter book."

"People would *kill* for that," said Molly, her voice cracking with excitement.

Toots inclined her head. "They would, yes. Sure. But Abigail has two of her own pattern books coming out this year, and what with Lizzie and the new baby coming . . . And now she's recovering from the accident . . . She's swamped. And Cade, well, he's not much for writing. Maybe they'll let you do it!"

Lucy laughed and felt the wine swim to her head. "Me? No."

Toots said, "Why not?"

"Because I'm not a writer, Mom."

"But it would be editing, not writing. And besides, you're the writer in the family. It's what you always wanted to do, isn't it? And your name, on a book of Eliza Carpenter's work. You and Eliza. Like a collaboration?" Toots's voice was so warm, so proud. Lucy hadn't heard that tone directed at her, not in years, not since she won the lead in the school play when she was nine and played the Thanksgiving turkey.

Lucy let herself bask in the warmth of her mother's smile for a moment and then exhaled. There was no way she could do it.

She sold books. She didn't write or even edit them.

The standoff between herself and Owen, which was probably imagined on her part, she knew that, had gone on long enough. Almost a week since the lightning. And he'd said for her to come by anytime and they'd go to the storage unit . . .

Tomorrow, then.

She'd talk to Owen tomorrow and see if he had any more papers, then she'd get him to take the boxes to Abigail, and that would be that. They weren't theirs. They had to give them back. It broke her heart.

Toots held up her hand and said, "In light of that wonderful news, I have some of my own. I have an announcement. Daddy already knows, but you should all know that I've started a new venture. I'm opening another chapter in my life."

Lucy exchanged worried glances with her brothers.

"Going into business sticking people with tiny needles in my bar?" Jonas guessed.

"Don't be silly. That's just for fun, not for profit. No, I'm going into pleasure parties."

Oh, no. Lucy felt herself pale. Jonas, apparently, didn't see Silas frantically drawing his finger across his neck, and asked the fateful question of doom. "What's a pleasure party?"

"It's a sex-toy party, darling."

Jonas blanched. Lucy put her head down on the table and rocked it back and forth.

Bart nodded proudly. "She's designated me the research and development department."

There was a long, awful pause. Jonas and Molly stared at their plates. Silas whispered something inaudible.

Then Toots said, "Does anyone want to see my new vibrators?"

# TWELVE

> Sometimes a knitter will need rescuing, and we must be ready to come to her aid, just as we would want her to do for us, were we in her handknit socks.
>
> — E. C.

Owen wasn't sure if there was anything worse than dealing with your mother's accumulated shit, piled into a ten foot by ten foot space, seven feet high, with only the narrowest walkway through it. It felt like something out of *Hoarders,* only he didn't have the promise of a job well done at the end of it glimmering like a beacon.

Standing in the middle of the storage unit, he stood up slowly from where he'd been bending over boxes of old photographs and rubbed his hip. These were the tricky things. What the hell did he do with them? Enough photos to choke a hippo, but he had no idea whose they were — had they been of his father's family? His mother's? He could take a few to his mom and hope for some kind of response, but he wasn't sure if he'd trust anything she said anyway. Photos were only memories as long as they were attached to a memory that could be trusted.

What he really wanted to do was throw all of it out. But family photos? Wasn't there some kind of son law prohibiting that? He moved it to the side.

Just like he'd been doing all day.

Damn, his body hurt.

Was this all he had left? In the whole world? This is what he had left to look forward to? Going through a crazy woman's belongings? She sure had more than he did. . . . Owen bet Lucy's house didn't look like this. Someone who owned a bookstore, a person as careful as she was, probably organized the spices alphabetically and her clothes by color. Of course, she had bolted out into the storm to watch the lightning, even though he'd seen that it had scared the shit out of her.

So that meant she was probably sensible, with a dose of the unpredictable. You throw in a good amount of gorgeous, in that understated way she was, as if she didn't even know it, and Owen knew that came pretty close to kryptonite.

He opened another box next to the stack of photos, and found thirty cans of alphabet soup. Good. At least this was something he could chuck out. He might regret it when the Apocalypse came, but until then, he'd have five cubic feet more space in here.

As he tossed it in the storage yard's Dumpster, Owen thought he caught a glimpse of someone outside the fence, a girl, a block away. She reminded him of Lucy. That curve of the hip, that loose brown hair, that careful way of walking, as if not wanting to disturb anyone . . . Dammit. He *had* to get his mind off of her. Lucy wasn't good for him. Obviously. This morning when he'd been shaving, he'd noticed bruised-looking places under his eyes from not sleeping, and he hadn't had those since the shooting, since the investigation.

At night, when he closed his eyes, he saw Lucy. And it pissed him off. The way he'd practically chased her out of the parsonage the other night . . . He didn't deserve to see her again, to think about her. It would just cement in her mind what everyone in town already thought about him, and Owen just didn't have the time or the heart to watch that happen to her.

Back inside the storage unit, he kicked a recalcitrant door on an old sideboard to get it to open. It didn't help, but it made him feel better.

"This is insane," said a voice from behind him.

Owen flinched, stilled his reflexes, didn't reach for his gun.

"Yeah," he said, turning around.

"Hi," said Lucy. She held up one hand in greeting and rocked backward on her heels, her toes lifting. "How are you?"

"Been better." He hated his rough tone, but he'd been alone for days, and this was a horrible job. And here she was, showing up, fresh as a flower with that open face of hers, and he was astonished to realize he wanted to rush her like a linebacker — in less than the space of a second, he could cross the few steps between them and take her by the upper arms, pulling her against him, crushing her mouth with his, pressing his body against his own, showing her exactly how badly he wanted her.

To hide his eyes and his thoughts that had no place around her, Owen turned and stared at the countertop of the sideboard he'd been wrestling with. He pulled on a drawer. It, too, was stuck.

"This is even worse than I imagined," Lucy said.

"Yep," said Owen. She was more right

than she knew. He cleared his throat.

"How do you know where to start?"

Owen jerked his thumb in the direction of the piles of crap behind him. "I come here every day and I push things around until I can't stand it. When I get to the point where I'm considering arson, I leave."

"You mind if I help you? And look for more of those papers?" she asked.

"Your tetanus shot current?"

Lucy nodded.

"Good luck."

And then, very simply, she helped.

Stepping in next to him, Lucy moved boxes with him. She carried light pieces of trash to the Dumpster, and moved heavier things than he thought she'd ever be able to move, just by using her legs and pushing. She made short work of a file cabinet that Owen had opened more than once and closed again in despair. He watched in amazement as she pulled everything out, rifled through the pages, decided what to keep or recycle. When she passed him a stack of paper an inch thick and took out a Hefty bag for paper recycling, he was overcome again with the urge to kiss her.

Who *wouldn't* want to kiss this woman?

"How did you do that?" he asked, when she entered the storage unit again, bringing with her the scent of sun and flowers.

"What?" she asked, as she pulled down another box. "Oooh! Yarn!"

"How do you just dive in and get this done?"

"Not my stuff. It's easier." Lucy held up the ugliest-color yarn he'd ever seen, bruised yellow and acid green. She made a face. "I thought your mother was a *knitter.* This is acrylic. I'm horrified. This whole box has to go. At least there are no moths. Guaranteed."

"I don't know what to tell you."

Still moving, still emptying boxes at the speed of light compared to the way Owen moved through them, Lucy kept talking. "So Eliza Carpenter, the woman who wrote these papers I'm looking for, the ones we need to give back to Cade and Abigail, she was my friend as a child. She was the one who really taught me to knit, and more than that, she told the best stories in the whole wide world. Instead of laughing at a little kid, or ignoring me, she listened. She always had time for me."

Owen, in the same amount of time, had done half what Lucy had. He shuffled a box of old, chipped mugs. How could he just throw these out? His mother had loved this one with the cow on it. "So that's why you want these patterns."

"Yep. But what I still don't know is why your mom had them in her storage unit. Why wouldn't Cade have them? When Eliza died, she'd left Abigail's cottage full of things that Abigail would need to run the yarn shop, and she had everything else with her in San Diego. Were Eliza and your mother that close?"

Running his finger along the sharp edge of ceramic mug, Owen thought. "She was the one with the long hair and those eyes . . ."

Lucy grinned. "They sparkled when she laughed. You couldn't forget her."

Funny, Owen actually remembered that sparkling. As a kid, he'd been drawn to that woman who knitted in the kitchen with his mother. It was one of the few times his mother would relax and really laugh. Once, when the woman who must have been Eliza was visiting, Owen had passed through the kitchen, and his mother had put her knitting on the table and reached out, pulling him to her, giving him a spontaneous hug as the other woman looked on, smiling.

He remembered that hug. They were few and far between.

Then Eliza had left for the day and his father had come home. The screaming had started again, and everything had gone back to ugly. Busted.

Normal.

Hell, it's probably how most of these mugs got broken. Owen took the box outside and threw the whole thing into the Dumpster, listening as the ceramic shattered inside.

Three hours later, they'd settled into a rhythm. Owen wouldn't call it comfortable — how could anything be comfortable when he was so close to a woman who set his nerve endings on fire like she did? — but it felt good, this shifting of bodies in such a small space. She was good at it, so damn fast, and when he was stuck, she saw it and made the decisions for him. "No, not that, yes, keep that, no, are you crazy? Throw that out."

When she laughed, he did, too. She was infectious. It felt as if she was getting into his bloodstream.

And then, in the early afternoon, he looked around and suddenly realized that he could see around the whole space. They'd done most of the work. He'd been dicking around by himself for a week and getting almost nothing done, and she'd been here for mere hours, and they were almost finished.

Owen looked at her. She had smudges of dirt across her nose and cobwebs in her hair. "You're amazing," he said. The words were out before he thought.

Then Lucy looked into a box and made a small squeak, which turned into a full-blown scream as something small and fast moving jumped out of the packaging and ran across the storage-unit floor. Her scream grew in volume and intensity as she stood, putting her hands to her mouth.

"No, no, it's only a mouse, Lucy, it's okay," Owen yelled, moving as quickly as he could toward her. He wrapped his arms around her, and her body was rigid against his. Her screams tapered off, but she still shook.

"It's okay, you're all right." All this for a mouse?

Then something like a choked laugh broke through and she finally said, "I'm sorry, it's a phobia. It doesn't make any sense. Right up there with heights. I hate rats and heights. And probably tall rats. Rats on ladders." She gasped. "Oh, hell."

"It was a mouse, I think."

She shuddered. "Only slightly less loathsome. *Stupid.* Hate being scared."

Owen drew her closer and used his thumb to stroke the side of her face. "You're doing good, heart."

He didn't know where that last damn word had come from. He wanted to take it back, to swallow it and hide it, put it away forever. And he wanted to hang it on a golden chain around her neck.

"Oh!" She didn't even seem to have heard him, thank God. She was peering down into a box at their feet, where the mouse had come from.

"What?" Owen asked.

"More! More papers. Eliza's papers." There was wonder in her voice.

God, if she ever spoke to him like that, with that tone — what he wouldn't do . . .

Owen had to get a damn hold of himself. This storage space was just too small, that was all.

She knelt. "This was the last box I had to open. And here they are." Lucy looked up at him and smiled. Stars danced in her eyes.

He wouldn't kiss her.

No.

He would *not* kiss her.

"Thank you," Lucy said, reaching up to brush his hand with hers. "Thank you so much. Do you want to come . . ."

And for just a moment, Owen stopped breathing as she looked up at him. He could feel her thinking about it, too, watched her eyes move to his lips and then back to his eyes. Her cheeks colored.

She went on, her words hurried, "I mean, what I meant to say, is do you want to drive over to Cade and Abigail's with me? To tell them about all this? I haven't yet. I've been waiting until Abigail was out of the hospital. And now she's home . . ."

"I'd love to." Owen grinned.

"You would?"

"Yep." He wanted to go anywhere she was going. Owen didn't care. He just wanted to be near her for a while longer. She could end up being more dangerous than any gun he'd ever held, but God help him, he'd always liked risk.

# Thirteen

Humble pie is a dish not unfamiliar to the new knitter. Sadly, it isn't that unfamiliar to the veteran knitter, either. Miscrossed cables and dropped stitches lurk, waiting for a moment of vanity to showcase themselves in their full and obvious glory.

— E. C.

An hour later, Lucy led Owen up the dirt driveway to Eliza's, the yarn shop Abigail had named for her mentor and her husband's great-aunt. She looked in her rearview mirror, still almost unable to believe that the same blue Mustang that could set her heart to racing as a teenager was rumbling behind her, hitting the same potholes that her trusty little compact car was barreling through.

Lucy's heart sank when she saw the small parking lot — it was full of cars, and heaven help them, there was a tour bus parked next to the alpaca shed.

This was going to be trickier than she'd thought.

She pulled into a spot next to a small red car with a license plate that read K2TOG, and Owen barely fit into the last available space.

Normally, she enjoyed the view. Cade ran sheep on the property he'd inherited from Eliza Carpenter, and they dotted the low green hills around them. Under an oak tree, a couple of pygora goats, raised for fiber, grazed. A footpath was well worn into the grass between the main house and the smaller, matching cottage, which housed Abigail's yarn shop. Lucy had spent many a happy hour fondling the yarns, taking classes, just hanging out with other knitters. It had been too long since she'd been out here.

Owen matched her stride as they walked toward the shop. "All these cars, are they employees of the sheep ranch?"

Lucy said, "Nope."

"This is all for the yarn."

"You're starting to get it now."

"Damn."

"Yep." Lucy pushed open the screen door of Eliza's.

Inside, it looked as it always did: like

paradise. High bookshelves ran along the walls, filled with every colorway of yarn imaginable. Blues and reds and yellows, the softests merinos next to coarser handspun local yarn made from Jacob sheep, showing off their natural black-and-white coloring. Yarn was heaped on dark wood tables scattered throughout the large room, every shade imaginable, silk and angora, alpaca and bamboo. Baskets sat on the floor, filled with sale skeins, castoffs that knitters hungrily pawed through.

And everywhere there were women. Women chatting, moving, reaching, laughing, hugging, sitting, and knitting. Women on chairs, couches, and a few on the floor. Lucy knew a few of them by name, some by sight, but most of them she didn't know at all. There had to be at least forty women in the room, as well as four or five men who were just as comfortable with the language of yarn as the women were.

Owen, on the other hand, looked as if he'd put his shoes on the wrong feet. Lucy wanted to laugh but then decided it would be unkind, so she touched his elbow. He jumped.

"It's okay. None of them will hurt you. Not unless you stand in front of the cashmere, anyway."

He turned his head to look behind him, even though it was obvious he didn't know what he was looking to avoid. Lucy left her hand on his elbow for longer than was necessary. She liked the way his arm felt.

She liked it too much. She drew her hand back.

Mildred popped out from behind a spinner rack of patterns. "Hello, you two crazy kids! Will you settle a bet between Greta and me?" Greta followed behind her, quieter, as usual.

Owen smiled. "Hi, Greta," he said.

Greta looked pleased to be noticed.

Mildred steamed ahead, still working on the sleeve dangling from her needles. "Did you, or did you not, date in high school? Greta says you didn't, I say you most certainly did. And I'm always right about these kinds of things. So she's going to owe me a milk shake at Tad's Ice Cream."

Lucy felt her face flush as red as the display Koigu shawl hanging over Owen's head. Should she answer this? Or look to him to do so?

"We didn't . . ." Lucy started.

"I kissed her once," said Owen. "Best kiss of my young life. Never forgot it. I should have dated her. But I didn't. So I think both of you are wrong. No one gets the milk shake, except maybe for Lucy, if she lets me buy her one."

Both women looked pleased by his answer, and Lucy pretended interest in a row counter that she already had a million of at home.

A small, round woman wearing orange wool from head to toe tugged on Lucy's sleeve. "Do you know this store?"

Lucy nodded, relieved. "What are you looking for?"

"I can't find the Cascade 220. Everything here is so expensive, and I just want to make my husband a dang hat. Is that so hard?"

"Well, I can understand that; some of Abigail's stuff is very nice . . . if you just look over here," Lucy started to lead the woman toward a corner piled with neat skeins in a dark wooden bookcase.

"Nice is one thing," the woman snapped. "Extortion is another."

Lucy slowed and looked over her shoulder at the woman. Was she intending to sound that surly? It wasn't a tone usually heard in Abigail's shop. Maybe it was accidental.

"Well, I'm sure you'll find what you're looking —"

"I'm sure I won't. I don't even know why I came on this tour. I never thought Eliza Carpenter was that special, and now I'm certain of it." The woman's voice got louder. Hisses of indrawn breath could be heard around the room as the other shoppers stopped talking. "This tourist trap is probably full of moths. I bet that Abigail they talk about never even really knew Eliza like she said she did. Just married her nephew and turned this old crap cottage into a place to fleece us." The woman barked an ugly laugh. "Get it?"

From her spot behind the register, two red spots flamed on Abigail's cheeks.

Lucy, still standing near the woman, desperately wished for something to say. Anything. *Come on.* But all words had deserted her. Just embarrassed anger that had nowhere to go.

One small woman who had been bending over a basket stood up. "Beatrice, now stop it. You know you always overreact when —"

The woman in orange continued. "I'm outta here. I'll be in the bus, waiting for our ride back to the hotel. At least there I have real wool to spin, not like this junk that's got more VM than my vegetable garden."

"Hey!" Lucy managed to squeak, but it was all she got out. Her heart was pounding too hard, and her hands were clammy. She had to defend Abigail. To say something to stand up for Eliza. But nothing came to her, the words were stuck in her throat. *Dammit.*

In her ear, Owen said, "What kind of bitch was that?"

Lucy shook her head, still mute. She led him to the back of the room.

At the wooden counter, Abigail clapped her hands when she saw Lucy, the color still high in her cheeks, warring with her bruises. "Oh, hooray! You're here! I'm so glad! And that witch is out in the bus, so all's right with the world." She came around the register, her belly slowing her progress. After she'd hugged Lucy, she embraced Owen. He looked startled, as if he hadn't seen the hug coming.

"What about that . . . ?"

"Who cares about her? I get at least one like her a week. Most knitters are nice, but there's a bad apple in every bunch. Not worth our time. Now I've got to take a break, and you're the perfect excuse. Sara!" she called to a small, pretty woman with glasses who was helping a customer figure out how to Kitchener an underarm. "I'm going up to the house for a few, do you have it?"

Sara waved. "Got it. No worries."

Expertly, Abigail wove her way through the crowd, nodding and thanking the customers that complimented her on her selection, murmuring the right things when they gasped their love of Eliza, leading Lucy and Owen out the front door and down the path to the main house.

As they followed her, Lucy wished she'd said something to that woman. Something snarky. Something smart, clever, quick. But even now, she still had no rejoinder. Gah.

In the hallway of the house, Clara the border collie padded out and lifted her head for petting. The kitchen was lit by sunlight. Lucy looked closely at her friend for damage. The side of Abigail's face was bruised and mottled, and she still had a bandage on one arm, but other than that she looked fine. Recovered.

Abigail sank into the kitchen rocker with a huge sigh, her arms cradling her belly. "Oh, Lord. They're wonderful. Did you see them? They have a tour bus! They're from Michigan! They drove all the way to California to see Eliza's ranch. Just to do this. To buy wool from her sheep. I still can't believe it. I *never* believe this stuff. They're amazing." She laughed, and Lucy laughed with her.

Abigail could have died, but she hadn't. Lucy's heart soared.

"How are you feeling?"

Abigail smiled. "I'm fine. Thanks to you

two. Don't think that we're going to let you forget it." She looked down at the swell under her hand and then back up at Lucy, blinking away tears. "I didn't want you to come see me in the hospital because I didn't want to cry there, but . . . thank you."

Lucy, overwhelmed by the tone of Abigail's voice, didn't know where to look. "We were just in the right place at the right time. And you're welcome. You would have done the same thing."

"But it was you. And I'm here . . . and . . ."

Lucy leaned over and kissed Abigail's cheek. Abigail grabbed Lucy's hand and clutched it tightly. For one long moment their eyes met. Lucy felt the gratitude and accepted it.

Then Lucy gently took her hand back. She said, "Is your hunky husband around? We need to talk to him, too."

Abigail appeared relieved. "You're lucky you just caught him. He's got Lizzie upstairs, and then they're going to town, to Tillie's. Good timing. He'll have heard us come in and be down in a second."

Sure enough, boots clomped down the stairs. Cade, dressed in a rugged brown sweater and Wranglers, held his small daughter in one arm. The other arm carried a very pink backpack.

"Hello, Mama," he said, and dropped a kiss on Abigail's head.

Lucy melted a little.

Abigail looked sheepish but grinned.

Cade nodded at her. "Look what the cat drug in. Hey, Lucy."

Lucy had known Cade since she was small. They'd run through the hills together while her mother knitted with Eliza in this very kitchen. Cade hadn't settled down until Abigail had come to town. Then they'd fallen in love — the danger of proximity, he called it — and the rest was history.

Cade handed a still-sleepy Lizzie to Abigail and then, before Lucy could take a breath, he enveloped her in a hug as tight as she'd ever been in before. For several long seconds, she was pressed against the wool of Cade's sweater. Then he let her go and took Owen's hand, pumping it up and down, seven, eight times. Owen's had to use his other hand to steady himself on the kitchen counter.

"You two saved my wife's life. If she'd been driving her truck, she probably would have been dead —"

"Or fine, because I would have been going faster, so I wouldn't have been there," said Abigail, in an argument that had obviously been ongoing.

"But instead, she was in that little family car I made us get, and you were there to pull her out, and I owe you one."

Lucy shook her head. She hadn't expected any of this. She'd come to bring them a ghost of the past, not to be hailed as a hero. "You don't owe us anything."

Cade moved behind Abigail, taking a bite of muffin that was left on a plate next to the sink.

"Lucy needed to ask you something, cowboy. Don't go running off just yet."

"Oh." Lucy watched Cade put on the brakes. "All right, Lucy. Shoot."

Abigail shushed Lizzie, who was beginning to fuss.

"I found something." Lucy rummaged in her bookbag. "A bunch of somethings, actually. Knitting patterns. At the store, in an old box."

Cade and Abigail looked at her blankly.

"They're Eliza's."

Abigail, visibly startled, reached for the stack. "Eliza's? Are you sure?"

"Damn sure."

"Unpublished patterns. Oh, my God," said Abigail. Cade just stared.

Lucy took a deep breath. "They were in Owen's mother's storage unit. We just finished going through it. There are a total of four boxes."

"But . . ." started Cade.

Lucy held up a hand. "I know. Legally, I know the rights are yours, as her heir. And you already have one knitting writer in the family. Abigail, I know you'll want to edit the patterns."

Abigail pulled out a piece of paper and turned it over, nodding.

Lucy smiled and dropped her eyes. "It would be the book of a lifetime, don't you think? It's what knitters have been waiting for. The unpublished works of Eliza Carpenter. Journal entries, too, that sound as if she's sitting next to you, telling you stories. They're fantastic." Lucy's voice broke — she couldn't help it. Part of her heart was breaking, too.

Abigail looked at Cade. They seemed to have a conversation in front of Lucy, although neither of them said a word. Cade nodded, and so did Abigail.

"So basically, we'd be hiring you to edit the patterns, right?"

Owen's head swiveled to look at Lucy. She dug her nails into her palms.

"No, no. I'm just bringing them to you. I bought them from Owen, but they're not mine, they're yours. He didn't understand what he was selling, and I didn't understand what I was buying. None of it was fair. We're returning all of it to you."

Abigail rubbed her forehead. "Why did your mother have these, Owen?"

"My mom and Eliza were friends. I'm remembering that now, and I'm starting to remember what she was like." Owen shot a look at Lucy that made her heart flutter in her chest. "I remember a time that she gave me a bike — I'd forgotten that until just this morning, and I don't know how I'd blocked that out. No one had ever given me anything like that before, and God knew my parents couldn't afford anything like that. It was secondhand, a beater — I was probably eight or so. Green, with twisted-back handlebars, and it squeaked when it went up hills. But man, I loved that bike." Owen paused. "She did nice things for my family. I'm not sure why."

Cade had been putting milk back into the fridge, but paused, the door standing open. "Green, with an orange racing stripe? Black spokes, and a rip in the green seat?"

Owen's eyes widened and he nodded.

Cade grinned. "She bought me a ten-speed and told me my legs were too long for that one. I'm what, three, four years older than you? So that's where my old bike went."

"Sneaky!" exclaimed Abigail, kissing Lizzie on the head. "Sneakiest knitter I ever knew."

"And once," said Owen, "when my mother sent me a Christmas gift, there was a pair of socks inside. With a card that just said 'E. C.' I never knew what that meant, and I only remember that because I still keep the socks, with the card still attached, in my sock drawer."

Lucy gaped at him. "You have socks hand-knit by Eliza Carpenter and you don't *wear* them?"

"They're bright green."

"So? They're handknit by Eliza! How did you . . . ? Why did she . . . ?" Lucy shook her head. Then she asked what she wanted to ask. "Why you?"

Owen shrugged. "I have no idea."

Cade laughed. "She got funny ideas sometimes. If she met you once or twice as a kid, if she liked you, you could turn into a pet, just like that. Eliza had her favorites, and if you were one, you were just lucky."

Abigail said, "He's right. And Lucy, the weirdest part is something you couldn't possibly know, though, and I don't think I've ever even told Cade. When I first made friends with Eliza in San Diego, I wanted to write her biography and pull together some new patterns, and she said no, that a girl with a bookstore would probably do it one day."

Lucy took a step backward and almost tripped over an uneven edge in the old linoleum. "What?"

Abigail said, "Then, years later, I moved here and met you and thought of it once, tossed it out of my mind, and never thought of it again until now. But I don't understand how the papers got into Irene Bancroft's storage unit. Why wouldn't they have been in my cottage? Or with her in San Dicgo? So she and Irene were friends, sure. But that implies a certain closeness, to leave your journals with someone."

Lucy shook her head as Owen lifted his shoulders.

Cade's eyebrows lifted. "So you think Lucy should write this book, am I right?"

"You're smarter than you look, cowboy," said Abigail, but her smile belied her words and Cade grinned at his wife.

Lucy took another step back. "Oh, no. You're the writer, Abigail. Not me."

"Come on, tell me you didn't think about doing this. Tell me you didn't dream of it. You're the bookstore girl. Books are your life. You told me once you wanted to write, when you were a little girl. And you're a knitter, to the bone. You loved Eliza, and I'm under contract for three books right now, and I don't have time. Cade certainly can't do it, and this would be a way of thanking you for what you did. Right, Cade?"

Cade put his arm around his wife. "It's a done deal. You're hired."

Next to Cade, Abigail nodded. "We'd have to pay you for the work you do."

Lucy held up her hands. This conversation had spiraled out of control. "If I did it, it would be because I loved Eliza and her work and it's important to me. I don't need money."

Abigail laughed. "That's what a writer always says in the beginning, for sure. And you'll use my yarn."

Lucy flushed with excitement. "Oh, it could be part of the draw of the book — patterns by Eliza, and kits with your yarn from her ranch."

Abigail's grin grew wider. "We'll need sample sweaters."

"I can start anytime. She wrote a pattern for Grandma Ruby, a bookstore sweater — this one I'm wearing now. You can see I've worn it into shreds. I want to remake this one first, if I can find the sleeve part of the pattern."

"What color?"

Lucy thought. "Yellow, again."

"Gauge?"

"Four and a half stitches per inch. I think."

"The softest merino, single spun. I have the *best* stuff for you."

"But . . . I don't know how to write a book." Doubt crept in, little tendrils of fear twining around her spine.

"You'll figure it out. Can I see the work as you go along?"

"Of course." Lucy hugged herself and gave a little bounce of joy. She lifted her eyes and Owen Bancroft's blue ones met hers in a gaze that almost felt like a caress, and there, in the sunlit kitchen where Eliza Carpenter used to live, Lucy felt, for a moment, like everything could work.

Then the kitchen door flew open, and a woman yelled, "Lucy, Sara's having a seizure. We need you!"

# Fourteen

Have faith in your knitting skills. You already know what to do.

— E. C.

Lucy flew out of the house at a run, Cade and Abigail following close behind her. Owen was the last to exit the house, feeling at a distinct disadvantage, hobbling over the small rocks and uneven ground.

Damn, Lucy was fast. And even with his daughter in his arms, Cade had crossed the ground quickly — they were both already in the shop. Abigail and Owen moved more slowly — Owen slowed by his disability, Abigail by her belly.

Why did they ask for Lucy? Owen felt like he was missing something obvious, something everyone else already knew. And he didn't like it.

Inside the store, a knot of concerned knitters were huddled near the couches, where

Abigail's employee had fallen. Sara was still twitching, jerking, her eyes closed, her mouth contorted in a grotesque, silent scream, her hands twisting painfully behind her on the ground.

Lucy was already speaking in a voice Owen hardly recognized.

"So the paramedics are already on the way. That's the most important thing. Good job, Martha. Now the only thing to do is just let her have the seizure."

One woman cried softly behind Sara, looking terrified.

"I know it looks scary," said Lucy over the noise of the jerks and guttural exhalations, "but she won't remember this at all. It's really okay."

The woman in orange, Beatrice, the awful one who had left the shop earlier, was back, and muscled in through the group holding a huge wooden knitting needle. "Move out of my way! You're doing it wrong. Here, use this size fifteen, we have to put this between her teeth."

Owen stepped forward. The woman was wrong — that was an old wives' tale, and could do more harm than good, but Lucy got between the woman and Sara first.

"No! Do *not* touch her." Lucy's voice was strong, confident. She didn't look like the same Lucy who couldn't stand up to Beatrice earlier.

"You don't know what you're doing. Get out of my way."

Lucy widened her stance. "You take one more step toward my patient and we're going to have a really big problem. I need you to stay back, ma'am."

"You idiot, she'll choke to death on her own tongue." Beatrice tried to push past Lucy.

But Lucy held her ground, her stance firm. "Her jaws are stronger than you can imagine. She'll snap that needle — she could splinter it and choke on the pieces. Now, if you get out of my damn way, I'll be able to monitor her airway until the paramedics get here, but *back off.*" Lucy said the last part low and strong, and Beatrice gasped in anger.

But she turned and retreated just as Sara started to come out of the seizure. At the same time that Sara's breathing became more regular, a siren whooped up the driveway.

"You should probably turn her onto . . ." Owen started to say, but Lucy had already done it, gently rolled Sara onto her side. Someone offered Sara a sip of water as her eyes started to flutter and Lucy refused on her behalf.

"No liquids. They'll check her at the hospital. For now we're just monitoring her." With one hand she brushed the hair out of Sara's face. "There, you're all right. We're right here. You're just fine."

Lucy was a different person — she practically glowed with purpose and authority — and Owen was transfixed. He watched as she greeted the ambulance personnel by name, joking with them personably, helping them load up Sara.

Once they'd driven away with her, only after the dust had cleared, he said, "Yeah. Wanna fill me in?"

Lucy looked down at her Keds and lifted her toes. "I'm an EMT. On the volunteer fire department for Cypress Hollow."

Owen bit the inside of his cheek, and the gun he still carried under his shirt felt heavy on his useless hip. "You're a first responder."

"Kinda. Only when I'm on call, and mostly I do backfill to the stations. But sometimes I go out with the paramedics, and sometimes I work fires. It's only a few times a month, but . . ." Her face lit up and it was as if the sun had been behind a cloud and had just come out. "I love it."

She wasn't just a citizen.

She was a goddamn *firefighter?* All right, a

volunteer one, but come on, really?

Lucy turned to speak to Abigail, and Owen pushed his way through the knot of women still talking about Sara and made his way to his car. He leaned again, breathing as hard as if he'd been the one doing the lifting of the gurney, which he hadn't been.

He looked up into the clear blue sky. Nearby, a lamb bleated and jumped straight up as if it had been stuck with a pin, and then it raced to join its mother and several other sheep grazing on the bright green grass.

Idyllic. This was the kind of place people dreamed about retiring to. A black truck rumbled down the main road, a low trail of dust following sleepily behind it. A hawk circled high above.

He could just get in his car and drive away. They hadn't come together. He'd followed her here. She had her car. Owen didn't even need to say good-bye. He could get back to town, back to concrete sidewalks, or better yet, he could just keep his foot on the gas and pass his mother, keep driving all the way to San Francisco, wrap the arms of the dirty city around him, put himself into the bowels of the Mission by nightfall. Have a burrito on Eighteenth, a drink on Valencia, and a girl on Columbus by midnight.

Dammit. No he couldn't.

He looked at Lucy again, that yellow sweater wrapped around her perfect curves, those brown eyes smiling in warmth at something an older woman had said. She laughed and hugged the woman.

Lucy wasn't the city. Lucy was this place, Cypress Hollow. Owen had no idea what he was doing. Firefighter, EMT, bookseller, writer — whatever the hell she was, he only knew one thing.

He wasn't going anywhere.

Across the dirt parking lot, Lucy couldn't read Owen's face. He wasn't leaving, that much was clear. Leaned up against his Mustang like that, he looked like the guy he'd been in high school. Was that a smoldering look he was shooting at her? Her stomach flipped before she remembered that just like back then, that was just the way he looked, just the way his dark blue eyes burned. At everyone.

He came forward toward her. Even with the hitch in his gait, she loved the way he moved, his long legs eating the distance, the sun hitting his broad shoulders . . .

Man, she had to get a grip.

He'd obviously been thrown by the fact that she was on the volunteer department. Maybe she could have told him earlier, perhaps she should have thought about the fact that it might have been important for him to know. She opened her mouth to speak, but before she could say a word, Owen slung an arm around her waist and pulled her against him.

Her hips fit against his and her breasts pressed against his chest. His mouth claimed hers in a brief, greedy kiss. There, in the parking lot, in front of at least twenty knitters, the dust still settling from the ambulance's tires, Owen kissed Lucy, hard.

Then he pulled his head back but kept his hips pressed against hers. His arousal was blatant.

Lucy gasped and swayed forward. God help her, she wanted more.

"Will you go out with me tonight?" His voice was low, but Lucy knew it was traveling to their audience.

All she could do was blink.

"Is that a yes?" he asked, and a grin tugged at the corner of his mouth.

She nodded and then shook her head, suddenly confused. "But I don't date."

"Neither do I," he said. "Why don't you?"

"Because . . ." *No one stays.*

"It's just one night."

Lucy said, "Why don't *you* date?"

"No one would have me now," said Owen, and Lucy felt something inside her crack.

"I'll have you, if she won't!" called Mrs. Luby, who was ninety if she was a day. Lucy jumped and turned her head. The knitters, en masse, had left the porch of the yarn shop and had sneaked closer. She felt a blush steal across her cheeks.

But Owen used the moment. "So? Her or you? I guess I have a choice tonight."

Lucy looked at his facc, thc rough stubble coming up along his jaw, a longer patch that he'd missed shaving that morning. She longed to touch it, to run her fingers along that bit. Behind his ear, she could see Cade's flock grazing on the hills, and behind that, the eucalyptus grove.

Then she looked up into Owen's eyes. His arms tightened and pulled her closer. God, he was strong. She loved the way he felt against her.

"Me," she said.

"I'll pick you up at seven," said Owen.

"Dammit," said Mrs. Luby.

# FIFTEEN

Flirt with the yarn. Dance with your designs. Make your knitting want you as much as you want your knitting.

— E. C.

It was official.

Owen had lost his mind. He jammed the car into third as he turned onto Main Street. He took the corner too fast, his Mustang fishtailing exactly like it used to when he was eighteen years old.

What could he have been thinking, kissing Lucy like that?

Owen didn't lose control. One more second, one more taste of her, and he'd have wanted all of her, damn all the consequences, damn what her family thought, damn what town he was in. She'd been right there with him, too. He'd felt it.

But God.

Owen didn't lose control with any woman,

especially not the girl next door who happened to be his high-school tutor, current landlord, and worst of all, *firefighter,* not even if she was white-hot, which Lucy was. Only she didn't seem to know how hot she was, which made her even more appealing, if such a thing were possible.

A date with a firefighter.

God, what a joke. The guys at work would have his head if they knew. Contrary to popular citizen belief, in many cities, cops and firefighters didn't always get along. Cops thought firemen had too many rules and took too long getting water on a fire. Firefighters thought cops were dangerous cowboys.

And she was an EMT, too? Sheesh. He just hadn't seen that one coming.

Minutes after driving up the dirt road and hitting the highway back into town, an even worse reality hit Owen. Lucy Harrison had just been being polite. Probably. Yeah, she was attracted to him, he could feel it in her kiss. She couldn't fake that. That was real.

But she didn't date? Of course she did. She just didn't date guys without jobs. Without a career.

Without direction.

He parked in front of Tillie's and yanked up the parking brake. The diner would be as good a place as any to kill time until he picked up Lucy for their date. He supposed he should figure out where to take her.

On their date. He hadn't taken anyone out since his last girlfriend, Bunny. He'd loved her, in his way. They'd spent many nights together, usually at her place, and he'd even let the discussion turn to kids every once in a while, before he shut it down. But a year into it, he'd found out from a friend that she was seeing an Oakland officer, too, earning her the name "Badge-bunny Bunny." The worst part had been realizing that while he'd been embarrassed, he hadn't been brokenhearted.

Staring through the window of the boarded-up old movie theater, he switched his memory search to Cypress Hollow again, for the thousandth time.

Memories from high school were a jumble — there'd been a lot of late nights and a shitload of parties, nights that he couldn't really and didn't want to remember. Before that final fight, Owen's father had been more than willing to provide booze to Owen and his friends, and the only way Owen had managed to graduate was to hire Lucy as his tutor. He'd never have passed math without her, no way in hell.

And then there'd been that kiss at the

graduation party, the kiss that hadn't been like any other before it, or if he really admitted it to himself, like any other since, not until he'd kissed Lucy again. She'd always done something to him. . . .

Dammit. How was this for justice? He'd come back to Cypress Hollow hoping to figure shit out. Not to get confused all over again. Time to make a list while he waited for it to be time for him to pick her up. Lists helped.

Owen strode into the diner. This place never changed — Old Bill, rag in hand, nodded at him from the register. That was Owen's cue to pick his own booth. They didn't stand on ceremony here — it was the one place the beach tourists had never taken over. The side room was still unofficially reserved in the mornings for the ranchers who drove into town after their chores were done, and God help the random tourist who sat themselves there. Owen had seen the ranchers actually pick up the tourists' plates and move them into the front room. Old Bill would only stare and wipe the counter again with a grin. Tillie's was a self-policing place.

Owen sat at the window, two booths away from Mayor Finley — he'd dated her briefly in high school, and knew that her brother had been drinking heavily, even back then. He nodded at two women in the booth behind him. They looked familiar, but he couldn't place them.

The whole town felt like that. Like he knew it but couldn't place it yet. It was like putting on old pair of jeans that didn't quite fit anymore.

Would it ever fit again?

Shirley nodded at his request for extra cream for his coffee, but didn't smile at him like she did the other customers. Screw it.

"You mind if I borrow a piece of paper?" Owen asked.

Shirley raised her eyebrows but tore off a sheet from her order pad and left it on his table with the creamer.

At the top of the page he wrote *Reasons For Staying.* Under it, he drew a heavy line and then sat thinking. He wanted to write Lucy's name but he wouldn't. That would be stupid. His mother. Of course. Her name went first. Then he wrote the word *Home.*

Owen looked at the word and scratched it out. That was ridiculous. Home. He barely knew what that was. The people in Cypress Hollow who remembered him certainly didn't want him back. Why, then, was he so drawn to this place? Why was he lured back here? Why was this the only place he could think to come when he was injured enough that he'd never work as a cop again?

He drew an *X* through the entire top half of the page and wrote on the lower half *Things To Do.*

*1. Handyman*

He could fix just about anything. It had always been a talent of his. He could get a business license, like he'd told Lucy, and set up a little shop somewhere. Hang a shingle. Fix things for little old ladies and pretty single ones. Wear a tool belt.

But the tool belt would hang sideways, wouldn't it? Off his damn crooked hip, and he'd probably fall off a ladder working some job alone trying to compensate for his aches and pains, and he'd break his neck and not be able to reach his cell phone and die alone in someone's backyard while trying to paint a trellis or something.

*2. Fisherman*

Owen stared across the street at the surf pounding the shore, and at the pier that made a long, straight line into the cold water. Men stood in the wind, their rods leaning against the railing. They stood there for hours, watching, waiting. Didn't look like a bad life.

It did look like a *cold* life, though, and God knew that Owen felt the weather in his joints now like he never had before.

*3.*

All right. He didn't even have a number three. He was shit out of things to write down. He couldn't be the only thing he wanted to be: a cop. Cops had to be in good physical shape, able to run, jump, leap.

And he hadn't passed the testing. That moment, when the doctor had denied his back-to-work clearance . . .

The pier swam in his vision, the ocean blurred by fog. Owen gulped his coffee like it would save his soul.

Molly, Lucy's best friend, entered the diner. She waved at a couple of people, touched Old Bill on the shoulder, and walked to his table.

She was all smiles. "Ooh, I love lists. I'm one of those organized types. I have to be. Can I sit down?"

Owen said, "Sure." And why not? She was one of the few people in town who didn't look at him like he had three heads.

Man, she was his type. Long black hair with a dyed red streak that looked like a racing stripe, and a rack that entered the room three minutes before she did. Gorgeous smile, dangerous laugh, sexy red heels.

And she wasn't doing *anything* for him.

He kept seeing Lucy's wavy brown hair and funny blue-and-green canvas shoes instead.

Focus. Molly was saying something.

"What are you doing that for?"

Owen flipped the paper over. "Nothing. Just trying to figure out what I'm going to do next."

"I love that kind of thing. Lay it on me. Let's brainstorm. Shirley, can I get a cup of coffee, please?"

Molly was hard to resist, Owen could tell. She was one of those girls who could bed a man and fix his life by morning. But not him. Shaking his head, Owen said, "I'm good, but thanks anyway."

"No, you're not, but okay. Just let me know. I'm kind of an expert on getting people back on track."

"What is it you do again?"

"What *don't* I do is the question. I don't bake, I suppose. I leave that to the Whitneys in town. I do anything that keeps me in the house I love here. Couple of real jobs, and then I pick up odd jobs, too."

"How are the odd jobs treating you?"

She shrugged. "Those are the ones that are harder to find."

"Oh," he said. Damn. If he stayed, those would be the ones he wanted. It wasn't like he really needed the money. His retirement and careful investments had left him enough money to live on, and the sale of his mother's house left enough to take care of Willow Rock. But he would need something to *do.*

If he stayed. He couldn't believe he was thinking long tcrm.

Two older women at the counter started arguing about something, one of them holding a green ball of yarn, the other one trying to pull it out of her hands. The discussion ended when Shirley said something sharply to them, but it led Owen to ask Molly, "Are you a knitter? Like the rest of this crazy town?"

Molly dug into her purse and pulled out a tattered ball of pink yarn. "Yep! I'm making socks. Or I was. A while ago. I'm not as good as they are, but I'm always trying. If you stay, you'll have to learn."

Owen's laugh surprised him.

"And you'll have to buy a house," said Molly. "That's where I come in."

"Ahhh. I see." But he didn't mind. "No, I'm fine living in the parsonage."

Molly shook her head, and said, "Oh, no, you're not. You just don't know it yet. Do you want a big house, a little one, a new one, an older one? Do you want a backyard? A condo? A Victorian? What's your price range?"

She had balls, and he liked that. "I guess, if I had to say, I like those older big houses, like on Encinal. They look comfortable. Maybe a fireplace would be nice."

Lucy in front of a fireplace, yarn cascading around her. Kissing her in front of the flames so that she lost count of her stitches.

*Pull it together.*

Molly gave him an inquisitive glance. Had he gone red? But she only said, "Okay. That's a starting place. So you like a multistoried Craftsman, huh? That's kind of rare here, but it's out there."

She made a note in a small notebook. "You were a cop, right? I used to date a cop."

"I'm sorry."

"Are they all like that?"

"Almost all of them. When it comes to women."

"That's a bad way to be."

"I'm reformed. Don't hold it against me."

She gave a smile that read both professional and sexy. "Price range? What are we talking?"

"I'd have to be able to afford the mortgage on my pension." He named a price that made Molly nod.

"Even around here, we can do that."

A male voice boomed behind his head.

"What's going on here?" Owen instinctively stood and turned to face the man, his hip and knee screaming in protest at the sudden move. His right hand twitched to his side automatically.

Jonas laughed. "I'm just kidding. What are you two kids up to?"

Owen pretended to be stretching, rubbing a muscle in his back. He hoped liked hell he'd played it off, and that Jonas didn't know that for one short second, Owen had touched the butt of the gun he still carried concealed.

He'd been startled. That was all.

Molly waggled her fingers at Jonas in a shooing motion. "Get out of here. I'm working."

"Teaching him Chinese?" Jonas seemed more relaxed this morning, almost human, and Owen was grateful for it — he didn't want to be eternally on guard around Lucy's brothers.

"No, selling him a house, dumbass. Now, go away."

Instead, Jonas pulled up a chair from the four-top behind him and straddled it, backward, scooting up to the edge of their table.

"Whatever." Molly tossed her hair and made another note on her pad. "All I know is this: I'm going to find Owen a house he can't live without, and I'll have him into it in a matter of weeks."

Owen felt too much caffeine sloshing in his veins. "Hey. I'm not committed to staying yet, anyway."

Molly shook her head. "Not with me as your new agent. We'll get you into something fast. I can bang any escrow through quicker than anyone else."

Jonas leered, looking younger than he had tending his bar. "Ha. You said 'bang.' "

"Ew. Shut up, Jonas."

"Make me."

Molly said, "Seriously, why are you so annoying? You're not helping anything." But her cheeks betrayed her: they colored, and she was smiling weirdly.

Lucy's best friend and Lucy's brother? Huh.

Jonas said to Owen, "Watch this one. She's a little *too* busy, if you know what I mean."

Molly made a whining sound and hit Jonas lightly on the arm.

They were flirting. Owen didn't know why he felt surprised. He didn't know them, after all. Did Lucy know about it? Somehow he thought she didn't.

"Just because I have a bunch of jobs, just

because I'm trying to get ahead in this poky little town, that isn't a bad thing."

"I wasn't talking about your *jobs,* but now that you mention it, sure: Chinese translator." Jonas held up one finger. "Realtor." Then he put up another. "Dog walker. Are you still selling makeup?"

Frowning, Molly said, "I've got a garage full, if you're interested."

"I'm good, thanks. The only thing you don't do in town is tend bar."

Owen just sat and watched. It's not like he could do or say anything that would drag their attention away from each other.

Molly tossed her head. "I'd be a kick-ass bartender."

"No way. You wouldn't be able to handle it."

"You kidding me? I mixed every drink my parents ever had. I know how to make everything. I can make a green-apple martini with my left hand while shaking a screaming orgasm with my right."

"Nah, I'm not buying it. Show me. Tonight. It's been way too busy for me lately, but I don't feel like interviewing anyone."

"You're on. I'm gonna kick your drink-mixing ass."

"Fine."

*"Fine."*

Owen cleared his throat.

They didn't notice.

It was Shirley who broke their eye-flirt showdown. "Jonas, you want something else, or are you gonna get out of my way?"

Jonas scrambled back in the chair and stood. "Sorry, Shirl. No, I'm good."

Shirley held up the pot. "You kids want a refill? Any food?"

Owen seized the moment. "No, we're about to get out of here. Thanks, though."

"Yeah, okay," said Jonas. "See you tonight, Molly. Bring your best game."

Molly just gazed at him as he left.

Owen said, "She know you two feel that way? Lucy?"

"What way?" Molly's finger went up to fuss with her hair.

"Come on."

"He's like a brother to me. It would be way too weird."

"And illegal if true."

"I don't know. I guess it's obvious." Molly sighed and touched her hair again. "This weirdness is new."

"Looks like it's mutual."

She leaned forward eagerly. "You think? Do you really think?" Then she leaned back and took a deep breath. "I mean, I date a lot. He knows that. We've always been friends. We talk about . . . stuff. You know? Everybody needs a Jonas. A pal. No, he doesn't look at me that way. I know he doesn't."

Owen picked up his spoon and put it back down. "So you really think I could afford something in town?"

"Why would you say it's mutual?"

*This* was why he didn't talk about these kinds of things with women, especially not women he barely knew. "I don't know. It just looked like he enjoyed talking to you."

Molly nodded. "Yeah. That's all it is. He enjoys my company. He's not attracted to me. Not like that. I'm sorry. I'm being ridiculous. Isn't it stupid?"

"What?"

"You know, when you're attracted to someone who could never, ever work out?"

Owen pulled his debit card out of his wallet and avoided her eyes. "Yep."

# SIXTEEN

Knitting is a quiet art.

— E. C.

Lucy, by six o'clock, had done just about everything she could think of to calm herself down. She'd dug through the boxes in the coat closet and found her old journal and sat with it on the front porch, pen in hand, waiting for inspiration. She'd scribbled a few words before feeling stumped and frustrated. She used to love writing — she'd wanted to *be* a writer, as a kid, all the way through high school, before she'd decided to sell books instead. But she hadn't thought about writing in years. And now she was going to edit a whole book? Nerves danced in her belly again at the thought.

She'd gone for a walk around the block, but had turned her ankle twice because she'd forgotten to watch where she was going. She'd taken a bath with a lavender bomb that had cost a ridiculous amount of money when she'd been out shopping with Molly, but the scent had put her into a sneezing fit.

Wrapped in an old yellow flannel robe, she wandered from room to room, picking objects up and putting them down again. She knocked over a vase that held knitting needles in the living room, sending them flying with a clatter that brought her back to herself.

Holy crap.

Owen. A date.

It came down to two things.

First thing: She had nothing to wear. Absolutely nothing. She had overalls. Jeans. Sweaters. A green dress that she'd worn to Abigail's wedding, but it was gauzy and way too sheer for a cold spring night. Owen was probably used to girls who wore high black boots and black tops that fell casually, perfectly, off the shoulder at just the right moment. Girls who knew how to walk in heels. Lucy wasn't that girl.

Second thing: Lucy couldn't stop thinking about that kiss. The way he'd just walked over to her. Grabbed her. *Kissed* her like that. In front of everyone. It should have embarrassed the hell out of her, or pissed her off, being manhandled like that, instead of making her melt, instead of heating her up inside in a way that she still hadn't recovered from.

Trudging upstairs yet again, Lucy made her way back to her closet. She opened it for the fourth time, hoping that somehow, since her bath, a miracle might have occurred, that a fairy godmother had sneaked in and filled her closet with pretty things.

No such luck.

Lucy's cell phone rang.

"Am I bothering you?" Whitney's chipper voice was too loud, and Lucy had to turn the volume down.

She sat on the floor in front of the hopeless closet. "No."

"I just wanted to talk to you about the possibility of that celebration for Abigail, honoring you and Owen, with a —"

"No, thanks."

"Just like that?" Whitney laughed lightly. "What about if you and I got together and put on a —"

Lucy interrupted her again. Whitney knew what men liked. "If you had a date, and you had my closet, what would you do?"

Whitney said, "Oh, no."

"That bad?"

"I'd go shopping."

"No time."

"What time is the date?"

Lucy leaned backward so she could see the clock next to her bed. "Forty-seven minutes from now."

"Black skirt?"

"No."

"Oh, dear. Black pants?"

"Only some corduroys."

Whitney sighed into the phone. "How wide are the wales?"

"What?"

"Never mind. Wear those. Now, white tank top?"

Lucy shook her head. "It's spring."

"It's called layering, Lucy. Do you have one or do I have to come over there?"

This was bad enough. "I have one."

"Good. That, and that blue sweater you knitted last year, the one with the lace edges. And a black belt. You do have one of those?"

"Of course." Lucy thought she did. Somewhere.

"And black ballet flats or pumps or heels or boots or something, anything other than those Keds of yours, can you do that for me?"

Lucy remained quiet.

"Do you *have* other shoes?"

"Yes."

"Will you wear them?"

"Oh, all right." Lucy decided it was just easier to give in than argue. And if she wanted to wear the Keds, she could. But Whitney was probably right.

"Now," said Whitney. "The date. It's with Owen?"

God, she hated to admit it to her. How did she end up having this conversation with Whitney, of all people? "Yeah."

"Awesome. He's always been so hot. Oh, boy, I remember him in high school . . ."

No, no, *no!* Lucy didn't want to walk down memory lane with Whitney and what she remembered about Owen.

But Whitney only giggled. "Just don't sleep with him on the first date, you wouldn't want him to get the wrong impression of you. No one else seems to stick around, do they? Maybe you can keep him hanging around if you play your cards right, and deal 'em out slow, huh? Okay, hon, I gotta run. Put on some blusher, too, you looked a little pale the last time I saw you. And think some more about that party for Abigail. I'm convinced it's a good idea. We'll talk later."

Lucy sat, staring into the closet, but she didn't see the clothes hanging in front of her.

*Deal 'em out slow.*

She always dealt them out slowly. One card at a time, one base at a time, just like a good girl should.

Maybe that was her whole problem.

She pulled out the black strappy heels that she'd bought with Molly that she'd never worn and held them up. They were sexy. Even kind of comfortable.

Why not?

Lucy changed and put on makeup, trying to remember Molly's tips. She looked at herself in the mirror and decided she looked nothing like herself. She looked . . . good. The white tank dipped low, and the blue sweater draped open. The heels made her taller, longer. Her eyes looked smoky with the MAC eyeliner that had cost more than her first used car.

She shook her head and stuck out her tongue. There. That was more like it.

The doorbell rang. Lucy jumped.

Owen leaned against the porch railing, a half smile on his lips. "You wanna shoot something?"

# Seventeen

Surprise yourself. Use a paper clip instead of a stitch holder. Knit with twine, or grass, or dandelion stalks. Dance while you knit. Sing.

— E. C.

In Lucy's mind, the gun range was going to be a sexy place to be. It would be a dark, narrow chamber, much like the barrel of a gun, slim and dangerous. Scary-looking trench-coated men and women in stilettos wearing European glasses would slink by her on their way out, casting shifty glances to planes flying low overhead.

Instead, the range was a squat concrete building that looked like it had been dropped in the parking lot temporarily and no one had remembered to come back for it yet. It was smack-dab between the Costco and the dump, and Lucy couldn't believe she'd never noticed the crooked wooden sign that said, rather grandly, CYPRESS HOLLOW GUN CLUB.

Inside, a balding man wearing grubby camo sat reading *Guns and Ammo,* looking bored. Maybe he'd cheer up when he saw a girl. Lucy gave him a bright smile.

He didn't even look at her, just slid a clipboard to Owen and said, "Sign in. Both got eyes and ears?" Owen nodded. "Twelve each. Ammo? Targets?"

"Nope."

"Pistol?"

"Yep."

"Lane eight."

The sound of wild and careless gunfire ricocheting around inside the room they were headed for didn't seem safe, not in the slightest.

Lucy was terrified.

Just out of sight of the clerk, as Owen started to pull open the heavy side door, Lucy clutched Owen's sleeve and pulled out one of the earplugs he'd motioned her to put in. "Hey."

He removed one of his earplugs, too. "You okay?"

"What if . . ." Oh, she should just say it. "What if I shoot and kill someone? Or someone accidentally kills me?"

"In the range? That really doesn't happen

that often."

"That *often?*"

"I'm kidding."

Lucy scowled. "If you think that's funny, then . . . You don't want to be the first casualty, is all I'm saying."

In a low voice close to her ear, in a tone that gave her shivers, Owen said, "You're going to be great at this. And it's fun. It's like this." Putting one hand at the small of her back, Owen put his lips against hers. Parted, his lips whispered against hers, a kiss and a promise. "You can do this."

Lucy wanted more. More of what his lips said to hers. She kissed him, hard, shocking herself, and she felt him react. The same electricity that jolted her must have shocked him, too, because the hand at her back tugged her in even closer, and she felt how ready he was, hard against her. His mouth became hotter, heavier, and his tongue demanded something she was almost ready to give him right there, against the ugly concrete wall. Owen scrambled Lucy's brain cells, and God, she wanted more.

But then Owen stood upright and put his earplug back in, looking straight at her. His eyes didn't so much dare her to do the same as much as expect that she'd be able to.

Sure.

Lucy took a deep breath and put her shoulders back, willing her heart to slow down and her jelly-filled legs to hold her up. "Right."

She reinserted her earplug and pulled open the heavy door before Owen could reach for it.

There weren't even that many people inside the range tonight. She expected that it would be packed, but of approximately twenty shooting lanes, only six or seven were occupied, almost all taken up by men, which didn't surprise her. And all of them, turned to watch her go by, which did.

And of course, this being Cypress Hollow, she knew most of them. Two volunteer firefighters looked like they were having some competition with masking tape and a target drawn to look like a recently ousted political figure. Don Beadle, the head of the Chamber of Commerce, was firing rapidly, emptying one pistol and then the next. The only woman, little old Mrs. Luby, was in the lane next to his, shooting a tiny, pearl-handled gun that looked more like a toy. Lucy smiled at her, but Mrs. Luby didn't smile back.

Ahead of her, Owen motioned her into a narrow space, set off from everyone else by two tall cubicle-like walls on either side that stretched to the ceiling, open in the back to the room they'd walked through and in the front to the target area.

Owen set his gun box down on the waist-height counter and took out two pairs of clear plastic goggles that looked like something welders would wear.

"Wow, hot."

He ignored her and pushed a red button. Their wire above started to move like a clothesline and a clip at the end of it got closer. When it reached them, Owen unfolded a target from the gun box and clipped it so that it hung freely. It was the image of a man's torso, the upper head and heart highlighted in red.

"Now push this button here, and send it out." Owen spoke a little louder than normal — his voice sounded muffled to her but it was clear enough over the loud pops from the other men shooting.

"Don't I get the bull's-eye ring to start out with? It has to be a guy, huh?"

"The hardest thing about shooting is being able to reconcile yourself with the idea of being able to take another person's life."

Lucy shook her head. "I don't want to do that. If I had to shoot someone, I'd just shoot them —"

Owen interrupted her, "In the leg. Sure.

That's what everyone with granola running in their veins says. But then the guy on crack breaks into your house and he's out of his fucking mind and you shoot him in the leg and it just pisses him off. Now he has your gun because he took it away from you *and* he's tied up your mom. And he's going to do bad things to her. While you watch."

Lucy's eyes widened. "How did my mother get involved?"

"I put her in the house with you."

Lucy imagined coming into her parents' home to find her mother tied up and hurt, to find a strange man standing over her, and then she imagined having a gun in her hand. "Nope. I'm granola, all right. I'm a Northern Californian. But I'll blow him away and pay for the therapy later."

He looked delighted. "This is what I carry, a Glock twenty-two, compact, takes a ten-millimeter round. Or forty Smith and Wesson, which is easier to find."

"Yeah. I have no idea what that means." Lucy leaned forward. "Is it loaded?"

"Not yet. You bring it to the range unloaded. Usually they ask to check at the desk. I think your beauty might have blinded him a bit."

Lucy snorted and then said, "Can I touch it?" Oh, no. That sounded way more intimate than she had planned it to. "The gun, I mean. Can I touch your gun?" She was making it worse.

Owen nodded and pushed a button on the side of the gun, and the bottom part of the handle dropped out. "This is the magazine. See? You put the bullets in here."

Lucy leaned closer. Oh, Lord, he always smelled good, like laundry soap and something more masculine. He made her a thousand times more nervous than the weapon did. Guns could only shoot.

"I'm going to put a round, just one bullet in, snapping it in like this, see, then I push the magazine up, then I pull back on the slide until it snaps back. Now there's a bullet in the chamber ready to be fired."

Drawing back on the main metallic part, he said, "See that round in there?" He angled it back so that she could see into the cavity on top, so that she could see the bullet resting there, looking innocuous and insidious at the same time.

"I just shake the gun to the side, like this, and it falls right out. See? Now I'm sure the gun's not loaded." He put the bullet on the counter.

Owen drew the slide back a couple more times, pointing out where the bullet had been and no longer was.

Lucy felt jittery. "Is there a way to be *sure* there's no bullet in it?"

He smiled. "I know how they work, and I know there's no place for a bullet to hide. But there's one surefire way to find out."

Snapping the slide back into place, he pointed the gun down-range.

"You're not going to . . ." she started. But if he did pull the trigger, it would just click, right? It wasn't going to fire, she knew there was no bullet. . . .

But he didn't do anything. Owen just held the gun out in front of him, his eyes narrowed, arms outstretched. A muscle jumped in his jaw. He looked down and straightened his right foot.

The barrel of the gun started to waver. His hand was shaking. Lucy's heartbeat, already erratic, raced into overdrive.

"Owen. What's going —"

Lucy watched him take a deep breath. He pulled the trigger.

*Click.*

Lucy jumped at the startling snap. "What happened?"

Owen didn't say anything. He lowered the gun slowly and then looked at it, turning it over, examining it first on one side, then on the other.

"What's wrong?" asked Lucy. She wished

she could take the earplugs out, but the gunfire from the other shooters kept a solid blanket of noise around them.

"Nothing," said Owen, but his voice was wrong — off, somehow. "Nothing at all. Your turn."

He handed her the gun, his fingers brushing hers as he passed it over. Her own hand shook, too. She'd blame the gun for her jitters.

He was even closer now. *Think, breathe.*

"So the first lesson is never, ever point it at anyone unless you're trying to kill him," Owen said hoarsely.

"But it's not loaded, right?"

"Never, ever point it anywhere you don't want to hit. Not even when it's unloaded. If I'd screwed up when I pulled the trigger a second ago, I would have only damaged the target. It's harder to fix a bullet wound." He winced as he moved to lean against the plastic dividing wall.

"Good, like that," he said. "Now, always keep your index finger straight, just below the slide, until you're ready to shoot. Don't ever rest it on the trigger."

"Don't I have to take the safety off?"

"On most guns, yes. On this gun, the safety is that little toggle on the trigger."

"This thing? So if I pull the trigger I pull

the safety, too? How is that safe?"

"Satisfied the letter of the law, I guess."

"So pull on the slide to cock it?" An almost unbearable giggle rose in her throat at the word, which she normally didn't have reason to say. She choked it back. She would *not* laugh.

He ignored her. "Yeah, good. Now point it at the target and squeeze the trigger. Gently. Just one, slow, steady pull."

His voice reverberated in her ear. Never had a thing made of plastic and metal felt so sexy in her hand, not even the toy she kept at home in her nightstand.

*Click.*

Lucy jumped again, as if it had really fired. She took a deep breath. "Show me how to load it."

Owen demonstrated snapping the rounds into the clip, pushing it up into the handle until it clicked. "Cock it. Yeah. You're good to go."

Lucy felt wild heat flush her face, and it wasn't just the gun. "So I shoot?"

"Wait." Owen pushed his weight away from the wall and moved behind her. "Right foot forward a bit. Left foot back. Now raise your right arm like this."

While he was talking he brought his arms around her, guiding hers. "Left hand here, as support. Both eyes open, look down the sights." His breath was warm in her ear, causing her stomach to jump. How the hell was she supposed to shoot a gun when he made her more jittery than firing a lethal weapon for the first time?

"Don't jerk it. Just one long, steady stroke of your finger. Keep the pressure nice and even. Let it do the work —"

*Boom.*

"— for you."

With trembling hands, Lucy carefully set the gun down on the counter in front of them, a tiny wisp of white smoke curling and immediately vanishing from the barrel. Owen was still behind her.

"Damn. Nice shot," he said.

"That hole? In the middle of the chest. I made that?"

"You did."

"That was really scary." Lucy glanced over her shoulder. "And it was awesome."

"You loved it." Owen smiled, but his face looked gray. "Now do it again."

She shook her head. "No fucking way. Are you nuts? Let's get out of here before one of us passes out."

# EIGHTEEN

Once I kissed the wrong man, holding the needles in my lap. They stabbed his leg like a dowsing rod gone wrong. Trust your knitting.

— E. C.

Owen hadn't had the clam chowder at the pier since he'd been at the roller rink back in high school, before it closed. The pier always struck him as too touristy to consider visiting. But now Lucy sat cross-legged on top of the picnic table, a bread bowl full of chowder in one hand, a spoon in the other, looking up into the night sky. "God, this is good."

She leaned sideways and pulled a bottle of Tabasco out of her pants pocket and dumped some in her soup. "Want some?"

Shooting on a date was an idea whose time had come. It had taken some fast-talking on his part to get her to take that second shot, though. She'd been so spooked by the bang, she'd almost bolted like a deer.

And fuck, he'd been no better, had he? As he'd picked up the gun and held it down-range, held it on the target, all he'd been able to see was the last time he'd aimed a gun. The last time he'd fired. The flower of blood that had bloomed, the river of gore that had run into the gutter, taking Rob along with it.

How was he able to pick the gun up every single day of his life, check it, cock it, put it in his holster, without seeing that reaction coming? If he'd predicted that, he wouldn't have brought Lucy along to witness it.

But talking Lucy into sticking it out and staying at the range, that had helped him get his mind off his own stupid, unexpected terror. Not that Lucy needed much coaching. Lucy thought she was scared of things, he knew. But inside, she had guts of steel — he could see her strength as clearly as he could see her amazing curves.

At his encouraging, she'd picked the gun back up and shot again.

And when, half an hour later, the other five guys in the range had been standing behind them, hooting at her shooting the ace off a playing card? That was a moment he was going to have to work on accepting.

Owen was a crack shot. Had been training for years. He was good.

She was better.

And she was hot. A damn gunslinger. She'd known just how to hold the weapon, just how to gaze down the sights, exactly how to line them up and acquire the target without getting rattled, the whole time, her ass looking so perfect in those black pants that he could barely look up to see if she'd made her shots. He'd been hard-pressed to keep his hands to himself in front of all those guys, and now, if he wasn't careful, he was going to get all stupid out here in the beach moonlight, seagulls wheeling overhead.

That's what it took? A little gunpowder?

Well, okay. Nothing wrong with that. He wouldn't think about that whole firefighter thing. Not right now.

He mentally shook himself and took another plastic spoonful of the chowder. Sitting on top of the table next to her, his feet perched on the bench below, Owen said, "I can't believe you stole the bottle of Tabasco. I should arrest you."

She stuck out her tongue at him. "You're not a cop."

"Citizen's arrest."

"We'll just put it back as we walk past on

our way to the car. It's what I always do."

Owen pretended to make a note. "Chronic offender."

She balanced the bread bowl on her knee. "You miss it?"

He didn't pretend not to know what she meant. "Every minute of every day."

Two boys skimmed by on skateboards, both texting while they kicked with their right legs, their phones glowing in the dimness. A woman walking a white mutt smiled in their direction. The air was cool and damp.

Lucy looked at him, and the space she left between them felt so open, so . . .

So exactly what he'd been waiting for.

What he'd been wanting. And what he hadn't even known existed.

With all that was holy, he didn't want to have to tell the story. Not to her. She'd look at him with those dark, liquid eyes and his heart would break all over again. But without knowing what he would say, without any planning at all, Owen put his bread bowl on top of the picnic table.

"Is it very bad?" Lucy asked.

"It's not good."

"For the love of wool, just tell me. You can't bottle it up, you'll make yourself sick."

"You don't happen to have any acupuncture needles concealed on your person I need to know about, do you?"

"Come on, tell me."

Owen nodded. "When I got hurt, someone else did, too. Worse."

Her eyebrows shot up, but she didn't say anything.

"My best friend was a guy named Rob Marlowe. We were hired at the same time, and we did everything together. From rookies, to graveyard shift, to days. Moved up to detectives at the same time. He was local. His mom loved me. Fed me lasagna and enchiladas twice a week, whether I needed it or not." Owen picked up his plastic spoon and bent the tip of it. "She always said that Rob hadn't appreciated her the right way, that he'd been too stringy as a kid, and stayed too skinny. Never filled out. Me, I lifted weights and had filled out, so I ate a metric crapload of her spaghetti and pasta carbonara and garlic bread. Ate anything she put on my plate, and then I'd eat Rob's leftovers, too. It got so that on our weekends I'd stay at his place, and we'd both go to his mom's for dinner every night. The guys teased us about being a couple. I guess, in a way, we were."

Lucy grinned, her eyes gentle.

"Then Rob worked vice, undercover, with

a cop named Scotty Tucker. Rob starting using."

Lucy looked shocked. "Drugs?"

"I wish it was that unusual, but it's not. It's tricky — you're undercover working dope, and if you're selling, buyers want you to use with them, to prove you're not a cop. There's a bunch of ways to get around it, to fake it, but you're in dangerous situations all the time, and no one trusts anyone else, and if you just take one real taste, they'll get off your back and believe who you say you are. A lot of guys go down that way."

"Wow," Lucy said softly.

"So Rob got hooked, and his partner, Scotty Tucker, knew it. He milked Rob, threatening to go to the brass if he didn't pay him off. Rob started dealing from the evidence locker, and got more on the street on his own. He was losing weight and tweaking." Owen paused and took a breath. "And me, I didn't notice. He said he was on a new diet, and he'd always been so skinny. I just thought he was working too hard, too many hours. Scotty started hanging out at Rob's house more and more. I'd never liked the guy, but I was doing overtime on dogwatch patrol, so I didn't get over there for months. I'll . . ." He cleared his throat. This was harder than he thought.

"I'll never forgive myself for that."

Lucy just looked at him, her eyes full of something he didn't recognize. His heart thumped in a way that was almost physically painful.

"Then what happened?" Lucy's voice was gentle.

Owen twisted the spoon in his fingers. He would *not* rub the scar on his hip, which suddenly burned. "One of my narcs rolled, told me about a major deal that was going to happen at Rob's house one night. It involved everyone — Rob's biggest dealer, buyers, distribution, all at his house."

God, it was harder than he thought, to tell her all this. "There's nothing like setting up one of your own. I ran point, since I knew him the best. My lieutenant, I remember, told me that if I could enforce the law and bring down someone I loved, then I was worthy of serving that law. I believed it at the time."

Owen stopped.

Lucy scooted over so that her knee pressed into his. She rested her hands on top of his thighs, a light, warm weight.

"Go on," she said.

The astonishing thing was that he thought he could.

"We got to the house, a routine SWAT

alignment. We were in the right shape, but we were amped to the maximum: these were our guys. All of us hated every fucking second of it. Then, at the exact moment that we had the house surrounded, when we were about to make entry, he came out. We didn't think he'd do that, we thought we'd have to extract. No one saw that coming. Then everything went to hell."

Lucy took the now mangled plastic spoon out of his hand and then threaded her fingers through his.

Owen cleared his throat. He had never had to say this part out loud — anyone he'd ever had to talk to about it already knew the lay of the land.

Lucy's hand stilled in his.

"Rob came out, his arms up. When he realized we were really going through with it, really going to take him in, he pulled a gun. I shouted at him, warning him, but he wouldn't drop it. Then he cocked it and put his finger on the trigger. He pointed it at the lieutenant."

Owen's voice ground to a stop, and it was almost impossible to start it up again.

"Five of us shot. Rob got Steve Moss in the stomach, and me in the hip and knee. We kept shooting until he stopped."

"Holy shit," Lucy whispered.

Dropping his eyes from hers, Owen watched Lucy's pulse flicker rapidly in the hollow at her throat. For a moment there was no sound but the crash of the waves below.

Then she said, "Do you know . . ."

"They don't release ballistics in officer deaths like that. No one knows who killed him."

*"Good."*

Owen nodded. "The look in his eyes . . . When we were shooting, when he was hit, it was the same wide-eyed, scared, betrayed look I've seen in kids' eyes, kids who've had their arms broken by their parents for the first time."

Lucy scooted farther forward and pressed her cheek into his, and he could feel her tears. "You loved him."

"To have him die like that — in that kind of terror and pain —" Owen gasped. "I fucked up. It was my own shortsightedness. I was too close to him. He was lying to me, and I never noticed."

He laughed and the sound of it was like ash in his throat. "My job was to catch liars. The one thing I know is lying. And he was so close to me. . . ."

"Owen," said Lucy. The tears he couldn't shed were in her voice, and then her mouth was on his, and she was somehow tangled on his lap, his hands in her hair, her arms around his neck.

Murmuring something he couldn't quite hear, she spoke something into his mouth, words that made him regret the fact that they were in full public display. If they weren't, if there was anything they could possibly hide behind, he'd have his hands up her shirt, under her bra — he'd suck on her mouth until she bit his lip even harder than she was now. And if they were behind a door, her pants would be a ball on the floor, and he'd be inside her within thirty seconds.

It took the two teens on skateboards shattering the air with ear-piercing whistles to break them apart. Gasping, Lucy pulled back first. Her lips were swollen, and Owen was astonished to find that he loved that fact. Good God, for the first time in seventeen years, he felt like marking someone with a hickey. Just a small one, on the side of her neck. A barely-there red mark.

Maybe he'd get a chance to leave her one later. She could give *him* one if she wanted to.

What the hell was this feeling in his chest? A lightness, like a damn hummingbird got loose in there? He wasn't altogether unconvinced he didn't need a medic. No, no left-arm pain, nothing like that.

He'd talked about Rob. Out loud.

To someone who mattered.

And she'd kissed him anyway.

# Nineteen

> Knit in public. Show them what they're missing, and then put the yarn in their hands. Be the doorway to our world.
>
> — E. C.

Owen's grin was so big it looked like it was going to split his face. It was one of the cutest, sexiest things Lucy had ever seen.

But Lucy knew if she didn't get off this damn picnic table in about a second, she was going to fly apart.

"Want to get a drink?" she asked. She couldn't ask him back to her place. Not this second. She knew he'd say yes. He wouldn't even have to say anything — he could just look at her one more time like he had a second ago, and she knew that they'd run to his car and they'd be in her bed within eight minutes. She didn't live far away, and she'd take any bet that he'd break every speed limit to get there.

*Deal 'em out slow.* Whitney's voice rang in her head. If she took Owen home, there would be no slow — there would be hot, and fast, and hard.

Lucy didn't know if she was ready. She didn't know if she was brave enough. She needed a minute to clear her head.

And that minute should probably be in public, where other people in direct view would keep her from removing first his clothes and then her own.

Or at least she hoped they would.

Owen held her hand on the walk to the Rite Spot, only releasing it as she darted inside Clamtacular to drop off the Tabasco bottle. He even held it as she pushed open the door of the bar.

She hadn't held someone's hand in here since . . .

Lucy couldn't remember the last time. Stephen, maybe, although he'd been a bit shy about public displays of affection. He'd had rosacea and PDAs always made him blush. That was before he left her for his aesthetician.

Jonas. Oh, God. She hoped Silas wasn't inside the bar, too.

But of course everyone was there.

Her father was playing checkers with Elbert Romo at the corner of the bar. They were both drinking frothy concoctions with pineapple toppers and pink umbrellas.

"Hey, Pop! Pretty drink you got there," said Lucy. It was futile to try to slip under the radar.

"Honey!" said Bart. "Have you ever had a hurricane? Elbert here said he invented them when he was stationed in the Pacific."

Lucy shook her head. "You have no shame at all, do you?"

"Nope," said Elbert, as he jumped three of Bart's pieces.

Bart nodded politely at Owen and Owen nodded back. Lucy was glad. Her father had been well trained by his wife — no matter what her brothers might think of Owen, Toots was a force to be reckoned with, and she'd embraced the idea of Owen Bancroft, so Bart would do the same.

"Perhaps you'd like to play the loser, son?"

Owen's eyebrows shot up. "I'd like that very much another night, sir. Tonight I'm spending time with your daughter."

Bart inclined his head and sipped his umbrella drink. "Well, I suppose that's all right, then."

Silas was in a booth with his iPod cords trailing out from under his red earflap hat, reading his Kindle in the dim light of the pool table. A plate of what looked like mini-cupcakes was at his right hand, and he moved them to his mouth automatically, one after another.

Whitney flitted from table to table, seemingly the ambassador of goodwill, doling out smiles and light kisses, along with more mini-cupcakes. No one seemed immune to her charm, and even Lucy found herself craving the chocolate, to her deep dismay. She was relieved when Whitney moved toward the dartboards.

Mildred and Greta were in the back of the bar in front of the karaoke machine, singing Patsy Cline's "Crazy." Each held a mike, each trying to drown the other out. Luckily, the volume had been turned low.

Molly and Jonas were both behind the bar. Lucy did a double-take. Jonas, sure. But Molly?

And even stranger: they were locked in prime flirt position. Lucy had seen Molly like this a million times before — when Molly cocked her hip at that angle, thrust her ample chest just a little higher than natural, dropped her chin to the right, lifted her eyes to the left, and looked dreamily angelic yet devilishly suggestive, all at the same time, she never failed to get her man. And yes, there it was, the patented sweep of the long black hair over the shoulder, leaving her fingertips to trail over her clavicle.

And Lucy's brother Jonas was falling for it, hook, line, and swizzle stick.

Of course he was. He hadn't had a girlfriend since his wife, Aggie, chewed him up and spat him out two years ago. And Molly was gorgeous.

Well, sure. Jonas and Molly were really good friends. They got along great. Lucy loved that her best friend was so close to her older brother.

But friends didn't look at each other like that. Uh-uh.

Molly licked her lips in the way that had once garnered her a trip to the Caribbean, and then looked across the bar to meet Lucy's eyes. Her posture straightened suddenly, and she reached for a bar towel.

A bar towel?

Lucy dropped Owen's hand and sat on a stool.

"What's going on?"

Molly leaned forward on the bar as if she belonged behind it. "Lucy! Hey! What's up? You want a drink? I can fix you one! How about a gimlet? Totally the rage. Your Manhattan is *très* over."

Confused, Lucy nodded.

While Molly — *Molly!* — fixed her drink, Lucy had no idea where to look. There wasn't a single comfortable place for her eyes to rest. Her mother had arrived, and was showing off various nipple clamps to her knitting group. Jonas and Molly were touching each other completely inappropriately behind the bar, bumping into each other while reaching for bottles, and laughing every time they did.

And each time she ventured a glance at Owen, the heat in the room seemed to rise so high she thought she might spontaneously self-combust. Just the side of his jaw, the stubble along his cheek, was almost enough to make her lose all impulse control. What would that feel like under her tongue? What about that soft spot right under his ear?

Why couldn't she stop thinking like this? When had her hormones started raging like this?

As soon as she'd seen him enter her bookstore almost three weeks ago, that's when.

Molly slid her gimlet to her, and Lucy took a sip of it. Too sour. She should have stuck to her tried-and-true Manhattan, two cherries, no ice. But Molly wasn't paying attention to Lucy's reaction; she was too busy winking at Jonas.

Winking. What the *hell* was going on?

Owen gestured to Silas, still sitting alone at his booth. Whitney walked up to him and said something, moving the emptying plate of mini-cupcakes closer to him, but he barely looked up. "He seems pretty solitary."

"He's always been that way." Lucy smiled. "Even in grade school, he sat alone at tables and talked to trees. He's the smartest one in the family, and has no interest in anything but fixing things and reading his books. I wish he'd get a girlfriend, though."

"Being alone doesn't mean being lonely."

"I know."

"Sorry," said Owen.

"But when you lost Rob —"

"Could we not talk about that?" Owen's voice was sharp.

It felt as if she'd been slapped. Lucy stared at her drink, suddenly uninterested in it. She wanted to be home, in her bed. Alone.

"Sorry," Owen said. "It's just that . . ."

"Owen, it's fine."

He had told her the awful story of his own volition. She hadn't wheedled it out of him. She hadn't begged him to tell it. Lucy'd thought it had meant something to him — she'd felt special that he'd chosen her to talk to.

She tried to speak without betraying the wobble she felt rising. "I've had a great time tonight, but I'm pretty tired. I'm thinking we should wrap it up?"

"Lucy, I didn't mean —" Owen's cell this time, jangled over the jukebox noise of the karaoke in the back corner. Mildred and Greta were still back there, now launching into a rousing rendition of "Walking After Midnight."

Owen looked at the caller ID. "It's Willow Rock. I'm sorry, I have to take this."

Lucy nodded and then watched as Molly dodged a playful tap Jonas directed at her rear.

Molly would use men to line a birdcage. Jonas thought women were something breakable to place on a shelf. They had no common ground. They would never, ever work. She hated to think of how hurt they could get.

Why hadn't she seen this coming? What could she do about it? Even if she confronted Molly, would she be able to find the right words to tell her how she felt? Lucy's left foot jiggled so hard on the footrest of the barstool that it slipped off with a bang.

She flagged down her friend. "Molly?" said Lucy.

"What's up? You want another?" Molly looked pleased.

"Can we talk in the bathroom?"

Inside the restroom, Lucy leaned against the bright pink sink. "What's going on?"

"Me? What's going on with you? Were you holding Owen Bancroft's hand out there? Because you have a lot to catch me up on since that kiss you told me about."

"My brother?"

Molly turned toward the mirror and reapplied a layer of gloss to her lips. "Don't change the subject."

"You were behind the bar."

"I'm helping him out."

*"You flipped your hair."*

"It was in my way!"

And suddenly the words were right there, ready to bc spoken. "Molly! I know you better than anyone else. You flip your hair right before you flip a guy onto his back and ride him like a circus pony. And you do *that* right before you call him a cab and forget how to pronounce his name. If you ever knew it, that is."

Molly recapped the gloss and put it in her purse. Then she said in a low voice, "You've never judged me before."

"You've never tried to jump my brother before. And Jonas doesn't date girls like you." God, it sounded so much worse when she said it out loud.

Molly's face, when she turned back to face

Lucy, was serious. "You're my best friend. I'm going to try not to take offense at that last comment, even though it sounded ruder than anything you've ever said before. But Jonas and I are really good friends, too, you know that. We've been friends for years now. He's my confidant. He knows every conquest I make, and he laughs at me. No one but you laughs at me like he does. I'm not going to hurt him, Luce. I need you to trust me."

Lucy took a deep breath, and at the same time, her cell phone beeped with an incoming text message.

"Well, at least I know it's not you texting me," said Lucy. This wasn't over. Not just yet. Molly, hitting on Jonas. It was going to take more than just a quick chat in the ladies' room.

Flipping open her phone, she clicked on the text.

*I have to go — Owen.*

"Lucy? What's wrong?"

She looked blankly at Molly. "I think my date just split on me." Without saying anything else, Lucy left Molly in the bathroom, the bathroom door slamming behind her. She felt awful.

Owen was still at the bar, shrugging into

his jacket. He was pale. “My mom. She’s gone.”

Lucy’s hands flew to her mouth. “Oh, my God. Owen. I’m so sorry. I can’t imagine . . .”

Owen looked horrified. “No! I didn’t mean that. She didn’t *die*. She’s just missing. I have to go help search —”

“Let’s go.” Lucy picked up her purse.

“No, no, I’ll take you home and then go search for her. Okay?” The final word sounded tacked on at the last moment.

“I’m good at finding things. I get it from my mom.”

Owen shook his head, and then exhaled with a whoosh. “Are you sure?”

She nodded. The sooner they got out of here, the better. She felt, rather than saw, Molly come out of the bathroom behind her.

Her best friend, whom she loved more than anyone besides blood relatives.

Then she thought again of Molly and Jonas, together.

Molly didn’t stay with anyone, she took what she wanted from men and left them crying in station wagons on dark highways. Lucy had always thought it was a trait of strength — something not enough women had. But when it came to Jonas . . .

Lucy and Owen left the bar without looking back. Her heart pounded a fast, steady rhythm, and once in the car, she tucked her hands under her thighs.

The night was even foggier now than it had been when they'd been sitting on the pier. Lucy almost mentioned that it was a good thing, that the fog would keep it from being as cold as spring on the coast could sometimes be, but the atmosphere inside the Mustang was heavy enough.

Instead, she held her tongue and they rode in quiet, uncomfortable darkness. Owen smelled almost as good as a man should legally be allowed to smell, of wood and soap and of something that she now knew was totally, completely him.

She cleared her throat. This silence couldn't go on or she'd jump out of her skin. "When did she go missing?"

"They noticed she was gone two hours ago. But she could have been gone for four. Ever since they checked on her at bedtime. Who knows? She's wandered away before, but they've always found her fast."

"Where are we going to start looking?"

"They asked me to go down to the water. Near the lighthouse." His voice was strained.

"Seriously? They want you at the beach?"

"They have police officers already out looking for her, going in toward town. And they're working near the riverbed themselves. But no one's gotten to the beach yet."

"She can't have gone far."

"They move fast sometimes. One time . . ." His voice trailed off.

"One time what?"

Owen turned onto Main, his hands tight on the steering wheel. "Usually when we got those calls, someone called dispatch within minutes to say they'd found a lost old person. Then we'd go get them and return them and everyone was happy."

"But what was different this time?" Lucy kept her voice soft.

"An older Filipina immigrant had walked away. She had Alzheimer's. We couldn't find her. We looked for hours and then we had to go off shift, so we told the family to keep looking for her. I wrote the missing persons report. When I got back to work three days later, after my weekend, my voice mail was full of frantic messages from the family."

"She still wasn't home?"

"She hadn't been in the country long, didn't speak any English, had no money. She was scared of strangers."

"How long did it take to find her?"

"A week and a half later, a guy at a gas

station called. She must have walked for about a week, every day, with no food. They found her in a shed in the back. Hadn't eaten, no water. Dead, of course." Owens voice was flat. Hard.

"That's *awful.*"

Owen pulled into the parking lot at the end of Fifth. He shut off the car with a deliberate twist of the key.

"Think about how many people saw her. Think about how many people probably thought she was a bag lady by the end. Didn't talk to her, didn't try to help."

"But this isn't the city. This is Cypress Hollow. We'll find her." Lucy was frightened by the despair that radiated from his posture. If the hero was worried, where did that leave her?

"We have to."

# TWENTY

> When your knitting scares you, when you dread picking it up and it stares at you from the corner where you threw it last, you're either getting it very, very wrong, or very, very right indeed.
>
> — E. C.

Lucy watched Owen climb down the rocks awkwardly, one hand on his hip. Just like her, though he'd probably been doing it all his life. Everyone who'd grown up in Cypress Hollow had spent time down here in the tide pools, away from the touristy soft sand. Balancing on slippery rocks, racing away from waves, it was a part of life here. High-school kids snuck bottles onto the beach and trysted in the small caves at low tide. They dared each other to climb up the rickety stairs of the old lighthouse, to hang off the top rail, counting the stars. Lucy, scared of heights, had never been up it, of course, but she loved the look of it outlined against the sky.

Lucy wondered how many women Owen had wooed down here over the years. God knew her first boyfriends had lured her to the beach with the promise of bonfires and s'mores, when in reality they just had forty-ounce beer cans and hickeys to give her.

Over his shoulder, Owen said, "It's colder here."

"It's okay." Lucy tried to sound reassuring, but it *was* dark and much colder here with nothing to protect them from the ocean wind.

"You want to go left, and I'll go right?"

"Yeah." Lucy didn't want to, not at all, didn't want to leave Owen, but she knew it would be better if they split up.

He nodded. "Check the crevices, okay?"

Of course she would, even though it was dark as hell out here, even with the flashlight. Her head ached, deep inside.

Setting off across the hard, packed sand, Lucy called Irene's name into the wind. For a while she could hear Owen behind her, and then she could only hear the pounding of the surf. Thank God it was low tide; this beach could be treacherous for those who were careless when it was high. They could get stuck out here. She'd have nothing but her purse. Her knitting. And Owen.

What would it be like to be stuck with Owen on a rock all night?

Hot. Scorching. No way to be cold. She might not knit that much.

What a fantastic way to think about him while they searched for his missing mother. Lucy blushed in the dark. Stupid.

"Irene? Irene!"

The wind blew her words inland. The blackness of the night sent shivers up her spine that had nothing to do with the temperature.

Lucy went all the way to where the beach ended and the high rocks started, looking into each small cave, and then she turned around and headed back. Owen was doing the same thing from his end and it took everything she had not to run toward him.

When they were close to each other, he shook his head.

"Nothing?" Lucy wanted to take back the stupid question as soon as she'd uttered it. Of course there was nothing. Irene wasn't with him. They'd struck out.

Owen's lips pressed together in a fine, determined line. He shook his head. "I'm not sure where else to go. I suppose we can help them by the river . . . I just have to get out of here." Looking up at the old lighthouse, Lucy saw him suppress a shudder. "I hate it down here."

Lucy stumbled as fast as she could through the rocky sand behind him. Damn these stupid, strappy, sexy shoes. If she'd been in her Keds, she could have gone fast, instead of tripping like she was now. She followed him up the short incline through the ice plant to the car and looked at him as he leaned against his Mustang. "Should we go?" she asked. "To the river?"

Owen looked back up at the lighthouse. The white, peeling tower rose above them into the foggy sky. As if he hadn't heard her, he said, "You ever go up there?"

She shook her head, feeling fog-clammy strings of hair hit her ears. "It's been closed and falling down my whole life."

"Never stopped anyone from breaking in."

Lucy admitted, "I'm terrified of heights."

"That's the last place I saw my father."

Lucy put her cold hands into her pockets and ducked her head in what she hoped was an encouraging gesture. A minute to listen while the searchers looked for his mother wasn't going to hurt.

"That night." Owen glanced at her. "You know the one."

The night they'd kissed. The night he'd left town and never come back.

"He hit my mom."

"Oh, God, Owen."

Owen laughed, but it was hollow. "Oh, that was nothing special. That happened all the time. Just another Sunday night at the Bancroft house. But that night, after kissing you, I wanted more than just an awful family with no hope. I wanted something better. I told my mother she had to choose. Him or me."

He closed his eyes and then opened them again, looking up at the lighthouse in the fog. The auto-beam swung from a small electronic box at its base.

"And she chose him," said Lucy, the fingers of her right hand worrying a beaded stitch marker she found loose in her pocket.

"Yep. I ran out of the house, calling him a fucking asshole and her a whore." He shrugged. "I was eighteen. I was stupid and brokenhearted. He chased me. We ran all the way down here. Up the steps of that fucking building," Owen jerked his thumb at the lighthouse. "On the top deck there, he beat my ass so bad I couldn't see out of my left eye for a week. Broke my wrist and my collarbone. I passed out."

"Oh, Owen."

He ran his fingers along the trim of the window and then down to the passenger mirror. "I think he thought he killed me. Or something. He must have said something like that to my mother, because she called the cops and told them where both his counterfeit machine and his drugs were stashed. They put him away long enough for him to get killed in prison, shanked in a dining-hall fight two years in. But I didn't know that she'd called, not when I woke up. I snuck into the house, got a backpack full of clothes, wrote you that note, and left town. Never looked back."

Lucy took her hands out of her pockets and hugged herself. She was getting colder by the minute. "What note?"

The query seemed to jerk Owen back to the present. He stared. "You didn't get the note I left in your mailbox? I put it there the morning I left. Sealed. With your name on it."

"I never got a note."

"Well, damn."

Lucy bit her lip and tried to still her heart. Then she said, "Will you tell me what it said?"

"Maybe someday. Now we have to find Mom."

Lucy nodded. Later. His mother was the important thing. "What about her house?"

"Her old house? It's vacant right now.

They said that was the first place they checked. But the house was locked, and the gardens were empty."

"They didn't check inside?" Lucy pulled on the door handle. "She's in the house."

"How would she get in?"

"Does it matter how? A woman knows how to get back into her house if she's locked out. She's there. I'd bet my own house on it."

# Twenty-One

Home is where your stash is.

— E. C.

Owen fought the idea with every fiber of his being, but what if, on the off chance, his mother was inside the old place? It was cold tonight, and they had to find her before she hurt herself by accident.

Even if it meant going home.

Going back to the place he swore he'd never return.

God*damm*it.

Parking in front of the crooked mailbox, Owen said, "So now what?"

"We check doors."

"You think they didn't do that?"

"All of them?"

"Of course they did . . . *Shit.* What if they missed the side door? It's pretty hidden by that old camellia bush."

"I bet she still had a key in the backyard

hidden somewhere, and that she's safe inside."

Owen felt wings of panic in his chest. "It's not safe. It's dirty and cold and torn apart and awful."

"Hurry, then," said Lucy.

The worst part was the roses.

It was bad enough that that the past owners had let the lemon trees go unpruned, the lawn be taken over by Bermuda grass, and the paint peel off the house in long, awful strips. It was hard enough to see that the house he'd grown up in had suffered from an extreme amount of neglect.

But the roses broke his heart.

It had been such a place of beauty. Floribundas and tea roses, twiners next to climbers. His mother had other plants, too: lavender bushes and rosemary, lilac and jasmine. She loved everything that gave off a sweet scent. But her passion had been the roses. When she was in the garden, she was happy.

Now, all but the rugosas were long and spindly, and even those weren't flowering, though they looked like they'd survived. Barely. They hadn't been pruned. Owen guessed they hadn't been touched even once since his mother moved out. Many of them had grown tall and fierce, with thickets of thorny canes. Well, at least they were protecting much of the house. What was that fairy tale with the hedge of thorns? That must have been about roses.

His mother's garden was ugly.

Owen pushed his way through the knee-deep weeds along the pathway to the old iron bench at the back of the yard near the creek. It was the only place that wasn't a rose thicket. But if these weeds were knee-deep now, after a relatively dry winter, what would they look like by summer? Tripping over a low knot of some sort of rosebush that he couldn't identify, he almost went down. *Shit.* The sudden motion wrenched his hip.

He caught himself on the edge of the bench and felt underneath it, running his fingers along the bottom of the iron for the hidden house key. Yes. There it was. His mother had always been good at routine. He'd known, if she'd unlocked the door with this key, she would have put it back before letting herself in.

Guilt, ugly as the rose stumps, washed over Owen as he stared up through his mother's ruined paradise. She couldn't have stayed alone in the house, though, not after those small fires, and back then he couldn't afford both Willow Rock and her mortgage, as well as his own.

"Owen?" Lucy's voice broke through his painful memory. "We should hurry."

In the dark, the tangled mess of the garden was difficult to negotiate, even in the thin beams of their flashlights. Lucy cursed as she tripped.

"Hey! Last thing you need is a concussion tonight." Owen held out his hand. "Come on, I'll lead." He wanted to touch her. That was the problem. He wanted to touch her too much.

Lucy hesitated, just for a second.

Owen said, "Fine. Just follow close."

"No, wait." Lucy put her warm hand in his callused one. "It's dark out here."

Walking ahead of her, Owen guided her over the exposed roots and low-lying stalks and branches. "Here, this way. Almost there."

The back door looked like an afterthought, without even a porch or stoop attached, almost hidden behind an overgrown camellia that hadn't been pruned in years.

"Goes to the laundry room."

The key turned in the lock. Inside, the dim beams of the flashlights did a poor job of lighting the rooms they entered but Owen could see that trash littered the floors. The kitchen sink stood a foot away from the wall. Glass from shattered windows glinted in the dimness. The air stank of standing water and something bitter. The walls were graffitied with tags that hit the ceiling, green, purple, black.

"You *lived* here?" Lucy whispered.

Owen ignored her, but tightened his hand on hers. "Mom! Mom?"

There was a noise, a rustling in the next room. He hit a light switch as they walked into the next room, praying the electric company had forgotten to turn the power off, but no luck. Just a dull click.

Then they were in a living room of some sort, and the rustling grew louder, then suddenly stilled. The flashlight's beam lit up a pile in the corner near the fireplace. A tangle of sticks that looked like it had been picked up from outside in the unkempt garden and plopped in the corner seemed to jerk, and then still. Small eyes winked at them. The shushing sound went silent as the nest froze.

A rat's nest. A literal rat's nest. God*damn* the last residents.

He heard Lucy take a deep breath and stifle a scream. Her hand tightened in his, but she did well — she didn't bolt.

"Shit. *Mom!*" Owen pulled and Lucy followed, stepping on his heels. "Through here, hurry. There's a sitting room in front. She had flowers in there."

He kicked through litter and detritus in the small front hall, and carefully pushed the glass door.

"Mom?" Owen kept his voice soft.

"I can't find the watering can."

Irene was crouched on the floor, squatting, her hands on her knees. There was nothing in the small glassed-in space except a few ripped and flattened old cardboard boxes. Even the graffiti artists had been kind here, leaving this room mostly alone, apparently content to break only a few of the small panes of glass.

"Mom. We've been looking for you." Owen's voice shook.

"Help me look for it."

Owen hugged his mother. "Are you okay?"

Irene pulled away from Owen's embrace and stuck her index finger into his chest. "If you just put things back where you got them . . ."

"Are you hurt? Are you cold? Of course you're cold." Owen looked at Lucy. "It's freezing in here. And wet. I'm calling the paramedics." He got out his cell phone to dial 911. "I'm seeing way too much of these guys," he mumbled. "I used to be the one who *got* the calls, not the one who called them."

Lucy took off the blue sweater she'd been

wearing all night.

"Irene? You want to wear this?"

Irene shook her head.

Lucy said, "I knitted it myself. Angora from a spinner out past Mills Bridge."

Irene looked at her hands in the dim light from the outside streetlight. "Does she have her own rabbits?"

Owen rolled his eyes. "We just need to take her with us. She's not going to make sense."

Lucy ignored him and spoke to Irene. "She does have her own rabbits. About two dozen, I think, but they're all like children to her. You should see the time she spends grooming them. She usually cards the fiber and spins on her wheel, but I've also seen her sit there, a bunny on her lap, her drop spindle spinning the fiber off the rabbit, right on the spot."

Irene's eyes crinkled as her face broke into a smile. "That's something."

"I'll take you out there one day, if you'd like me to."

"I used to knit, too."

"I know. Do you still knit?" Lucy eased the sweater over Irene's head, and Owen assisted, directing Irene's arms into the sleeves.

"What?"

"Do you still knit? I can get you some wool and some needles if you like."

"I don't know how." Irene looked warmer already.

"Yes, you do."

"I can't remember. I can't even remember, going back. You know. Like reverse."

"Going back? You mean purling?"

Irene nodded hard. "I can't do that."

Owen took Irene's hands. Poor thing, they were freezing, stiff. This was awful. Her lips were tinged with blue. It couldn't be much below fifty degrees in the house, but it was colder in this glass room.

Lucy said, "Your hands never forget. You still know how. I can show you. Would you like that?"

Irene stood still, her eyes filling with tears.

Owen said softly, "Come on, Mama. No crying. We have to get you home. Are you tired? The nice ambulance is going to check on you."

Sirens wailed in the distance, and then got closer, the fire engine pulling up in front, the ambulance not far behind. Its flashing lights danced through the glass windows of the porch, and Irene covered her eyes and whimpered.

"It's okay, Mama." Owen had a hard time injecting sympathy into his voice now, though. Anger was setting in. What the *hell* had she been thinking, wandering away like that? Oh, yeah. She hadn't. She hadn't thought in years.

And Willow Rock. What was he paying them an arm and a leg for, if not to prevent exactly this from happening? He was going to have a talk with them that would leave their ears bleeding, see if he didn't.

The firefighters were the first through the front door, tumbling over each other like puppies, and Owen remembered why he loved being a police officer. Order. Precision. Not like a damned volunteer fire department in a sleepy beach town. How could Lucy do this on her off time? Impossible to imagine.

"Hi, Jake," said Lucy to the tallest man.

"Lucy! What's going on in here?" The firefighter looked down at Irene, still seated on the floor. "Ma'am. You okay? How long have you been in here? Jones, start vitals," and with a few directions, he had two other people checking Irene over.

"Captain Jake Keller," he said to Owen. He was obviously the one in charge. Good. He didn't look like a complete idiot. "Your mom? How'd she get in here?"

"Owen Bancroft, and this is my mother, Irene. She's been in here for at least a couple of hours. I'm going with maybe hypothermia, some dehydration."

Jake nodded and gave the female firefighter a few more instructions. Owen glanced at Lucy. The ambulance medics had entered, and Lucy watched them, as if checking their work.

The paramedics wrapped a heating blanket around Irene and loaded her on a stretcher. She'd gone silent again, and her eyes were closed tight. Owen didn't think she'd speak again for a long time. Maybe days. More.

He was so furious *he* could barely speak.

"Thanks," he managed, as the firefighters cleared out.

The door shut behind them with the distinctive click-snap he'd heard all his life — he'd forgotten that sound, how he'd hear it in the middle of the night when his dad would try to sneak in, unheard, way too late.

God, he hated this house. He should buy it just so he could burn it to the ground. Raze it. It was all it was good for.

Lucy pressed her face to the window, watching them carry Irene to the ambulance outside.

"I should take you home now, then I'll go to the hospital," Owen said. Even the very words felt as heavy as lead, dropping like bullets to the ground.

"You kidding me?" she said. "I'm staying with you. Now that we've found Irene, this is officially the most exciting night ever."

And the way her smile broke across her face was like dawn, come early.

# Twenty-Two

> And never, ever be scared when knitting. Holding your needles with that much tension will only do bad things to your neck and your poor, muddled psyche.
>
> — E. C.

Irene didn't have to stay long at the hospital — her vitals were surprisingly strong, and she didn't display any signs of dehydration. They released her at two in the morning and Owen drove her back to Willow Rock, Lucy sitting in the backseat, her needles clicking quietly, as they had at the hospital.

Lucy had waited for him in the car while he took his mother inside, not wanting to introduce anything unfamiliar into Irene's bedtime routine. When he'd come back out and eased himself down into the driver's seat, she'd moved into the passenger seat and looked at him expectantly as he started the car.

An almost overwhelming urge filled his body, the desire to reach out and stroke her arm, to touch her face, to kiss the side of her neck and breathe her in. Instead, he stared at the gas gauge, struggling to still his breathing. Wordlessly, he started the engine.

After another moment of silence, she prompted, "So? Is she okay?"

It took all his concentration to put the car in reverse. "She's fine. We changed her clothes and she doesn't even have any scrapes or bumps. Miss Verna will have the on-call nurse check on her again first thing in the morning." Owen glanced at the dashboard clock. "Which, since it's already three, I guess won't be very long from now."

"The medics were great with her, weren't they? I love watching them when I'm not on call. I learn so much. They're volunteers, you know. Mostly. I mean, Jake's paid, but . . ."

"Oh, for fuck's *sake.*"

"What?" Lucy was clearly startled, her eyes wide.

"She's been wrapping her own shit and drying it. Keeping it in her dresser drawer and calling it diamonds. They just told me about it."

"Wow."

"They should have told me sooner. They hid it from me. It's their *job* to keep me apprised of everything that happens with her. It's just one long downhill slide, and I like to know how far down that slide we are." Owen hated the break in his voice. "How close we are to the very bottom."

"Oh, damn." Lucy slid low in her seat and pulled her knees to her chest. Her hand went to her head.

"How do you feel?"

"Me?" In the light of the streetlamp they passed, she looked surprised. And worried.

"You must be exhausted."

"I'm fine. Bed will be good." Her words fell away.

Owen pictured her in bed, and imagined himself next to her, kissing her good night, stroking her arms, her sides, making sure she was comfortable. He imagined watching her eyelids droop slowly, watching her breathing slow and grow deep.

He imagined watching her every night.

"Careful! That speed bump there's a doozy."

Christ, he hadn't even been paying attention to the road. Slowing, he took the turn for her street. He wouldn't push. If she wanted him, if she needed him, he was there.

He was so there.

When he said he wanted to see her safely inside the house, she didn't argue. Then she didn't seem to want to go right to bed, and even though he wanted to insist that she do so, he controlled himself. He didn't say anything. They danced around each other, instead. In the kitchen, she made tea and gave him a cup without asking if he wanted it or not.

Lucy sat on the couch, knitting. He sat on the chair opposite her. How was she not dropping from exhaustion? Shouldn't she go to bed? But her eyes looked strangely bright, and her cheeks were flushed.

Instead, he asked, "What are you making?"

It was the right question. He loved the way her eyes lit up as she smiled at him, holding up the small piece of yellow fabric that dangled from her long needle.

"I'm swatching. It's going to be a remake of that ratty cardigan I always wear, the one I told you about, the one where I've only found the body pattern so far. Eliza Carpenter designed it for my Grandma Ruby. Even though Grandma was always knitting something for someone else, she never made herself anything. By the date at the top here," she held up the page she'd placed in a plastic protector, "Eliza wrote this pattern just before Grandma died. It was the last sweater Grandma ever made, and it means everything to me. I just need to find the sleeve directions."

He could listen to her talk about knitting terms all night, words that bounced nonsensically around inside his head, as long as that look stayed on her face. Owen loved her smile. "They were really close, huh? Eliza and your grandmother?"

"Eliza always had women surrounding her, following her. My mom was one of those, even though she was so much younger. It sounds like your mom was one. Mildred and Greta, the two older women you've met who are attached at the hip, were in her knit cadre. But Grandma Ruby and Eliza were like sisters. They spoke the same language."

Lucy knitted while she spoke, her fingers flashing. How did she do that? She wasn't even looking at it. Owen never knew that knitting could be so damn sexy, but she made it look good. Nimble fingers. He knew what she could do with those . . . She was still talking. With effort, he dragged his attention back up to her eyes.

"I think that was the hardest thing for Eliza about moving south. Leaving my grandmother, and leaving her land."

"Why did she go?"

"She needed more help than Cade could give her, more medical attention, and a lot of the older knitters had gathered into this one assisted-living place right on the beach. She was the queen of them all. My grandmother would visit Eliza there once a year for a week, and it was like knitting camp while she was there. Grandma would come home, and it was like her . . . I don't know. Like her spirit was glowing or something. God, now I sound like my mother."

Owen smiled. "Your mom isn't like anyone I've ever met before." *And neither are you,* he thought, but he didn't say it. He couldn't say it. "Is knitting hard?"

"You want to learn?"

"No!"

"Why not? Threatens your manliness?"

"As if anything could. Come on, now." He was rewarded by her laughter.

"I could teach you and reteach your mother at the same time. . . ."

"You're serious?"

"Hey, knitting is *way* more soothing than yoga. Yoga's hardcore. Traditionally, knitting was considered man's work. Think about it, it's just loops and knots. How much more manly can you get? And you could always knit a beer cozy or something."

"A beer cozy."

"Keeps your beer cold, and your hands warm."

"Is there seriously such a thing?"

"I've even seen a gun cozy."

Owen took a sip of his tea. "That's a joke, right?"

"I think the pattern was meant to be ironic, yeah, but it exists. I can make you one for your Glock, if you'd like."

"Keep my hands warm and the bullets cold?"

"Something like that," she said.

Her eyes dropped to her work as she turned it, tucking a trailing piece of yarn out of the way, flipping the long, oddly flexible needle around and starting to knit back the other way. He didn't understand anything she was doing, but it was nice to watch. Soothing, somehow.

Owen said, "I remember my mother knitting."

Lucy didn't look up at him, just kept her hands in motion, and he felt mesmerized by her.

He went on. "The click of the needles is nice."

Lucy shook her head a little and then said, "I'd really like to help her remember how to do it. It'll come back to her as soon as she touches the yarn, I know it."

"Will you teach her again sometime?"

"Really?" She sounded eager, like she really meant it.

"I'd love it if you would. Anytime. Don't even ask me first. I'll put you on the list of approved visitors, and you can go see her."

"I will, then."

"They should have told me about her fake diamonds." He knew it was apropos of nothing, but Miss Verna's words nagged at him. "Think about the health violations. Digging around in a toilet bowl? For the love of Christ. I can't even wrap my head around it. And then to not tell me."

Lucy changed the subject as fast as he had. "Jake Keller's a good guy, huh?"

Owen frowned. "Well, it's not like she was hanging from a ledge or anything. . . ."

"But if she had been, Jake and his crew would have been there. Just like they were at the fire, taking care of Abigail. That's why I love working with them. . . ."

Lucy was forgetting something important, though. "*We* were there," said Owen. "We saved Abigail. And if my mom had been hanging from a ledge, *I* would have saved her. They're just firefighters, and volunteers at that. They're not gods." He thought of something. Something he didn't like at all. "Are you dating him or something?"

"God, no! He's my boss when I'm on call. He's full-time, one of three firefighter/paramedics. The rest are volunteers. They're combined, both firefighters and EMTs. It's just that . . . tonight reminded me of —" Lucy stopped talking and picked up her mug, looking into it as if it held the answers to life's most important questions.

"Reminded you of what?"

"Damn, I need more honey in my tea," she said, and it sounded like a tragedy.

"Is it in the kitchen?" Owen asked. "Let me get it for you." He wanted to take care of her.

"No, I'll get it."

He followed her into the kitchen.

She added the honey and leaned both arms on the countertop. "Hell," she said.

"Tell me."

Lucy stared at the tile backsplash behind the sink. "It reminded me of being on the beach with my grandmother. When she collapsed in front of me, under the lighthouse."

In Lucy's voice, Owen heard the same caliber pain he'd felt as Rob had fallen to the ground, the gunshots still ringing through the cold San Francisco fog.

She went on, "I called 911, and the medics came. They worked on her. I couldn't do anything. I didn't even know CPR, had never taken a course. Turns out, they couldn't save her. But I couldn't even try, didn't know what to do except hold her hand and cry."

"Sometimes that's the best thing you can do." His words were hollow, he knew it. He took the bear-shaped pot from her hands and added a long stream of golden honey to her tea.

"I was just scared." Lucy looked up at Owen, and her eyes sparked, making his heart beat so hard it almost hurt. "That's why I joined the department. I was always scared. Quiet little bookstore Lucy." Her eyes darted downward again.

Owen used the spoon to swirl the honey. "So, pulling people out of burning cars? Holding people back while others have seizures? That's not brave?"

"That's different. That's just helping."

"You know what?"

"What?" she whispered.

"I've always known you were brave. Since the moment I saw you in high school. Quiet, smart, and daring. Since I kissed you that first time. Since you knocked me over with the way you kissed me back."

"Oh." The word was a breath.

He didn't plan it, didn't think about it, didn't wonder if it was going to be the right thing or the wrong thing to do. But in the space of a sigh, she was in his arms.

She wrapped her arms around him so tightly he could barely get air, but he didn't care. Her mouth met his, and he didn't know who was kissing harder, deeper, but it didn't matter.

He wanted her like he'd wanted no other woman, ever.

But she needed to make the decision. He wouldn't make it for her.

He pulled back, breaking the kiss. Looked into her eyes. Waited. Hoped.

And she said one word.

"Now."

Then she gasped and pushed her mouth to his, her breath sweet against his tongue. She pulled up on his shirt, ripping it up and over his head. His holster, the gun still in it, hit the floor with a metallic crash. Owen opened the fly of her pants and tugged the zipper. She broke the kiss to lift her shirt up and over, and then flung off her bra, dropping it to the tile.

His pants next, and the condom came out of his wallet, and they were naked against each other in the dim room. Putting his hands to either side of her face, Owen kissed her eyelids, her nose, her cheeks, back to her mouth.

The backlight from the living room lit her brown hair to flames of russet and gold and her eyes sparked bright.

"You are so beautiful," he gasped. She pressed harder against him, her hands pulling him against her.

"Just . . . I just need . . ." Lucy bit his bottom lip and lifted her naked leg to wrap around his hips. He could feel her heat, her wetness.

Owen groaned. He couldn't take much more of this. He had to be inside her.

"Hang on," he growled in her ear. Putting his hands under her buttocks, he lifted her, turning them so that her back was against the wall. He held her up so that her other leg could wrap around him, and she shifted in just the right way, tilted his hips, and he was suddenly inside her, all the way, as far as he could go.

Lucy made a high-pitched noise in the back of her throat. As they kissed, he felt the keening sound inside his mouth. Her tongue was hot silk, demanding and brazen.

Her fingers curled into the small of his back, holding on as he lifted and thrust into her again and again. She ground her hips against him hard, harder, every time he pushed. He'd never been this far, this deep before. He'd never felt like this.

The coil of heat inside him spiraled higher as he watched her face. Her eyes were screwed shut, and she seemed to be climbing. He could watch her forever. But he wouldn't be able to hold out much longer.

Lucy's eyes flew open, and she stared into his with an intensity that went beyond passion, beyond lust.

"I'm right here," Owen said. "I'm not going anywhere. I'm not leaving you." Her legs wrapped tighter, her fingers pulled him against her. "I'm right here."

*Now,* she mouthed, and he felt her contract around him as she came. "Now," she whispered against his mouth. "Now, now, now."

He thrust into her again, hard, harder, and joined her, his face pressed into the soft place at her neck, in front of her ear.

"God, oh, *God.*"

For a moment, he stood there, trying to slow his heart rate. He still held her up against the wall, her arms around his neck.

He took a deep breath.

"You want to put me down now?" Her voice gave her away, and as he carefully slid her off him and down, she gave in to the laughter that he'd felt building up against his chest. Bringing him with her, she collapsed onto the large green rug that lay in front of the washer and dryer. His hip felt like it was on fire, but it was worth it.

"Oh, Lord." She laughed.

Owen managed to say, "Wow." Her hands were perfect, soft and strong, fit perfectly into his.

"You're really here," Lucy said. "Back home."

"I am," he said.

Her laughter was the happiest sound he'd ever heard.

# Twenty-Three

When in doubt, you'll never go wrong with a knit-two-together. Simple and attractive. Easy. Fun.

— E. C.

Lucy woke purring. Warm, lying on Owen's shoulder, splayed out, smack-dab in the middle of her huge bed, she was exactly where she wanted to be.

And Owen was with her.

Good Christ on a pogo stick, how had she managed this one? She'd dealt out all the cards at once. In the kitchen. And then again, an hour later, in the bed. Maybe a few more cards had been played at dawn, as well, slower that time.

Lucy was exhausted. And better than that, she was happy. She'd made a decision not to be scared. And he'd met her there.

She rolled off Owen with a sleepy, contented groan. Lying on her back, she looked out the window. Lazy wisps of fog curled past the window. A perfect, cool spring morning. Her favorite kind. And soon, coffee would make everything even better.

She wasn't going to think about Jonas and Molly — that was for later. She must have gotten some of that wrong, right? They could have been flirting, but Molly had always flirted a little with her brothers, just like she did with everyone. Harmless. That's all it was. Lucy shook the thought from her mind.

From behind her, Owen's arm went around her waist. He pulled her in against him, and moved so that she was flush against his long lines. Was he even awake? For one long moment, Lucy lay still, waiting to see what he would do next.

God, she wanted him so badly she felt dizzy with it.

What if he touched her? What if he wasn't sleeping, and he was just waiting to see what *she* would do, and if she encouraged him, he'd take her, just like that. First, his arm would move from her waist up to her breast, then he'd press against her from behind, and she'd feel just how much he wanted her. . . .

No, he was asleep. Lucy felt his long exhalation against her neck. She'd go make coffee, instead. She sighed and lifted his arm so she could slide out of bed without waking him.

Without a word, Owen pushed himself up. With one hand on her hip, he turned her to face him. In the early morning light, she stared.

His eyes were as dark blue as the water at the end of the pier, and even as Lucy felt herself sinking into them, he moved, fast, just like he had in her brief fantasy. His lips came down on hers, hard, hot, and ready. His tongue slipped against hers, gentle only for a moment, and then insistent.

Owen made it perfectly clear what he wanted. Pushing Lucy down onto her back, the kiss intensified, and his hands moved to her breasts.

Arching her back, Lucy pressed up against him. She couldn't think. Wouldn't think. He had to . . . oh, God, yes. He caressed her nipple while she moaned and bit his lip. His hips ground against hers, and she could feel how much he wanted her.

Damn all of it, she wanted him the same way.

Fast.

Hard.

*Now.*

Her hands pushed against his chest, breaking the kiss, even though moving away from him was the last thing she wanted.

"What?" Owen said. "Is this okay?"

Her daring was back — that rush she'd felt, right before she'd run out into the lightning storm, right before she'd told him last night she wanted him, damn the consequences. Lucy didn't know if it was smart or not, but she didn't care. "Shut up and *hurry.*"

Owen's answer was a laugh that turned into a growl as she bit his ear. He held her wrists against the bed and kissed her again.

"Owen?" she murmured against his mouth.

"Yeah?"

"What did the note say?" Lucy dragged her tongue along his jaw.

"What note?"

"The one you left in my mailbox when you left."

"Secret. Maybe I'll tell you someday," Owen said, and his smile was wicked.

He was even more perfect by the light of day than Lucy could have imagined, with definition where normal people were soft, tautness where most were slack. As he turned to throw his pillow onto the floor, muscles rippled between his shoulder blades.

The scars, though. They caught her eye, even though she willed herself not to look at his left knee. A long rippled mark. And the one above it, on his hip . . .

But it was what was next to the scars, just between them, that caught Lucy's attention. Owen was huge, and ready. Again.

Thank God she had that box of rainbow-colored condoms in her nightstand. Lucy'd been so embarrassed when her mother had put them in her Christmas stocking that she'd almost thrown them out, but then she'd stuck them in the drawer on an impulse fueled by irrational hope.

It had been a really long time.

"Red? Blue? Green?" Lucy held out a selection.

He laughed. "I'd like yellow, please."

Lucy frowned. "I don't think . . ."

"I'm kidding. Pick whatever you want, Lucy." Owen knelt on the bed next to her, his mouth against her neck. He nibbled the skin below her ear, across her clavicle, and started trailing down. "You're amazing." He pulled back his head and looked at her. "You're so beautiful."

Lucy felt even more naked than she'd been even a few seconds ago, but it was a wonderful feeling. It felt like what she imagined jumping out of an airplane would feel like, with none of the fear of dying and all the excitement. She smiled up at him. "So are you."

Owen grinned and picked the red one.

He couldn't breathe right when his lips were touching her, and it didn't matter where — if his mouth was against her breast, he couldn't get enough air into his lungs, and if his lips were against her neck, there wasn't enough oxygen in the whole wide world, and there probably never would be.

Owen didn't get it. She was put together like a normal woman. She had two arms, two legs, and all the requisite parts. He'd checked. As soon as he caught what breath he could, he was planning on checking all over again. But as he slipped two fingers inside her, catching her lower lip with his teeth as he did it, he knew that no one had ever felt like this before, that no woman had ever been this silky and wet and as hot as a furnace inside, and at the same time, no woman had ever been this much fucking fun.

Because she was laughing up at him. Laughing as if she were having as great a time as he was, which was maybe the most fun he'd had in memory. She was like a ride on a roller coaster, only it didn't come to a stop. Just when he thought he'd reached the highest part of the ride, he got higher.

Keeping his fingers inside her, he trailed his tongue down her body, taking his time, licking and teasing each sensitive point he found, her waist, her hip, the inside of her thigh, and then, when she was tensing around his hand, at the moment when she was gasping, he lowered his mouth to her, pressed his tongue against her most delicate spot, kissed her while his fingers kept up their motion, until she writhed under his mouth and hand, her hands wrapped in his hair, pressing him into her, her voice above him, begging him never, ever, to stop.

And when she'd stopped pulsing around him, when she purred and pulled him up her body, laughing, when she finally wrapped her legs around him and he pushed into her, it was as if she'd been made to fit him — she breathed into his mouth and gasped against him, pressing back against him in perfect rhythm, as if they'd been doing this for months, for years, forever. His cock found purchase and friction, heat and speed, and oh Christ, she was so fucking wet, and she screamed into his mouth, and then he came, and she did, too, and it wasn't like anything else — she was with him.

Those incredible eyes, the way she stared into him as he spiraled down into her, as his breathing eased, as they panted against each other . . . Her grin was huge and open, and his heart lurched.

An hour later, in the most massive bed he'd ever been in, Lucy dozed on his shoulder. Owen was limp-limbed, the sheets damp and twisted around them. God, where *had* she found this bed? It looked like it had been built with the house, at the turn of the century. It matched the bookcases downstairs, tall spirals of decorative wood. The huge mattress didn't even really fill the whole frame. Owen stretched as far as he could and his feet still didn't hang off the edge. It was great.

And that was indubitably the best sex of his life. The way she had sounded when she came, the way she looked when he did, the way she kissed him at the last minute, the way she laughed as he fell against her, the way she tucked herself around him and closed her eyes, her cheek against his. The way her heart slowed to a steady thump.

Sure, the last time he'd had sex wasn't even that long ago. That gal had been fun and sweet and came with no strings attached.

Whereas Lucy had strings. Lots of them.

Strings all over town.

And she felt more perfect lying next to him than anyone ever had.

Goddammit. Inside his head, he groaned. He'd really done it now. Why didn't he see this coming? He should have guessed this would happen if he spent the night in her bed.

He groaned softly. He'd screwed up. As usual.

How was this possibly going to keep him drama-free?

It wasn't. Nothing about Lucy made him feel sane or calm.

Lucy stirred, her hand running across his chest, down his torso. . . . He had to get up before she got to . . .

There. Yeah, before she got to there.

"Mmmmm. Hi," Lucy purred in his ear. Damn, she was *blazing* hot. How could he be ready again, when he'd thought he'd given her all he had, just minutes ago?

"Um," Owen said. He scooted sideways and started to sit up. His hip protested. It made sense; he'd been using the hell out of it all night. "I have to . . ."

"What?"

"I should . . ."

The curtains were closed, but a ray of early-morning light had found its way in and was draped over her shoulder, grazing her cheek, the side of her face.

He'd never seen anything prettier in his whole damn life.

Something must have shown on his face, because she put her hands to her forehead and whispered, "What? My hair must be a wreck, I know."

Owen just shook his head and leaned down to kiss her, one more time. "You're gorgeous."

Lucy wrapped her arms around his neck and kissed him back. He lost his breath. She drew him down to her so that he was lying down again. Then she pulled the blanket back over him.

How was it possible that her mouth fit his like it did? Like they were born to kiss each other? He tried to breathe, to will himself to break the contact, but it was proving impossible.

There wasn't really a reason he had to stop, right? Maybe there was, but he couldn't remember it. God, she was so soft, so warm. . . .

The door of the bedroom flew open.

"Lucy? Do you know where Owen is?" Lucy's mother, Toots, walked past the bed without looking at it, and went right to the window. She pulled the curtains back and turned to face the bed, hands on her hips. "He's not at the parsonage and his car's in front of your house."

Lucy had turned to stone in Owen's arms. She had her eyes squinched shut, as if she was going by the old if-I-can't-see-you-you-can't-see-me principle. Owen thanked every power there was that Lucy had pulled the blanket over them both.

"Oh, how cute! Look at you both! You're cuddling! Owen, good morning. Good to see you. I thought I might find you here."

How was it possible that his head hadn't exploded?

"Good morning, Mrs. Harrison." Shit. It had been twenty years since his voice broke like that.

Lucy's mother flapped her hands. "Call me Toots. Mrs. Harrison is Bart's dead mother and I never liked her very much. Now scoot." With both hands, she pushed on the blankets where Owen's and Lucy's legs were still intertwined. "Let me sit here."

Toots perched on the side of the bed.

Lucy still hadn't opened her eyes.

"Oh! Look!" Toots grinned and picked up the box of condoms from the nightstand. "The rainbow pack from Santa! I'm so glad they're getting some use, you sweet little bunnies."

Lucy moaned as if she were in pain. Hysterical laughter rose in Owen's throat that he prayed he'd be able to bite back.

Toots leaned forward and whispered to Owen, "Bart likes the green ones best, but I like the purple."

Groaning louder, Lucy pulled the covers over her head.

"Of course, we don't need to use them. Obviously. I'm a few years past baby age, thank God. But a little color always adds spice, doesn't it?"

Owen nodded dumbly.

"Now," Toots went on, "Are you ready for yoga?"

*Hell.* That was it. He'd agreed to this, hadn't he? At the bar with his mother, Toots had asked him about his hip and leg injury. She'd said yoga would help it, and she'd offered him a private lesson Wednesday morning. He'd said yes, even though if his cop buddies ever found out, he'd have to leave the country.

Today was Wednesday. She had tracked him to *here?* Could there possibly be worse timing?

"So you two get dressed and come down to the living room. I brought you a mat, Owen, and Lucy, I'll pull yours out of the hall closet, okay?"

Lucy squeaked and went farther under the sheets.

"Good. I brought sage — I'll go smudge." Toots left the room with a jingle.

Owen lifted the sheet. Lucy's huge brown eyes looked up at him in horror.

"This is a nightmare, right?" she asked.

"I hope so."

"I'm never leaving this room. You can just tell her I died. She won't mind."

"Are you kidding me? You think I'm facing her without you?" Owen pulled the sheet back. "Impossible. You're coming with me."

Lucy's hands moved to cover herself, her breasts swaying softly as she pulled the sheet.

"Wait," Owen said. "Let me look at you."

"My *mother.*" Lucy rolled onto her stomach to glare at him. "Is *downstairs.* We're going to do *yoga* with her. And all I can see are colored condoms dancing in front of my eyes."

Running a finger down the soft, straight line in the middle of her back, he said, "We'll make it work, heart." That name again. That he couldn't stop saying. Where the fuck was his edge? And how could her skin possibly be this soft?

Lucy's eyes crinkled at the edges as she

smiled. She hesitated and then said, "You're a nice guy, huh?"

"Well, this morning I wasn't." Even though he'd had the time of his life, Owen mentally kicked himself again. He shouldn't have. "I might have . . . Well, I took advantage of you."

Lucy laughed and slipped out of bed on her side, wrapping a pink knitted afghan around her body as she moved. "You're implying I didn't want my advantages taken. What if I took yours instead and you just didn't notice?"

He sat up halfway. "Did that happen?"

Lucy looked down at the ground and back at him. She grinned, and her smile lit her whole face. "Oh, yeah. I took 'em good."

# TWENTY-FOUR

There's no need to be careful in knitting. The worst that can happen is a hole, and you have the tools to fix it. You can fix everything.

— E. C.

"Now, lift thc sit bones and let the inner thighs roll forward. That's it, the ischial tuberosities feel as if they're floating up into the air as your feet ground into the earth, bringing you into alignment. Good, Owen, good. You're getting it."

Lucy shook her head and hung upside down in downward dog. She cheated in the position and tucked her head and bent her elbow so she could peek under her arm at Owen. Four feet away from her, on his mat, he was also in an upside down vee, and his face looked bright red and unhappy.

Toots said, "Rest in the breath. Move deeper with each exhalation, lengthening your spine. Now, on the inhalation, move forward into plank pose. Eliza Carpenter always liked this one best, even more than downward dog. Said it was good for the wrists. Strengthens them for knitting."

Lucy came forward into a high push-up. Owen swiveled his head up and around to look at her and then followed her motion.

"Lucy, breathe deeper, that's it. Move that oxygen. Good, good. Now, stay here in plank. Pulse up just an inch, take a breath, moving up between your shoulder blades, and now, breathe out, remaining in plank."

The move was subtle, and should have been barely visible, but Owen managed to make it almost a military push-up.

Toots sighed. "All right, lower yourself to the floor. And cobra, good job, Lucy. Much better than you usually do. That's odd. Owen, not like . . . Well, okay, push back into child's pose. Oh, Owen."

Lucy turned her head to the side to look at him again. This really wasn't going well.

"Maybe this isn't your thing," she whispered.

Folded forward into a truly uncomfortable-looking crunch, Owen looked at her. "You think? She's trying to kill me."

"It's just yoga. And wasn't it your idea?"

Toots snapped her fingers. "That's it. Thirty minutes will have to do."

"That's it?" said Lucy. "Really?" Usually her mom made Lucy go at least an hour, and a session taught by Toots at the local studio was ninety minutes.

"Owen's going to hurt himself." Toots's voice was sympathetic, but Lucy knew the tone. When Toots had decided something was done, it was done.

"What about savasana?" It was Lucy's favorite, the corpse pose. Really, it was the only move she was any good at.

"Fine." Toots looked disappointed. "Lie on your back, feet outstretched, hip distance apart. Hands open, close your eyes." She flopped back on her own mat, and gestured that Lucy and Owen do the same.

A minute later, Owen said, "I like this one."

"Me, too," said Lucy.

"Quiet, both of you. Rehearse for death."

Lucy snorted.

But the ten minutes that followed were excruciating. Why had she asked for this again? She should have just let her mother wrap up the session with no fanfare. Instead, Lucy was lying next to Owen, just feet apart, listening to his breathing.

And thinking about how his breathing had

been earlier, ragged and fast. In her bedroom. Oh, God. Lucy grew warm in places she had no business growing warm in, not with her mother in the same room.

Think about something else. Anything.

That swatch for Ruby's bookstore sweater. Think about how it had come out perfectly at four and a half stitches per inch, as if Abigail's yarn from Cade's sheep had been meant for the project, even though Eliza Carpenter had died two years before her nephew's yarn began being commercially produced.

Squeezing her eyes more tightly closed, Lucy tried not to think about what was really racing through her mind — whether or not she could still taste Owen on her lips. About how her hands had fit interlaced with his, during the last moments of being together, as he'd pushed into her, their eyes locked.

Later. She'd deal with that, pay for it, later.

"Enough! Owen, honey," said Toots, sitting up. "Namaste. Namaste, Lucy," Toots folded her hands in front of her and gave a quick bow.

"Was I awful?" asked Owen.

Toots nodded. "Horrible. But it's about the practice, not the execution, thank God, and I'll make you do it again sometime.

Don't you worry about that. Lucy, can you give me a ride home on your way to work? Dad dropped me off but he was going to the hardware store, and that way I don't have to bother him."

"Of course." Now Lucy had to look at Owen and deal with him sensibly, in front of her mother. "So . . ."

Toots interrupted her. "Go upstairs and get ready for work. I'll make Owen something to eat."

She took a quick shower and changed, and when she came back down, Toots had made Owen breakfast with ingredients out of Lucy's cupboards that she didn't even know she had.

"You made pancakes?" Lucy was flabbergasted. "I had them here all along?"

"I had to improvise a bit, but yes."

"Can I have one?"

Toots grimaced. "Oh, no. I only made enough batter for three, and I gave them all to Owen. I'm sorry."

Owen, to his credit, looked horrified. "I'm so sorry, I didn't know that was all there were. I would have saved two for you."

"Mom!"

"I'm sorry, hon. I forgot you were up there."

And that's where the truth resided. Toots

didn't leave Lucy out on purpose, maliciously. She never had. But a combination of Toots always being busy with side projects, important community ventures, and Jonas and Silas being bigger, louder, and stronger, meant that Lucy had always come downstairs to find the pancakes were already gone.

She sighed. "That's okay. I'll get a doughnut at work."

Toots brightened. "I'll go to Whitney's and we'll get you something really yummy, how about that? Wouldn't that be nice?"

"It's fine. Are you ready?"

Toots nodded.

Owen rinsed his dish and flipped the switch on the garbage disposal, which made a groaning, heaving noise.

"Oh, don't do that! It's broken." Lucy leaped to switch it off. "It ate a spoon and I haven't been able to use it since."

He leaned against the sink and said, "You want me to fix it for you? I'll start my handyman business with you. Maybe you can give me . . . a good reference."

And just those words, rumbled near her, reminded her of what his voice sounded like in her ear, what he sounded like when he was inside her. Lucy's knees went to jelly and she touched his elbow, trying to ignore her mother's curious stare.

"Yeah," said Lucy. "That would be nice."

"It's okay if I stay?"

"There's a tool box in the pantry."

"I'll be creative."

Lucy knew he would. Oh, God, would he ever.

In the car, her mother said, "Owen's very attractive."

Well, Lucy should have expected this. "Yeah."

"And probably really hot-cha-cha in the sack, huh?"

"Mom!"

"Good," said Toots. "I know that your dad and your brothers don't trust him, but I'm fine with him, I really am. I swear it."

"Really?" Lucy said. "You sound like you're protesting a little much. And besides, it's not serious. I'm just having fun. Doing something exciting. For once."

Of course it wasn't serious. It couldn't be any kind of serious.

Toots nodded and looked out the car window.

"You always tell everyone to have fun, Mom."

"Yep."

"You gave me those condoms."

"Honey, I just said it was good that you're having a fun time. You always take everything to heart. Weigh things out, plan your life so carefully. And I agree with you. It's time for you to embrace danger, have a fling, throw caution to the wind. Fall in love. Even if it means certain heartbreak."

"I don't think mothers are supposed to say things like that."

"Watch out for the mailman. He's going to pull out."

"I'm a proficient driver, thank you. Been doing it for twenty years."

"Just be careful."

Lucy tucked the nose of her car into her mother's driveway. "I don't understand. You want me to go crazy, get all wild. But I should be careful?"

"Are you falling in love?"

Lucy didn't answer. When she was around Owen, she wondered if she'd even really been in love before. She had no idea what she was doing.

And God, she'd wanted to talk like this, heart to heart, woman to woman, to her mother for so long. Lucy opened her mouth to ask her for advice, to ask how she'd know if, when, it was love.

But then her mother said, "Let your body have fun. But keep your heart from taking things so seriously. You don't deal that well with change, and when I look at him, I don't see his aura staying in Cypress Hollow long, so be a tiny bit careful, okay?"

Lucy wrapped her fingers around the wheel and pulled it toward her like it was the yoke on a plane, as if could pull herself up and out of the car. "There you go again. Do you want me to be wild or cautious?"

Toots went on as if she hadn't heard her. "And let me know if you want to try this new thing out that I just got for my pleasure business. It's this cone-shaped thing that you get on top of, and then I think the man positions himself behind —"

*"I will die if you don't stop right now."*

"Love you, too," said Toots as she leaned to kiss Lucy's cheek.

# TWENTY-FIVE

The best way to peek inside a woman's mind is to steal a glance into her notions bag. If her stitch markers are jumbled, so are her thoughts, I'd bet my last tape measure.

— E. C.

Owen gave the wrench one last twist and was tempted to stick his head under the cold water faucet.

Lucy was gorgeous. Even when presented with the disgusting slime at the bottom of her disposal, half his brain was still thinking about her.

Hell, she made overalls look sexy. Before he'd seen her wearing them, he would have said that it was impossible.

He rolled over and stared at the underside of the sink.

She was more than just sexy. He was in deep. Holy shit.

Owen had dated Bunny for only a year. Before Bunny, he'd been with a woman that he'd ditched after an argument over taco seasoning.

He'd wondered if he'd been broken — if in fact he'd spent so long outrunning his fractured childhood and chasing his career that he'd just never understood what his friends talked about, or couldn't make sense of the reason they fought so hard to work the long overtime hours in order to pay for the weddings, the houses, the kids that made their faces light up like Christmas trees.

And then along came Lucy.

Owen twisted himself out from under the sink and felt suddenly nervous in a way he hadn't felt in a long time.

No way in hell could she be a firefighter, paramedic, EMT, or coastal search-and-rescue *anything* that required her being anywhere that wasn't safe. At least, nowhere that he couldn't protect her. And with the way that he got around nowadays, that was just about everywhere.

Owen knew too well it was the quiet nights when things went wrong — the simple calls, an old man having a heart attack, the medic not watching his back, completely unaware that the son was off his meds and triggered by a stranger touching his father, still writhing in pain. Or a simple domestic, and the brother-in-law no one mentioned pulling up with a gun. The medics were the ones in the most danger. They weren't armed, not prepared, not trained. And in a sleepy town like this, where meth was going to be a problem, where the volunteer department did it all, combined firefighters and medics, cobbling them out of *citizens?* Hell, no.

Not Lucy.

Not after he'd found her. Shit, he couldn't even run after her right now, and he'd been the fastest in the academy.

Owen stood slowly. Goddammit, his hip hurt. This was the worst pain he'd felt since recuperation, in fact. And damn, it was worth it.

Owen ignored the fact that it was already too fucking late, that his heart was already involved. It probably had been too late since she'd kissed him on the porch of the parsonage. Maybe since she'd kissed him at that high-school party seventeen years ago, if he looked the truth straight in the eye.

He'd left his holster and overshirt upstairs in her bedroom. It took him a long time to make it up the stairs — he could barely remember climbing them last night, which was a miracle in itself. He'd kissed her on every step, he did recall that. Now he took his time with each one. Stairs were the one thing that were sometimes almost unnavigable for him, and he breathed carefully, using the banister for support.

He liked that, last night, when they'd tumbled into her room, still wrapped around each other, the immense bed hadn't been made. He didn't trust anyone who was neat all the time. The downstairs was tidy enough, but this looked like she really lived here.

Now, he saw that a pair of jeans was in the corner of the room, next to an old wooden upholstered armchair, as if she'd shucked them off over there, in front of the window. An old lamp that matched the intricacy of the carved bedposts stood next to the armchair, which looked like an ideal reading spot. He could picture her there, her legs kicked over the arms of the also oversized piece of furniture, book in hand.

A nice, safe image. See? He wasn't too sprung over her yet.

Unless she wore sexy librarian glasses when she read. Owen bit back a groan.

As he slung his holster on and then buttoned his shirt, he pulled open the closet door.

Nothing but clothes.

There. That should satisfy him. No skeletons. No ex-boyfriends' bodies, no counterfeiting supplies. *Get over it,* he told himself.

But once a cop, always a cop. It wasn't something he was going to be able to just turn off, not so quickly, not this soon.

He moved out of her room and down the hallway. In the bathroom, he took a quick peek into her medicine cabinet. Nothing but over-the-counter pain relief and three different kinds of toothpaste.

Behind the next door was a small office: a desk, two chairs, some boxes. A long bookcase ran the length of one wall.

*You're not a cop anymore.* Owen breathed more easily. What the hell was he looking for?

Pulling back the sheer curtain, he peered down into the backyard. A wooden table, flanked by four big wooden chairs, sat next to a barbeque grill. Lots and lots of trees. A small shed in the lower garden.

And a man, creeping through the yard, looking over his shoulder.

A man going toward the shed, and moving quickly.

Owen moved as fast as he could to the top of the stairs and then went down them slowly, clutching the handrail. God, that hurt. His hip protested so much he was surprised he couldn't hear it grinding through his skin, and when his knee locked, he stumbled for a second.

Fuck.

But he'd be damned if fell down a flight of stairs while a burglar broke in to Lucy's shed. He spun to the side and grabbed the handrail with both hands. He steadied himself. He was okay.

Owen felt himself switch into cop mode. The training hadn't left his body. His heartbeat wanted to pick up speed, but he concentrated on slowing all his motions, all his reactions. And thank God he hadn't stopped carrying his gun yet.

He didn't go through the rear kitchen door; that was too obvious. He went out the front door, after checking out the windows in the living room. Nothing on the street but parked cars.

Owen moved to the right of the house. The gate that had been closed when he arrived now stood open.

He consciously lowered his center of gravity. Moving slowly, he kept to the side of the house. Whoever was out here was obviously stupid, moving through the yard, out in the open. He wouldn't expect Owen, so he had the advantage of surprise.

He heard a scraping noise behind the large oak tree. The small storage shed's door stood open. Good. Just a petty burglary. Easily handled. Small-town criminals didn't want anything other than to find something of value to sell, usually so they could buy meth. They didn't tend to have weapons, since they'd already sold them long ago.

Each one caught was another off the streets. For a couple of days, anyway.

Owen ignored the protest of his hip as he eased forward, staying behind the oak. A good look around the yard showed that the burglar appeared to be alone. If he'd had any kind of lookout from the front, Owen would have already known it — the lookout would have blown the warning, and the criminal would have run.

This was almost too easy.

At the door of the shed, he paused. Waited. Listened. The person inside rummaged through something. A scraping noise. A cough.

Owen took a breath. Slowed his heart further, moving the calmness into his abdomen. Seeing it exactly as it would happen.

He broke leather on his holster as he had a million times in training drills and on the street, and his Glock filled his hand as easily as air filled his lungs. Finger next to the trigger, not on it, but close, always so close.

And suddenly, it wasn't easy anymore.

An image of Rob flashed into his mind — Rob, dying, bleeding. The report of the guns. The blue of the uniforms huddled around him, the roar of confusion, the stench of panicked sweat.

Owen's gun felt foreign. His gut clenched.

*Fuck that.*

He spun around the door and into the shed, his arm outstretched. His legs were strong, his stance unmovable.

"Freeze! Police! Hands *up!*" he roared. His voice filled the small metal shed. His finger ached to pull the trigger, and at the same time, he was terrified he would.

The man in front of him was bent over something — all Owen could see was the ass of his jeans. He dropped what looked to be a pair of bolt cutters. His hands flew up, and then he froze, his back still to Owen. A red hat, something familiar . . .

"Lace your fingers behind your neck. *Now!* Back toward me, slow. *Slow!*"

Owen backed out of the door, into the yard. "Keep coming backward toward me. All the way out of the shed. One false move and I'll blow your fucking head off." He knew his words were true. He knew now he would shoot. Fifteen years of being a cop, and he'd only had to actually fire once. And he'd shot his best friend.

"No, n-no. B-borrowing."

They all said that they were just borrowing something, picking up something promised to them.

*"Turn around."*

The man turned.

Silas. The red bobbles dangling from the end of his cap jumped.

Owen's breath left his lungs as if he'd fallen from a great height. "Fuck. Oh, fuck."

"What the *hell?*" said Lucy from behind him.

"Fuck," said Owen. There was no better word — it didn't exist. No apology was going to take care of this one. "Why didn't you *say* something?"

Silas opened and shut his mouth in what looked like fury.

Owen holstered the gun. He tried to snap the leather and found himself completely unable to manage it. His fingers felt like pieces of cold meat dangling at the ends of his hands. "Why were you in there anyway?" His voice was rougher than he intended it to be.

Lucy spoke instead of Silas. "I keep the hedge clippers in there. He was going to help my mom later. Not that it's any of your damn business."

Hell.

"So, you mind explaining what exactly is going on here?" Her voice was cold as she faced him.

"I'm sorry. I thought your brother was a burglar. I saw him creep into the backyard." Owen spoke the words, knowing them to be true, but he wasn't thinking about them. He was thinking about the fact that he'd almost shot Silas.

He'd almost shot Lucy's brother. In cold blood. An unarmed man, who'd been in a place he was legally allowed to be.

"Didn't . . . c-c-creep."

Lucy looked madder than a pissed-off yellow jacket. "I can't believe this. And I only find out because I forgot the bank drop and came back for it."

"I couldn't be more sorry. I just looked down and saw him, and I thought . . ." Oh, shit.

But it was too late. She'd picked up on it. Of course she had.

"You looked *down?*"

"Well, I was — um —"

"Looking for something? My bedroom doesn't look down here."

"I . . ."

Lucy's eyes shot ice. "The only upstairs

room with a view of the backyard is the spare room."

Owen didn't say anything. His heart was racing as if he'd run up a hill.

"I see. Find anything you like?" Lucy's cheeks went red. "You violated my privacy." She sounded more disappointed in him than anyone had ever been, and he'd let a lot of women down in his past.

"Not . . . cool," said Silas, who looked a lot more comfortable now that the gun was put away. "Wait . . . *in* your bedroom?"

Lucy ignored her brother and stared at Owen.

Owen said, "Lucy, I won't even try to offer an excuse. I'm a cop. We're nosy, and . . . I needed to know that you were legit. That everything was . . ."

She cut him off. "You *were* a cop. I think everyone but you is aware of that. The sooner you get that through your head —" Lucy shook her head as if to clear it. "I can't believe you did that. *Snooped.* And then almost shot my brother."

Lucy shook her head. "I'm going to get the bank drop. I need both of you gone when I come out."

Silas wandered toward the gate, as if to give them some privacy. But Owen held his ground.

"I'm sorry," Owen said, again. "But I think I'm so thrown by the thought of you being an EMT, fighting fires. It made me wonder who you were, I guess. I can't handle the thought of you being in danger. I don't want you to ever be at risk. Ever. I couldn't be with someone who . . ." His voice trailed off. He meant the words to carry the weight of his worry. He needed them to carry everything he meant, all of his heart. But instead they landed with the force of an anvil, and he knew he couldn't take them back.

Lucy met his gaze.

It was cool out here. He could see the outline of her nipples under the thin cotton of her tee shirt. A blue and orange college football shirt was right up there with overalls in the category of garments he never would have thought sexy. But he was wrong again. He forced his gaze to stay on her face.

"Just go," she said.

If she'd shot him in the heart, it would have hurt less.

# Twenty-Six

Patterns are good and well, but when you know how to knit, forget about them. Use them as a jumping-off place. Don't live in them. If you lose a page, take it as a sign. You always know best.

— E. C.

Elbert Romo was standing in front of the Book Spire, tapping his toes and jiggling.

"Hurry, hurry," he said.

"One of these days I'm not going to let you use my bathroom. I'm just flat-out going to refuse and let you explode out here on the sidewalk." But Lucy opened the door for him. He raced through the dark store in front of her.

"Wait!" Yesterday she hadn't put away the . . .

The postcard stand left in the back room crashed to the ground, and the next thud was Elbert.

"Goddammit! Elbert! Are you okay?"

More thuds. Lucy snapped on the lights. Elbert was already up and racing again for the bathroom. "I'm fine!" he called as the door slammed behind him.

Postcards littered a six-foot radius. There wasn't a single one that had landed with its mates. It would take hours of sorting.

Lucy couldn't imagine being in a more foul mood. She was spoiling for a fight — she could feel it in her veins.

Five days now, she'd been like this. Five days of leaving her cell phone off inside her overalls pocket. Five days of avoiding Owen.

He could have easily come into the bookstore, she knew that. He must have walked right past the door as she was inside, working. He was mere paces away, at any moment, inside Grandma Ruby's parsonage. He was inside the space she knew as well as any building in the whole world. But he must have been avoiding her, too.

The bookstore, usually a balm in times of trial, wasn't helping her. Sitting in the children's section on the cushions didn't soothe her nerves. Knitting in the craft zone when the store was empty only ended in dropped stitches. And even though Lucy knew it was probably only her imagination, her customers seemed as petulant and cranky as she was. Mildred and Greta had had a heated argument about which cast-on was better, long-tail or cable, which was unlike them. Lucy hadn't even dared to insert her own opinion, emotions had been so high.

And at the end of each night, as much as Lucy's body longed to run down the path and throw herself into Owen's arms, she walked home instead.

Lucy had taken action, had made that decision once. She'd acted foolishly five nights ago, she'd dealt out those cards. And it proved *exactly* why she didn't make rash, hasty decisions, why she kept things the same, why she stayed safely in the same box, keeping things the same way, year after year.

Because when she didn't, men pulled guns on the wrong people in her backyard. For Pete's sake.

Owen had told her she shouldn't be on the volunteer fire brigade, which meant he didn't understand her at all. That he couldn't be with someone who was. But wouldn't that be exactly what he *would* understand? The need to help? To rush in? Why didn't he get that?

And he'd snooped in her house while she was gone, which meant he didn't trust her.

Worst of all, he'd held a gun on her

brother. It would have been something she could forgive if she'd trusted him with that gun, if it had been a simple misunderstanding, if it had been what he'd said it was — a case of Owen thinking he'd caught a burglar in the act.

But Lucy had been able to read the doubt in Owen's eyes. Owen hadn't trusted himself. He'd almost shot her brother — he'd almost made a deadly error, at the cost of her little brother's life.

Lucy couldn't trust Owen. And Owen didn't trust her.

And now at the store, all her emotion didn't seem to fit inside her body, her head. She tried to tamp it down, but it boiled under her skin. She whacked her shin on the book cart that was parked in exactly the same spot it had been left in for the last ten years and cursed, violently. It didn't help.

Elbert Romo came out of the bathroom, none the worse for his tumble. "Coffee ready yet?"

Lucy sighed. "It's ready, Elbert."

Tunelessly whistling like he did every morning, he grabbed the latest copy of *People* and flipped through it, dropping the blow-in subscription forms on the floor as he walked.

Mildred and Greta came in. They smiled

at her and poured themselves a cup of coffee and sat with Elbert at the table. Mildred took out a piece of knitting that looked like it was made of plastic rope. She held it up. "Dish scrubbies. They're tearing up my hands, but you can wash them in the dishwasher to clean them!"

Greta rolled her eyes.

Mildred said, "I saw that. What?"

"I keep telling you. If it's a dish scrubby, then why on earth would you wash it in the dishwasher?"

Mildred humphed and kept knitting.

Lucy took a deep — and what she hoped was a steadying — breath. It just made her choke instead. She coughed for a moment.

Just something to do. That's what her store was to them, wasn't it? Just a place to hang out, to kill time. It was one of multiple places in town where people could find coffee in the morning: the Rite Spot usually had coffee for whatever meeting it was hosting, and Tillie's most popular meal of the day was breakfast.

She didn't even charge them for the coffee. She thought about changing that — suddenly asking for money for refills — then she thought of the sad eyes that Elbert would give her, and the soft dollar bills that Greta would press into her hand, the quarters that would slide across the countertop. They might even stop coming altogether. She knew they were all on fixed incomes.

Lucy closed her eyes and listened to the click of Mildred's needles and the scratch of Greta's pencil as she worked the crossword in the paper that she'd bought down the street at Tillie's — not even from Lucy's stack.

Whitney was probably right. They should work together. Whitney was a smart, savvy professional woman who was making a good life for herself from a small-town business.

While Lucy was losing money on coffee.

She sighed again.

Well, at least Lucy could use the time to work on the book. She brought the knitting bag full of Eliza's papers out of the back room and set it on the counter, next to the register. The ideal place to work would be at the large table, but that looked good and occupied already, what with Elbert, Mildred, and Greta all sitting there.

Lucy squared her shoulders. She was a writer now. She had a book to put together.

She had to find the sleeve part of the bookstore cardigan pattern. It would be the first pattern in the book, holding the place of honor, if she was able to find it. She set down her cup of coffee to her right side, and to her left she placed the sweater swatch; then she centered a dusty, cat-hair-covered box in front of her on the counter. Sigur Rós played on the stereo and when she looked out the narrow clerestory windows, fog that looked like gray angora fiber drifted by in wisps.

Lucy opened the flaps of the box, the last one she'd found in Owen's storage unit. The one with the mouse, or rat, or whatever it was. At the thought, hairs rose all over Lucy's body and she shuddered, but she kept going.

Three whole packets of Eliza Carpenter's notes were in the box, scattered in among old romance novels, tied with lengths of faded blue handspun yarn.

She tugged at the first knot and started to read.

Oh, the voice. That had always been Lucy's favorite thing about Eliza Carpenter, that personable voice that could never be mistaken for anyone else's. She didn't tell the reader to use U.S. size-8 needles — she asked them to find their very favorite pair of needles and adjust the pattern to suit the joy of their own hands.

It made for reckless knitting sometimes. But always beautiful.

What if she were not only to rewrite these

lovely patterns into different sizes, in standard writing, coding each the way knitters expected to find them — what if she also somehow managed to pull out the sections of Eliza's voice and leave them intact?

Lucy's mind started to race as she put pieces of patterns next to jotted notes, mixing the pages she'd been carrying around with these newly found ones.

It could be more of a coffee-table book. Big glossy pictures of the sweaters, beautifully photographed. One page of Eliza's conversational writing, facing Lucy's scrubbed-up version? Or all together at the back?

Then she wouldn't lose passages like this one:

> Once, walking along the beach with Joshua, we clambered up a high, huge rock the size of a house and sat, staring at the ocean, watching the sunset. When we turned to climb down, we found we were stranded, the water too high and dangerous to swim to shore, even though it was less than ten feet away. I pulled my knitting out of my bag. His head was cold, and he'd forgotten his hat, as he always did, so I fashioned a double-stranded garter stitch rectangle that I

put over his head, and fastened it with two cable needles. And then I did my own knitting, and by the time we got down, I had most of a sleeve, the cuff of which was stained by moss in a careless moment. I love that bit of discolored sleeve now, my souvenir of the night on the rock with my beloved.

These vignettes were tucked among her patterns, as if Eliza had just wanted to put them somewhere, just in case.

They would *be* the book. The patterns were what the world clamored for, but the parts that Lucy knew were the best were these, a non-pattern for a garter-stitch rectangle to fit a cold, loved head on an unexpected evening.

A simple, one-stitch pattern like that, vying for space next to the next one — Lucy's fingers drifted over the page titled "Seven Seas," a shawl that was separate oceans of lace joined by rivers of I-cord that didn't make any sense at all until the knitter attached the last little bit and shook it the right way, and then the shawl fell into perfect proportions to drape across cold shoulders on a breezy seaside evening.

"Genius." Lucy breathed the word. It would go perfectly with the "Cypress Hollow Lighthouse" sweater in *Silk Road,* the new companion piece. . . . Knitters would line up to make it, place it in their Ravelry queues, discuss it on knitting forums. She could see it perfectly.

Lucy pulled out another packet of yellowed, folded sheets, tied together with three or four plies of a creamy handspun yarn. Eliza's dark, spare script was the best thing she'd seen today. At least she had this. Lucy placed her hands flat on the papers and closed her eyes. She breathed in slowly. She wouldn't think of walking down that back path to the parsonage. But her traitorous cheeks heated anyway. Just thinking about him did this to her? She was pathetic. No better than when she was in high school.

Think only of Eliza.

Between a pattern for a raglan pullover and a cabled scarf was a page covered by a long paragraph.

> We had to put Old Daphne down today. She was a good sheep, my sheep, one of my very favorites. She never liked Joshua, which set her apart from the other sheep. They always love him. Instead, she was ornery and grumpy and liked only me and warm, sunlit grass. And her wool was the finest we ever

raised. Even spun in the grease, it was lovely, and when washed and carded, it practically spun itself. A breath was all it took to lock the twist, and it always plied up into a lofty, bouncy, strong yarn that over the years has made three of my most favorite sweaters, including the one I'm wearing in the barn as I write this. I'm watching Joshua clean out her stall, pretending the end of her life doesn't matter to him. But it does. He'll tell me so later, and I won't say I told you so.

Another page, a sketch of a cardigan with a crazy zigzag collar at the top, and below:

We had to call the fire brigade out yesterday afternoon.

Lucy's heartbeat quickened, and she held the paper closer to her eyes. What were the chances of this?

Joshua has a stronger nose than I, and he smelled smoke while we were having coffee on the back porch. We thought it was Hooper's controlled burn up on the ridge at first, but it turned out to be a small fire in my kitchen. It started in the electrical outlet next to the stove. I can't remember, in all my years of living on this ranch, and everything we've gone through, ever being that scared. I felt like a goose. I still do. Joshua was perfect — threw baking soda on it, when I would have thrown a bucket of water. The brigade came out, volunteers, all of them, and they tromped around my parlor, and they couldn't tell us anything that Joshua didn't already know, since he put the wiring in this house with his own two hands, but it was them being here that mattered. It calmed me down like hands on a skitterish lamb. They were exactly what I needed. I can't imagine this valley not having that brigade, and the town would be less without their bravery.

Lucy put the paper down slowly, reverentially. It felt like a sign.

A benediction.

The next page was less yellowed, and the date seventeen years past. When Lucy saw the names mentioned, her eyes moved faster across the page than she could keep up with, and she had to reread it.

Ruby thinks her granddaughter Lucy will take over the Book Spire someday, but I've told her she must let her find her own way. Give her a nudge and let her make mistakes, let her make a big mess. They're so alike, I think: Ruby never makes a single error, never shoves things around, never mixes up the colors when we're dyeing fiber until she gets a big accidental brown blob like I do. Sometimes you have to mess up. I hope they both learn that. Joshua always said I mustn't meddle, though. Let me sit here in the sun like the cat next to me and think for a minute about meddling. I like that girl and I think she's strong and a good little writer, from what Ruby's shown me, stories and poems. Maybe I'll meddle, just a tiny bit. Or perhaps I'll fall asleep in this puddle of warmth instead.

Eliza Carpenter. Writing about *her.* Lucy felt herself blush. Immortalized by Eliza Carpenter. She wanted to frame the page, and show everyone, and she wanted to keep it a secret at the same time.

The bell on the door jingled. Lucy jumped. A real customer.

"Hi, kids," said Molly as she entered the store. "How's everyone?"

Lucy smiled. Okay, not a real customer, but a friend, at least. Maybe they'd be able to talk about Jonas.

Molly hugged Mildred and Greta and kissed Elbert on the cheek and then approached Lucy at the counter.

"Here, your swift and ball winder. Thanks for the loan." Molly's voice was warm. Normal. Maybe Lucy had imagined it all the other night at the bar. Molly was flirtatious. She and Jonas were friends. There was nothing wrong with that, nothing at all.

"You're welcome. It's good to see you."

"You, too." Molly gave her a hug, hard, and she smelled of her normal citrus shampoo and jasmine body lotion. Lucy felt like she was home.

Sitting in her regular perch, the stool on the other side of the counter, Molly said, "Tell me everything. What's up with Owen?"

Lucy hadn't even been aware how much tension she'd been holding in her neck and shoulders but as she leaned in and caught Molly up on everything that had happened, she felt knots loosen as she spoke. Molly gasped in all the right places and said all the right things. How had Lucy gotten through all this without her best friend?

"Well, hell. And all I've done looking for a house for him to buy, too."

Lucy spun on her stool and hit her elbow on the cash register. "*Ouch.* A house?"

"He said he wanted me to look."

Raising her eyebrows, Lucy stared at Molly, who had the grace to look sheepish.

"Okay, okay, I might have badgered him just a little bit. But by the end, he did seem interested, and I told him I could get him into something fast. But there's actually not much moving in town right now, nothing in his price range, just a Victorian with water damage, and a Craftsman on Clement that's torn up and infested with rats."

"Oh, God."

"What?"

"That's his childhood home. The one on Clement."

Molly pursed her lips and looked thoughtful. And then, like Molly always did, she moved into devil's advocate. "Okay. So he opened a door and looked out a window. That's not cool, at all, but he wanted to make sure you hadn't killed anyone. Of course, he probably knows as well as we do that going through your things isn't going to tell him whether you're trustworthy or not."

"Why not just check my criminal record?"

"Wouldn't you mind that just as much?"

"Well, yeah, but then I wouldn't know. Victimless crime." Lucy frowned. Molly wasn't being very encouraging.

Greta said something at the table and Mildred hooted with laughter. Elbert clapped his hands, and then they huddled together again, whispering.

Molly went on, "And he doesn't want you to run into burning buildings, but none of us do. That's because we love you."

"That's because he's a control freak."

"Or . . ." Molly touched her arm. "Because he's always been the one doing all the saving. And suddenly he can't. You ever thought of that? That maybe that's his real problem? That maybe he was looking for an external reason not to trust you to make it easier to justify his feelings?"

Lucy leaned back. "That's not fair."

"And holding a gun on Silas was just him trying to regain some of what he's lost. Period. And he was showing off, just like any other man. Like when Jonas does that Tom Cruise flip of the tequila bottle before he pours a shot. Does he really need to do that? He wastes money in booze every time he does it, as the liquor hits the floor, but he does it anyway. . . ." Molly gazed up into the ceiling vaults, where the sun danced in motes of dust.

Lucy stared.

Molly was dating Jonas. She really was.

But Molly didn't seem to notice Lucy's

sudden mood change. “Lord, I have to pee. I’ll be right back. You think about that man in the parsonage. I think he’s something different, and I think you could be good together. That’s all I’m saying.”

As Molly went in the back, the door opened for the next person.

“Yoo-hoo! Hello!”

Whitney. Fantastic. Just what Lucy needed. The sour icing on one crappy cupcake of a day.

Whitney looked like Donna Reed come to life. She carried a small red basket that matched her black dress covered in red cherries. Her hair was curled so that it made a delightful flip against her shoulders. Even her lipstick was perfect: a pale, pearly pink.

“I’m just popping in to — good grief, Lucy.” Her head swiveled slowly, looking around the store, which apart from the three gossiping quietly at the table, was empty. “Where are your customers?”

Lucy’s hackles went up immediately. “It’s a quiet time of day.”

“Well, it *shouldn’t* be. The ladies’ auxiliary just got out — you should know things like their routine and be offering them something for stopping by. And after three o’clock this afternoon, the Kiwanis let out, and I usually bake them something special.

You could offer them a special discount on magazines or something. I'll make you up a list of who does what in town."

Lucy wanted nothing more than to let her knees bend, to fold herself into the small space behind the cash register and pretend she wasn't even there, but instead, she didn't. She imagined Eliza. Eliza never would have let her get away with that. Eliza had thought she was strong.

"I'd appreciate that, Whitney." Instead of tasting like ash, as she'd thought the words would, the sentence made Lucy feel lighter, freer.

Whitney grinned. "Great. I'll bring it to you. Anyhoo, I have a surprise and a bigger reason for being here than just bringing a basket of snickerdoodles. There should be . . . just behind me . . ."

She looked over her shoulder at the door, which flew open to reveal Thomasina, Whitney's sole employee, who came in carrying plates and platters of cookies and baked goods. Lucy thought Elbert Romo's eyes might pop out of his head.

Mildred and Greta started giggling. They were in on something, the sneaks. Lucy felt something sneak up the back of her spine, a warning.

Trixie Fletcher, the local reporter for the

*Cypress Hollow Independent,* came in next, mumbling into what looked like a voice recorder.

"What the hell's going on here?" Lucy didn't like surprises. She didn't even like going to other people's surprise birthday parties, because she didn't like the feeling of stress it gave her waiting for the guest of honor to show up.

And exactly *where* had Molly escaped to? Lucy realized she hadn't heard the telltale creak of the bathroom door.

Whitney placed a huge plate on the table and whipped off the fabric covering it, revealing a staggering pile of chocolate-chip cookies, steam still rising. Lucy felt her traitorous stomach growl.

Lucy walked toward the plate of cookies that called louder than the town's volunteer fire brigade siren. They smelled better than anything Lucy had ever smelled before, creamy butter and intoxicating vanilla, and deep, dark chocolate.

And even while her head screamed at her to stand up for herself, to not roll over like this at the first hint of chocolate chips, she couldn't stop herself.

Whitney was a drug dealer. That was it.

And she still didn't know what was happening. But it didn't matter.

Whitney knew it, too. She smiled and appeared totally satisfied. She pushed the cookie plate out of Elbert's reach, who already had a cookie in his mouth and one in each hand, toward Lucy.

"Still warm."

Lucy nodded and reached for the closest one.

This was the best cookie she'd ever had. It was so good that it was totally worth making nice on a permanent basis with Whitney. In fact, why weren't she and Whitney closer friends? She couldn't remember now.

"Honey," Whitney said as she put one long, slim arm around Lucy's shoulders, "You remember when I told you that you and Owen were heroes?"

Lucy choked on a cookie crumb and nodded.

Trixie walked up to them, holding the recorder almost under Whitney's chin.

"And remember when I said that you and I should partner up and do more things together, the bookstore and the bakery? Together, as a team?"

"Um . . ."

"Today is that day!"

And the marching band entered the store.

# TWENTY-SEVEN

> One of the nicest things about knitting is that you can hear all the wonderful sounds going on around you.
>
> — E. C.

Both the front and side doors burst open at the same time and a blast of noise entered as two halves of the high-school marching band played "For He's a Jolly Good Fellow," meeting to convene in between Self-help and Literary Fiction.

"Whitney's Bakery brings a hero's celebration to the Book Spire, in honor of Lucy Harrison and Owen Bancroft!" shouted Whitney over the music.

"Are you *insane?*" Lucy yelled.

Whitney beamed as Mildred, Greta, and Elbert climbed carefully up onto the nearest bookstore pew, holding onto one another, to watch. The marching band filed in, filling up the children's section. The tuba player took out a spinner rack of Richard Scarry books without noticing.

Behind the band, a line of people entered the store. First came Lucy's family — all of them. Toots and Bart, huge smiles wreathing their faces. Her father, in particular, looked as if he might fall right over, his chest was so puffed full of pride. Lucy knew it was all for her. And in the midst of a wave of what felt like near panic, she realized she'd never, ever seen her father look like that before. A lump centered in the middle of Lucy's chest and then moved to her throat, and when Whitney put her thin hand in hers, she clutched it gratefully.

Behind her parents came her brothers. Jonas winked at her and stood behind their mother near the metaphysical section. Silas winked at Whitney — *Whitney?* — and stole a cookie from the table before grabbing a book from the gardening section and starting to read.

More people flowed in. It was as if Tillie's and the ice-cream shop and the drugstore had been tipped on their sides and emptied all at once into the Book Spire, as if all of Main Street had been lured in by the scent of Whitney's baking and the oompah-sound of the band which had now switched, for whatever reason, into playing the theme song from *Rocky.*

Then Cade MacArthur entered, carrying little Lizzie on his shoulder. Behind him came Abigail. A cheer went up as she entered.

Lucy went even redder than she already was. She felt her hand going clammy in Whitney's, but Whitney held tight.

"Just a second, honey, the other guest of honor should be coming in . . . right . . . *now!*"

The side door of the transept opened again, and Molly entered, looking triumphant. Behind her trailed Owen, and Lucy's heart leaped in a way that almost hurt. The deep blue cabled — but store-bought — sweater he wore matched his sea-swept eyes perfectly. His limp seemed a little more pronounced, and his face seemed tired.

Lucy's heart pounded harder.

Across the room, over the low shelving next to the counter, over the table stacked with baked goods, past the heads of people seated on the reading pews, they locked eyes, and it was as if all the air had been sucked right from the huge room. Nothing existed but the two of them.

For one second, time and sound stopped. Lucy only heard her own breath. His lips moved, and she longed, with everything within her, to fly across the room and press her mouth against his, to bury her face in his neck, to feel his arms come around her. She stared at his eyes, his mouth, the plane of his jaw, the side of his neck. Maybe it was the cookie, the taste of chocolate still filling her mouth. Maybe it was the way the morning sun lit up the tops of his cheekbones. Lucy couldn't remember it ever being so *necessary* to be near someone, to the exclusion of everything around her.

Instead, she wrested her hand from Whitney's and held her own elbows, tightly. Her stomach knotted as she turned her head to look at Abigail and Cade, who beamed in her direction. Then they stepped up into the reading nook. They were higher now than anyone else except for those standing on the pews, and they raised their hands for silence.

"Everyone! Thank you for coming," said Cade. "This wouldn't have been possible without Whitney's Bakery, so thanks for that, and Trixie, thanks for getting the word out in the paper so we could all show up."

Lucy resolved to never miss a day of the *Independent* again.

Abigail, wearing a green handknit sweater that couldn't disguise her huge pregnant belly, stepped forward. "Owen? Could you come stand up here with Lucy? We promise we'll make this short. Neither of you look like you're breathing."

The crowd laughed, but Abigail was almost right — Lucy's breath got shorter the closer that Owen came. When he was standing with her, when she could smell the scent of his soap and something that was uniquely, perfectly him, she bit the inside of her mouth.

She stole a glance at him, and his eyes met hers. Something in his gaze looked broken, and he glanced away quickly.

Lucy felt empty. Alone, surrounded by everyone she knew and loved.

Abigail and Cade held hands as baby Lizzie made a loud crowing noise that wowed the crowd.

None of this seemed fair. She couldn't even remember if she'd brushed her hair this morning. Surely she had, right?

Crap.

And Whitney was taking photos, the flashbulb popping. Of course she was. Just like at the party in high school. All Lucy needed was to throw up on everyone, and the circle would be complete.

Abigail grinned and said, "Everyone knows that we named our daughter Lizzie after my mentor and Cade's great-aunt,

Eliza Carpenter. That name was easy. Well, we've been at a loss for what to name our next child when he or she arrives. We've spent some late nights arguing about who's more right than the other one. But after that day almost a month ago, when these two angels pulled me out of a burning car that I was trapped inside, the decision has become clear to us. If it's a boy, we're naming him Owen. And if we have another girl, she'll be called Lucy." Tears filled Abigail's eyes and her voice broke. "And we couldn't ask for finer, more heroic names than those."

Lucy felt her own eyes fill with hot tears and saw a suspicious sheen in Cade's eyes, too, as he stood next to his wife on the steps. Sniffs in the crowds told her she wasn't alone.

"And if it turns out to be a girl, then Owen gets to pick the middle name. And vice versa," said Cade. "That'll keep it fair. Thank you, you two, for saving the life of my wife. She means everything to me. She *is* my life." He cleared his throat and dropped a kiss on top of his wife's hair. "Now, you two, is there anything you'd like to say? Lucy?"

Lucy just shook her head. She wouldn't have been able to speak around the lump in her throat, even if she'd wanted to.

Cade nodded. "Okay, Luce. Owen? How about you?"

Owen said, "Thanks for . . . this. You didn't have to, though." He stepped forward, and Lucy could only see the side of his jaw which clenched before he went on. "Lucy may have a burning need to save people, after watching her grandmother die in front of her, but I've gotten over it during the course of my career. Honestly, you save some, but you lose more. The good guys die, and the bad guys get away. Nothing personal, but it didn't matter who was in that car. Coulda been a child molester or a murderer, and we would have dragged him out, just the same."

Whitney dropped the cup of punch she was holding. Toots reached for extra napkins and started mopping up the pink liquid while Owen kept talking.

Lucy dug her nails into her palms and felt fury rise in her chest. This wasn't fair of him, and not kind at *all.* If Cade and Abigail wanted to thank them, even if they didn't want it, the least they could do was accept it, even if they hated it. She willed words to come to her, something that could ease the sudden tension that crackled under the high ceiling, but she was still unable to move her vocal cords.

Cade looked confused and hastened to wrap it up. "Well, anyway, we sure appreciate that you were there. Both of you. That's all, folks. Now, everyone get some of Whitney's great baked goods and buy some books from Lucy!"

In the crush of awkward hugs and congratulations, Lucy was pulled away from standing next to Owen before she could formulate the words she was searching for, and in the next half hour, she lost track of him altogether. When the Book Spire finally emptied of everyone except Molly, almost two hours later, Lucy walked through the store, stooping to pick up dropped napkins and stray receipts.

Owen was gone. Again.

Oh, the *gall* of him, to bring her grandmother into it! And to make Whitney, and worse, Cade and Abigail, feel stupid about their sweet surprise plan.

Fine. Whatever. What an ass. How could she have ever seen anything in him? Lucy kicked the side of the trash can by accident as she tried to lift the bag out and stubbed her toe so hard she saw stars. *"Shit."*

"You okay?" said Molly, tucking another paper plate in the bag.

"No."

"Where did Owen go?"

"I don't *know.*"

"His speech was weird. But do you think that baby-naming thing will help you work it out with him, though?" said Molly with a saucy wink. "Double date? With me and Jonas?"

"Molly, no!" Lucy's voice came out even more horrified than she felt, and that was saying something.

Molly's smile fell away. "All right. We need to deal with this, *now.* Which is the part you hate more, exactly? The part with you and Owen? Or the part where your slut friend is dating your brother?"

They stared at each other.

Lucy opened and closed her mouth, and then said, "You're not a slut. You just sleep around. A lot."

Molly gave a high screech and clenched her hands into fists. "What is *wrong* with that?"

"Nothing! There's nothing wrong with that!" said Lucy. "But he's my brother and I just don't want —"

"— him to get hurt. Obviously," said Molly. "In the meantime you're about to lose your best friend if you keep this up. You need to think about what you're saying, and I'm not kidding here."

"I . . ." There was so much to say Lucy

didn't know where to start. She loved Molly, so much. But for Jonas? For sweet, injured Jonas? She didn't want to hurt her friend, but how could she make Molly understand that Jonas wasn't ready for her? "He's just so . . . Look, Molly. You're an erotic novel."

Molly cocked an eyebrow and a hip at the same time. "I'm porn?"

"No, they call it erotic. It's totally acceptable. It's hot. It sells, and it's good stuff. Well-written and fun. Very, very popular. But Jonas, he's an inspirational romance. Maybe historical. Like on the prairie. He's looking for marriage material. Someone for the long haul, someone to help him . . . pull his tractor or something." Lucy's voice trailed off.

Molly's mouth opened and then snapped shut. Her freckles stood out in sharp relief on her angry face. "I hate to break it to you, Lucy, but that's not what he wants pulled. He's looking for someone to screw on my back-porch swing while I'm giving people instructions on how many baby aspirin to take for their chest pain in Cantonese. Then he kisses me and goes home. He's the best lay I've had in years and the kindest person I know, and we're not looking for anything right now but fun, and I would have shared that with my best friend if she'd been able to get the stick out of her ass for even one second." Molly's façade was broken only by the sheen of tears in her eyes, but not a drop fell. "Call me if you grow up a little bit, okay? I need a friend. Not judgment."

Lucy felt sick as she watched Molly leave. And there was nothing she could say as she stood there, more alone than she'd ever felt in her life.

# TWENTY-EIGHT

> Knit like you love — with your heart, hands, body, and soul.
>
> — E. C.

Parking in front of Willow Rock, Owen sighed.

His mother was the last item on his list. As usual. But on any given day, being with her was the roughest, and longest, part of his day. Could anyone blame him for putting it off as long as he could?

Owen shouldn't have left the bookstore. He should have insisted on staying with Lucy. But he'd been so stupidly stunned by the way he'd felt standing next to her that the instinct for flight had kicked in when that crush of people had set upon him, when all he'd wanted was to hold her, to put his arms around her. And at the same time, he was so mad at her — that she'd even consider placing herself in danger, putting herself in places where he couldn't follow her. Sure, it was the twenty-first century, and women were just as good as men when it came to being heroes. He knew that. He'd worked alongside women on the force who were head and shoulders better than any men he knew at their jobs. But when it came to Lucy . . .

When he imagined her running somewhere when that pager went off, someplace that he couldn't go, where he couldn't help? Unarmed? Impossible. Even if it made him an asshole of the first order, *he* was supposed to be the rescuer, the hero. Didn't she know that?

But after all that, he still just wanted to take her to bed and keep her with him, safe and warm. And if it moved to hot and bothered . . . Okay, so sex with her was the hottest he'd ever had. Every time he thought of her, he had to balance his concern with his lust.

But she wasn't just a good time, a great lay. Lucy was so damned much more than that.

That was the problem. She couldn't be more than that to him.

Not when he had nothing to give her.

He'd been running errands all afternoon since the surprise marching band . . . *thing,* trying unsuccessfully to drive Lucy's dark eyes from his mind — maybe searching his mother's chest of drawers for more tissue-wrapped shit would distract him.

In her room, his mother was showing Miss Verna a piece of knitting.

"Sleeve," she said.

"Mmmm." Miss Verna nodded.

"And heel."

"Are you making a sweater or a sock, Irene?"

His mother scowled and put the knitting under her pillow.

But Miss Verna grinned at Owen as she slipped past. "She's feisty today. Your visitor did her good yesterday. Get hcr to wash her hands, would you? It's almost dinner."

"What do you mean, visitor?"

"You know, that pretty girl. The short one. You put her on the list." Miss Verna looked suddenly worried. "Lucy?"

Owen said, "She came? Already? To see Mom?"

"Was here all last night, knitting with your mother. Kept her quieter than I've seen her in months, and she's been in a good mood all day. Now get her hands washed for dinner, if you don't mind. It'd be a help."

Owen nodded, trying to picture Lucy seated in this dark room with the drapes always drawn, leaning over his mother whose breath was probably not so fresh. "Hey, Mom, wanna wash your hands?"

Irene drew the knitting out from under the pillow again and focused on it, bringing her nose dangerously close to the sharp tips of the needles.

"Mom?"

Dammit, where had she gone? She'd been right there a few seconds ago. "Mom. Please. Get up. You need to wash your hands. Almost dinner."

Glancing up only for a second, Irene hissed. "I'm *knitting.*" But the yarn wasn't moving through her fingers anymore.

Owen rubbed his eyes with his hand. He leaned on the wall.

How did people do this all day? How did people manage this at home, taking care of the people they loved without help? They were fucking saints and he wasn't worthy of being in the same room with them. He wasn't even good at being able to handle this for a small part of every day. Couldn't even do *this* right.

"Mom. *Now.*"

She ignored him.

He had an idea. Probably a stupid idea, but it was all he had.

"Hey, Mom. Would you help me wash my

hands? Please?"

Irene looked up, and it was as if she had put on a different face entirely, as if she were a different woman. "Always had dirty paws."

In the bathroom, Owen stood next to her, the water running over their hands. "Like this?"

"Let me, let me. Lather, lather."

Irene's hands were still strong, and she rubbed the soap into his, turning them so that she didn't miss a spot.

In the mirror her eyes met his. They were his mother's eyes again. Without thinking before he spoke, Owen said, "Why didn't you ever leave him, Mom?"

Irene looked into the sink. "Didn't want to go."

It *was* his mother. She was here for the moment. "But he lied. And hurt you. All the time. And he had nothing to give you. *Nothing.*"

"Love is love is love." Irene sounded disgusted with him. But at the same time, her hands never slowed, still pushing and rubbing his under the water.

And Owen, in a blinding moment, got it. Even if his dad had had the world's shittiest way of showing it, his father had loved his mother. And Owen was rocked to the core as he realized for the first time in his life that his mother had loved his father back.

And as she scrubbed Owen's hands with hers, her arthritic, knobby fingers cleaning his as they had a thousand times when he was young, he understood something else: Irene loved her son, but she would never say it.

She'd chosen his father that awful night. But she'd put his father in jail when it mattered, and she'd always loved her son.

Owen leaned hard against the toilet tank as the truth sunk in. "Thanks, Mom. You did a good job," he said gently.

"That girl needs the boxes."

Owen said, "What?"

"Eliza boxes."

*"Lucy?"*

"For her. Eliza's boxes." It was a long string of thoughts for his mother, and the words were sharp.

Owen's brain stalled like a car running out of gas.

"Mom, do you —"

The water was getting colder, and Owen added more hot. He'd be lucky to have any skin left, but Irene's pale eyes that met his in the mirror were completely clear, without shadow.

"Mom, do you mean the boxes in your storage unit?"

"Eliza made you socks. She always said you'd come home. To me. To her." Then Irene looked down and said. "Clean. All clean."

Owen dried both their hands on the scratchy white towel hung on the rail. "My hands are clean now. You did a wonderful job. And I'm home now, Mom."

He beamed at his mother, and Irene gave him a shaky smile back. The shadows were back again, behind her lids. "Turtles."

"You bet," he said. "Turtles are totally where it's at."

Not tonight. Today had been too much, and he'd been a royal asshole at the bookstore. No surprise there. Tomorrow. He'd go to Lucy tomorrow. They'd probably never know what Eliza Carpenter had meant by leaving those papers with his mother. But it was enough that she had.

And love was love was love, according to his mother. God knew Irene Bancroft wasn't the best model for romantic bliss, but maybe telling Lucy what his mother had said about Eliza would be enough to gain a small fraction of forgiveness, to earn back a small bit of her trust. He hoped to God it would.

Because it hit him with the force of a bullet. Bancrofts weren't good at this. Owen was in love with Lucy Harrison, and he was scared to death.

# Twenty-Nine

Use a bright light to look for moth holes. Face them head on. Admit that you have a very, very serious problem. You might have to have a wee cry. I wouldn't blame you.

— E. C.

Lucy slept fitfully that night, fighting through dreams of tubas blaring and babies crying. She woke, wishing the bookstore were open, but it was Monday. Of course, she was the owner. She could open the Book Spire if she wanted to. But that would be admitting failure somehow, and she grimaced at herself in the mirror as she brushed her teeth.

She could handle a day off, right? She wasn't some crying fool, sick to the gills over some guy, lost and brokenhearted.

Why did it feel so much like she was, then?

Lucy eschewed making her own coffee in

favor of heading for Tillie's for breakfast. She pulled on the same dang pair of old overalls, Ruby's bookstore cardigan and blue-and-green Keds. She made sure the fire-department pager was in her pocket — she had duty for the next twenty-four hours.

"If it ain't broke, don't fix it," she muttered to herself, as she pulled her door shut behind her. Mr. Kento across the street looked at her in surprise. Yep. Now even the neighbors who thought she was semi-normal would think she was batshit crazy, finally gone 'round the bend and talking to herself. Just as well.

As she sat at her booth in the diner while Shirley poured her coffee, Lucy fought back tears. There, at the front of the restaurant, was a big flyer advertising tonight's intro class for the next session of the volunteer fire brigade training. Captain Jake Keller's smiling face beamed down on the diner patrons, and even the handlebar mustache someone had penciled in on the poster couldn't detract from the commanding presence he had. VOLUNTEER. SAVE LIVES. CHANGE YOUR OWN.

She loved volunteering with them. It was part of who she was. Sure, it was a sleepy town, and in the last four years, she'd only been able to actually help on a few fires, and usually she only did rehab on them — fire watch, handing out sandwiches afterward. Mostly the pages that went out were handled by the people actually paid and on duty — the volunteers handled backup. But she *had* handled real medical calls. Difficulty breathing. CPR, those few times, and it hadn't been like it had been with her grandmother. She'd known what to do, she'd trusted in her training, and in the volunteers at her side.

But Owen didn't trust her, obviously. Not to help people. He'd actually said that, in her backyard. He couldn't be with someone who put herself in danger, he'd said. Because she might hurt herself? Or someone else? Which one did he mean?

He'd said once that he thought she was brave. Guess he'd changed his mind.

*Damn.* She'd even chased her own best friend away, for God's sake. She had no idea how she was going to fix that, or even if she'd be able to.

She remembered seeing Owen's hand shake, the gun still in it, still pointed at his brother, and wondered if he'd felt the same way. Too late. Too broken.

What if they'd just screwed everything up so badly there was no going back?

Lucy ate her eggs without tasting them

and choked down half a piece of toast. At the back of the diner, a small group of women waved at her. Lucy waved back — she sometimes knitted with them on lazy Monday mornings. Betty, a rather new knitter and already a very good spinner, smiled and held up a promising-looking scarf. Janet, a local superstar known for her imports of luxury fibers, raised an important-looking eyebrow and winked. Mildred and Greta, always present at most of the local knitting groups, blew her a kiss each, but Lucy just paid her bill and slunk out of the restaurant, shooting the group an apologetic smile. She just couldn't handle small talk right now. They'd ask about Owen, she knew they would, and if even one of them hugged her, she'd come undone, and she *wouldn't* cry now.

No. No crying. Absolutely not.

Outside Tillie's, two seagulls squabbled over half a bagel, one pecking the other viciously, the other not giving up, beating and flapping its wings in a great show of loud force. Lucy shooed them, using her feet to drive them apart, then she broke the bagel into two pieces, throwing them in opposite directions.

"Gah," she said, looking at her fingers. The Rite Spot's doors were open. The bar, even at this hour, probably had a patron or two. She'd use Jonas's restroom to wash her hands, and maybe use the opportunity to ask her brother what he thought he was doing, if he was even thinking at all. God knew someone in this town should look before they leaped.

Or how about just not leaping at all? How about staying nicely in one spot where it had always been safe, how about that?

Jonas was behind the bar reading a book. For once he wasn't moving, not cleaning, not wiping anything down.

Lucy held up her hands. "Washing! I'll be right back."

When she came back out, she tried to get a look at the book Jonas was reading. "What's that?"

Jonas looked up and pushed the book beneath the counter.

"Was that . . . ? You didn't buy that from me; I'd remember. If you bought that on Amazon, I'll burst into tears, and you don't want that. This is not my day." Lucy meant it.

"No, no. It's just . . . I borrowed it. Not my normal thing." He held it up a J. R. Ward vampire suspense.

"Those are fun. Dark and scary."

"Don't tell anyone."

"Nothing wrong with them."

"If you're a *girl.*"

Lucy shook her head. "You're right. Absolutely. I forgot. You're such a vapid specimen of a man that reading a romance is obviously going to turn you into a female. Well, good. I always wanted a sister."

"Shut up."

"They're good books."

Jonas leaned forward and lowered his voice so the old man at the end of bar wouldn't be able to hear. "They're *great.* They're like candy. I can't put them down. Molly gave me one the other night at her house, and I'm totally hooked. This is my fourth already."

Perching her bag on top of the counter and leaning a hip on a bar stool, Lucy took the only opening she might get. "About that." Then she took the J. R. Ward book out of Jonas's hands and smacked him, hard, along the side of the head, before putting it back into his hands.

"Dammit! What was that?" Jonas rubbed his ear.

"What the *hell* are you doing with my best friend?"

"None of your damn business!"

"It *is* my damn business if both of you get hurt and come crying to me and I have to decide which one to have lasagna night for, and my lasagna isn't even that great, but it's the only comfort food I make, which'll mean I'll have to eat it forever and ever while you two rotate through my house on alternating nights."

"Or we'll be fine. She's a big girl, Lucy."

"*I know.* That's what worries me. I love her with all my heart, but she's the Big Bad Wolf and you might be . . . Well, you might be carrying a basket in the woods. Do you have any idea . . ."

"How many men she's been with this year? Last year?" Jonas nodded. "I have a more current tally sheet than you do. Molly doesn't tell you everything, you know that?"

Lucy sat up straighter. "She does, too!"

"No, she doesn't. She tells you four of five. She says you flip out regularly on the fifth so she leaves him or her out."

*"Her?"*

"Well, she usually leaves all the hers out when she's talking to you. Hang on."

Lucy took the 7UP Jonas slid to her while he went to serve a couple of beers to some truck-driver-looking types. She looked across the bar at her own reflection in the mirror, but quickly looked away. She had no idea whether or not Jonas was successful or not with his business. She'd always supposed he was, but she realized now that it was possible he was hanging by a thread. Maybe he was scared. Maybe he had a hard time trusting himself. Maybe she hadn't been looking hard enough at things that mattered, maybe not for a long time.

Was it always about control? And what the heart wanted?

Funny, last week, when she'd made love with Owen, as soon as she'd reached for him, even while she'd felt like she was spiraling out of control, she'd known exactly what she was doing. What she was choosing. What she was doing with her heart.

That was the worst part of it all.

Her stupid heart.

Jonas was back. "So what's all this really about? Is this about you and Owen?"

Lucy scowled. "Of course not. Besides, you hate him."

"Yeah. But I'll get over it if he's what you want."

Eying Jonas suspiciously, Lucy sipped the 7UP, feeling the bubbles on her tongue. Then she said, "I don't believe you. You're trying to trick me so I'll leave you alone about Molly."

"I don't think he's going anywhere, that's the thing. And I watched how he looked at you yesterday during that party Whitney threw at your store."

"How? What do you mean?" Lucy leaned forward.

"He looked at you . . . Okay, this is going to sound wrong, no matter how I say it, so I'm just going to say it, okay?"

Lucy nodded, hard.

"I don't even know if you remember. You know when Dad was on that trip to New York and there was something wrong with his plane, and it went down, but everyone was okay? And then he flew home and we picked him up at the airport? You know how Mom and Dad looked at each other?"

Lucy swallowed. She *did* remember, of course she did. She'd been clinging to her mother while they ran through the terminal, but then the gate's doors had opened and Toots had dropped her hand and covered her own mouth with a cry like Lucy had never heard before. And then her father was there, and her parents had looked at each other before running through the crowd to embrace, as if they were home.

It was the look she'd always measured everything else against. Butterflies beat inside Lucy's chest.

"He looked at you like that. No matter what he was saying, that's how he looked at you."

"Oh." The butterflies turned into sparrows that turned into something bigger, brighter. Something necessary and essential and scary as hell.

"And quit worrying about me and Molly. We're fine."

"But . . . you know she . . ."

"Eats men for dinner and spits them out behind her as she walks away. I know. But Lucy, have you maybe considered that that's all I want? Friendship and a fuck?"

Lucy's eyes widened. "Jonas! You don't talk like that!"

"We're just having sex, Lucy. No strings. For either of us."

"That's what you say, but — you want a girlfriend! To get married again someday! That's what we want for you!"

"No strings, Lucy. That's what we both want. And it's okay for us to do that. It had been a really long-ass time for me. I love Molly as my friend, and she's incredible in bed."

Lucy held up a hand. "There's a line that I can't cross in discussing sex — anything in regards to you. Or Silas. Or our parents. *Ew.*"

"And she's still my best friend."

"So when she sleeps with someone else, you'll be fine."

"I like hearing about it when she does."

Lucy put her forehead on the bar. "Oh, my God," she mumbled. "You are such a better Californian than I am. Where do you all go to school for this?" She raised her head. "Seriously? Is there a number I can call? I don't do drugs. Would wearing Birkenstocks assist me in my enlightenment?"

"How about not being a jerk about it, huh? Just try to support us both." Jonas's voice grew serious, and he put both his hands down flat on the bar between them. "Molly's really mad at you, kiddo. I don't know how you're going to fix what you broke between you two. But sometimes you just have to trust the people you love."

Owen's face flashed through Lucy's mind.

In a small voice, she asked, "With all that . . . in mind. If you don't know where anything is anymore, how anything works, how can you be sure that what you need will still be there when you open your eyes?"

"You don't. Sometimes it's not there when you look the second time. Sometimes it's just gone. And sometimes you get hurt." Jonas raised his hand to brush the hair from her face. "And then you move on. You always do."

Lucy took a deep breath and released it slowly.

Then she said, "I have to call Mom. But hey, I have books five through the end of that series at the store. Make sure you get them from me, not some internet retail giant. Okay?"

# Thirty

A little knitting shores you up.
It always does.

— E. C.

Toots answered on the first ring, and of course she wanted Lucy to come over, she said, but yes, there *was* something Lucy could pick up on the way over. An apple galette from Whitney's Bakery would hit the spot, wouldn't it?

Lucy closed her eyes. It was her punishment, she supposed. Just what she got. She wanted her mother — and the universe wanted her to pay for the comfort up front.

Lord, even the cutesy font on the bakery sign bothered Lucy, all lace curlicues and cotton-candy paint. The front window was done up with half curtains and doilies. Maybe Whitney was going for French chic, but it really came off looking more like French bordello from the outside.

Right. She'd be quick about it. Get this over with.

Lucy pushed open the door. She did it briskly, with authority.

And promptly knocked over a little old lady standing on the other side of the door.

"Oh, my God!" Lucy pulled the door back toward her, to the outside, the way it should have been done anyway, now that she saw the big Pull sign.

"I didn't see you!"

The old lady moaned.

"Are you hurt?" asked Lucy.

"No, it's just my pies . . ."

Whitney pushed Lucy aside. "Mrs. Irving. Oh, dear. Are you injured? Do we need to get help?"

Mrs. Irving held up her hand. "I'm fine. Don't be ridiculous. I'm quite cushioned, and I didn't hurt myself. Someone take my arm."

Whitney, still looking darling although presumably she'd been actually working, helped Mrs. Irving up. "There now," she cooed. "Are you all right? I'd hate to think that you'd even hurt just one tiny muscle. Everything okay?"

"I'm fine, dear. But I do think my pies are ruined."

Lucy scrambled to try to pick up the

boxes that littered the floor. There were four of them. Two were upside down, and one was on its side. She'd just assume all those were done for. "Look," she said, picking up the last box triumphantly. "This one might have made it. See?"

As she held it up, the bottom of the box ripped and the cherry pie dropped to the ground, its cherry contents splashing to the floor and back up, splattering onto the counter, the glass case, and Whitney's dress.

"Shit!" Lucy said.

"Language!" said Whitney. "Mrs. Irving, you just get on home. I'll personally deliver four fresh pies, no, make it five for your trouble, in the morning. I'm sorry you won't have any tonight, though. Any cherry on you, dear? No? She just got me, I see. I'm glad none hit your clothing. Off you go, I'll see you first thing."

"Very sorry!" Lucy called as the door swung shut.

Whitney turned to face Lucy and said, "Nice job."

"I *said* I was sorry. I didn't see Mrs. Irving there."

"She's wide as a barn, which is the only thing that prevented her from breaking a hip."

"I was in a hurry. I'll buy a pie, though, if

it helps."

"*You'll* buy a pie? Don't you need five? And if you want to buy another one for yourself, that's fine by me."

Lucy sighed. "Fine. Whatever. And I'll take an apple galette, too."

Whitney said, "Oh, I suppose you really didn't mean to knock Mrs. Irving over. But I wouldn't turn you down if you offered to dry-clean my dress. It'll be ruined if I don't get it treated professionally."

Lucy grimaced. "Of course. Tell me how much it costs."

"I'll just add another twenty to your bill here. That should do it. Just call it a nice round hundred and ten?"

"Dollars? Are you *kidding* me?"

"Well, fifteen each for five pies and one apple galette for you, plus twenty for the dress."

Lucy ground the words out from between her teeth. "Will you take a check?"

"Of course, silly! I know where to find you if it bounces. Now, let me get your galette."

Lucy concentrated on making her handwriting clear. While she was paying for her sins, she might as well go all the way. "Thank you for the nice party yesterday, Whitney."

Her voice rang out from the back room.

"Oh, darling, you're so welcome! Wasn't that fun? We should do more things like that! Together! Don't you think?"

Gritting her teeth, Lucy signed her name, pressing so hard that the paper ripped a little. "I think once was probably enough, but it sure was . . . fun."

Whitney's gleaming curled bob popped out from behind a rack of cinnamon buns. "Didn't you have a good time?"

"Well, of course I did . . ."

"Lucy. *Oh,* I was so proud of you." Whitney put the white box on the counter, and then came around and embraced Lucy tightly in a hug that smelled of chocolate and butter.

Lucy extricated herself as carefully as she could. "I didn't do anything."

"That was the point, you goose. It would have been so easy for you to have done nothing. Like you've always done. Just like *most* people do. You've always kept everything the same, haven't you? Just like your grandmother did. But that night, you did something, you saved Abigail. And now, with me, you're moving ahead with your business. And as businesswomen in our town of Cypress Hollow, a small town traditionally run by the good old boys, I'm proud of us." Whitney raised her fist. "We are women with a mission! Hear us roar! We shall not be moved!"

"I think you're mixing your metaphors. Or your marching slogans or something. I don't want to change my business, Whitney."

"Oh, come on, sure you do. It's exciting, isn't it? You're a writer now, as well as a bookseller. People already love us in this town, and as a combined force, we'll only do better!" Whitney was pretty all of the time, but she was really gorgeous when she smiled like that. Lucy felt a headache starting, just looking at her.

"Why are you on my side?" The words were out of Lucy's mouth before she could stop them. But she meant them — wanted the answer, even though it came out sounding wrong. More and more lately, she'd found herself drawn to Whitney. What had she missed all these years? Had an actual friend been hiding next door to her all this time, and Lucy had been too busy being caught up in old, tired drama to notice? Was that possible?

Whitney's smile slid sideways. "Oh, Lucy. Never mind. Thanks for the check. I'll lock the door behind you."

"I'm sorry." Lucy *was* sorry. She hadn't meant it like it had sounded and she wished with her whole heart she could take it back.

"No, you're not."

"Whitney . . ."

"I'm not after you, you know. I'm not out to get you."

Lucy shook her head. "But . . ."

"When I proposed having a night where our businesses merge, like a cookbook night here or a cupcake night at your bookstore, guess what? It was because I want our businesses to succeed. *Both* of our businesses." Whitney picked up a napkin holder and then set it down. "I'm a good businesswoman. I might even go a step further and say that I'm a great one. I could retire in two years if I wanted to, did you know that? That's how lucrative sugar and flour has been for me. But I'm not going to, because I want to do even more. I look around our town and I've seen a lot of closed stores and shuttered windows, but the only store that concerned me was yours. Because we went to high school together, and because sometimes, every once in while, I thought we might end up being friends. Finally."

"Whit—"

"But guess what?" Whitney raised her hands and then dropped them. "I'm done. I won't be bugging you anymore."

No, Whitney didn't understand. "In high

school, though, you remember that night at the party? Haven't you hated me since then?" Lucy clung to the edge of the countertop.

"*In high school?* The night I took that picture, the night you threw up? You know I threw up, too, about two miles down the road? We were all drunk, and we were all stupid, and we were all kids, and we've all forgotten about high school. We aren't the same people. We've all grown up, Lucy. For God's sake. It's time you did, too."

Lucy felt desperate. "No, you don't get it. . . . It's all changed. Molly, and Jonas . . ."

"Are sleeping together. I know. And guess what? I'm taking advantage of your other brother. And what's more — I like him a lot, too. Didn't see *that* one coming, did you? No, you never do. Now get the hell out of my shop, little girl. Come back when you grow a pair."

# Thirty-One

When you think that the knitting is all that matters, it's time to put it down and look up to see the person sitting on the couch across from you. You may have forgotten who you're knitting for.

— E. C.

She was right. Whitney was right. Everyone had grown up. And Lucy was still wearing the same shoes she'd been wearing in high school because she was too scared to change them.

As she walked to her mother's house, the world's most expensive apple pie dangling from a pink pastry bag in her right hand, she thought about the Book Spire and what she was doing with the legacy her grandmother had left her.

Whitney and she *would* work well together, especially if they combined the cooking/reading thing. It was hot right now. People would love it. Whitney was smart.

Lucy knew — she'd known for a long time — that she could be doing more. She could set up a better online presence. And there were book clubs that wanted to meet at her store, but she'd been happy to send them over to the Rite Spot instead. What was wrong with her? There were other nights she should be hosting. She had the room — why not have knitting nights here? Abigail had her knit groups over at her store, but there were other knitting groups in town, the ones that Lucy belonged to, not to mention the crocheters and quilters. For that matter, Toots was always looking for other venues for her various klatches, as well as her tarot groups, her spiritual cleansers, and her meditation groups.

Lucy had been a fool. Her family had always thought she was scared of trying new things, and they were right — she was. Anything a little different, a little out of the box, and Lucy hid her head in the sand, lest she do something wrong, make the wrong decision and cause the worst to happen.

But Lucy'd been as scared of losing the store as she was of losing people. And now she'd lost Owen *and* Molly, and suddenly, in light of that, the store didn't seem to matter at all.

She'd probably make a hash of the Eliza Carpenter book, too. Who was she, to try to pull together a new Eliza book? What right did she possibly have? Why were Abigail and Cade allowing her? It was ridiculous.

Lucy wished the pager would go off in her pocket. Give her something to run toward, something that she would know how to handle, something she could *do.* But it remained stubbornly silent.

The first few raindrops of a spring storm rolling in off the ocean hit Lucy's face as she turned to walk down her mother's street. She blinked the drops away. She tripped over a crack in the sidewalk and only caught herself by windmilling her arms. Panting a little, she stopped and turned, the Eliza papers tucked in a knitted bag under her arm. The small town spread out along the shore, blooming against the low, spitting clouds. She knew every roof down there, and as always, her eyes rested longest on the spire of her bookstore.

Home.

And the gray roof behind it, the parsonage.

She hurried faster to the only other place she wanted to be.

"Mom?"

Faintly, she heard her mother's voice from

the backyard. "Out here!"

Toots was lying on the chaise longue outside.

"It's cold out here, Mom. And it's starting to rain."

"I love it. Gives me a chance to wear the sweater I just finished." It was a stunner, all right, pink chenille with embroidered green . . . what were those things?

"Wow. Snakes, huh?"

Toots grinned and sat up. "You like them? I thought they were quirky."

"That's a good word for them."

"Is that my apple galette?"

Lucy nodded and thrust the bag toward her mother.

"Isn't Whitney a genius baker? She can't do anything wrong, can she?"

"Did you know . . ." Lucy's voice trailed off. "About . . ."

Toots nodded smartly, approvingly. "About her and Silas? Of course. Don't you think it's sweet? Silas, finally getting a girl, and *what* a girl. Good for him."

And then Lucy burst into tears.

Toots was many things as a mother, and preoccupied was usually part of the equation. But her shoulders were the best shoulders Lucy had ever known for crying on, and she sat inside her mother's embrace as they rocked in the cool air.

"There," Toots said into Lucy's hair. "There." She didn't ask questions; she just held on.

Long minutes later, Lucy choked back the last sob, her cheek against a chenille reptile.

Toots said, "A little better?"

Lucy nodded and hiccupped.

"It was your father's and my thirty-ninth anniversary last week."

"I'm sorry, I forgot!" Check off yet another thing Lucy had screwed up.

"Not your anniversary, is it? You're not supposed to remember." Toots touched the tip of Lucy's nose with a finger. "Your father reminded me of what twitterpated fools we'd been, and how our energy had thrown things off for a while. In our first two apartments, clocks would never keep time right. Always went too fast, even when they were plugged in to regular house current. Just being together caused things to break. So many negative ions."

"Mom, come on."

Smiling ruefully, Toots said, "Sometimes love doesn't run smoothly."

"What if it doesn't run at all? What if someone does something that breaks it?"

"Did you lie, cheat, or steal?"

"No."

"Did he?"

Lucy shook her head.

Toots gave a small humph. "You want some hot chocolate?"

Lucy nodded again.

In the kitchen, Toots hummed while Lucy got out her knitting.

"Pretty yellow," said Toots. "So much lovely stockinette. So relaxing."

"It's Grandma's sweater, in Abigail's yarn." Lucy paused while she held it out.

Her mother kept humming.

"I don't think I'm the right person to edit the Eliza patterns and put her book together."

"I saw Irene Bancroft at Willow Rock last Christmas, when we were caroling, and she said something about boxes that should be taken to the Book Spire. I didn't know what she meant, didn't even remember she had a son Owen's age. Didn't pay much attention to her, to tell you the truth. I was just sad she seemed so lonely. But I do know this: the only thing that made Eliza happier than knitting was love."

Lucy's heart raced. "What?"

Toots dropped a flotilla of marshmallows on top of the hot chocolate and set it in front of Lucy. Then she added even more to her own.

"Well, I guess we'll never know what she was thinking when she left the papers there. Her being dead and all. But sometimes I wonder . . . if she didn't think that you and Owen might hit it off . . . You just never knew with Eliza."

"Oh, brother. Why not just have a séance, Mom?"

"Oh!" Toots clapped her hands and leaned forward. "We *do* know Miss Potts on Beach Road."

"I was *kidding.*"

"Shoot." Looking disappointed, Toots sat in the chair opposite Lucy. "Are you in love with him?"

Lucy clutched the needles so hard they bent a bit. "Yeah, Mom. I am. Crazy in love."

Toots smiled. "Good. Accept that. Revel in it. I'm glad."

"But it's broken. Mom, we're two broken people, and it's not easy like you always say it is. I can't just . . . wave a magic wand and work on my aura or buy some magic beans and it'll just be fine."

"So you have to *fix* it," proclaimed Toots with a flourish of her hands.

Lucy buried her face in her hands. "How?"

"We can just do a little hypnosis, honey." Toots looked at her as if it were the most natural thing in the world.

"*Mom!* No. No way."

Toots raised her hands to her hair where the curls were frizzing around her face. "Okay, okay, fine. I'll come up with something. Give me a minute." She reached for Lucy's bag. "Oooh! Can I take a look at her papers, honey?"

Fine. Lucy let her change the subject and drew out a random pile for her mother to go through.

While her mother flipped through pages, dipping in and out of the notes and patterns, Lucy knitted. She was going to have to rethink where to start the raglan to make Eliza's rough notes work. She was thinking of making it a spring cardigan. If only she had the sleeve instructions. She didn't trust herself enough to just make them up. It wouldn't be an Eliza Carpenter sweater if she did that. It would be a hybrid, and that's not what she wanted. But she'd been through all the boxes now, and she didn't think the missing page was going to show up. Lucy made herself a note and then knitted a few rows.

*Knit through everything.* Eliza's motto. She'd take it for her own now. Lucy wouldn't think of Owen or of everything she'd lost, and she wouldn't think of the look on Molly's face as she'd run out of the bookstore yesterday.

How could her heart hurt this much and still keep beating? How could her hands keep knitting?

Knit through everything. Even after she'd screwed everything up so badly she'd never get the skein of her life unknotted.

But the sound of the house was comforting, as always. Her father collected clocks, so the four in the kitchen ticked companionably, never quite on the same exact beat. The heater clicked on automatically, and the house *wooshed* as the furnace started. Was this small garter edging going to be enough to keep the piece from curling? Oh, well, blocking would cure all ills, just like Eliza had always said. And the crocheted edge would also help. When Owen's dark eyes crept into Lucy's thoughts, she resolutely thought about small pearl buttons instead, ignoring the sharp stab of grief.

As she turned the row again, her mother made a small noise. Was she crying? Granted, her mother cried at the drop of a double point, but it always undid Lucy.

"Mom? What is it?"

Toots wiped her cheek and held up a yellowed piece of lined paper. "Have you seen this one? Oh, we have to give this back to them."

Shaking her head, Lucy reached for it. She'd seen it but hadn't read it. "I knew it wasn't Eliza's hand."

"Read it. Oh, read it now."

The script was in pale blue ink, and some of it was smeared.

*November 4, 1969*

Eliza,

Were it not for you, I'd be gone. M would be alone, and I would be somewhere far away, brokenhearted and bereft. The world itself told us we were wrong, that we were unnatural. Even, perhaps, evil. Even though we knew we weren't, knew it with every fiber of our beings.

So we hid.

And when that rumor started and blazed (oh, but it was true! The worst kind of rumor), we considered leaving, packing our bags and heading for a different town, where no one knew us. But M is so attached here, her roots so deep, that she would wither and die anywhere else, and I felt it was my responsibility to leave, to protect her, to save her.

You, my dear Eliza, when you stepped

into our house to knit with us, when you invited us out with your knitting friends, when you included us, together, you changed everything. I stopped mentally packing my bags every time I heard a whispered comment behind my back, and I stopped worrying about bumps in the night.

And last week, when you asked in front of all those women what day we celebrated as our anniversary . . . Well, this isn't New York. We hear about people marching for rights, and we'll never do that. We used up all our bravery when we moved in together as roommates years ago, and we were about to run out of that little which we'd held in reserve against emergencies.

Last week, we left your home with our heads held high. You included us. You've always loved us, but you included us in the conversation that day, and your friends followed your magnificent lead.

We are validated by your friendship and we remain eternally in your debt,

G.

Toots clapped her hands delightedly and wiped away another tear. "Isn't that just so Eliza? If she couldn't matchmake a couple, then at least she could help keep them together."

Lucy shook her head. "Who is this?"

"You silly thing. Think."

"All I can think of are Mildred and Greta, but they're not . . ." Lucy's hand flew to her mouth.

"You didn't *know?*"

"I just thought . . . I thought they were best friends."

"Well, of course they are. In the same way your father and I are best friends."

Lucy's knitting slipped from her lap, and she caught it by the working yarn. How on earth could she have missed that for all these years?

"You know," her mother continued. "In the sleeping-in-the-same-bed way, the having-sex way."

"Mom! I get it!"

"In the way you and Owen —"

"Quit it!"

"Are you uncomfortable with them being gay?"

"Of course not. Who do you think you raised?" she said.

Toots nodded, with patience in her eyes. "That's all right, then. I can take clueless. I can't take bigoted, but clueless is just fine."

Lucy looked at her knitting. She thought about her mother and father, happy in the same bed for thirty-nine years. Mildred and Greta, happy, presumably, for decades, and Lucy, because she didn't see change, because she'd seen them as friends since her childhood and had never seen fit to revise that vision, had no freaking clue about their happiness.

Lucy officially knew nothing about other people's relationships. She wasn't allowed to judge anymore.

But she could try to understand. And she could ask the question that had been bothering her for the last week. She took a deep breath. "Mom. In high school, did you ever . . . preempt a letter to me from Owen?"

Toots glanced sideways at Lucy and then back down at the papers. She didn't pretend not to know what Lucy was talking about. "I wondered when you'd ask me that. I didn't open it, I can promise you that. I'm not a snoop. But still, it wasn't my proudest mothering moment, and I've regretted it. But I had heard he'd left town, and I didn't think you needed the distraction. I threw it away. It was your senior year, honey. And you were so preoccupied with thoughts of him. I didn't think you'd ever get over that boy — it hurt you so much when he left."

"Oh, Mom. I wish you hadn't done that."

The corners of Toots's mouth quivered.

"I'm sorry. And then the others, your other boyfriends. They kept leaving. I wondered if it was my fault somehow — I should have worked outside the home, made you a latchkey child, more independent. Or something . . ."

"Oh, stop. Don't cry. You did everything right." Lucy just needed to move forward. "Mom, I need your help."

Oh, she didn't know if this would work. This might just be too much. It might be *way* too much.

Toots pushed the papers to one side and sat forward on the edge of her chair, the tears still welling. "My sweet little radish. Anything."

"I need to buy some . . . things."

"Things?"

"From you."

Toots brightened. "Sex toys?"

"*Gah.* Can you please go get your trunk or bag of tricks or whatever it is you have? And if you tell Dad I'll have to kill myself. Probably with a butter knife. Positively, absolutely. So never, ever tell. This is not a dinner story, capisce?"

Toots made a locking motion in front of her lips and threw the invisible key behind her. Then she stood up. "For you and Owen? Yes?"

Lucy groaned and covered her eyes with the half-knitted sleeve. "No. For Molly. And whoever she wants to use them with. *Please* don't ask."

"Darling. I don't judge. I just hope she picks Jonas and that he has a good time. I have something he'll like, in fact . . ."

Lucy wondered if it was possible to die of embarrassment.

Or of hope.

# Thirty-Two

Always be brave.

— E. C.

Lucy carried in the big brown Trader Joe's grocery bag and thumped it down on Molly's kitchen table. Molly wasn't home, but thankfully, she had Molly's spare key for times exactly like these.

Times when she needed to scatter sex toys all over her best friend's table, willy-nilly.

Well, willy, at least.

Lots of them.

Lucy started at the top of the bag and worked her way down. First the dildos. They ranged from small to large, seven of them. There was a purple one, a blue one, two pink ones, and two that looked way too realistic for Lucy's comfort. Did they have to have simulated veins? Was that really necessary? One was double-ended and Lucy couldn't figure out for the life of her the logistics of it. She quit trying after a moment.

Lucy stacked them like Lincoln Logs on the table and then stood back to look. They looked more like dog toys than sexual items, like those Kongs people filled with dog treats.

Next came the nipple items. There were vibrating nipple clamps, ones with feathers, ones with chains. Nipple oil that heated when blown upon, and tiny little clothespins that looked like they were supposed to hang up doll clothes, although Lucy supposed they weren't. Not with that packaging.

Then the little pink whip and the black paddle with the heart cut-out — it was kind of cute, in its own way, Lucy thought. Not that she'd ever have sex again anyway. Without Owen, what was the point?

At least Molly might have fun.

She laid the pièce de résistance on top of the stack — a butterfly-shaped remote-control operated vibrator. Bright purple, it gleamed at her like a wicked Jell-O mold. It looked like it wanted to have fun, like it was ready. If it hadn't been Lucy's mother selling the product, she would have wanted one herself. Just in case.

Lucy stepped back and admired her handiwork. It looked like a dirty display window in Molly's kitchen, next to her spice rack. The only thing missing was a flashing sign advertising LIVE NUDE GIRLS.

The side door opened, the one that led to the garage. Good, just in time. Molly was home. This was going to be the apology to end all apologies. If this didn't prove to Molly how sorry she was, then she didn't . . .

Molly entered, followed by Janet Morgan and her husband Tom, all laughing and shaking off the rain.

"Oh, holy hell," whispered Lucy as she moved to stand in front of the tower of sex toys.

Molly's mouth opened and shut, just once. Then she put her head to the side and rested her fingers along the side of her nose, as if she had a headache.

"We just finished looking at a loft on Skyline and we were going to talk about the comps. Would anyone like a glass of wine? I know I would."

"That sounds great," said Lucy. "A big one."

"Darling," purred Janet. "That *is* a big one, isn't it?" She lifted the largest purple toy out of the pile and held it up for Tom to see. "It'll match the rest of our collection, won't it, lover-boy?"

Tom, a cowboy from the top of his worn

hat to the tips of his scuffed boots, blushed. "Janet. Stop. We'll leave these girls to . . . whatever it is they want to do." He ducked his head and didn't look back up.

Janet put the toy back on the table with obvious regret. "It does seem you have certain interesting *things* to discuss, sweet-hearts. Molly, call me tomorrow. My sheep-wrangler isn't going to go for the loft unless we get a compost heap somewhere along with it, you just know that." She kissed the air on both sides of Molly's cheeks and gazed at both of them with admiration. "If I was a bit younger, I would have a*dored* this generation's freedom. Not as if I didn't have enough of my own, you know . . ." She followed Tom, leaving a wake of expensive fragrance trailing behind her.

As soon as the door shut behind them, Lucy dropped into a kitchen chair with a wail. "I'm sorry! I'm so sorry. I didn't know."

"The biggest commission of my career. Janet Morgan. The cashmere mogul?"

"I know who she is! I've knitted with her at Abigail's place and at the Monday group at Tillie's and I'm still scared to death of her. And I could have killed her by accident. Death by dildo avalanche."

Molly snorted. "Is this supposed to be

some kind of apology? Is that what all this insanity is?"

Lucy looked down at the overflowing table and sighed. "Yeah."

Molly gave a short giggle. "It's good." Then she laughed. "It's really good."

Lucy smiled, her heart leaping hopefully. "It is?"

"Yeah. This is an apology I can get behind. And in front of." Another gale of giggles. "And on top of."

"Stop!" Lucy could feel herself going even redder than she had at her mother's house, which was hard to imagine. "I just wanted to say this: You can do what you want."

"Lucy." Molly's voice was soft, and the laughter died away. "Honey, I love you, but I don't need your permission."

"No, no, that's not what I meant. I mean I know that you, as a grown-ass woman, can do whatever, and *whoever,* you want, and if my brother is one of them, then he must be pretty damn special to be picked."

"He is, Lucy. You know he is."

"And you're my best friend. Nothing changes that. I'm sorry I was the biggest ass there could possibly be."

Molly's eyes sparkled as she looked at the table. "You were an ass. But you're forgiven, my little vixen. Your mother must have *died* and floated up to heaven when she got out all this stuff."

"Why are you sure I went to her?"

"Because, dollface, there's no way in hell you went to a store for this. You would have needed me for that, and I wasn't around to help. Now, there are a few things here," she lifted up a particularly lurid purple toy that was curved to look like a dolphin leaping, "that I already have in my stash that perhaps you can use? I don't need duplicates, after all."

Lucy took a deep breath. "No, thanks, I'm good." She smiled and felt tears fill her eyes. "Don't make me any more beet red than I already am."

Molly leaned forward. "And what about Owen?"

Lucy shook her head, the lump in her throat preventing her from speaking for a moment.

"It can't be that bad."

"It is. We messed things up too badly. Yesterday, at the store, when he said those things, that's when I knew. He's seriously over me. And honestly, if he feels that way about what I do with the fire department, I can't be with him, either." Lucy looked at the black-and-white tile of Molly's kitchen floor and her heart fell into her Keds again.

"He's gone." Her voice broke. "But I don't know what to do about this pain."

Molly's mouth twisted sideways, and then she put her arms around Lucy.

Lucy took a deep breath and leaned into her best friend. "At least I have you," she said.

Molly said, "Oh, honey. You always have me."

Lucy let the tears come.

# Thirty-Three

> And always, in knitting, as in life, have an open mind. You'll see there might be another path open to you, one you almost missed. Stockinette never looked so good from a garter-stitch road, did it?
>
> — E. C.

Huddled under an oak tree in the rain, Owen stood outside the firehouse, his heart in his hands. Okay, it wasn't his heart, it was a Ziploc container of homemade chicken tikka masala that he'd made himself, but it was the best he could fit into plastic. Owen had wanted to make a great dinner, something interesting, different. Something people didn't get every day, something with flavor, depth, richness. Something romantic, full of spice and passion.

Owen didn't have much else to offer Lucy. It wasn't lost on him that his life echoed his father's a little too closely at this point. No job, an old Mustang, and soon he'd be in the process of repurchasing the same damn house his father had owned. He'd talked to a delighted-sounding Molly on the phone an hour ago, and she was getting the wheels in motion for him to buy back his mother's house.

Again. The same house he'd sold for her when she'd gone into Willow Rock. He was buying it back at a fraction of what he'd sold it for, thanks to the recession, and it would be his first big project in Cypress Hollow — he'd fix it up and use the before and after photos to launch his handyman business. As long as there weren't too many stairs in a project, he could do almost anything, he knew he could.

And he'd repair his mother's garden, bring the roses back to life, and on sunny days, he'd bring her from Willow Rock to sit in the garden. Maybe, just maybe, it would be like she'd never left. He could hope, right?

Owen could become a part of Cypress Hollow again.

And most important, Lucy would see that he was serious as hell about all of this. About staying. About her.

Owen would wait all night if he had to, holding the container in his hands. Tonight was the first night of the new recruits' training for the fire brigade, and Molly had told him that Lucy always helped with the classes. When the class let out, she'd come out, and knowing Lucy, she'd have stars in her eyes from helping someone learn something new and exciting.

It was still terrifying, the thought of her being on the department. His stomach churned thinking that at any moment, anywhere in this little town, an old man could drop his cigarette onto his couch and set his whole house on fire, thus putting Lucy's life in danger. *Lucy's* life.

But maybe, if he took his time about it, he'd bc able to talk her out of it. He wouldn't try to force her. That was the wrong approach with Lucy. But maybe, with the horror stories he'd stored up over the years, and he had a million of them, he could convince her that she'd be better off safe with him, not running around all over town, chasing after car crashes and gas explosions and house fires . . .

And he hated the niggling jealousy he felt, low and deep inside, that she got to run toward the problem, while he would always, from here on out, have to stay behind.

But Owen was going to work like hell on getting over that feeling. He was. He knew everything depended on it. He took a deep breath to even out the nerves that jangled electrically through every part of his body.

He could see the tops of their heads in there milling about, the meeting over, and if just the force of his will could drive those citizen rookies out, they'd be flying out of the building as if shot from the end of a fire hose. He hadn't seen her, yet, though. She was probably still at the front of the class. Helping someone learn something extra. That would be like her.

There, he could feel that dumb-ass grin again. He loved her. Hot damn, he'd finally realized it.

He wasn't stupid enough to think it would be easy. He'd broken her trust, and he knew that it would be hard won back. Lucy was smart, tough, and strong. His equal, in all ways. But he'd do what it took to prove that he was worthy of her.

Of course, figuring it out while he'd been with his mother was one thing. Knowing it inside the parsonage was just fine. But knowing it here, when she was about to face him with those cool, beautiful dark brown eyes, accepting that she was just as likely to blow him off with a few well-chosen words that would turn him into tiny pieces of jelly quivering on the ground, well, it was taking all his remaining courage to stay here, standing up, holding his damn cooked chicken in a plastic bowl, holding it tight so that it didn't drop, because, fuck it all, it was all he had to give her.

Those stars in her eyes would dim when she saw him, he knew that.

But God, if he showed her this container of tikka masala, and maybe if they sat in the Mustang near the water, where they'd had their clam chowder, and if he took his time, maybe he had half a chance. Okay, a tenth of a chance. He'd take those odds. He'd take any odds at all.

If he told her he loved her . . .

His gut churned as the front doors opened, light and laughter spilling out into the rain. Everything that had ever happened in his life depended on this moment. He was more frightened, more alive than he'd ever been before.

Just her. Owen waited for Lucy.

He recognized some of the people who came out of the firehouse by sight, and some of them looked suspiciously at him from under the edges of their umbrellas. Owen knew that old familiar feeling of being sized up, being categorized as Hugh Bancroft's son, and relegated to either being not important enough to being thought about again, or the opposite, being worrying enough to warrant constant vigilance. What was he doing out here? Lurking in the dark?

Owen, perversely, found himself enjoying it. He hunkered deeper into his leather jacket and shrouded himself further into the overhang of the oak tree he was leaning against. The man who ran the hardware store who thought Owen had stolen paint from him every time he'd come in as a teenager — Owen had never stolen more than a couple of penny nails, to prove a point — hurried his wife down the sidewalk.

But then Tony Castello and Charlie Foscalina, two of the old ranchers from up the valley, came out, eyeing their new pagers suspiciously. When they saw Owen under the tree, they jerked their heads in greeting, something they didn't bother doing for anyone who hadn't lived in town at least twenty-five years. Owen tried to be cool in his chin-nod back but felt inordinately gratified.

And then Jim Younger, the town vet, came right up to him and shook his hand, telling him it was a good thing to have him back in town, and that Molly had told him he did odd jobs — was there a way he could build a shelving unit for his files in his new extended office next month? Was that something he did?

Owen nodded. "Hell, yeah. I'd love to."

"Great," Jim said, struggling as his umbrella blew inside out. "That would be great. Can you get me a quote? Just for the bean counters, you've got the job. I don't care, I just want it done fast."

Owen had the feeling his new life was starting, and the only part of it that mattered still had to walk out that door.

He waited until the flow of people flowed to a trickle. Then no one. Just that fire captain, Jake Keller, who pulled the door closed and locked it, with him still inside.

"Wait!" No matter how fast Owen tried to move, after standing under the tree so long in the cold night air, his hip hurt too damn much to get rolling quickly. So he yelled louder. *"Wait!"*

Through the glass, Jake looked up in surprise. He unlocked the door and pushed it open a crack.

"Help you? If you're here for class you missed it by a long shot."

"Looking for Lucy Harrison."

Keller frowned.

"Owen Bancroft. You picked up my mom the other night in that old house on Clement. Lucy was with us. She was supposed to be here tonight and then we had a date after." Okay, that stretching the truth a bit, but Owen was getting worried.

Jake lifted his wide palms, face up. "Your guess is as good as mine. Better, probably. She's usually my right-hand man at the orientations. Missed her tonight. You tell her that when you find her, okay?" The door shut with a cold thud.

"Well, hell." Owen looked at the stupid container of chicken. "What next?"

The front of the Book Spire was dark. It didn't stop Owen from prowling the back alley, though, to see if Lucy was perhaps in the back of the shop, in the storeroom. But the lights were out back there, too.

Actually, now that he noticed it, everything was dark. The streetlights were out, and he glanced down Main to the one stoplight down on Oak. It, too, was dark. Must be a power outage from the storm. Owen used the small Maglite on the end of his keychain to light up the back of the alley. If Lucy was inside, she'd have lit a candle at least, right?

Should he go to her house? Was that pushing it? At least the Book Spire was literally on his way home to the parsonage, and he could justify poking around.

But looking into the windows, he could

see she wasn't there. He'd blown it again.

Right now, he knew kids were studying in Tillie's for their upcoming SATs (if they had their generator working), and he knew the local ranchers were already asleep in preparation for getting up at four in the morning, and he knew that skaters on the pier were probably illegally jumping off benches in search of the perfect height, rain notwithstanding.

And he was alone.

*"Dammit."* Owen threw the tikka masala into an open trash bin that sat between the bookstore and Whitney's Bakery. It exploded with a loud *thunk* that made him feel worse. He was an idiot.

He should just go home and rest. He was cold and wet, and it would probably help if he were able to sleep at all, but sleep had been elusive. Even when he felt most exhausted, as soon as he closed his eyes, all he saw was her.

Lucy.

The woman of his dreams. His heart.

In the alley next to the bookstore, Whitney's purple Phrosting-mobile was parked near the back door of her bakery. The headlights had been left on, and he waited for a moment to see if she'd just arrived, in case they were automatic and would shut off shortly. When they didn't, he tried the car doors, but they were locked. Great.

The back door of the bakery had been propped open with a milk crate. He knocked, but no one answered.

"Hello?" he called. The door was heavier than it looked.

"Over here," a high, flirtatious voice called.

Weaving around huge bags of flour and stacks of boxes, he navigated through the dim interior using his flashlight. He went through the door on the left, toward where he'd heard Whitney call out.

And he found her. She was mostly naked, propped up on a marble slab that was lit by flickering candles. Naked, that is, except for the frosting.

Whitney was decorated like a bachelor's party cake. Red frosting formed a tiny bra, and pink frosting served as panties. A white frosting necklace framed her throat. She wore silver high heels, and had her ankles draped over an enormous mixing bowl. Candlelight danced across her body, flashing against the silver dragees in her belly button.

Owen could think of three health codes being violated, and he bet that was only scratching the surface.

"Jesus Christ!" Whitney screamed as she hurled herself off the worktable. "What the *hell* do you think you're doing?"

"Expecting someone?" He tried unsuccessfully to silence his involuntary burst of laughter.

"Sure as shit not you! What do you want?" Whitney breathed hard. She held an empty paper flour bag in front of her, attempting to wrap it around her body. She had pink frosting in her hair from her mad rush off the table. She reached out her hand to steady herself on a stool. Then she gasped.

A roar came from behind him, and Owen was body-tackled before he could spin around. Twisting on the ground, he struggled to roll to his back so he could have a fighting chance at getting in a punch.

"I'll kill you, you son of a bitch!" Silas, Lucy's brother, saying more at one time than Owen had ever heard him say before, hit him in the face. Owen saw a flash of light behind his eyes and felt the impact snap down his spine. He shot his fist up into the air and managed to connect with what felt like a jaw.

Silas yelled again. Apparently, he thought getting Owen in a headlock would be a good idea, which was fine by Owen. He hadn't taught fighting in the police academy for five years for nothing. Owen waited for his time, until he was in a good position. Silas took a breath and started to say something.

But before a single word left his mouth, Owen swept his left leg out and to the side. Silas's feet were kicked out from under him. He released his hold on Owen, and crashed to the ground, where Owen pinned his arms behind him.

Leaning forward, he said to Silas, "Are you gonna try to hit me some more? Or can I let you go?"

Silas muttered something against the concrete and then went limp under his hands. Owen released his hold.

Whitney's paper wrapper shook as she stared at them. "What's going on, Owen?"

Silas growled something unintelligible and wiped blood from below his nose.

Owen said, "You left your damn headlights on, Whitney. I was looking for Lucy. Can you put on some damn clothes? Silas, I'm not interested in your girlfriend, so you can chill the hell *out.*"

Whitney held up a finger. "Neither of you move a muscle. I mean it. Not a hair on your head, and don't say a word." Her voice brooked no argument.

Whitney disappeared with a bag into a side bathroom. While she was gone, Silas and Owen stared straight ahead, both breathing hard, neither saying anything. Whitney came out three minutes later, looked perfectly composed in a pale peach dress and matching heels. Not even a trace of frosting gave her away.

"Well, all right boys. Silas, it appears as if this date is over, although I'd love a rain check. Owen, Lucy rushed in just before I closed and she picked up a box of brownies, said she was taking it —"

"Yeah, yeah," Owen interrupted her, "to the fire brigade meeting. But she didn't go."

Whitney frowned. "No. She said she was volunteering her time teaching knitting at an old folks' home. And she asked if I wanted to be part of it with her, to provide the treats if she provided the books. She wants to get Abigail in on it, too, to bring the yarn. And I thought it was the oddest thing, since we'd had a fight earlier in the day, and I thought she'd never talk to me again."

Owen narrowed his eyes at her. Could he trust her? Jesus Christ, she'd been covered with powdered sugar a few minutes ago. But hell, he would head to Willow Rock, on the off chance Lucy was there, as fast as the old Mustang would get him there.

Silas picked his red earflap cap up from

where it had fallen under an industrial-sized mixing bowl, pulled it tight down onto his head, and then stuck out his hand. “Sorry, man. Mix-up.”

“ ’S okay.” Owen shook Silas’s hand. “Could happen to anyone.”

# THIRTY-FOUR

Knitting lessons aren't for the
faint of heart.

— E. C.

The first thing Lucy thought when she saw Owen stride into the lobby of Willow Rock was, *Finally.*

Then she thought, *Too damn late.* Her legs, which had been shaking for the last ninety minutes, threatened to go out, but she rushed to the front door and folded her arms in front of her chest.

"Where the hell have you been? Why haven't you answered your cell phone? We've been trying you for an hour and a half."

Her fingers hit the silence button on her pager, which had been beeping nonstop for the last fifteen minutes as it called in the volunteers for the search. She should probably just take the batteries out and save herself the trouble.

Owen gave her a wild-eyed look, and she didn't blame him. Two police officers spoke quietly to Miss Verna and Janie, who were filling out paperwork behind the desk. Everyone in the lobby, including herself, was soaked. The power had just been restored, and under the fluorescent lighting, they all looked like drowned rats. Lucy knew she was freezing, but she couldn't feel it. Not yet.

"Tell me what happened." Owen pushed past her, his gaze already fixed on the staff.

Lucy grabbed his arm. She'd be damned if they took the heat for this. It wasn't their fault. That was the worst part.

"It's nobody's fault but mine. They had nothing to do with it."

"Where *is* she?"

"Everyone's already out looking. We'll go back out, too."

"The house? Have they been to her house?" Owen pulled his cell phone out of his pocket and flipped it open. "*Shit.* I turned it on silent when I was here earlier. I always do. I forgot to turn it back on."

"The cops have been to her house, and I went, too. I searched every room, and the garden, too. She's not there, Owen. Or anywhere in between here and there."

Owen covered his face with his hands and scrubbed, hard. "I don't get it. How did she get out?"

One of the officers approached him. "Owen Bancroft?"

He nodded.

"Officer John Moss. We've got six officers searching and our K9 tracking now. The dog's scented toward the river, but with the rain we're not sure about the trail. You have any idea about where she might have gone?"

"No." Owen's voice was strangled. "If she's not at her old house, I have no idea where she might be. How did she get *out?*"

Lucy threaded her fingers through a hole in the left front of her sweater. She felt it ripping, the yarn running even more than it already had, and she didn't care. "We'd been knitting together. She was doing great. Not talking much, but just knitting along. This was my second time coming to see her." Oh, God, she didn't want to tell him. She'd lost his mother. It was the worst thing she'd ever done. Lost a person. *His* person.

"And then?" Owen's eyes burned into hers.

"I went to the bathroom down the hall — I didn't want to use hers. It seemed to upset her when I opened that door. So I just went down there for a minute, but when I was gone, the power went out, and Janie called out for me to come get a flashlight, and when I got back to her room with the light, she was gone."

"In the rain."

"Miss Verna said they put an alarm on the side door since the last time she got away, but with the power being out, it didn't sound. And the backup battery failed."

Owen dropped his head back, staring at the ceiling. "She got out."

Pressing her lips together, Lucy nodded.

Miss Verna came around the lobby counter and stood in front of Owen. "Mr. Bancroft," she started.

"Don't call me that," he said.

Lucy started. Was he going to scream? Yell? How bad was this going to be? She bit back tears for the hundredth time since this all started.

"But . . . I'm so . . ." Miss Verna held out her hand and Owen caught it in both of his.

"I'm just Owen, you know that. I've never been Mr. Bancroft to you. My mother is sick. Very sick." Owen's voice was professional, firm and direct, and Lucy got the feeling that this must have been how he'd sounded when he'd been on the job. "You can only do the best you can. You can't control when the power goes out, and you can't be everywhere at once. She doesn't wear a tracking device. We'll go out and find her, don't you worry. Just stay by the phone for when we call you, and take care of Janie and the other residents, can you do that for me?"

Tears were streaming down Miss Verna's face by the time he finished speaking. She nodded, and then she pulled him into her arms, pressing her cheek against his. "Go find her. I love her, and I'm sorry."

Lucy bit the inside of her lip and took a deep breath. Then she said, "I'm coming with you."

Owen looked at her, and she couldn't read what was in his turbulent sea-dark eyes. He didn't say anything, just nodded.

The inside of his car smelled of wet leather — the windows steamed almost instantly. Owen cranked the defrost without saying a word.

Was he too furious to talk? Could she blame him?

"Do you have any idea where to go first?" she asked.

"Not a clue," he said. He rolled his window down and shined his flashlight with its surprisingly strong beam into the bushes they passed. "Just driving."

He still didn't sound angry, though. Lucy

didn't get it. She didn't get *him.*

"Owen, I can't tell you how sorry I am." It was all her fault. Miss Verna hadn't been actively watching Irene because she'd known Irene had been with Lucy. Safe with Lucy.

Owen shrugged. "Shit happens."

"You can't just say that. It's not that easy."

"You know what?" He looked at her for a moment, and Lucy's breathing quickened in the darkness of the car. "Sometime it is. Sometimes life just goes wrong, and there isn't anything anyone can do. You had to go to the bathroom. Not a crime. The power went out because of the storm, no one's fault. Mom got out. Now we find her."

How could he be so calm about this? Lucy wanted to scream. She wanted to cry. And she wanted, more than anything, for him to pull over, turn off the car, and take her in his arms and kiss her senseless, but she knew that was the most stupid thing she could want — there was no time for that, and worse, she knew the divide between them was too broad. He'd made that perfectly clear at the bookstore.

She sat straighter and held tightly to the seat belt, looking out her own window into the rain.

"Why were you there, and not at the

brigade orientation? I saw that captain, and he didn't know where you were."

Lucy turned in surprise. "You went there? I'm always at those meetings. I'm good at those, good at motivating recruits. But I figured it was my turn to take a break. I left Jake a message at his office, and I guess he didn't get it. But doing something like teaching knitting, doing something in combination with Whitney, working on my business at the same time . . ." She fiddled with the fraying edge of the seat. "I suck at that. And I'm working on things I suck at."

"You could get hurt."

Her head swiveled so fast her neck hurt. "Teaching knitting?"

"Trying to save lives. In this podunk town where the closest trauma center is a thirty-minute helo flight away."

"So you're telling me I can't?" Words were coming to her now. She had to get them right. And no one, not even Owen, would tell her she couldn't do something.

Not even if it meant losing him.

"Shouldn't, I said." Owen's voice was still calm. Strangely so. As if he knew something that she didn't. "I don't want you to do something that I can't. Especially if I can't follow you. I never said that you couldn't.

Of course you can. I know you're great at it."

*"What?"*

"You're a natural. I saw you with my mother that night in her house. You have the touch. You're brave, and strong, and you're wonderful. I'm just jealous. And stupid."

Lucy heard his words, but they didn't make sense to her brain. It almost sounded like he believed in her again.

Still.

Hope rose, that tiny beating of butterfly wings in her chest, and she pushed it down. They just had to focus on one thing at a time, and right now, it was fixing what she'd screwed up. Before it was too tragically late.

"We have to find her, Owen. Before we talk about anything else, we have to find your mother."

Owen nodded and turned the wheel so they were driving down Main Street alongside the shore, shops to their left, dunes to their right. "Did she say anything, anything at all tonight? Any place name? Any word she said tonight would be freshest in her mind, might act like a homing device."

Lucy thought over every word they'd spoken since she'd arrived at Willow Rock, but it was hard to remember — so much of

Irene's speech had seemed disjointed, fractured. Single words, hung on threads of sound that didn't seem to be sentences as much as random thoughts, like floats of yarn, carried behind colorwork.

"It was difficult. . . . She didn't make sense."

"I know. Take your time."

She thought harder. "But I did talk to her about Eliza. She perked up when I did, got brighter. I told her about finding the box with *Silk Road* and the papers. Talked about the 'Cypress Hollow Lighthouse' pattern. I asked if she'd ever made it, since it was such a popular pattern when the book came out. She did repeat the word *lighthouse* a few times."

Shivers of horror rippled up and down Lucy's spine as Owen hit the accelerator, speeding past the pier, headed for the curve of the cove where the lighthouse stood, still invisible to them.

"It's too far," she gasped. "She couldn't make it on foot, could she?"

"My mother?" Owen said. "She could make it in forty-five minutes, even with the rain. It's less than a mile and a half from Willow Rock. She's there, I'd bet everything I have on it. She hated that my father chased me up there — she ranted about getting it pulled down when they put in the auto-strobe. I've never known her to actually go there, but I can't imagine that's stopping her now. God*damm*it."

They were almost at the parking area. The dirt lot under the looming building was empty as Owen fishtailed the Mustang into it with a spray of mud.

"Wait," he said, as Lucy reached for her door handle.

"What?"

"You're taking your bag?"

She nodded. "I can sling it over my back like a backpack. It has Band-Aids in it. . . ." The words sounded idiotic to her ears. Band-Aids? The cowboy Band-Aids that she'd put on Owen the first time he'd been in the parsonage? What good would they do in a medical emergency?

But Owen groped in the back of the car, bringing out a small first-aid kit. "Good. Put this in your bag, too. It has iodine and gauze and a couple of bandages. Not much, but it's something." Then he changed the subject abruptly, and his words were rushed, pushed together. "Lucy, I can't make it up those stairs, not up more than one flight. If she's not at the bottom, if she's gone up, you're going to have to bring her down."

"But —" Her head swam. In her whole

life, she'd never been higher than the second story of her house. She was unable to even go onto her roof. "I don't think I —"

His right hand, warm, perfect in the way it fit hers, grasped her left. "I believe in you, heart." He lifted it to his mouth and kissed the back of her knuckles, grazing them with his mouth. The butterflies in her chest turned into fluttering sparrows. "I always have."

Irene was nowhere to be found on the bottom floor inside the lighthouse. By the look of the inside, the graffiti and the broken beer bottles, many had forced their way in over the years. Owen's flashlight, which had seemed so strong earlier, seemed dull now, lighting only small swathes of rubble in front of them. The interior smelled harshly of seaweed and oil and decay.

Lucy clutched the back of Owen's leather jacket and hoped he wouldn't notice.

They entered a small kitchen, which led into a machine room that opened onto the bottom of the staircase. It spiraled overhead to the left and made Lucy dizzy as Owen swung the flashlight up the broken steps. Pieces of the staircase were missing altogether. Irene could never have made it up those steps. From here, she and Owen could only see the very bottom portion, and they were in such bad repair that she wouldn't trust them to hold a person who weighed more than a child.

And then the flashlight's beam hit something on the bottom step.

One pink slipper, covered in fresh mud.

Owen groaned. "Fuck."

"Oh, God. I can't."

Owen put his hands on Lucy's shoulders and moved her toward the bottom of the stairs. "I'm calling 911. You have your phone? As soon as I'm done calling them, I'm calling you. Open the phone, lock it, and put it back in your pocket. It'll be an open line, and I'll be able to hear you."

Lucy wanted to say, *I'm so scared, I'm too scared, I can't,* but she folded her lips and looked at him instead. She wouldn't say the words.

"Goddammit, I wish I could go instead," he said as he handed her the flashlight. "But I'd make it one flight and they'd have to send the paramedics for me, too. I just can't . . . There's nothing more in the world I want to do. There's nothing I used to be better at. And I know —" His voice broke, and then he started speaking again. "I know you probably don't think much of a man who can't do the job he's meant to do. But

I can't do it. I need you to, Lucy."

Lucy felt fizzy, feeling the blood drain from her head, her face, and dug her fingers into his jacket. What the hell had she been thinking? This was worse than the night of the car fire. So much worse.

But so much more depended on this. Owen needed her now. No one else could help him.

Owen looked at her. In the darkness, she could barely see him, and behind her something rustled, something that didn't bear thinking about. But suddenly, Lucy thought she knew what might be in his eyes.

"Lucy . . ."

"Okay," she said.

"Okay?" he asked.

"Yes."

"Be careful." And with those two words, Owen kissed her. It felt as if she'd been waiting for this kiss her whole life. His mouth was heavy on hers, and she kissed him back, greedy for the days, for the years, they'd missed. She pressed against him and felt him, how they fit each other, perfectly. And as suddenly as the kiss had started, it ended.

His fingertips swept her jawline, and he whispered the same words, "Be careful," but it sounded like he was saying something else.

Lucy nodded and turned, adjusting her bag behind her so that her hands were free.

She took the first few steps carefully. They creaked, swaying under her weight. Good God, they should have torn this place down years ago. Why hadn't they? People kept talking about turning the lighthouse into a hostel or a resort, a moneymaker for the town, but this was ridiculous. She could hear nothing but the blood pounding in her ears, a constant, throbbing roar.

One flight up, just out of sight of Owen, her foot plunged through a rotted board, but most of her weight was still on her back leg, and she caught herself on the railing. The rail itself swayed treacherously, and as it curved ahead of her, she could see it was broken into splinters.

"Oh, Jesus," she gasped.

In her pocket, her cell phone rang, making her jump. She answered.

Owen said, "You're doing great."

"You can't even see me."

"I can hear you haven't crashed to the bottom floor yet."

"Thanks for that vote of confidence." But the sound of his low laugh in her ear made her go limp with relief, and Lucy remembered to breathe again. "I'm locking the phone open now."

"Good."

She put it back in her pocket, knowing that whatever she said, he'd hear. And if she told him something . . . something terrible, he'd be able to disconnect and call 911 back with an update.

But she prayed to God that wouldn't happen.

Another flight. She wouldn't think how high she was. The steps were worse here — two were gone entirely, just missing. A hole gaped down into blackness, and even when she swept the flashlight's beam into it, she couldn't tell its depth.

What if Irene had . . . ?

No. She hadn't. That was all that mattered. She was either up above, or she wasn't, and there was only one way to find out.

Lucy leaped from the whole step she stood on to the next partial one. The staircase sighed and seemed to sway, but it held. Lucy exhaled with relief and kept moving up.

Too scared to rely on the rickety railing at all, Lucy pressed the palm of her left hand against the clammy wall, cupping the peeling paint as if it would give her purchase.

She leaned forward and swept the beam of the flashlight forward a few steps with her right hand, and then used the same hand to feel the next step, to test its weight first before putting her foot on it.

About two thirds of the way up was a small landing with a window with no glass left in it. Rain lashed through the opening, and from here, Lucy could see the lights on Main Street. They were so far down. And she was so far up. No, no, no, she should never have looked. . . .

But knowing Owen could hear her on the open line, she said, "I'm still going. I haven't found her." Her voice was breathy, so she cleared it. "It's pretty high, but I'm good."

It was a damn lie. How kids came up here for fun was beyond her. This wasn't fun, this was pure, sheer hell. Scary, and so flipping high up . . . Lucy's palms sweated and she felt a dizzy sickness at the base of her skull. She wished she could hear Owen's voice in her ear, telling her she was going to make it, but stopping now to talk would be ridiculous.

She could do it. She *would* do it.

Just a few more steps. The wood here was a little better up on this last stretch, as if the higher the stairs went, the less they'd been used over the years. Lucy understood.

God knew on a normal day she'd never have made it this far.

Finally, at the top, Lucy ducked her head to pass into the lantern room.

The old shattered light stood in the middle of the circular space, but the glass walls themselves stood mostly intact. Lucy tried to peer out, to see if Irene was outside on the deck, but since the beam never had to shine inland, the room had been supported by a wall on the inland side, making it impossible to see all the way around. If Irene had made it up here, and if she was on the other side of that wall, Lucy would have no way of knowing it. Except by going out there.

A door to her left hung open on one remaining hinge. Outside, a metal railing fenced in the iron deck that creaked in the wind. Lucy could almost see it sway, just as she swore she could feel the building itself move in the storm under her feet. She would *not* think about earthquakes, not right now.

Lucy inched her way to the door, and then sat down, feeling like a child too scared to go down stairs standing up. She swung her feet out into the rain, feeling the biting drops soak through her jeans, and she prayed like she'd never prayed before that

Irene wasn't up here, that she was hidden someplace safe. Locked in the bathroom at Tillie's, maybe. Or in the back storage shed at the public library, sleeping. Anywhere but up here, alone, in this storm.

Her feet hit thc iron deck with a clang. "Owen, I'm on the outside now, at the top." She did well, she thought, at keeping the panic out of her voice.

Then she made the mistake of looking down.

She could see through the iron slats. Of course. All the way to the rocks, so far below. When Lucy raised her eyes, all she could see were the clouds huddling over the breaking waves, the enormous surge of the tide below. And she was so small, up here, so high, alone . . .

She backed up, pressing herself against the wall of the lighthouse as flat as she could, as if that would save her from falling.

And a knitting needle in her bag poked her sharply in the back.

Eliza Carpenter.

Lucy shook her head, sharply. *Eliza* wouldn't have been scared up here. Eliza would have thought it was an adventure, one she would have told Joshua about later, and jotted down in her notes. Eliza would have thought it was exciting. Maybe she'd been up here, in this very place, in a storm before. Maybe that was the inspiration for the cabled sweater.

She'd be Eliza, then.

Pushing away from the wall, but not trusting the railing, Lucy walked carefully to the right, using the flashlight to make sure she stepped only where the decking looked strong. Up here, too, there were holes in the iron, where the deck had rusted and actually fallen away, spots that took Lucy's breath away with abject terror.

But she kept moving, just like Eliza would have.

And as she came around the back of the light, where the solid wall joined the glass, she found Irene.

She was huddled under the only overhang available, a small wooden eave, her knees pulled up against her under her nightgown. One bare foot stuck out, the other still slippered. She was soaked, and even though she was partially sheltered, the rain was flying sideways now, pummeling her. Her eyes fluttered and her hands shook.

"Owen, she's here, she's here, she's here."

He'd hang up now, she knew, and call and confirm with the medics that Irene had been found.

In the meantime, though, Lucy was in charge.

"Irene, oh, Irene."

But Lucy didn't look down, didn't check her footing, and as she rushed forward, her left foot went through a hole in the deck. The section she'd been standing on folded, crumpling like it was paper, swinging downward, smashing off. Lucy wasn't aware of conscious thought — she reacted, exploded into motion. She kicked forward with her right foot. With both hands, she grabbed the next section of deck, dropping the flashlight, which tumbled, end over end, until it finally hit the rocks with a tiny, faraway clatter.

There, in the darkness, alone, Lucy swung by her arms from the iron deck.

# Thirty-Five

Knit through everything.

— E. C.

Strangest of all was the silence — the rain ceased for a moment, and the wind died down. She heard nothing but the beating of her heart, a rapid, steady rhythm.

Then as if he were standing next to her, a breath away, Lucy heard Owen say, "You can do it, Lucy."

Lucy counted the beats of her heart as she felt the blood pump up to her fingers, clutching the metal rail. One, two, three. Then she did the first, the only, and the most important pull-up of her life. It wasn't like in the movies where the protagonist pulls herself over an edge with cat-like grace — it was ugly and painful — she clawed and scratched her way up, swinging her right leg up so that just her heel caught the edge of the deck and then she finally managed to get her torso up and onto the deck.

Still on her belly, Lucy slid forward, breathing hard. Sound came back, and the storm's raging filled her ears — the roaring wind, the pounding rain, the creaking of the metal.

Irene watched it all with uncomprehending eyes.

And she was most important. Not the fact that Lucy had almost died by falling from a height that left her breathless with horror. That, right now, didn't matter at all. Irene was okay. She had to stay okay.

Grandma Ruby's bookstore sweater was wet and torn even worse than it ever had been, but it was warm from Lucy's body heat. She took it off and put it over Irene's shoulders, tucking her arms into it, one by one.

"Wool keeps its warmth, you know," Lucy told Irene, her voice shaking as much as her hands. "Even when it's wet. It stays warm. It's f-f-fire retardant, as well, did you know that, Irene? Now, let me see, your arms are okay, how are your legs?"

The bottom of Irene's bare foot was, unsurprisingly, cut in several places, but the blood came in a slow trickle. Lucy decided against trying to treat it herself. It didn't seem to be bothering her, and she didn't want to upset or scare her. They couldn't move from this spot, now that Lucy had taken out the one exit route.

Lucy didn't see any other obvious injuries. Irene was cold, obviously, and hypothermia, she knew from their last visit to the emergency room with Irene, was serious in older patients. Lucy pulled out her cell phone and then wrapped her arms around Irene.

"I'm just gonna hug you warm while I call your son, okay?" Lucy hoped like hell it was okay. If Irene freaked out right now, that would be the end. For both of them, probably, because she wouldn't let Irene move away from her without a fight. And it was a long way down. Too far down to think about. Her breath juddered in her chest.

But Irene tucked her chin down and leaned into the circle of her arms, as if she wanted to be close, to be held.

Lucy's phone rang in her hand, Owen's number on the display.

"She seems to be okay, but she's cold and wet and we have to get her off of here. Fast." Lucy could finally — *finally* — hear sirens getting closer. "We can't carry her down the way we came. Trust me on this one. She's got to come down on a ladder from right where we are, at the back of the top deck. They're going to have to carry her down somehow —"

"They're almost here. We'll send up a Stokes basket. Are *you* okay?" Owen's voice was sharp, alarm in every word.

"I'm fine. We're fine." Then Lucy pressed her lips together, hard, suddenly unable to breathe.

"Just hold tight. It's still going to be at least ten minutes before we get set up down here with the ladder and the basket. You gonna be okay?"

"Yep."

But as soon as Lucy hung up, Irene started to fidget in her arms. First she pulled away from Lucy, then she started to cry. Then Irene made a motion like she was going to try to stand up.

"Oh, no, honey, you can't. We can't move, not even an inch, okay? It's not safe."

They weren't the right words. Irene got more agitated.

"Owen," Irene said. "Owen, up here."

Lucy said, "He's okay, Irene. He's fine."

"Owen," said Irene, more firmly, and looked around as if she realized where they were. "The lighthouse. Owen. Up here."

"Owen's fine." Lucy pulled down on Irene's arm. She didn't want to hurt her, but she had to keep her right here. This was the only safe place in the whole damn lighthouse, and she wasn't even totally sure about that. If Irene leaned on the railing in front of them, Lucy didn't trust it not to give way as the deck had, just feet to the left of them.

It was strangely light now — the rain eased, and the lights of town bounced off the low cloud layer. Irene looked into her eyes and Lucy could see the wariness there. "I put him away. And then he died."

Did she mean Owen's father? Could she possibly be remembering that night Owen's father had chased him up here in high school?

"Owen," said Irene. "Go." She stood halfway up, her legs wobbling, her torso swaying.

"Irene," said Lucy, injecting all the urgency she could into her voice. "I brought my knitting up here. I was wondering if you could show me how you hold the yarn."

Irene shook her head, but she slid back down beside Lucy. "What?"

Lucy's freezing, wet hands had a hard time pulling the wool out of her bag, and she could feel several stitches slipping off the Addi Turbos, but it didn't matter. "Look. I hold my working yarn like this, with my left hand. But you hold it with your right, I think. Can you show me?"

She put the needles into Irene's hands. Irene looked at it as if she'd never seen knitting before.

"I know, it's wet out here, isn't it? Your hands are probably pretty cold. Maybe if you go really slowly, though, you could show me. I'd sure appreciate the help."

In the low light, Lucy knew Irene probably couldn't see the knitting well. Lucy could hardly see the stitches herself. But Irene's hand started moving, slowly at first, wet stitch by painful-looking wet stitch. And then her fingers caught the rhythm and garter stitch dropped from Irene's needles, and she relaxed against Lucy's shoulder.

The fire truck below began extending its ladder toward them.

Lucy had been in the middle of increasing a swathe of stockinette, heading for the armscye, and she knew that most of this would have to be ripped out later, but as the firefighters ran around and shouted from below, she found herself wishing that she could keep a stitch or two of Irene's in the work.

Somehow, she decided, she would. In the replica of Grandma Ruby's bookstore sweater, the pattern that Eliza had written, the pattern Lucy would rewrite by adding her own sleeve design, there would be a stitch done by Irene as she perched on the edge of the lighthouse.

A sweater made by all of them.

Lucy put her arms around Irene and let her knit. She closed her eyes and could see, as plainly as if he were in front of her, Owen, below, waiting for her.

She couldn't wait to get on the ground.

# Thirty-Six

Wool has as much memory as love does.
— E. C.

The hospital kicked them out after a few hours. Irene was going to be kept overnight for observation, but the warming fluids and heat packs had brought up her core temperature, and they thought she was going to be okay.

Again.

Lucy had never seen a person actually, literally, sag with relief, like Owen had done when the doctor told him the news, but he had — his back hit the wall, and his good leg held him up while his bad leg gave out. He'd held onto the back of a chair bolted to the wall and listened to the doctor, and then he'd looked at Lucy with so much emotion in his eyes that it had made her hands shake.

She'd led him out to the Mustang, and then she'd asked for his keys.

"You're driving?"
She'd nodded.
"No girl's ever driven my car before."
"First time for everything."
The clock on the dash read two in the morning. They drove past the Rite Spot, and Jonas was out front locking up. His eyebrows rose in surprise to see her driving Owen's car. But he raised his keys and jerked his head. It felt like approval.
They passed the pole Abigail's car had hit almost a month ago, where everything started.
They didn't speak. Owen put his head back and closed his eyes.
Lucy turned left on Fourth Street, and right on Walnut, and then pulled up in front of her own house. She shut off the engine, and they both got out.
Without saying a word, she led him inside.
At the bottom of the staircase, she waited while he put his hand on her shoulder, and they took each step slowly, one by one, together.
In the bathroom, Lucy lit three candles and filled the clawfoot tub with hot water, and then turned around. It was only then that she started to shake again. But they still didn't speak.
Slowly, they both removed their clothing.

Lucy didn't take her eyes from Owen's as they moved as if in slow motion, first their shirts, then their still damp and muddy jeans.

The tub full, she turned off the tap.

The room was silent.

And then finally, an eternity after Lucy first wanted to, she stood on her tiptoes and kissed Owen. His lips came down to meet hers, and in that perfect instant, she knew she was home.

He tasted of night and rain and smelled of the ocean. He was everything she wanted, everything she needed. And as he kissed her back, she felt her heart expand until she didn't know how it could possibly fit inside her chest.

They got into the tub together, laughing as it splashed over the rim onto the tiled floor. Owen washed her first, moving his hands slowly, tenderly. Then she washed him, running her hands down his legs, his arms, the side of his jaw, pausing all the while to turn her head to kiss him, to breathe him in.

Then she leaned back in the candlelight, cradled in his arms, the water lapping over their shoulders. It would have been easy, natural, to roll over and move against him, to take him inside, to have him that way.

But Lucy hoped there would be time for that. She hoped with every part of her soul that there would be all the time in the world.

Finally, Owen said, "I saw you fall."

Lucy stiffened, and her foot pressed against the end of the tub. "You did?"

"I thought my life was over. Did you hear me shouting at you? You must have. I could hear every creak of the metal, I could practically hear you breathe."

She shook her head, her wet hair against his warm chest. "It was so loud up there, but then so quiet when I fell. Then I thought I heard you. . . ."

"I said, 'You can do it, Lucy.' "

Lucy closed her eyes. She'd heard that, loud and clear. She'd believed it. He'd been right.

"You were amazing."

Lucy smiled. "I know." She held her hand up and watched the water run off it. "But I only went up because you believed in me."

Owen's arms tightened around her. "I realized when you were up there that I was wrong, that I've been wrong this whole time about you and the fire department."

"Figured." Lucy had heard that in his voice, too.

"Good."

"But you don't mind?" Lucy stared at the

candle perched on the edge of the sink but listened intently for the timbre of his answer. Not that she would stop. But it did matter.

"I think I'll always mind not being able to follow where you go, especially if you're in a dangerous position. But Lucy . . ." Owen shifted so that she slid halfway off him, so that they were facing each other in the tub. Candlelight lit stubble on his jaw and highlighted the shadows under his eyes. He looked exhausted.

And he looked like the man she loved.

"Lucy, I don't know how long you'll let me nag you and worry about you and let me be the one you come home to, but I want to be that man." He smiled, and his sea-dark eyes were clear. "I love you. Before you say anything, I have nothing to give you. But I'm going to start that handyman business, like I told you, and I'm buying back my mother's house, and I'm going to fix it up. I'm going to ask Silas if he wants to be my partner, and maybe, if that goes okay . . . then maybe —"

Lucy silenced him with a kiss that left them both breathless. "You've always been perfect."

Owen just stared at her.

"Ever since high school," she said, "when you missed tutoring half the time because you were in detention. When you called me the wrong names on purpose. When you kissed me in that bedroom at the party. When you left and never came back. You were always the right person for me. I think I've loved you since then. I just didn't know it. You were perfect then, when you weren't a cop. You're perfect now, as you are. I love you, Owen Bancroft."

Owen's eyes caught fire and Lucy felt the flames reflected in her own.

"Tell me what you said in the note you left, the note I never got."

He laughed and wrapped his arm around her waist, pulling her closer. More water splashed over onto the floor.

"It said that I'd be back for you. That I would come home."

# Epilogue

Love through everything.

— E. C.

Lucy's only regret was that Owen's mother couldn't make it to the launch party. They'd had a good day yesterday — a really good day. Irene had been strong and alert enough for them to bundle her up in the car and take her to the house. Owen had taken her carefully by the hand, and it had twisted Lucy's heart to see them both leaning on each other as they moved around their old home.

Irene had shown little interest in anything beyond the garden, though, and only wanted to sit in the old metal bench at the back of the yard. She'd stared at the roses as tears rolled off her cheeks. She hadn't said much besides "rugosa" and "Owen," but they hadn't needed much more than that. She'd also smiled, two heart-stoppingly huge smiles when she'd seen the way the Lady Banks was blooming again, scrambling over the support Owen had built for it. It was a smile they hadn't seen for a long time. She was getting worse, of course, but days like this were good and they held on tight to them.

Out there, on the bench, Irene was the third person to see the finished book. Lucy put the gleaming, dust-jacketed copy of *Eliza's Road Not Taken* into Irene's lap.

"It's my book," Lucy said. "This is your copy."

Irene nodded and turned the pages. On the front flap was a large black-and-white photo of Eliza and Joshua, both wearing homespun, handknit Ganseys, leaning against the barn wall. Irene touched the paper and smiled again, then she'd closed both the book and her eyes, turning her face up to the sunset. The three of them sat in the garden, listening to the waves crash on the beach, two blocks away.

Then they'd taken her back to Willow Rock and put the book on her nightstand.

It had been enough.

Tonight, though, Lucy was almost sick with excitement that felt too close to dread.

"What if no one comes?"

Owen leaned against the bookstore register and laughed. "They'll come."

"No, really. They're bored to death. Or just tired of hearing me talk about the book for a year and a half. No one cares anymore. Why should they? Why would they come to a book-launch party of a knitting book? A novel, sure. Or when Bill Hildebrand self-published his memoir on sailing to Fiji, yeah. *That* was a party, but you know what? He roasted a pig in the ground, didn't he? Yep. We're not roasting a pig. All we have are cupcakes!" Lucy gave a wail and covered her face with her hands.

She felt fingers lift her hand and then a kiss was placed on her forehead. "Okay, now open your eyes and look at me," said Owen.

Lucy shook her head. "I'm terrified."

"You're not terrified of anything. What about that three-alarm fire last week up in the valley when that firefighter fell off the ladder? You were on the rapid intervention crew? You can't tell me you're scared."

"That's different. I'm with everyone else when I'm on a fire. This is just me. *Alone.*"

"You'll be fine."

"What if they've published this book and they've made it look so gorgeous and we're throwing this party and *no one ever buys it?* No one, anywhere, ever."

"I'm sure that's what the publisher intended. A loss. You must have been a real fast-talker to pull that one off."

"I wasn't —"

"I know, heart. That's the point." Owen laughed again. "They had a plan. It will sell. It's your book-launch party. This is your day. And Eliza's. She can't be here to enjoy it, and by all that's woolen, if you don't enjoy it for her, then I'll know the reason why."

Lucy gaped at the man she'd always loved. "Did you just swear by fiber?"

Owen shrugged. "What can I say? It's catching."

In the space of half a heartbeat, Lucy wrapped her arms around Owen's neck and kissed the breath right out of him. When she was done, he was gasping and clutching the book cart behind him. "What was that for, woman?"

"Knitting is *sexy*."

"I know that now," he said.

"You really think they'll come?" Lucy asked again.

Owen nodded.

Everyone arrived at once, of course.

Elbert Romo came straight from a Bingo championship at the VFW, so of course he scuttled straight through into the bathroom without saying hello or looking at the book.

But Mildred and Greta came in with gusto, arms raised high, tears already streaming down their faces.

Greta said, "Oh, look at all the decorations! It looks like a wedding, with the bunting on the pews and all the flowers and candles!"

Mildred was already flipping pages frantically, her handbag forgotten at her feet. "But look at the book! And Greta, just look at this picture of Eliza! Oh, turn to page seventy-nine! Do you remember that day? I know just where that was."

"You've outdone yourself, Lucy." Greta's smile was quiet, and lovely.

Lucy stood straighter in her red dress and touched the front of her yellow cardigan. It was the prototype for Ruby's Bookstore Cardigan, and she loved it more than any of the other sweaters in the book — the soft, old-fashioned curved edging, the waist-shaping, the short sleeves, the pearl buttons. It made her feel pretty and feminine, and it made her feel like she was continuing something important, like she was continuing both Eliza's and Ruby's work, and that both of them had their arms wrapped around her at the same time.

Whitney and Silas came in carrying huge trays of more goodies than Lucy thought she'd ever need. And even though it was still almost eighty degrees outside on a warm fall evening, Whitney was wearing the red earflap cap Silas had knitted for her. She took it off and folded it, placing it carefully in a side pocket of her bag.

"You're going to be fine. Remember the other night at the ganache class? Every single woman was planning on being here tonight, and you didn't even know all of them. And some of them didn't even knit. They'd just heard the buzz."

"About a knitting coffee-table book."

"About *the* knitting coffee-table book. Now I have to go guard the goods before our men devour them all."

Lucy grinned at Owen and Silas, hovering over the trays, sniffing ecstatically. "They're good together, huh?"

Whitney nodded. "Did Owen tell you yet about the job they got today?"

Lucy bit her bottom lip. "I'm the worst person in the world. I forgot to even ask."

"Today is your book-release day. I think he'll forgive you. Silas said the house was in such bad shape that they're going to have to gut the place and fix everything, do a complete overhaul for the owner."

"So they're in heaven."

"Completely. Utterly."

"Good." Lucy was glad for Owen. He worked so well with Silas. Owen handled the visible stuff, the counters and floors and walls, and Silas did the insides, the plumbing and the wiring. Owen had only pulled a gun on him one more time, for dramatic effect. As a joke. And Silas had been *really* late that day.

Molly and Jonas came in through the front doors, Toots and Bart hot on their heels.

Toots was saying in a loud voice, "But Bart, I told you, if we lead a Tantric class, you *have* to be naked. At least part of the time."

Bart walked past Lucy, shaking his head. "You may have hit the point where I draw the line, wife. I never thought I'd say it, but this may be it."

"You knew when you married me . . ."

"We can discuss this later, Toots."

"The kids don't mind."

Jonas said, "The kids mind, Mom. They really mind. We're at Lucy's party now, look, Mom! Her book!" He held it up and waved it as if waving a red cape at a bull.

Toots scowled at Bart. Then she beamed at the book and then at Lucy. "Darling. My clever little rutabaga. How gorgeous is that book? And you did this? With Eliza? And Abigail? Where is she, by the way?"

"They'll be here soon," said Lucy. "Lizzie woke up late from her nap and little Owen is teething, but they're on their way."

Molly came up next to her and squeezed Lucy until she could barely breathe. "It's wonderful. I'm so proud of you. Show me where your picture is."

Lucy blushed but flipped to the back flap to show her the small black-and-white photo that Owen had taken of her down by the pier.

Molly touched it with her finger. "Lucy Harrison. That's you." Then she looked around the store. "And this is you. Look, I see people from three different knitting groups, from the fire department, from Willow Rock, and from City Hall. This is *all* you. I'm so proud of you, Luce."

"Thank you," Lucy whispered, and she kissed Molly's cheek. She *wouldn't* cry. Not now. That would be silly. Instead she grinned and said, "How's my brother?"

Molly shrugged. "Good. We're hanging out tonight."

"Like last night. And the night before."

"Like we always tell you, it's not a big deal."

"Right, right." Lucy said. "You're just hanging out. Dating other people."

"Whenever we want to. We can totally see

anyone else."

"Totally. And the last time you slept with another person was . . ."

Molly turned a page in *Eliza's Road Not Taken* and said, "Did you know there's a typo on page eighty-seven?"

"No, there's not. And it was like, a year ago, right?"

"But we could. Anytime we wanted to."

"You just keep telling yourselves that." Lucy loved the flush that stole across Molly's face.

"But there *is* a typo."

"Crap."

Thirty minutes, half a glass of champagne, and many congratulations later, Owen caught her eye as he slid two snickerdoodles at the same time into his mouth. He didn't look repentant at all. He looked delighted.

And in the russet sweater she'd made him from Abigail's pattern and Cade's wool, he looked delicious.

It had been the busiest year and a half of her life, but what with editing the patterns and Eliza's vignettes, and moving out of her house and into Owen's, Lucy's life had gone from peaceful and stable to unpredictable, loud, and filled with love. With the money she made renting out both her house and the parsonage, she finally had enough to feel comfortable experimenting a little with the bookstore. The cooking nights with Whitney and the craft nights in the store were going like gangbusters; the waiting lists were always long, and word of mouth sold each class out. During her evenings and days off, she wore the brigade pager and responded for station coverage, medicals, and the occasional fire. It was exciting, sometimes scary, and she loved it.

Owen, in the meantime, was intent on making his childhood home into a house that would be for both of them. Not a repository of memories, but a place for the two of them to make new ones. He was always trying something new in the living room or kitchen, adding an island, or building a bookcase. When she got home from work in the evening, the furniture was never where she'd left it in the morning, and she was getting used to it.

Kind of made things fun, actually.

Just like he did.

Owen winked and Lucy's toes curled inside her blue-and-green Keds.

■ ■ ■ ■

# A+
# Author Insights, Extras & More . . .

FROM RACHAEL HERRON
AND WILLIAM MORROW

■ ■ ■ ■

## Ruby's Bookstore Sweater

### Finished Measurements

**For more detailed photos, go to yarnagogo.com/rubysweater.**

Bust: 34 (38, 42, 44, 48, 52) inches

Length: 23 1/4 (23 1/2, 24, 24 1/4, 25, 25 1/4) inches

**Gauge:** 18 stitches and 28 rows = 4 inches in Stockinette stitch

### Materials

Lorna's Laces Shepherd Worsted wool, 4 (4, 5, 5, 6, 6) skeins

One US #7 (4.5mm) 12-inch circular needle or set of DPNs (or size to get gauge)

One US #7 (4.5mm) 32-inch (or longer) circular needle (or size to get gauge)
Once US #G (4mm) crochet hook
4 stitch markers
Stitch holders or scrap yarn
Yarn needle

**Sleeves — Make two**

Using shorter circular needle or DPNs and a long-tail cast-on, cast on 52 (56, 60, 64, 68, 72) stitches. PM and join to work in the round.

**Round 1:** Purl.
**Round 2:** Knit.
**Round 3:** Purl.
**Increase Round:** K1, M1, knit to last st, M1, k1 — 2 stitches increased.

Continue in Stockinette stitch (knit every round) and repeat Increase Round every 6 rounds 7 more times — 68 (72, 76, 80, 84, 88) stitches.

Work even until sleeve measures 7 inches from beginning (fudge last increases if necessary, as Eliza would). At end of last round, work to 5 (6, 6, 7, 7, 8) stitches before marker, slip 10 (12, 12, 14, 14, 16) stitches onto scrap yarn for underarm. Put the rest of stitches onto stitch holder (or second piece of longer scrap yarn).

### Body

Using longer circular needle and a long-tail cast-on, cast on 152 (168, 188, 196, 216, 232) stitches.

**Row 1 (RS):** Knit 38 (42, 47, 49, 54, 58) stitches, PM, knit 76 (84, 94, 98, 108, 116) stitches, PM, knit 38 (42, 47, 49, 54, 58) stitches.

**Row 2:** Knit.

**Row 3:** Knit.

**Row 4:** Purl.

Begin pattern:

**Row 1 (RS):** Knit.

**Row 2:** K2, purl to last 2 stitches, k2.

Repeat Rows 1 and 2 until piece measures 4 inches from beginning.

### Waist Shaping

**Decrease Row (RS):** * Knit to 3 stitches before marker, k2tog, k1, slip marker, k1, ssk; repeat from * once, knit to end of row — 4 stitches decreased.

Keeping first and last 2 stitches in Garter stitch as established, repeat Decrease Row every 6 rows 3 more times — 136 (152, 172, 180, 200, 216) stitches remain.

Work even for 7 rows.

**Increase Row (RS):** * Knit to 1 stitch before marker, M1, k1, slip marker, k1, M1; repeat from * once, knit to end of row — 4 stitches increased.

Repeat Increase Row every 8 rows 3 more times — 152 (168, 188, 196, 216, 232) stitches.

Work even until piece measures 14 1/2 inches from beginning or adjust to your preferred length.

### Join Sleeves to Body

With RS facing, work across right front to 5 (6, 6, 7, 7, 8) stitches before marker, slip 10 (12, 12, 14, 14, 16) stitches onto scrap yarn for underarm. Continuing to work body and sleeves in pattern, PM and work across 58 (60, 64, 66, 70, 72) stitches from first sleeve holder, PM, work across back of sweater to 5 (6, 6, 7, 7, 8) stitches before marker, slip 10 (12, 12, 14, 14, 16) stitches onto scrap yarn for underarm. PM and work across 58 (60, 64, 66, 70, 72) stitches from second sleeve holder, PM, work across the left front to end of row — 248 (264, 292, 300, 328, 344) stitches.

Keeping first and last 2 stitches in Garter stitch, work even for one inch.

### Raglan Decreases

**Decrease Row (RS):** * Knit to 3 stitches before marker, k2tog, k1, slip marker, k1, ssk; repeat from * 3 more times, knit to end of row — 8 stitches decreased.

Repeat Decrease Row every other row, 26 (27, 29, 30, 32, 33) more times — 32 (40, 52, 52, 64, 72) stitches remain. (4 stitches remain in each sleeve section.)

### Collar

Work in Garter stitch (knit every row) for 5 inches. Bind off all stitches loosely.

### Finishing

Graft (kitchener stitch) underarms together.

### Crochet Edging

Body crochet edge: With US #G (4mm) crochet hook (or size that suits you best) work around the sweater, beginning at the mid lower edge back:

Round 1: 1 sc, ⋆ 1 ch, skip approx. 1 cm, 1 sc in the following st/row ⋆, repeat from ⋆-⋆ all around sweater. Bonus points if the number of ch-loops are divisible by 8, but you can fudge this later if necessary.

Round 2: Crochet ⋆ 1 sc in the first ch, skip 3 ch, crochet 5 dc in the next ch, skip 3 ch ⋆, repeat from ⋆-⋆ and finish with 1 sl st in the sc from beg. of round.

Sleeve crochet edge: Work the same as body crocheted edge.

## List of Abbreviations

ch — Chain
dc — Double crochet
DPNs — Double-point needles
K — Knit
k2tog — Knit two together (decrease stitch)
M1 — Make one stitch (increase stitch) by knitting in front and back of stitch
P — Purl
PM — Place marker
sc — Single crochet
sl st — Slip stitch
ssk — Slip two stitches, one at a time, as if to knit, then knit those two stitches together through the back loops (decrease stitch)

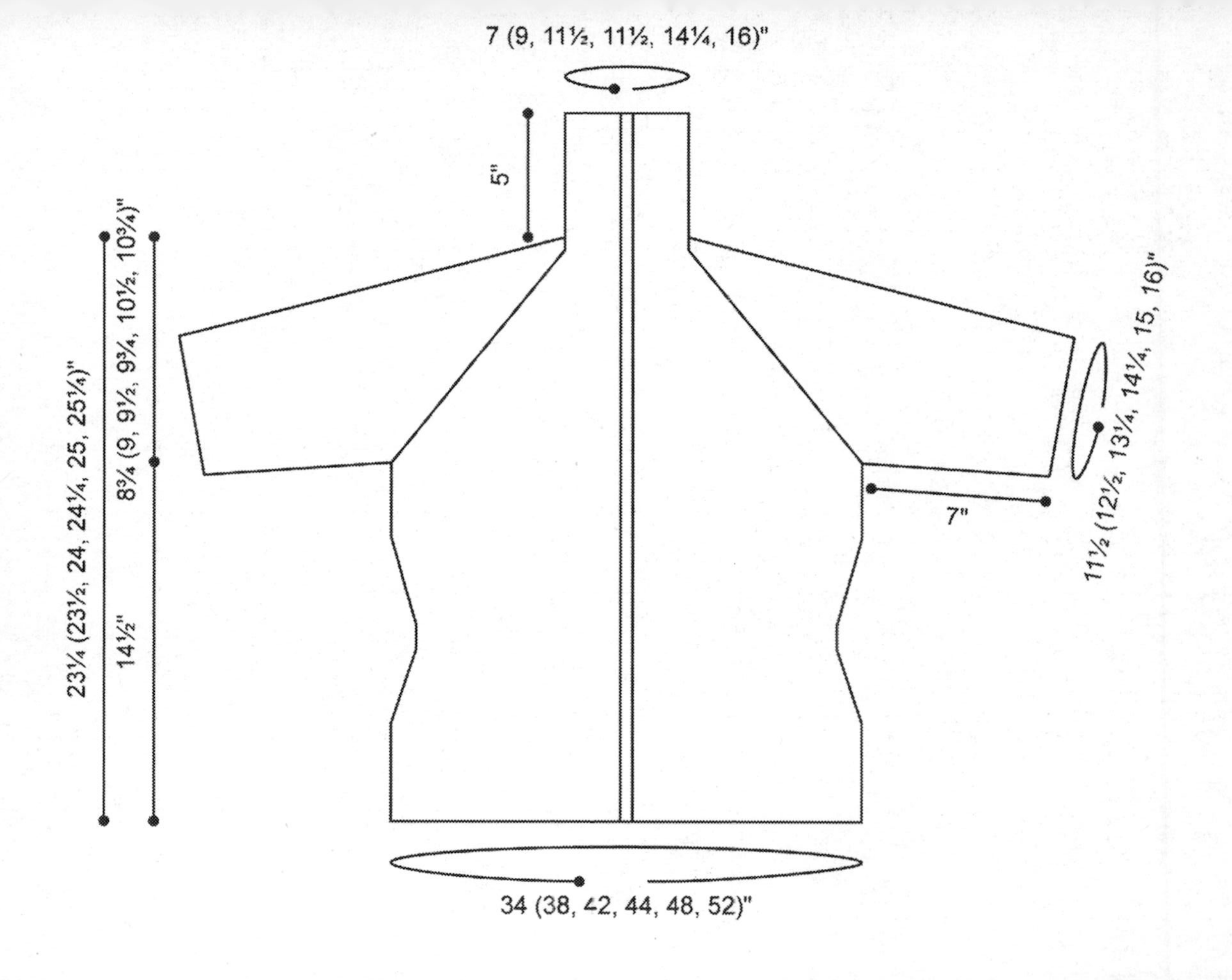
7 (9, 11½, 11½, 14¼, 16)"
5"
23¼ (23½, 24, 24¼, 25, 25¼)"
8¾ (9, 9½, 9¾, 10½, 10¾)"
14½"
11½ (12½, 13¼, 14¼, 15, 16)"
7"
34 (38, 42, 44, 48, 52)"

# ABOUT THE AUTHOR

**Rachael Herron** received her MFA in English and Creative Writing from Mills College. She lives in Oakland, California, with her family and has way more animals than she ever planned to, though no sheep or alpaca (yet). She learned to knit at the age of five, and generally only puts the needles down to eat, write, or sleep, and sometimes not even then.

**www.RachaelHerron.com**

The employees of Thorndike Press hope you have enjoyed this Large Print book. All our Thorndike, Wheeler, and Kennebec Large Print titles are designed for easy reading, and all our books are made to last. Other Thorndike Press Large Print books are available at your library, through selected bookstores, or directly from us.

For information about titles, please call:
(800) 223-1244

or visit our Web site at:
http://gale.cengage.com/thorndike

To share your comments, please write:
Publisher
Thorndike Press
10 Water St., Suite 310
Waterville, ME 04901